lethal

legacy

lethal legacy

by

Gerald Myers

CYNTOMedia
CORPORATION

Pittsburgh, PA

ISBN 1-56315-363-7
Trade Paperback
© Copyright 2005 Gerald Myers
All rights reserved
First Printing—2005
Library of Congress #2004117515

Request for information should be addressed to:

SterlingHouse Publisher, Inc.
7436 Washington Avenue
Pittsburgh, PA 15218
www.sterlinghousepublisher.com

SterlingHouse Publisher, Inc. is a company
of the CyntoMedia Corporation

Cover Design: Jonah Lloyd - SterlingHouse Publisher
Book Designer: N. J. McBeth

Printed in The United States of America

Dedication

To Mark and Jeff, two guys who, for me, have defined friendship.

Chapter I

The mournful wail of the ancient shofar filled the mosque-like synagogue before seeping into the night. A thousand members of Congregation Rodef Shalom stood reverently as the cantor appealed to God while acknowledging his sovereignty over all.

Outside the spacious temple, more of the Jewish community hurried down Fifth Avenue, then amassed outside the thick oak doors awaiting the evening's second service. It was *erev* Yom Kippur, the evening before the Day of Atonement, in the autumn of 1989. Upon hearing the wail, the newcomers hushed their chatter and stood reverently in place, steeped in a warm sense of tradition, part of a civilization that had survived four thousand years of human history. Just as the somber tone dissolved into the lingering twilight, a sonorous, more ominous sound filled the air.

Less than a mile away, in the affluent community of Murdock Farms, a huge mansion exploded, then burst into flames. Seconds later, drawn by the deafening roar, dozens of horrified neighbors bolted from their own magnificent homes. An elderly shut-in living across Bennington Street stared out her bedroom window, then had the presence of mind to dial 911. Almost instantaneously a convoy of fire engines arrived, lumbering down the narrow thoroughfare, their sirens melding with the shouts and shrieks.

The police arrived quickly and acted with cool efficiency. In minutes, they had the two-block area surrounding the burning structure cordoned off. Beyond the hastily constructed barriers, a growing number of excited thrill-seekers joined the cluster of shocked neighbors gaping at the spectacle. The squad of harried looking officers was kept busy restraining the crowd. A narrow path was cleared for authorized officials to enter and leave the site. One of these officials was detective Carmen Vitale.

Vitale, short and stocky, with a mop of jet-black hair and a round weather-beaten face, had almost toppled his TV dinner when the bulletin of the explosion crackled out of his Bearcat scanner. Explosions were hardly a common occurrence in Pittsburgh—and especially not in Murdock Farms.

Grabbing his tan blazer he raced down the steps, hit the garage door opener in full stride, swung into the driver seat and slid the revolving blue emergency light up onto the roof of his rusting, green Fiat. Five seconds later, he was out of his Shadyside high-rise and screeching toward the blaze.

"What's the story, Mahoney?" he shouted at the fire chief as he approached the burning house. "Anyone inside?"

"The whole damn family, Carm. According to one of the neighbors they were headed to the late service at Rodef. We think the furnace blew."

"Ah, shit!" cursed the detective. Sick with worry, he started toward the mansion's massive, front door. A pair of burly, soot-covered firemen roughly detained him.

"Where the hell you think you're going?" screamed the Chief.

"I gotta get in there!" he snapped back.

"You can't go in there, you stupid dago. It's a fuckin' inferno. A couple a minutes ago two men tried and the roof almost buried them. No one's makin' it outta that place alive. And I can't afford to add a dim-witted dick to the casualty list."

"But she might be in there!" Carmen cried. His overwhelming anxiety deteriorated into a mind-numbing paralysis.

"Who's she?" the Chief asked.

But the detective's state of shock rendered him oblivious to the question. Semi-conscious, he stumbled away from the hellish conflagration. Instead, he hid in the memory of the next to the last time he'd seen the girl who, on another starry night so many years ago, had stirred feelings that haunted him to this day.

Craning his short thick neck to peer over the row of booths between him and the front door, Carmen saw her checking with the hostess. Then she noticed him, smiled, and hurried over.

"You got the invitation?" she began by asking. "You're coming to the wedding, aren't you?"

"I don't know Rachael," Carmen replied hesitantly. "I feel a little funny. Won't your fiancé—what's his name—mind?"

"His name is Alan Weber and he hasn't got any say in the matter. You're my friend and I want you at the wedding. In fact, I'd make you an usher if I could. But that's not my choice. That's up to Alan."

"My, my," said Carmen, impressed. "Nearly an usher at my old girlfriend's wedding. Wouldn't that raise a few eyebrows?"

"Maybe. But it also shows how special you are to me, Carm. Those times we shared add up to plenty."

Yeah, plenty of shit, he thought bitterly.

Carmen couldn't escape the fact that Rachael had been his first true love. Though she'd matured since the last time they'd been together, he noticed how her face still retained its youthful beauty. Silently his heart ached at the sight of her soft, brown, puppy-dog eyes and that wide, full mouth. But his favorite feature was her hair, auburn, soft, and alive. He loved to watch it bounce gaily on her shoulders as she gestured animatedly.

Shaking off this reverie, he focused instead on the nasal twang in her voice. Probably something she picked up during college in Philly, he told himself, a realization that drove home the impact of their years apart, more evidence that she'd changed. An amused look in her eye reoriented him.

"So what's up, Carm?"

"What do ya mean, what's up?" he retorted defensively.

"I mean, what's going on in that meshugana Italian life of yours? Like, for instance, how much longer do you have left at the Academy?"

"Oh, that. Another year and I'm done."

"How do you like it? Is it exciting?"

"It has its moments. But I'll like it better when I'm done. This student crap is for the birds. Me, I'm itchin' to get out on the streets and start makin' a difference."

"No kiddin'? Don't tell me you're a real law and order type. You always struck me as quiet and reserved."

"That was just around you, Rach," he replied, feeling defensive again.

She reached across the table and patted the back of his hand. Instantly, his heart started to race. He withdrew. In order to mask the abruptness of his reaction, he reached into his pocket and pulled out a small jewelry box.

"I, uh, bought you something," he stammered. "You know, for the wedding. I hope you like it."

"A present, Carm? That's so sweet of you. Can I open it?"

3

"Sure. If you want to."

"Of course I want to, silly."

She lifted the hinged lid revealing a felt-lined interior. When she saw what was inside, her eyes brightened.

"Oh, Carm, it's lovely. You shouldn't have. It looks so expensive."

"I didn't wanna get you somethin' impersonal, like dishes or a veg-o-matic," he said, trying to explain. Rachael, meanwhile, eased the tiny chain off its mooring. "I was never any good at pickin' jewelry. But I saw this in Henne's window and thought you'd go for it."

"Carm, I love it. Here, help me put it on."

She set her heel on the bench and raised the cuff of her pants. Fumbling a bit with the clasp, he positioned the delicate ankle bracelet and snapped it into place, marveling at how elegantly her pretty Semitic name had been carved into the fourteen-karat gold plate. She left her foot on his bench, rotating it back and forth, letting the shiny strip catch the light. Then she looked up, gazed at him, and smiled.

Thirty minutes later, they left the restaurant and stepped onto bustling Murray Avenue. Despite the hour, it was still mild and breezy. Carmen zipped his University of Pittsburgh letter jacket and stuffed his hands in his pockets. Rachael slipped her arm inside the crook of his elbow.

"Just like old times," she commented pressing her comely body against his. This familiar sensation, absent for so long, aroused him. He pinched his arm to his side, drawing her close. She didn't resist. Briefly, she set her head on his shoulder.

"It sure is," he agreed, his excitement blunted by frustration.

They strolled along in silence. After turning at the corner of Forbes and Murray they passed the Jewish Community Center. "Remember the dances we used to go to in there?" Rachael asked pointing toward the red brick building. "You and Irwin used to hide in the corner near the punch bowl. Amy and I had to practically drag you onto the dance floor."

"I really hated to dance," he reminded her. "And besides, they had all those weird dances back then. I never knew which one to learn."

Counting on her fingers, she said, "Lets see now, there was the Monkey, the Mashed Potatoes, the Loco-Motion, and the Stomp. Once you got the hang of them, you got pretty wild."

"Blame my hot Italian blood."

4

"I got a better taste of your hot Italian blood during the slow ones," she reminded him, her fleeting smile a tad coy. Self-conscious, he hoped the shadows from the overhanging trees masked his blush.

They climbed past the stately, gray stone Temple Sinai Synagogue, crested the hill near the entrance to Schenley Park, then descended. Halfway down the hill they turned right onto Plainfield, then Bennington. Carmen regarded the row of magnificent mansions bathed in the champagne lamplight and thought they resembled Gothic cathedrals. Finally, near Maynard, Rachael indicated the eight-pillared white structure on the corner. But instead of escorting him to the front door, she headed for the rear entrance by the greenhouse.

"Mom's got quite a green thumb," she commented gesturing to the rows of potted plants and flowers. Carmen grunted in agreement. Then, as they entered the main foyer, she raised a slender finger to her lips and warned, "Shhh, I'll see if anyone's up."

To Carmen's chagrin, someone was. Malcolm Rosenberg, Rachael's father, reclined in an easy chair a few feet away in the family room. Shit, he cursed, shouldn't that old man be in bed by now?

They approached. Dr. Rosenberg stood up to greet them. Carmen thought his manner a bit too formal.

"Ah, Vitale!" the robust thoracic surgeon said, peering down at Carmen. "Rachael told me she'd scheduled a little meeting with you. But I see by my watch that it's getting a bit late. I'd hoped she would have been home hours ago."

Carmen struggled to suppress his anger. *I wonder if he'd a treated me so condescendingly if I was Jewish, or maybe a hotshot surgeon like him. But since I'm just a lowly Police Academy student—and a dago to boot—I guess I'll never know.*

"Come on, Dad," Rachael interceded with a wink at Carmen. "I'm not a kid anymore. My company can bring me home anytime they want."

"Just let me remind you, young lady," her father countered as if he'd missed the meaning of her comment, "you happen to be engaged to Alan. It's highly irregular for you to be out this late with anyone, let alone an old boyfriend."

"Carmen wasn't a boyfr…" she began, then caught herself. "Well, I guess he was. But he's a good friend now. And if I want to spend time with him, you can't stop me."

"That's probably accurate," the older man conceded. "Just keep it clean." He gave Carmen a sharp glance. The Academy student returned the old man's glare. Tense moments passed. Rachel reached for Carmen's hand.

"Let's get away from him," she whispered. "I'm not going to win this one." They escaped into the kitchen. "Sorry about the inhospitable reception," she apologized. "He takes that hero-worship he gets at the hospital and in synagogue much too seriously." Carmen nodded, resisting making a comment he might later regret. "How about something to drink?" she added.

"No, I'm fine," he answered truthfully. "In fact, your father's right. It is getting late. I still have to walk home on those streets I'll be keeping safe someday."

"Sooner than you realize," she commented supportively. "What about a ride?"

"Naw. That's okay, I'd rather walk. It'll give me time to think about how it used to be with us."

She smiled tenderly and turned toward the front door. "Wait," she said. "This is the first time you've been in the house since Mom redecorated. How about a quick tour?"

Reluctantly, he agreed. They began in the formidable dining room dominated by a huge, rectangular, Henredon table flanked by twelve stately chairs, a dark wood China closet, and an antique breakfront. They then strolled through an archway into the stately, ultra-formal living room where they paused by a shiny, black baby grand piano. Without prompting, Rachael sat down and played him a flowery version of Beethoven's Fur D'Elise. After she finished, she escorted him to the rear of the house where a pair of French doors led out onto a huge veranda.

"And that's where the wedding will take place," she announced. In the silver light of a three-quarter moon, he discerned the white gazebo silhouetted against a stand of trees.

"I guess that's where you'll be the next time we see each other," he said pointing to the dainty structure. Moisture welled in his eyes. "You'll be all decked out in white."

"On that day, I become Mrs. Alan Weber," she said proudly. Then she caught herself. "Oh, Carm," she apologized, "I'm so sorry. I know this must be tough for you. But believe me, it couldn't have turned out any other way. For us, there were just too many barriers."

"I know, Rach," he agreed, his nod emphatic. He was being polite. In his heart of hearts, he believed otherwise.

Shit, he thought bitterly. Who says love conquers all?

And so must death, the detective conceded grimly.

"Hey Carmen," shouted someone, rudely plunging him back into the harsh reality of the moment. It was Mahoney. "We think we can get someone inside. We're gonna haul 'em out—one at a time."

The cadre of valiant firemen toiled for the next half-hour. For Carmen it seemed like an eternity. Drawing from his professional training, he worked at composing himself, preparing his mind for what would come next. He'd seen plenty of gruesome sights in his time. He could certainly weather another. But on the other had, it had never been this personal before.

Eventually, the six pairs of heavily clad firemen had the six body bags free of the badly, charred building. Hesitantly, Carmen walked over to where they were lined up according to their size on the lawn. A ghostly cloud of soot and smoke seemed to hover above them.

"Carmen," Mahoney instructed dispassionately, "tell me if you recognize any of these victims enough to I.D. them."

"I haven't seen Malcolm Rosenberg since seventy-three, Chief," Carmen noted. Mahoney nodded, walked over to the bulkiest bag, and unzipped it halfway. Despite Carmen's mental preparation, he was hardly prepared for what he saw.

The stench, a mixture of burnt flesh, cooked muscle, and human hair, wafted up, reminding him briefly of a time he'd inadvertently tossed a rancid, fat-laden steak on the grill. He winced and turned away. Then he forced himself to look.

Despite the scorch marks, the portly face appeared familiar. The skin on the forehead had completely melted away, exposing the bleached bones of the corpse's generous cranium. One cheek had coalesced into a matted mass of melted flesh, muscle, and fat, which, now exposed to the cool evening air, was drying into a crusty paste. The right orbit was hollow. Fragments of an exploded eye had speckled the congealed skin.

Carmen fought off a wave of nausea. Involuntarily, he gagged. "That's him all right," he said, his hoarse whisper barely audible. "That's old man Rosenberg."

"Okay," said Mahoney slowly, "let's see who else we got."

Working to quench the bile in his churning stomach, Carmen inched his way down the row, peeking into one thick green canvas bag after the other. Inside the next were the remains of an elderly woman. Amazingly, the fire had spared her soft, blemish-free skin, her gray, coarse hair also intact. Carmen easily recognized Rachael's mother, Sarah. But rather than her pristine complexion, the chilling expression on her postmortem visage was the aspect that fascinated him. White as a ghost, she wore a look he could only describe as one of unmitigated terror. It suggested that, instead of succumbing to suffocation or the heat, the poor gentle woman had merely died of fright.

A young man's body was also available for inspection. His facial remains resembled Dr. Rosenberg's, mostly a coagulum of melted skin and fat. Probably Rachel's brother Barry, Carmen decided, or perhaps another male relative, like a cousin or a nephew.

The next two bags seemed only half filled. Zipping them all the way down Carmen realized why. Inside laid the traumatized corpses of two young children. The first, that of a small boy, had the base of a silver candlestick holder protruding from the center of its chest. The other belonged to an older female child whose skull had been brutally deformed and smashed from the front. Amorphous material, loosely resembling a wad of sandy gray Jell-O, oozed onto its cheeks and ears. When Carmen realized that this substance was part of the child's shattered brain he gagged again.

A single bag remained. His heart racing with trepidation Carmen approached the soiled canvas. Cautiously he knelt low and spread the sack's edges. Despite his steely reserve and years of experience, when the moment came, he just couldn't bring himself to view this last mutilated face. Instead, he eased the zipper all the way down, focusing his attention on the victim's scorched right leg. What he witnessed there convulsed him more than all the repulsive, abhorrent mutilations that had passed before. There it was, just above the foot, slung securely around the ankle, a small delicate chain attached to a gold plate displaying the italicized name, Rachael.

Chapter 2

Even after consuming a fifth of Jack Daniels, Vitale couldn't sleep. A loop of heart-wrenching memories of Rachael Rosenberg kept swirling around in his head. Finally, around six a.m., he flipped on the television, dragged himself out of bed, and dressed. Two cups of black coffee later, ready to face the scene of the disaster again, he made his way back to the corner of Bennington and Maynard.

Except for the two police officers charged with the task of keeping looters at bay, the street outside the charred ruin was deserted. The lawn, littered with piles of wet moldy wood, twisted metal, and chunks of plaster, resembled a scene from a disaster movie. Carmen stopped by the front door and examined a splintered rent where eager firemen had hacked their way into the inferno. Flashing his badge toward one of the officers, he was permitted to enter the wreckage.

Upon initial inspection, the interior seemed gutted all the way to its brick superstructure. From the irregular mounds of rubble, it appeared that a section of the ceiling had crashed down onto the first floor. The living room was in shambles, shattered scorched furniture and charred cushions strewn everywhere. The once elegant baby grand piano had buckled, then crashed to the floor, its singed legs failing to support the formidable bulk.

The dining room had suffered the most damage. Here the non weight-bearing walls had literally buckled outward. The bulky furniture had apparently been propelled with extreme force in all directions, projected against those same walls by a blast which had opened a gaping hole in the center of the hardwood floor. Metallic-smelling dried blood had coalesced into tar-like puddles on the tattered Oriental rug or congealed on what remained of the walls, forming crusty rivulets that had slithered like rain on a dirty windowpane. Carmen walked over to one slender vein and scraped at it with his thumbnail. Like a chip of paint it flaked to the floor. Grimly, he shook his head, reluctant to imagine the grotesque horror that had created this mess. Then, uncertain whether the floor in this part of the house would support his weight, he gingerly tested his footing before backtracking into the front room.

Crossing into a hallway that bisected the first floor of the wreckage, he passed the broad staircase that led up to the second floor. Beyond it, he located the door to the basement, the same one he'd passed through during his only visit so many years ago. Fortunately for the purposes of his investigation, the fire had spared it. He descended into the murky darkness.

The structure's cellar seemed constructed of mainly concrete and cinder block. Carmen wondered why it had never been finished. Debris from the warped and frayed ceiling had plummeted into random heaps around the rectangular expanse. Except for the area directly below the dining room, most of the joists had held.

Flipping on his flashlight, Carmen traced a broad arc inside the giant enclosure. The yellow beam illuminated the laundry area off in the corner and a row of metal storage cabinets along one of the walls. A vault-like cedar closet filled the southeast corner flanked by piles of plastic storage boxes. The furnace, or what was left of it, looked to Carmen like a scrap metal sculpture, something he might see at the Shadyside Arts Festival.

Carmen examined the area around the gnarled appliance. There was nothing unusual here, just sections of pipe, and parts of gauges and valves. He was about to move on when, about ten feet away, a flash of metal caught his eye. It looked like part of an old-fashioned alarm clock with a single bell still attached. He found this curious. After donning a pair of cotton gloves he picked up the piece and placed it in a thick plastic bag. Then he poked around the wreckage for a little while longer. Eventually he came upon the mangled carcass of a storage battery, the kind he'd used in lanterns when camping with the Boy Scouts. This also went into the bag. Sniffing around the floor by literally putting his nose close to concrete, he detected a peculiar, almost acrid odor. It seemed to emanate from near the base of the furnace. Where had he appreciated this particular scent before? He couldn't remember.

When he was finally satisfied that there was nothing more to see down there, he trudged upstairs and headed into what was left of the family room. Standing there, uncertain what to investigate next, he felt a wave of exhaustion wash over him. Noticing a hassock that had, amazingly, been spared by the fire, he set his weary body down.

Suddenly, it was a cool Sunday afternoon in late spring. He was decked out in his navy blue church-going suit, his favorite paisley tie, and a pair of cordovan shoes that were killing his feet. Dozens of the other guests were mingling around the tastefully decorated rooms, many holding long stemmed glasses or plates of hors d'oeuvres. Several were engaged in animated conversation. A uniformed waitress offered him a glass of champagne. In the formal living room, an eight-piece orchestra, tightly arranged around the baby grand, played one of Bach's Brandenburg concerti.

Off to his right, he caught a glimpse of a woman in a white wedding gown. It was Rachael, of course. Compelled to stare, he watched her flit gaily about, charming her guests, conferring with her family, and briefly instructing the help. Finally glancing Carmen's way, she seemed to notice him sitting there. Waving a dainty, white-gloved hand she favored him with a warm, broad smile.

The reality of losing her hit him like a sledgehammer. A distorted newsreel started spinning wildly in his pounding head. There they were drinking punch at Irwin Goldberg's Bar Mitzvah, then slow-dancing at the Jewish Community Center, then strolling home on a spring evening through the narrow streets of Squirrel Hill. Their first kiss segued to a brief but passionate love affair. Suddenly they were hugging good-by at the airport where an incredible rush of joy was followed by a shudder of emotional pain.

The pair of police officers came running in to see what had caused the crash. What they found was Carmen stationed by the wall, his whole body trembling. In his hands, he held the shapely legs of the Victorian chair he'd just smashed to smithereens.

After a mobile lunch from the McDonald's drive-through, Carmen arrived back at the precinct building on Penn Circle. Captain Jackie Robinson Powell's office was situated near the far end of the second floor hallway. Distracted by concerns about why the Chief had summoned him, the detective covered the distance slowly. Absently he returned a few cursory greetings along the way. As he approached the enclosure, he glanced inside the opaque-glass window and noticed the two men in dark blue suits. Suddenly, things became a little clearer. Feds, Carmen thought grimly and pushed open the door.

Powell, a tall, broad-shouldered Afro-American with a neatly trimmed mustache and a close-cropped haircut sat behind his solid oak desk. "Oh, Carm," he greeted his inspector, "come right in." Then, nodding at the two visitors, he continued, "These are agents Jeffries and McCormick. They know you were at the scene of the Rosenberg house explosion last night."

Vitale nodded curtly at the two stiff-shirted visitors, then eased down onto a slatted wooden chair next to them. What the hell does the damn FBI want here? he asked himself. As if reading his mind Powell continued, "Let me get right to the point, Carm. I've already fielded calls from the Anti-defamation League, the American Zionist Coalition, and the Jewish Defense League on this one. It seems that this Malcolm Rosenberg was more than just some hotshot heart surgeon. He was also one of the most influential Zionists in this area. And those special interest groups are convinced that what happened at his house was some sorta terrorist act."

Perking up, Vitale offered, "The thought crossed my mind, too."

"The regional FBI office," Powell continued without acknowledging the comment, "has been authorized to take over jurisdiction of this case. Supposedly, there's a question of national security and they're interested in what, if anything, we've got so far. So in case you were wondering, that's why you're here."

Carmen eyed the two stiffs suspiciously. Their pretentious, overconfident manner really annoyed him. He sucked in a deep breath, then tried to sound professional.

"Actually," he replied in earnest, "not much Chief. I checked the site this morning, but all I found was nondescript rubble."

"Any sign of explosives?"

Vitale hesitated, loath to offer these two claim-jumpers anything concrete. "Well, I'm no ballistics expert," he continued slowly, "but I did find part of an alarm clock and the remnants of a lead storage battery. These items were in the general vicinity of the furnace, which was really mangled." Carmen caught the spark of interest in one of the Feds' eyes. He debated whether to mention the acrid odor which he now realized could have come from a brick of C4.

"That's really not of much help, detective," interjected the shorter of the two agents. "As you mentioned, you're obviously no ballistics expert."

"Yeah," replied Vitale, an eyelash away from reaching back and punching the asshole in the face, "you're certainly right about that."

"You finished your report yet, Carm?" Powell interrupted, as if trying to mitigate the growing tension in the room. "If so, I've got some other work I need you to get started on."

Probably another petty bust to divert me from the serious stuff, he thought to himself. But this time, it's personal. "So, I'm to assume that as far as we're concerned," Carmen said, staring directly into his boss' eyes, "the case is closed?" Powell nodded. Mirroring the nod, he slowly rose to his feet. Then, just as he turned to leave, he caught a glimpse of a manila folder sitting on the corner of the desk. "Is that the coroner's report?" he inquired.

"Why, yes, Carm," Powell replied, a little too matter of factly. "It is. Why?"

"Just curious," continued Carmen. "I tried to ID the bodies last night. But besides Rosenberg, I really wasn't sure who the victims were. Mind if I take a peek?"

Powell glanced at the FBI agents. The taller one returned an almost imperceptible nod. "No problem, Captain," the one Carm thought was called Jeffries responded. "We've got our copy. Just have Vitale send his personal report to the regional office along with the items he found at the scene. Even though we'll be conducting our own, more thorough investigation, his observations may be of some help."

Safely back in his own office, a Spartan affair consisting of an oak desk, some metal shelves for books and reports, and a dented four-drawer filing cabinet, Carmen plopped himself down onto a padded leather swivel chair. Before him sat the manila folder, its flap folded over but not sealed. Placing his palms on the blotter, he spread his chunky fingers wide, and considered what he would be doing next. The briefest wave of nausea rippled through his insides. Then, summoning a modicum of grim determination, he unwound the red thread and flipped open the flap.

Inside, he found a pile of Xeroxed papers, each covered with typewritten information. In the upper right corner of the first page, the name, Malcolm Rosenberg, had been recorded. Listed partway down the page and half an inch from the left margin was Final Diagnosis and Cause of Death in bold black letters. Under that was typed, "massive third degree burns covering seventy-five per cent of the body surface." The secondary diagnoses of myocardial infarc-

13

tion; old, mild chronic obstructive lung disease; renal sclerosis; generalized arteriosclerosis involving abdominal, cerebral and coronary vasculature; and duodenal ulcer, healed, with chronic scaring, followed in numerical order.

He burned to death, Carmen summarized.

The second report was a copy of Sarah Rosenberg's post-mortem examination. She, too, had demonstrated signs of extensive burns. But the cause of her death was listed as a massive, acute myocardial infarction. From Carmen's recollection of the expression on the poor woman's face, that look of sheer terror, it wasn't difficult to imagine how the explosion had caused her demise. He recalled an article he'd once read about how, when people committed suicide by jumping off bridges or tall buildings, they frequently succumbed to heart attacks long before they ever hit the surface.

The next report focused on a young male who Carmen now could confirm was Rachael's younger brother, Barry. Shutting his eyes for a moment, Carmen recalled meeting him many years ago. What came to mind was a bright, energetic teenager with dark hair, a round, boyish face, and a friendly, almost ingratiating personality. Rachael had once mentioned that her father was intent upon Barry following in his own surgical footsteps.

Carmen's last contact with Barry had been during the summer following the young man's freshman year at Penn. After college, he learned from talking to Rachael, the son had remained true to his father's wishes and spent four years at Johns Hopkins School of Medicine. Then, early in the summer of 1980, he'd returned home and started his cardiac surgery training at Northbanks University Hospital across the Allegheny River from downtown Pittsburgh.

For Carmen, however, an image of Rachael's brother from August of 1973 persisted. Barry, the detective recalled, had been an idealistic kid, thrilled to be in an ivy league school and even happier to have beaten the draft and the Vietnam War, which was all but over at the time. One balmy Sunday afternoon, while Carmen waited for Rachael to change out of her tennis outfit, Barry had paused to chat. During their conversation he'd confessed his secret desire to enter into the Peace Corps and then become a social worker. The last thing he wanted was the rigors of a high profile career in medicine. Apparently, the old man had prevailed.

They seemed like polar opposites back then, Carmen noted. What an irony that they ended up suffering identical fates, both succumbing to third degree burns covering most of their bodies.

14

Then there was little Melissa Weber. The coroner's report noted that the child had been ten years old when she died. Judging from her last name, Carmen assumed she was Rachael's daughter, probably her oldest. This unfortunate youngster had died instantly, succumbing to a violent blow to the skull delivered by a hard, flat object. In addition to being partially decapitated, her nose, cheekbones, and orbit had been pulverized. As an incidental finding, one of her legs had been amputated.

The next report documented the fate of Melissa's younger brother, Gary. Extensively burned, his six-year old body had been mutilated almost beyond recognition.

Even to Carmen's experienced eye, though these first five reports were simple and to the point, they were at best revolting. After digesting this simple fact, he braced himself for what he knew would be infinitely worse. Beginning by translating the technical jargon into laymen's terms, he transposed this final record into a gory image.

Rachael Rosenberg Weber's demise had been swift, if not merciful. Trying to visualize the scene in detail, all he could think of was a hapless execution victim being attacked by a squad of blindfolded knife throwers. What the report actually stated was that the only woman Carmen had ever loved had been skewered by no less then a half dozen shattered floorboards. The bomb blast had apparently transformed these usually blunt planks into an arsenal of razor-sharp projectiles. The largest one had pierced her chest. Another had smashed her skull. The image was almost inconceivable. Then, when he was finally able to incorporate Rachael's face into the gruesome picture, the usually hardened and emotionless detective felt his stomach churn once again. Involuntarily he gagged twice, pounded his clenched fist on the desk, listed to the right, and deposited his breakfast.

Chapter 3

I t was still dark outside when an exhausted Dr. Mathew Carson reached over and slapped at the snooze bar on his alarm clock. After three tries, he finally succeeded in extending his sleep. Nine minutes later Bruce Springsteen's, *Born in the USA*, stirred the bleary-eyed, thirty-four year-old psychiatrist out of bed.

After a shower and shave, he took a moment to regard his reflection in the bathroom mirror. With his short, light brown hair, thin stern mouth, gray eyes, and oval face, much of what he saw resembled someone he'd rather forget. Good old Mathew Wordsworth Carson II, he thought with a wince. It had been years since he'd officially renounced his esteemed parent. He desired nothing of him, now or ever, including his genetic endowment.

While dressing, Matt considered his own choice of profession. As a research fellow at Western Psychiatric Institute's Weimar Pavilion grinding through his first post-graduate year, he had plenty to consider. Last spring he'd completed his psychiatry residency. Unlike most of his classmates in the class of eighty-seven who'd gone directly into private practice, he'd chosen a research track. His primary interest was utilizing pharmaceuticals and environmental manipulation to modify resistant, socially maladaptive behavior. At one time this practice had been broadly termed, in quasi-Orwellian jargon, brainwashing. But with the prophecies of the famous work, *1984*, still unrealized fiction, Matt considered it worthwhile to apply certain concepts and methods developed by a few select branches of the worldwide intelligence community over the last forty years toward more humanitarian ends.

At 6:45 AM, he rotated the ignition key of his sleek Nissan 300ZX and was soon on his way to Braddock Medical Center's emergency room, a place where he occasionally spent his off-days, moonlighting for extra cash. As the engine hummed, he ran his fingertips affectionately along the smooth dashboard and took a deep breath of the scented, leather interior. With a tap on the accelerator, he left his sprawling, but pedestrian borough of Edgewood behind.

The once proud, but now decaying town of Braddock was nestled along a bend in the Monongahela River. Matt knew from stories told by some of the old-timers who tended to use the hospital's emergency room as a walk-in clinic, that Braddock, named for the famous pre-revolutionary army General, had once been a thriving community. For decades its businesses and shops had been supported by revenue from the US Steel's Edgar Thompson Works. But with the decline of the steel industry, the backbone of its economy had been shattered, and the middle class merchants and professionals had departed.

Now, to the casual observer, Braddock was a predominantly black ghetto comprised of rutted streets, boarded buildings, and broken down houses. At night, and sometimes even in the light of day, drunks, addicts, and derelicts roamed the once bustling streets, intimidating the last vestige of citizenry and frightening the motorists who were foolhardy enough to cruise the main drag. Matt knew from personal experience that carjacking at gun point while stopped at a traffic light was not an unusual occurrence.

After parking in the quasi-secure emergency room lot, he punched his three-digit call number in at the physician's entrance door, nodded to the guard, a man he vaguely recognized from earlier shifts there, and entered. A pretty receptionist sat primly behind the broad, registration desk lightly primping her stiff, tawny hair. She ran a polished pinky finger around the perimeter of her fleshy lips. Matt knew he might have been attracted to her if it weren't for the brown cigarette stains between her incisors.

"Morning Bonnie," he greeted, pausing by her gray-white Formica countertop. "How's business?"

"It's slowed down a lot, Dr. Carson," she cooed, her smile broad and inviting. "Truth is, you just missed most of the action. Hilda, my roomy, worked nightshift. The medics wheeled a stab wound in around four. She said he was a gory mess. They barely got him to the OR before he bled out. Housekeeping's tidied things up in there, but the nurses still seem all bent outta shape about it." She punctuated her report with a coy, little frown.

"*Muchos gracias, Bonito,*" he said with a nod. "Now, at least, I know what to expect."

"Anytime, *el doctoro,*" she replied in her own hackneyed Spanish.

Once inside the emergency room, Matt detected a vague undercurrent of electricity in the air. He knew that this kind of inanimate energy furnished the backdrop for the potentially volatile environment that could erupt at any moment. On the green linoleum floor, by an elderly woman pushing a scraggly mop, he noticed the ghost of a dark liquid puddle. The waste sack on her cart was chock full of soiled blue chucks, stained gauze pads, and used IV tubing— telltale signs of what indeed must have been a bloody ordeal.

After taking a deep breath, he eased over to the nurse's station and scanned the slatted, metal chart rack. From the intake times, he guessed that the two uppermost records had just been set there. He was about to attend to these patients, but paused when he saw the cream-colored stickers on the front of both. These were apparently patients waiting for the staff orthopedist who usually wandered in around seven to set any sprains or fractures from the previous night. A buxom Black nurse stood by the main counter delivering routine instructions to a thin, Hispanic-looking young man. Matt noticed the wrist splint and the thick, gauze bandage wrapped around his olive-skinned forehead. His glassy-eyed look and vacant stare suggested that he really wasn't interested in what she was saying. The nurse's impassive demeanor mirrored her patient's.

Probably a frequent flyer who'll be back soon enough, Matt decided.

In the cluttered workstation, harsh static crackled from a complicated looking radio-transmitting unit nestled by a row of reference books on the middle shelf. Below it, on the coffee-stained blotter, was a red telephone. A young emergency medical technician sat poised on his stool waiting for relevant transmissions. Matt knew that most of the real trauma was routed to the bigger medical centers like Regional in Monroeville, or Shadyside and West Penn in the city. But Braddock did occasionally cull some neighborhood action transported to their doorstep by the local police or nearby ambulance services.

Matt then noticed that Betty, an elderly woman with dyed blond hair and more than her share of wrinkles, was working the station. Hunched over the counter, clad in her standard white uniform and green smock, she checked the pile of charts from the previous night and confirmed that all the paperwork was in order. He was about to greet her when a whiff of a familiar perfume distracted him. It was Opium, his favorite. Turning around he saw Katie Conley, his most recent girlfriend, standing next to him, her bright blue eyes virtually sparkling with delight.

"Bonnie told me you were working daylight," she said softly, leaning close to his ear. "But I wouldn't believe it until I saw for myself. How'd you swing it, Siggy?"

"It was easy," he replied, still amused by the pet name she'd bestowed upon him, a stilted reference to the great Dr. Freud. "I'm about to start a new experiment at the Clinic. It doesn't start until five this evening. So I thought I'd hang out here for a while."

"Experimenting again, are you?" she said, her eyebrows elevated in mock interest. "And what pray-tell are you planning to do to those poor crazies down in Oakland?"

Chuckling, he replied, "Be civil, Katie. My patients happen to be very nice people. And they're no nuttier than you. Although, after seeing you do your thing at *Confetti's* last Saturday makes it a toss-up. Anyway, there's a myth that the full moon brings out the craziness in some folks. Well, I thought it would be interesting to test that hypothesis. There's supposed to be a big, bright one out tonight. That alone should provide some of my patients down at Weimar with some very compelling stimulation."

"I bet. Just don't go making them into werewolves."

"I wish I had that much control," he replied, flashing her a mischievous grin. "Unfortunately, all I'll be doing is EEG tracings and charting psychological maps. If I'm lucky, we should show a statistically significant trend toward the abnormal. If so the results may be publishable."

"Oh, no!" she exclaimed expressively, "not another celebrity in our midst. I'm not sure I can handle the notoriety. Quick! Hand me some sunglasses so I can block the glare."

"I'll try to tone it down, just for you, Kate."

She beamed at him again, then moved off to stock the crash cart. A few moments later, Big Alice, another daylight regular, waddled over with a chart. A five year-old girl with an earache was waiting with her mother in the ENT room. Matt scanned the face sheet. Despite the fact that he was scheduled to work in the emergency room, Matt knew that sore throats, sprained ankles, coughs, and colds filled up much of his shift. But he really didn't mind that the community used the facility as a walk-in medical clinic. Treating their ailments made him feel like a real doctor.

He reflected on this notion as he walked down the hallway. He knew that his chosen field of psychiatry seemed to hover on the fringes of conventional medicine. With its psychoanalytic roots, unorthodox treatments, and strange medicinals, it was sometimes regarded as little more than black magic. And he suspected that, despite a concerted effort by the psychiatric community to formalize their research practice and treatment using scientific methods and standardized therapy with field-tested pharmaceuticals, the unflattering reputation persisted.

So what if the public views what we do as mystical, almost supernatural? he asserted. Despite what the public thought he was still a highly motivated professional, compelled to take twisted, dysfunctional minds, uncoil them, and make them work properly again. And if he tended to utilize some unorthodox techniques in the process, so be it.

He knocked on the door, opened it, and smiled warmly at the screaming little girl with the cornrows in her hair. So begins another morning in Braddock's Community Health Clinic, he thought ruefully.

Matt introduced himself to the child's mother, not more than twenty years old herself, then removed the otoscope from its harness on the wall. After explaining what he was about to do, he enlisted the young woman's assistance and gently inspected her daughter's angry-looking eardrum. Red and pussy, it was infected all right. He charted his findings, scribbled a prescription for a mild antibiotic and recited a set of standard instructions. The scrawny, dark-skinned woman grunted her understanding, yanked roughly at the sniffling, little girl, and without a thank you, strolled out of the small, examining room. Matt followed her toward the workstation, shaking his head in amazement, wondering how such folks got along in the world.

When he reached the physician's corner of the work area, Matt noticed the stocky man in a blue uniform lounging by the coffee maker. The broad shoulders, gray wavy hair, and bulbous nose were unmistakable. Matt greeted Officer Jerzey Einhorn. Tipping his cap, the local police sergeant returned the favor.

"Hey doc. Did ya hear about the explosion over in Squirrel Hill last night?"

"Can't say I did, Jerz. I was listening to a medical tape on the way in this morning so I missed the news. Anyone hurt?"

"A whole family burned to death. Six people. Some doctor's mansion in what they call Murdock Farms. The guy's name was Malcolm Rosenberg. Ed Burns at Channel 4 said he was some big time heart surgeon over at Northbanks. Heard of him?"

"The name sounds vaguely familiar. But cardiac surgeons don't tend to hang out in my part of the hospital. Who else died?"

"The whole family—wife, son, daughter, and two grandkids. The local dispatcher's been monitoring the Pittsburgh police band since midnight. He filled me in on the situation when I punched in this morning."

"Sounds tragic," Matt replied absently as he flipped through a growing pile of charts. "What kind of explosion could have caused that much damage?"

"They suspect it the gas furnace blew. They was Jewish, though. The guys at the station been wondering if maybe it was arson or something."

"Arson? In Murdock Farms? Now com'on, Jerzey. This isn't Beirut."

"Yeah, but they say this Dr. Rosenberg was pretty outspoken when it came to the enemies of Israel. He might o' rubbed some loose cannons the wrong way."

"You mean a bomb? Isn't that a bit radical?"

"Ya never know what those lunatics'll do Doc. Ya just never know."

The rumble of traffic builds to a sonorous crescendo. As she stumbles around a right-angled bend in the road, the arrestingly, beautiful young woman is suddenly confronted by the expanse of concrete and steel. Speeding autos screech past only to disappear around the curve behind her.

Tentatively, heart flapping like a captured bird's wings, she tests the bridge's pedestrian walkway. Vaguely, her foot perceives the vibrations. She starts to withdraw, but fear roots her in place. A horn blast startles her. She hops back in panic. Turning, she begins her retreat.

A group of Blacks approach. Sauntering along, they push and shove each other with rough playfulness. One shouts, "Hey, you. Hey, white girl. Don'chu go nowhere. We needs to talk to you."

Horror, then confusion, fills her muddled mind. Disorientation and fear expand like a tempest inside her foggy head. She sprints in a panic along the concrete path hovering like a gangplank over the black waterway. The interlopers pursue. She retreats. Midway across the expanse she halts. A mere glance below reveals an ebony void that seems to beckon her. Irresistibly, she feels drawn toward the abyss.

Her head spins. Vertiginously, she peers over the rail at the meandering river. Calm and serene, it is a charcoal gray pool, faded to almost pewter in the early afternoon light. Then, to her distorted perception, a rent appears in the mirror-like surface. At first, it's just a narrow corridor, a black slit in an other-

21

wise unblemished expanse. Rather then provoking fear and repulsion, she senses how the deep, inviting gorge offers refuge and safety. Is this the womb from which she's estranged?

She glances left, then right. It seems to require little courage or resolution to act. Without hesitation, she climbs up onto the rail, teeters for a split second, then plummets head over heels into the enchanted deep.

By 2:00 that afternoon, the emergency room resembled a department store on Boxing Day. At both ends of the long central hallway uniformed personal scurried in and out of massive double doors. Respiratory techs with bags and tubing hurried by in one direction, while technicians with baskets jammed full of syringes and tubes pausing to pick up requisitions, moved off in the other. Aides and volunteers transported patients to x-ray or their rooms. Amid all this confusion, a harried Dr. Mathew Carson paused like a general to survey a map of the battlefield.

While he reviewed a two-yard long monitor strip between his outstretched arms, a bank of green and black oscilloscope machines chirped merrily behind his back. As he'd predicted upon arriving early that morning, the calm had erupted into chaos. He checked the digital readout on his Casio wristwatch. Only one more hour to weather.

"Hey doc," yelled the anxious EMT from across the nurse's station. "Unit Three's just checked in. They've got a fish in the water. Some young woman in her mid-twenties. Seems she went over the Rankin Bridge about twenty minutes ago. Their ETA is ten minutes."

The emergency crew's estimated time of arrival had been as predicted.

"We've got a Caucasian female here who appears to be in her mid- twenties," reported a tall, gangly young man in a powder blue shirt and navy blue pants. His bushy reddish-blond moustache twitched nervously as he spoke. He held a tattered, brown clipboard in his large bony hand.

"At approximately 1300 hours, she went over the south rail of the Rankin Bridge into about twenty feet of water. One of the local tugboat captains saw her jump and radioed the station. Four frogmen splashed down at 13:15 and rescued her. We arrived on the scene at 13:30. While CPR was being administered, approximately five hundred cc's of river water was evacuated from her chest. We attached the monitor and found her to be in a coarse V. Fib. We defibrillated her twice with 250 joules and restored her to sinus tachycardia. Initially, there were no spontaneous respirations. But after a couple of minutes of vigorous compression she had a massive emesis and began breathing on her own. We inserted the airway and secured her for transport."

"Anybody bother to get a pressure?" Matt asked as he signaled Katie to call anesthesia.

"Seventy-systolic at first." The tall medic nodded at his slovenly partner who was standing by. "Buddy, over here, got ninety over seventy in the van."

"Good job, Riley," Matt told him. "And thanks. We'll take it from here."

Matt leaned over and hastily scribbled his signature on the bottom of the medic's hand-written report. Then, with the help of two orderlies, he instructed Alice to help move the drowning victim's limp body from the gurney to the narrow bed. This young cyanotic drowning victim, he realized, was his responsibility now.

When he first saw her he thought she was dead. Her creamy white skin had that kind of bluish hue. Her long blond hair almost reached the floor. She was wrapped in thick wool blankets, olive green, like Army surplus and a length of plastic tubing snaked from her arm. The harsh white light from the fluorescent bulbs made her look ghoulish in a supernatural way. She was pretty, that was for certain, but pretty like the bride of Dracula might look.

At Katie's direction, the drowning victim was wheeled into room four, a cubicle designed for multiple-trauma victims. Rooted in his spot, Matt was left there amid the green tiled walls and black speckled linoleum floor, commotion swirling all around him. He had to shake himself into action. This seemed like one emergency-too-many for the day.

The first thing he noticed as he approached the bedside was her tremulousness. Gently, he placed his open hand on top of the moist blanket, so heavy and musty, and felt the fine fibrillatory motion, as if an electric current was coursing through her body. Then, he realized how cold she must be. This was the first time he'd ever dealt with acute hypothermia.

As Alice unwrapped the wet wool covering, Matt checked to see if his patient was breathing. Barely. The plastic airway moved gently up and down. He considered intubation.

Per protocol with trauma victims, an EKG was being obtained. Ripping the paper off from its origin Matt regarded the bold complexes and noted that the young woman must have a strong heart. Next, he checked her eyes. They constricted to light. Her pulse was thready but regular. Katie confirmed that her pressure was still hovering around ninety systolic.

Just then the blood gas results came back. She did need to be intubated.

Dora, a pert thirty-something respiratory technician, fitted an airtight mask over the victim's nose and mouth and delivered pure oxygen into her lungs from a black Ambu bag. Matt observed how, with each squeeze, the young woman's narrow chest, still boggy with river water, rose slightly then fell. While contemplating an effective management scheme, he couldn't help but notice how her small firm breasts and pale pink nipples moved rhythmically with each breath. That was until he glanced over at Katie who was observing him with annoyance etched all over her face.

"Nice melons, huh Siggy?" she quipped. "Don't get any ideas."

The clock on the cubicle wall said, two-forty. Matt, sitting on a stool at the head of the bed leaned over with an intubation speculum in hand. Uncomfortable moisture collected in his clammy armpits. A ripple of sweat trickled down his back. He stopped, straightened, and stretched. He knew her chances weren't good. And treating her was going to be tricky.

He listened to, rather than regarded, the cardiac monitor, which chirped brightly with each heartbeat. He estimated the rate to be about one-ten. Katie handed him the endo tube. He slipped it in just as the respirator was wheeled in.

The machine was connected. Matt called out the settings. A few seconds later, the young woman's saturated lungs began to inflate rhythmically. Next, Matt walked around to the side of the cart and plunged a needle into a crease in her groin. A tube full of bright red arterial blood pulsated back toward him. Just then Katie, with her cap a bit askew and a cool expression still on her face, rushed in with some bags of intravenous fluid. As per Matt's instruction, they had been warmed to 104°. Without checking with him, she substituted a heated one for a bag the medics had hung on transfer.

"Alice," he called, "could you give me an N.G. tube?" A few seconds later it was in his hand

While brushing a clump of the hair away from her face, Matt smelled the silt and slime of the river water. A strand of what he took for algae stuck to his palm. Then from his vantage point above her head, he noticed the thin, serious mouth, forced open at the corner by the protruding tube, the high cheekbones, and blond eyebrows. He had examined her eyes before and was struck by the pale-green irises speckled with brown. Yes, she was very attractive.

The insertion of a nasogastric tube went smoothly. Immediately afterward, he injected a syringeful of air and with his stethoscope listened to the young woman's abdomen. When he heard the bubbling, he knew the device was properly positioned. A suction pump was connected and copious amounts of viscous, greenish-black fluid began filling the large, wall-mounted reservoir bag. Matt noticed flecks of blood and coffee ground material mixed in with the gastric contents.

Next, he called for blood to be drawn. Three different antibiotics were hung. The last thing he did before stepping back was to order two grams of intravenous cortisone to be given, hoping to ward off the probable aspiration pneumonia.

"How about a Foley, Boss?" called Alice from the front of the room where she had been rummaging through a drawer. "She ain't about to ask for no bedpan."

"Sure, sure, Alice. Whatever you say."

The two nurses positioned themselves on opposite sides of the bed. Before they began Katie declared, "I doubt if we need an audience for this one, Dr. Carson."

The knife-like edge to her voice made him glance up. She returned his questioning gaze with a cold, hard stare.

I guess she's concerned with more than the patient's modesty, he told himself. Grabbing the patient's chart from the counter, he stalked out. When he saw the blank spots on the face sheet he strolled over to the workstation and asked, "Hey Betty. What's the story here? Doesn't this patient have a name?"

"Apparently not, Dr. Carson," replied the secretary in a raspy, cigarette-roughened voice. "The medics couldn't find any identification on her. Admissions listed her as a Jane Doe."

"That's just great! Now where the hell are we gonna get her medical records from?"

"That's the same problem I'm havin', Doc," interjected a gruff voice from the hall side of the counter. "Russ Franks, in case you were wonderin'," the shabbily dressed intruder announced holding out a nicotine-stained hand. "I'm a news beat reporter from the Post Gazette. I got down by the riverside a tad too late to see the heroics. So I was hopin' to get some info about the victim here.

Gerald Myers

The cops said she was clean when they found her. And it looks like no one who knows her has shown up yet."

"Well, I guess you know as much about her as we do, Mr. Franks," Matt replied wearily. "But then come to think of it," he added after glancing down at the empty data sheet, "you might know more."

"Then suppose we pool our data," continued Franks leaning his musty-smelling body over the counter. "For starters, can you tell me if she's still alive?"

"She was when I left her."

"And is she gonna make it?"

"Most likely. But she's got plenty going against her."

"For instance?"

"For instance; aspiration pneumonia, hypothermia, and probably sepsis to name a few. But if one can trust her cardiogram and what I'm hearing through my scope, she's got a strong heart. If her constitution's as good as her rhythm, I'd have to give her a better than even chance of making it."

"That's encouraging," commented the crusty, old reporter as he jotted down a few notes in his wrinkled flip pad. "Any idea why she did it?"

Suddenly distracted by an image of the woman lying there on the gurney, flaccidly unconsciously, rapidly accumulating a host of lines, catheters and tubes Matt asked, "Did what?"

"Took the plunge, Doc. You know, took the plunge. Did ya see any signs of previous suicide attempts? You know, scars on the wrists, healed fractures, rail-road tracks. That kinda stuff."

"Now that you mention it, I didn't notice anything suspicious. Why do you think it was suicide?"

"I don't know what it was," the meddlesome little man continued. "The word I got from the tugboat captain was that a group of black kids were out on the bridge, too. But they weren't close enough to give her a shove. He couldn't even say if she was bein' chased or not. So I ain't sure what happened, either. That's why I was hopin' you could help me out."

"Well, Mr. Franks," Matt replied, focusing a little better now, "I won't know anything much until she comes to. Right now she's unconscious and in critical condition. I expect she'll be moved over to the intensive care unit in a little while where Dr. Mobley, one of out staff internists, will assume jurisdiction. If she comes around, he'll probably get one of the staff psychiatrists to help figure out what made her jump. Maybe then we'll both know the story."

26

"Then it looks like, for now, my job is pretty much stymied," Franks conceded. "Mind if I stick around for a little while longer and see if anything else develops?"

"Suit yourself," replied Matt with a shrug. Secretly he was happy to be done with the journalist. "You'll have to wait in the waiting room or out in the hallway, though."

"No problem, Doc. I'm used to hangin' around and waitin'. And by the way, Sharon Winslow and her crew from Action News are on their way over. She's probably planning to run a spot on the six o'clock news. If you play your cards right, you may even get your mug on the tube."

Matt glanced over at him and nodded comprehendingly. *Just what I need,* he thought to himself.

Chapter 4

The Weimar Clinic, a futuristic looking, nine-story, concrete and glass structure, hovered above Bayard Street in the Oakland section of Pittsburgh. An exclusive research facility run by Pitt's Western Psychiatric Institute, on its seventh floor Dr. Mathew Carson, first-year psychiatry fellow, conducted his psychological experiment.

The walls of the main corridor were painted winter white, its brightly lit harshness offset by the plush green carpet. Nestled in ornate frames were portraits of the field's founding fathers, Freud, Jung, and Adler, who shared precious wallspace with the more contemporary experimental psychologists Skinner, Holland, and Wolpe. Another group, known as the neo-Freudians—Horney, May, Fromm, and Rodgers, to name a few—were mounted opposite. Strolling pensively down the hallway, Matt regarded the paintings reverently, hoping someday that efforts like his Full Moon trial would land his picture on a wall of some prestigious university's Department of Psychiatry.

Inside Room 703, formally known as the Sleep Lab, Matt was greeted by the hum of machinery and the murmur of whispering voices. After peering through the huge two-way mirror, he noted with satisfaction that three of his patients were resting comfortably on adjacent cots with thin sheets pulled up to their necks. A latticework of wires coursed from the patches on their foreheads and scalps to Matt's side of a two-way mirror. There, an elaborate electroencephalograph (EEG) machine tracked their brainwaves. Leaning over, he reviewed the squiggly lines on the broad piece of running graph paper, expecting a preponderance of alpha waves mixed in with some betas and thetas, each differentiated by the amplitude and frequency of their spikes.

Pointing to a particularly frenzied tracing, he turned to one of the female technicians and commented, "Ray must be having one helluva dream." The mousy-looking Pitt graduate student glanced up and smiled. Matt noticed her pale-green eyes that resembled those of that young drowning victim he'd helped save earlier that afternoon.

Although Matt had kept pretty busy since he'd left the emergency room, he couldn't seem to get the mysterious blond-haired woman out of his head. At three PM he'd left the small parking lot and turned onto Braddock Avenue. Up ahead, he noticed the long, narrow Rankin Bridge as it spanned the Mon. Immediately, an image of the slender female plummeting over the rail came to mind. Later, when he paused for a burger and fries at a fast food restaurant, a young woman sitting in the corner of the dining area could have been her twin. Finally, while accelerating his sports car up the steep hill toward the Clinic, an ambulance with red lights flashing screeched by, triggering a replay of the afternoon's activities. Something about this woman made her unique from the hundreds of trauma victims he'd treated over the years. Now sitting in the observation room in the clinic, aspects of her dramatic presentation replayed in his head.

Why had she impressed him so, he wondered? What made her seem so special? He shook his head. The image faded. The graduate student's face came into focus. Patting her on the back he acknowledged the quality of her work and slipped out of the room.

Next door, Matt went over to a square-backed, black, leather chair and sat down facing another two-way mirror. On the inside was another graduate assistant, this one a tall, dark-haired male in the process of interviewing a thin, sallow-skinned, middle-aged woman with a gaunt face and hollow cheeks. Her large, brown eyes darted nervously in all directions. She reminded Matt of a figure he'd once seen in a Modigliani painting. Long, bony fingers toyed with a soiled handkerchief in her lap.

Through a speaker mounted in the corner of the observation chamber, Matt noted how the formalized questions were met with hesitant, muted responses. But soon, his mind began to wander again. This time, an image of his father popped into his head. He wondered whether the "great" Mathew Carson frequently found himself in this same position, monitoring an interview while stationed on the covert side of a two-way mirror. After all, wasn't this one way CIA prisoners and detainees were questioned? Hadn't his old man, in his role as Deputy Chief of Covert Operations, been one of the department's top interrogators?

I doubt if Dad and his CIA cronies were this professional or courteous, he suspected.

In fact, wasn't it as a direct consequence of Matt's unwitting discovery about his father's inhumane methods of extracting information that sent him on his downward spiral? And wasn't it partially due to this psychological breakdown, and more specifically his vulnerable lottery number in the selective service draft, that drove him from his own country and into the uncertainty of a life on the run?

As it turned out, Canada wasn't so bad in the early seventies, he mused. In fact, after I got used to those brutally cold winters, it was pretty sweet.

Sporting shoulder-length hair, a boyish face discolored by a reddish-brown stubble, and a grim, stoic demeanor, he'd snuck over the border just south of Niagara Falls during the Christmas holidays of seventy-one. Hitching his way north past Toronto, for the next five months he secured odd jobs and laid low, sleeping in a series of boarding houses, cheap motels, and youth hostels. By late spring, he finally reached Halliburton and answered an ad for a position in the maintenance department of an overnight camp called White Pines. It turned out to be a typical upscale retreat catering to affluent, upper middle-class Jewish brats from the States. Midway though the first summer there he met Lauren.

Lauren Wescott, the camp owner's only daughter, had graduated from a White Plains prep school earlier that spring and was working the waterfront during her last summer before college. Watching her coach small groups of spoiled youngsters in diving, snorkeling, and canoeing, he found her pretty and perky, with a sharp wit and a friendly disposition.

On his occasional trips along Waterfront Road, Matt would slow to a crawl, lean out the window of the camp's old Ford pick-up truck, and study Lauren's sleek brown body as she edged to the rim of the ten-foot platform, flexed deeply at the knees, then plunged gracefully into the crystal blue lake below. Splitting the surface like a silverfish, she'd momentarily disappear from view, only to reappear seconds later with a big smile and a wave for him.

From the moment she invited him into her circle, he seemed determined to slip from under the yoke of his father's unwitting betrayal and reassume control of his life. With her help, he unleashed his anger, acknowledged his hurt, and gradually unburdened himself of the guilt and shame he'd assumed.

His love for Lauren had thawed his icy heart. Feeling safe around her, he was soon sharing stories about his childhood in Seven Springs, Virginia, where, in the years before Vietnam, he grew up just a few miles from the nation's capital. Then, in 1968, just as the social upheaval and the injustices of the Southeast Asian conflict began to dominate the headlines, he relocated to Pittsburgh and enrolled in Carnegie Mellon University. There his ultra-conservative Republican upbringing collided with the school's leftist campus politics and fomented a seething internal conflict that sent a series of mind-numbing shock waves through his psyche. This struggle intensified after he inadvertently witnessed top-secret video footage documenting the inhumane interrogation techniques his father used on a group of Asian POWs in South Vietnam.

After that idyllic summer, Lauren enrolled in the University of Toronto. In her gentle, persuasive manner she convinced Matt to join her. With little to dissuade him from this plan, in mid-September, he moved his meager belongings into a tiny one-bedroom apartment above a jewelry store on Young Street.

At first, with the hordes of American draft dodgers loitering around the hospitable Southern Canada city, it was difficult landing a job that paid a decent wage. But with the help of Mr. Wescott, Matt finally secured work in the construction field, working on a recreation complex being built near Lake Shore Boulevard called Ontario Place. The job kept him financially solvent and physically sound before the winter slow down.

Although the Wescotts believed Lauren resided in the women's dorm, in reality she lived with Matt. Within the intimacy of this little world they patiently explore the depths of each other's bodies and spirits in a way he doubted he'd ever feel uninhibited enough to do with anyone else again.

But after a year and a half, the idyllic nature of this arrangement began to falter, its shine starting to tarnish. Simultaneously, as he hung on the perimeter of the University environment, interacting with Lauren and her friends at concerts and plays, Matt felt drawn back to the campus. And so it was, in the spring of seventy-four, at the ripe old age of twenty-two, his goals and aspirations, once so muddled and indeterminate, came into focus.

Fourteen years later, seated in the darkened observation room at Weimar, Matt Carson MD, AACP, felt older and wiser. He smiled as he recalled that hardheaded, idealistic humanitarian he'd been back in Canada, who, after stalling long enough for his emotional maturity to catch up to his physical growth, he chose to pursue a profession where he served people as the antithesis of his father. Using the funds earned from the construction work, supplemented by money from the odd jobs he'd secured on campus, he covered both his tuition and living expenses. And four years later, in June of 1980, he graduated from the University of Toronto with a 3.75 grade-point average on a pre-med track.

Three years later, after President Carter invoked universal amnesty for all American draft dodgers, Matt discarded his standing as an expatriate and returned home. With the pre-requisite testing successfully completed, in the fall of 1981, Mathew Carson III was accepted at the University of Pittsburgh's School of Medicine.

But what about Lauren? As he now knew was a common fate of wartime relationships, their once quixotic romance gradually became routine and mundane. Although he continued to care about her, the intensity of his affection diminished over the years. First, covertly to himself, then more candidly out loud, he acknowledged that marriage was not in their future. Now, years later, Matt surmised that they had merely been victims of youthful lust, seduced by the excitement of exploring their disparate cultural backgrounds, trying to integrate them into a congruous whole. In the end, the lure of opposites, which had fueled their initial attraction, wasn't sufficient to sustain a lifelong bond.

The hollow-faced woman in the interviewing cubicle let out a yelp. Next, she leapt from her seat and pranced around the room. Her outburst snapped Matt out of his reverie. He watched with amusement as his flustered graduate assistant, clipboard in hand, followed her around like a confused puppy, while imploring her to sit back down. Matt reached over, pressed a button at the base of the microphone and spoke into it softly.

"Let her rant, Bob. This is the kind of stuff we've been hoping for. Mary's never exhibited this kind of behavior before. It may be significant that she's demonstrating it tonight."

The tall thin psychology student looked up with a start, nodded hesitantly, and sat down. Mary, after swirling around the room for a full ten minutes, executing awkward pirouettes, crossovers, leaps and spins, eventually exhausted herself. When she went to plop back down on her chair, the force of her descent sent the seat flying. She, instead, ended up on the floor sitting facing Matt with her legs spread apart. While observing these peculiar antics, something caught his attention.

"That scar on her thigh!" he shouted aloud. "That's it! Jane Doe from the ER had the same mark."

"What? What's that?" inquired the grad assistant from inside the room.

Matt, having inadvertently left the transmission button on, stammered into the microphone. "A-a nothing Bob. Just something that struck me. Continue with the interview, would you please?"

Chapter 5

A tired, frustrated Carmen Vitale leafed through a pile of notes and papers at his desk in the Precinct Building. Disgustedly, he shook his head. Set before him were a couple of personality profiles and a lot of unanswered questions. Since he'd been officially pulled off the case, his privileged channels of inquiry were off limits. And without this tactical edge, his meager effort at ascertaining meaningful answers was going nowhere. Determined to take matters into his own hands, he slammed his pen on the blotter, yanked his coat off the hook, and stalked out of the office. A few minutes later, he was back in his Fiat, heading toward the North Side.

Located across the Allegheny River from downtown, this part of Pittsburgh had once been famous for quaint, well-appointed homes and a proud ethnic mix. The ravages of time, however, and creeping poverty had led to squalor, dilapidation, and decay. Gloom and doom now infested the neighborhood, transforming it into a ghetto beset with starvation, homelessness, and a subculture of crime and vice.

Among the rack and ruin stood Northbanks University Hospital, perched like a citadel near the river, and shoring up one of the community's shaky borders by easing the human suffering that continually showed up on its doorstep. It was along these hallowed hallways that Carmen Vitale strode, determined to expand his inquiry into the violent death of Dr. Malcolm Rosenberg and family.

It was near the first floor executive suites that he collared a reluctant Henry Murdock, the hospital's chief administrator. But despite the use of some 'gentle' persuasion, the detective only managed to wrest a collection of xeroxed copies of the primary deceased's curriculum vitae and a biographical sketch which the hospital used for routine media releases out of the hardened CEO.

Undeterred by Murdock's lack of cooperation and fueled by his own inextinguishable mania for the case, Carmen then tracked down Dr. Douglas Cody, chief resident in the surgical program and a personal friend of Dr. Rosenberg's thirty-one year old son, Barry. Dr. Cody, in contrast to Murdock, turned out to be friendly and helpful, eventually introducing Vitale to Kathy Bentley, assistant head nurse on one of the med-surg units. Kathy, who Vitale decided was pretty, prim, and competent, had been a girlfriend of Barry's. From her input he formulated a tight character sketch of the now diseased junior surgeon. Beyond that however, Kathy could shed little light on the catastrophe that had befallen the family.

Later that afternoon, across town, in the synagogue's executive office, Carmen met with Abraham Cohen, President of Rodef Shalom Reform Congregation. There he finally made some headway. While reiterating how extremely influential Dr. Malcolm Rosenberg had been in the medical community, Cohen also pointed out that the famous surgeon was an ardent Zionist, a premier fund-raiser, and a generous philanthropist.

"A few specifics may help make my point," Cohen offered, in a thick Jewish accent that was more than a little distracting. "Back in 1975, for instance, when fund-raising money seemed particularly scarce, Malcolm served as chairman for the local Israeli Bonds Campaign. Single-handedly, he accounted for a half million dollars in donations. Two years later, he led the entire country in the amount pledged to the UJF."

"UJF?" Carmen inquired.

"The United Jewish Federation. Used to be known as the United Jewish Appeal. They coordinate most of the fund raising activities for *Eretz Israel* in the States."

Carmen nodded his understanding. Cohen then continued, describing how Rosenberg, in the late seventies, had become so active in the Zionist movement that his medical career took a back seat to his patriotic endeavors. In 1979, he was unanimously elected local chapter president of the Americans for Israel. In 1984 he became its national leader.

"Malcolm was a real firebrand," Cohen commented, his eyes, which had been wistful, coming alive with excitement. "Almost legendary for his fiery, no-nonsense position on our Jewish homeland, just after taking office he spearheaded a drive to meld the diverse factions within the pro-Zionist movement, unifying them under one banner. In the early eighties, this modern King David turned his attention to even more politically active pro-Israeli organizations. But that's where he stalled. Like everything else in his sadly shortened life—may his soul rest in peace—his revolutionary zeal seemed years ahead of its time. After banging his head against the wall for a while, he must've realized that the world of ethnic politics was much less malleable than the medical profession he was so used to commanding."

Finally, Cohen went on to relate, Malcolm, in the summer of 1985, at the not-so-old age of sixty-five, feeling personally defeated and morally exhausted, relinquished his position of power and prestige, and set himself adrift in the mundane world of semi-retirement.

That evening, back in his office, with the day's twelfth cup of coffee cooling on the blotter beside him, Carmen shuffled the papers around on his desk. Once again he reviewed his notes of the conversation with Abe Cohen. Perhaps, Carmen wondered, something buried in Rosenberg's past had returned to haunt the forthright surgeon so many years later.

Granted, he had probed and prodded Cohen for nearly two hours and seemed to have garnered little more than a handful of disjointed facts. Now, he reviewed these scraps of paper, focusing for a moment on some details about Dr. Rosenberg's military service. During late World War II, in the spring of 1945, as a lieutenant in General Omar Nelson Bradley's twelfth division, Rosenberg's company swept through Northern Germany. Perhaps it was then that he got a real taste of what it meant to be a Jew in Germany, Carmen speculated. Was this where his Zionist fervor was spawned?

Carmen took another sip from the Styrofoam cup, ran a trembling hand through his jet-black hair. With his thumbs he massaged his throbbing temples. From what he could deduce from his busy afternoon with Rosenberg's former medical colleagues and Abe, it was clear that the former heart surgeon had his share of adversaries—and perhaps some enemies as well. But Carmen also questioned if any of these individuals would be capable of, or have had the courage, to murder the venerable man and his entire family.

Cupping his hands behind his head, Carmen shut his weary eyes, then arched his back. In the gray-tinged darkness Kathy Bentley, Barry Rosenberg's old girlfriend came to mind, exactly as she had appeared earlier, perched primly beside him in the rear section of South Pavilion's fifth floor nurse's station.

"Barry had to be the sweetest guy I ever dated," said the petite, auburn-haired, young woman. Regarding him with her head cocked slightly to the right,

Carmen appreciated how her pretty brown eyes seemed speckled with spear-shaped flecks of green, radiating like a corona from her tiny, black pupils. Her pencil-thin eyebrows arched expressively as she continued. "Until he met that pseudo-Jewish bitch, that is."

The unexpected change in inflection took Carmen by surprise.

"What?" he inquired awkwardly.

"It started last spring while I was out of town. That's when Barry met that blond-haired, green-eyed monster. And she then proceeds to plunge her claws into him so deep I had no hope of saving him."

"You were out of town?" the detective asked, still a few laps behind.

"Uh-huh," replied Kathy, a rosy blush seeping into her complexion, perhaps a little embarrassed by her outburst. "It was during the first week-end of April. I was visiting my parents in Harrisburg. My sister turned twenty-one on April Fool's Day. We had a big party for her. By then, Barry and I had been dating for almost a year. I wanted him to come along. But he was on call in the hospital, so he couldn't make it."

"And that's when he met the—uh....," Carmen stole an unobtrusive glance at his notes, "blond-haired, green-eyed monster."

Kathy grinned sheepishly. "Yeah. One of Barry's old buddies from the neighborhood asked him to go to a Saturday night Jewish singles' dance. The bitch zeroed in on him there. After that, things between us deteriorated so fast it made my head spin." Carmen looked confused. The pretty young nurse seemed eager to elaborate. "Once they started seeing each other, he was like a different person toward me. The thing I always loved about Barry was his gentle compassion. From the moment we met, he was always considerate and tender, extra careful to regard my needs and wants before his. He never used to say or do anything that would upset or make me angry."

"And after he met this other woman...?"

"Almost overnight, he turned into a real jerk," she replied, her voice louder, the harsh edge back. "First he ignored me, then he avoided me completely. After I returned from Harrisburg, the few times we were together, he acted like he barely knew me. What kind of crap was that? After we'd been sleeping together for almost a year, for God's sake? It wasn't long before he stopped calling altogether."

Carmen nodded grimly, intrigued by this development. Without prompting, she continued, "I was so confused and upset, I could barely do my work. Every time I saw him around the hospital, I'd feel this knot in my chest. And it kept getting tighter and tighter. It was like he was playing out some Dr. Jekyll and Mr. Hyde routine. It was *her*. I know it was. She seemed to have this hold on him. The thing that amazed me most was how fast it happened. That's the part that destroyed me. One day we were lovers, the next we were history."

"Did he happen to share this woman's name with you," Carmen asked calmly, trying to conceal his hopefulness, "or anything else about her?"

"Only after I dragged it out of him during our last fight. Even though he'd dumped me, I still wanted to know. In fact, I needed to know, just to preserve my sanity. Her name was Lanie Richman. She looked about twenty-five— which was a little young for Barry to go begging after if you ask me—tall with blond hair and green eyes."

"How do you know what she looked like?"

"One of my girlfriends saw him mooning over her at the Watering Hole in Oakland one Friday night last August. The way she described her, the bitch sounded pretty waspy. Later I learned she's a grad student at Pitt in the International Studies Department—or at least was at the time."

"So she lives around the University?"

"As far as I could tell. Barry mentioned that she was renting an efficiency on McKee Place in lower Oakland. That's probably where he was hiding out on those summer nights I was trying to find him."

"Do you think she's still living there now?"

"How should I know?" she retorted. "The last time Barry and I spoke was in late June. That's when I told him I never wanted to see him again, which I realized later was a stupid thing to do, since we still worked in the same hospital. But most of the post open-hearts don't go to five-north anymore, so it turns out that we rarely ran into each other, anyway."

And now neither of you has him anymore, Carmen reflected as he stood up to stretch again. He thought how interesting it was that Kathy's bitterness over being dumped helped her ignore the tragedy of Barry Rosenberg's violent death. In fact, he recalled, it wasn't until he'd reminded her that Barry *was*, in fact, dead, that she began to mellow. It wasn't long after that she broke down right in front of him. And that's how he left her, slumped slightly forward in her chair, silently sobbing.

At a little past one, feeling exhausted and drained, Carmen grabbed his trench coat, and headed for the building's main entrance. Just as he was about to walk out, he heard the night sergeant mention, "That's him, Ma'am. That's Vitale."

Carmen turned at the sound of his name. In the waiting room's harsh florescent light, he noticed a wrinkled, gray-haired woman sitting on the edge of one of the wooden chairs. She clutched a black leather purse and what looked like a crumpled brown package close to her chest. Rising quickly, she hurried over to him.

"You are Herr Vitale, are you not?" she confronted him, her thick accent unmistakably German. "The one who the reporters interviewed the night the Jewish mansion exploded? You're the detective conducting the investigation? Yah?" The authoritarian tone made her questions sound like declarative statements.

"Well, sorta," Carmen replied, his own voice sounding a little flustered. "Actually ma'am, there's really no investigation in progress."

"Vell, there should be!" she declared, her weather-beaten face nodding decisively. "Violence like that should not be condoned!" Then suddenly, she shoved her crumpled package into his hands, so forcefully that it sent him backpedaling across the linoleum. He came to a jarring stop against the intake counter.

"The world must appreciate *die Geschichte meines Bruders!*" she declared loudly. Then, she turned and marched out the door.

Taken aback, Carmen struggled to collect himself. Self-consciously, he nodded at the desk sergeant then straightened up. More curious than concerned, he hurried after the fleeing woman. Dashing out the door, he bounded down the flight of concrete steps.

But when he reached the deserted sidewalk and surveyed the narrow streets near Penn Circle, his visitor was nowhere to be found. It was as if she'd vanished into the thin, night air.

Feeling the effect of the long, emotionally trying day, an exhausted Carmen Vitale staggered into his apartment in the wee hours of the morning. Without another thought about Malcolm Rosenberg, his daughter, Rachel, the explosion, or the strange old crone with her mysterious package, he crumpled, fully clothed, into bed. The next thing he knew, the alarm clock was blasting reveille into his ear.

On his way back to the office he began to consider everything he'd learned about the gutsy, old cardiac surgeon. The more he pondered, the uneasier he became. The whole thing just smelled fishy. His sixth sense told him that there'd been more than a faulty furnace at work here. But what he needed was proof. And fast. But without proper authorization to priority sources, he was stymied. A fresh mandate from the captain to officially resume the investigation was essential.

As Carmen strolled into his office that morning, Chief Powell was in an unusually foul mood. "What do you want, Vitale?" he barked uncharacteristically. "I don't remember calling you."

"You didn't," Carmen stammered. "I've got a request, that's all."

"Oh, you do, do you? I thought you were in McKees Rocks on that China White stakeout. Kelly's been calling every ten minutes to see where you've been."

"I'm on my way," Carmen replied defensively. "I stopped by the office to pick up my piece."

"Well, whaddya waiting for? Those boys've been up all night. They need relief."

"I'm going, Chief," Carmen insisted, the blush under his collar betraying his annoyance. "Just calm down."

"Don't tell me to calm down," Powell retorted. "Now what's that request?"

"I want to re-open the investigation into the Rosenberg mansion explosion."

"What? I thought that crap was history. Weren't you here when the Feds paid us a visit?"

"You know I was."

"Then what else do you need?"

"Well," Carmen said slowly, "I think we were dropped outta the loop too fast. It seemed suspicious to me. From my calculation, there's plenty more here than meets the eye."

"Such as?" Carmen related what he'd culled from his interviews with Peterson, Bentley, and Cohen. "Big shit," retorted Powell. "No meat to that at all. Where's the evidence? I need a helluva lot more than a good story to countermand a direct order from the FBI."

"I'm working on that, Chief," Carmen insisted. "I just need more time and the authorization to go through proper channels. There's stuff buried here that goes back a long way. I got a feeling it might touch on sensitive areas, maybe even governmental."

"That's bullshit, Vitale. You don't need time. You just wanna use department funds to head off on one of your half-cocked goose chases. No deal. I got more important things for you to spend your time on. Like those half-dozen cases I'm still waiting for reports on. And those field-based surveillance teams you're supposed to be backin' up. Not to mention that little investigation into the Homewood rapist you wanted to run. I don't recall having heard word one on that case."

"Bullshit? You want to talk bullshit, Chief? The way I see it, all you care about is having nice, neat little reports on your desk every morning. Then, when something important comes down, you can't even look past protocol to see the value in going after it."

The Captain leaned across his desk and met Carmen's glare. The two men stood nose to nose. "I don't know who you think you are, Vitale. You've been acting awfully strange, lately—and it's not just since this Rosenberg case, either. Maybe it's time you took a break—a kinda extended leave of absence—without pay, to cool off, to put things in perspective."

"That sounds just fine to me," Carmen rejoined. Turning to leave, he added, "Just don't call me when you need a scapegoat. I'll call you."

It was good that *Cappy's*, a local pub on Walnut Street, was almost empty when Carmen wandered in at eleven that morning. Company was the last thing he wanted. Finding an empty stool by the corner of the bar, he started firing down shots of his old favorite, Jack Daniels. By late afternoon, he was wasted. After an early dinner he weaved home in the Fiat, spent some time staring blankly at a series of sit-coms on TV, then thoroughly bored with it all, was about to turn in. That's when he recalled the old lady's bundle.

"Where the hell did I put that thing?" he slurred out loud. He spotted the package on the lamp table next to his recliner. He ripped off the wrapping, which turned out to be a wrinkled brown, grocery store bag, and found a hefty journal inside. The lettering on the shiny black vinyl cover was embossed in gold. He had to regard the title twice. It wasn't in English.

41

Gerald Myers

Meine Geschichte
By Hans Frederick Reichman

To Carmen it looked like German, or maybe Yiddish. He rolled back the cover and began to read.

My name is Hans Reichman. I was born in the beautiful city of Hanover, the capital of Lower Saxony, in what is now known as West Germany. But in 1920, when I breathed my first breath, we were all one glorious country populated by a single, genetically superior Aryan race. Granted, we had just been defeated in battle, thwarted in an effort to conquer the inferior peoples that surround us. And at the whim of the victors, we were maliciously stripped of our army, our wealth, and our national pride. But the world would soon come to realize that this humiliation was merely a temporary setback, a brief interlude. Soon the greater glory of Germany, guided by the steady, resolute hand of the greatest leader the world has ever known, would assert itself once again.

Initially, I learned about the magnificence of my Motherland and the purity of my people from my father, Hermann Reichman. A brilliant, articulate attorney, a politician, and a veteran of the The Great War, Father was a thin man with sandy colored hair and clear, bespeckled gray eyes. In springtime, on cool Saturday mornings, he would take me on a cable car ride down to the Trammplatz *to show me the impressive ministry building. Within that structure's great hall he had delivered numerous impassioned speeches to the assembly. After the tour, we'd move on, strolling hand in hand around the gold-domed Town Hall, before lunching by the blue waters of the* Maschteich.

And as we promenaded along or sat and ate, he would relate the history of the German people—my people—about the splendor of the race and about our date with destiny that was postponed by our humiliating military defeat. He shared tales of the Kaiser's war, the battles and the heroism, the brave men in his company.

"Someday, Germany will rise again," he insisted, "and you, my son, will be there to see it. You may even be fortunate enough to participate." From those talks I learned of my heritage and my calling.

I suppose that's why, in 1933, when Baldur von Schirach, a husky, sandy-haired recruiter for the Hitler Youth Movement came to my grammar school, I was immediately consumed with enthusiastic zeal. Despite his bulk, von

Schirach was still a boyish looking young man of twenty-six who seemed gentle and reserved. He spoke about loyalty to the cause, about health and might. But what he really conveyed in his manner was an unswerving devotion to and an unshakable belief in our leader, Adolf Hitler. And sitting in that auditorium, surrounded by my classmates, listening to him speak, I realized that Baldur endorsed the same ideals my father had; patriotism, loyalty, and the superiority of the German People. When he was finished, I was offered an opportunity to join this organization—one so dedicated to the glory of the Chancellor and to the homeland we all loved. It seemed natural to enlist.

My father, a member in good standing since 1927 of the NSDAP, the Nazi party, was thrilled with my decision. In the early twenties, he'd been a member of the Free Corps, a group of ex-military men who had made themselves available to the government and the party when force was required to accomplish political ends. And when a new organization, one of greater size and scope, one that promised to assist Der Führer lead the campaign to purify the country and restore the Aryan race to its appropriate place of prominence in the world, one that called itself the Schutzstaffel *or SS, my father joined that too. Almost simultaneously, I became a member of Hitler's* Jugend, *the organization of which Baldur had spoken so gallantly.*

Carmen skimmed over the next several pages which seemed laced with lengthy descriptions of Reichman's first two years in the *Jugend*, about weekends spent marching with backpacks and rifles through the *Eilenriede*, a large city park in the northeastern section of Hanover, of playing war games and learning marksmanship. Eventually, the now sober detective waded through a detailed account of classroom work in which German instructors attempted to rewrite entire sections of modern history, philosophy, political science, and genetics, in a distorted effort to promote the Aryan culture as intrinsically superior.

What a bunch of bullshit, Carmen critiqued with a snicker.

One time, for an assignment from class, I successfully charted our family tree, tracking the purity of my lineage back over two centuries without a break or contamination. My mother's ancestors were originally from Iran and emigrated to Europe in 1714, soon after Elector George Ludwig of Hanover assumed the British throne and became George I. My father's roots were in the Saxony area and stretched back even further, dating to the Calenberg family in the fifteenth century.

When I discovered all this it made me very proud to be a German and a warrior for the cause. I recall listening in our cozy living room to Der Fuhrer on the radio one evening. It was like he was speaking directly to me. I still have his speech recorded in my notebook:

> We must be dominated by one will. We must form one unity. We must be held together by one discipline. We must all be filled with one obedience, one subordination. For over us stands the nation. You must be loyal. You must be courageous. You must be brave and among yourselves you must form one great, splendid comradeship. Then all the sacrifices of the past that had to be made and were made for the life of our nation, will not have been offered in vain.

Carmen stifled an urge to spit on the page.

The earlier reference to my mother gives me pause. Her name was Katherine. She was kind, gentle, and extremely beautiful. Her skin was creamy white. Her soft, blond hair just reached her shoulders. Her deep, blue eyes were tender and calm. I will never forget watching those eyes, as she inched toward me at night, while I lie in my bed awaiting sleep. From her mouth sweet, soothing phrases would flow. Then she would bend over and kiss me good night.

My mother was a talented woman, a musician. She was skilled with the oboe and violin, but also a virtuoso on the piano. Our small home on Fundstrassen near Eilenriede was always filled with the lovely strains of classical music. I did not need to learn about the great German composers from that old, stuffy curmudgeon in my music class. All I had to do was open my bedroom door and let the rich, melodious sounds wash over me from the family room.

When I was a child, Mamma used to practice often. But as I grew older and my sisters Margaretta and Irma came along, she had less time to play. By the time my Wolfgang entered the world, the piano stood there most of the time, its cover down, its strings silent.

Despite the harsh, masculine road I've chosen to travel, I suspect that whatever sensitivity and artistic ability I still possess comes from Mamma. Sometimes I wonder if my life would have been more fulfilling had I done some-

thing more artistic. But such was not the reality. I did, however, for much of my young adulthood, indulge some instinctive need to use the written word to express myself. This drive manifested itself first in the weekly newsletter I wrote for the Jugend, then in a short novel I attempted during high school, and finally in my brief stint as a journalist for Das Schwarze Korps in Berlin just before the war in 1939. The fact that I've maintained a personal journal intermittently over the past fifty years attests to that compulsion.

Thus, in the end, as my final creative act on earth, I have endeavored to satisfy the creative forces my mother instilled in me by condensing my fifty years of recollections into this single, comprehensive work.

Chapter 6

Cupid targeted me on an historic evening during the early part of November in 1938. By then, at the age of seventeen, I had risen to the rank of lieutenant in the Hanover division of Der Führer's Youth Corps. As regiment leader I coordinated the activities of my six brigades of young soldiers during war games, scheduled marches, intra-mural athletic contests, and academic debates.

During the five years I'd attended the Jugend, the nature of the Jews in Germany and the world had been made crystal clear to us. During classroom lectures, in summer seminars, and through various newspaper articles, we learned that they were usurious moneylenders and unscrupulous merchants. They worked as unethical professionals and served as corrupt politicians. In a nutshell, the Jews were foul, diabolical, and distrustful. They had contributed to Germany's defeat in The Great War. As sure as an infection needed treatment or a cancer excision, the world needed to be cleansed of this inferior race.

In the summer of 1936, my father took me to a seminar on Social Darwinism. There, the great Nazi and SS officer, Julius Streicher, delivered a lecture on this very topic. Here's the portion I recorded in my journal:

> The Jew is a parasite. Wherever he flourishes, the people die. From the earliest times to our own day, the Jew has quite literally killed and exterminated the peoples upon whom he has battened, insofar as he has been able to do so. Elimination of the Jew from our community is to be regarded as an emergency defense measure.

On the evening of November 9, 1938, shortly after sundown, an important step in realizing that elimination was undertaken. In an action resembling a violent, destructive plague, similar to the plagues those same Christ-killers unleashed on the people of ancient Egypt, rather than play the perpetrators, the Jews of Germany became the victims.

Around 8:00 P.M., in the square Am Steintor, in the shadows of the Anzeiger tower block, twenty-four members of the first two brigades of the Hanover Jugend arrived. By 8:15 we had our orders. Fifteen minutes later, we were ready to deploy.

The peal from Sergeant Schmitt's police siren was the pre-arranged signal. As our commander had informed me, the Jugend would spearhead a campaign that would be spontaneously embraced by the German public. The Jews would be taught a lesson they would never forget.

Upon hearing the peal, I unleashed my troops. Their orders were to smash the windows and doors that belonged to the Jewish merchants in and around the Marktplatz. Looting was frowned upon in the commercial district of the Old Town, but not prohibited. Word came down that, if it occurred, the police would look not react.

Separate brigades of Jugend were dispatched to the Jewish residential areas, densely populated ghettos where the hated usurers lived, worked, and prayed. Systematically, houses, apartments, and community centers were targeted. Their evil places of worship would be burned to the ground. Casualties were expected as thousands of despised ones fled into the streets. I snickered to imagine them standing by while their precious homes and synagogues burst into flames. What a glorious night for the German people, one the Christ-killers would not soon forget. History would remember it as Kristallnacht.

But for me, despite its global significance, Kristallnacht would have a personal aspect. At precisely 8:35 I followed a quartet of my boys from the first brigade down Knochenhauserstrasse toward the Old Town Hall. The sound of shattered glass and the sight of fleeing individuals surrounded us. A cacophony of shouting merchants, wailing sirens, and screeching whistles hung like a cloud over the narrow thoroughfare. A small band of Hassidic Jews, men in black coats with coarse matted beards and old women in long cotton dresses and white shawls scurried past. One screamed about something called a pogrom. But instead of pity, their fear fueled my lust to take part in the action.

Across from the gray-domed Town Hall stood an open-air market. In daytime, the Jewish merchants operated their stands, bartered meats, produce, household goods, and crafts. But the tables and shelves were barren now, the merchandise carted off in trucks and cars. The musky odor of fresh fish, rare *beef, and ripe vegetables lingered. On the next two blocks stretched rows of densely packed stores, mostly owned by orthodox Jews, who sold appliances, clothing, and furniture at grossly inflated prices. When I reached this Satan-infested area my heavy, black leather boots crunched down upon a carpet of broken glass. Every storefront window had been smashed. The locked doors had been forced open. Inside, display cases and shelving were in disarray with mer- chandise strewn on the floor or dragged into the street. Proudly I watched my young troops, equipped only with rocks and crowbars, achieve their objective.*

Panicking merchants moved in every direction. Diatribes in Yiddish and German mingled with my shouted orders. As I stood, my fists on my hips, observing the carnage, a foul smelling old Jewish man in black baggy pants grabbed the sleeve of my brown shirt so roughly he almost ripped off my swasti- ka. In a pitiful, high-pitched voice, he begged me to explain why this was hap- pening. It took all my strength to shake him off so I could continue my inspec- tion.

And then I heard the weeping, a mournful sound that slithered through the chaos like a sinewy thread, distinct from the hysterical wailing that filled the night air. I sensed it originated from the alley between two rows of stores. Unfolding my jack-knife, I inched around the corner structure and slid cau- tiously along the wall. Away from the streetlights, the alley was dark and cool. The stench of uncollected garbage accosted my nostrils. The closer I got, the more pitiful was the sound. I fully expected to find some terrified child hiding among the refuse. Bu instead, I came upon a young female, nearly my age, crouched between two dumpsters. Seeing her straight blond hair reflected in the moonlight, I suspected she was not a Jewess.

"Come out Fraulein," I coaxed. "I will not harm you."

She peered up at me, her face as delicate as a rain-streaked flower. Now I knew she was Aryan. Regarding me anxiously she slowly rose to her feet then glanced past my right shoulder down the deserted alley. Perhaps it was the red, white, and black swastika on my upper arm that made her tremble.

"Please, there is nothing to fear. You are quite safe with me."

"B-b-but..." she stammered meekly, "all the violence." Her voice was a pale whisper, her eyes desperately imploring. "All the broken windows and loot- ing. What is happening?"

"The Jews are being taught a lesson, that is all. You mustn't be distressed. Surely you've heard about the murder of the German diplomat, Ernst Vom Rath

in Paris yesterday by the Polish Jew, Grunszpan. Der Fuhrer has issued a proclamation from Munich. Actions like these will not be tolerated. The perpetrators must be punished."

"But these poor people of Hanover haven't done anything," she objected.

"Forgive me for disagreeing, but these people are neither poor, nor innocent. And the sooner they are made to pay for their transgressions the better." She had no response to that. "Here," I urged. "Let me help you. No harm will come to you as long as I am by your side."

She allowed me to wrap an arm around her shoulders and guide her back toward the Marktplatz. We emerged from the alley into the garish streetlight. The riot was now at its zenith. A band of brown-shirted Jugend hurried by, their arms full of merchandise. Hordes of local factory workers joined in, burly men in tattered denims, women in tattered coats with their hair wrapped up in scarves, all claiming tables, chairs, radios, and Victrolas. A pair of local teenagers negotiated a wheelbarrow laden with loot past my feet, then disappeared into the shadows.

With a firm hand, I guided my frightened little bird past the commotion. We turned right onto Kramerstrasse and down to the Leine. After passing the Leineschloss, the seventeenth century palace of Duke Georg von Calenberg, we stepped onto the footpath along the riverbank.

She told me her name was Isle Hesse. She was soon to be sixteen. Her father, a farmer, owned nearly one hundred and fifty acres of rolling meadow on the way to Wunstorf, twenty kilometers west of Hanover. For the past four months, while she had attended St. Clemens near Goethe Pl., Isle had been living with her Aunt Karla and Uncle Klaus here in Hanover. Her parents, devout Papists, had encouraged her to enter the convent, but she was reluctant to commit to that course. So, instead, she had agreed to a formal parochial education from the inner city conservatory.

Once we were away from the noise and commotion, her shyness abated somewhat. Before long, she shared stories about how her friends made sport of the silly nuns. With a hand over an embarrassed expression, she described pranks and practical jokes perpetrated on the unsuspecting sisters. Chuckling, I found myself amused by her tales.

"But how did you happen to be out on the streets tonight?" I inquired in earnest.

Gerald Myers

"That is not as unusual as you might think," she replied. "Uncle Klaus works at the textile factory until eight tonight. We planned to meet for dinner at the Konigsberg Pub on Marketstrasse. After classes, I stayed at the school library and studied, then left St. Clemens at a little past eight. When I neared the Marktplatz I heard all that shouting and breaking glass. I didn't know what was happening. I became frightened and ran down the alley to hide."

"You shouldn't have worried. Any action executed by the Jugend must have the approval of the SS, the right arm of Der Fuhrer. Being a good German, you would have been safe no matter what."

"That protection was difficult to appreciate while rocks whizzed by my head," she interjected.

"I suppose so."

We strolled along for a short while longer, passing the Maschteich, then under the Arthur-Menge-Ufer Bridge. Timidly, I brushed my shoulder against hers then grazed the back of her hand. Withdrawing at first, she then eased closer. Finally, she allowed me to take hers in mine.

"My uncle is bound to be worried if I stay out much longer," she admitted. "I must be getting home."

Glancing at my watch I asked, "May I walk you? It's time I returned to the Marktplatz. But I won't let you go on alone." She hesitated for a moment, then nodded.

We doubled back along the dirt path to a point where the river makes an elbow bend to the left. Here we climbed back to street level. From there, she guided me to near her uncle's house on Schlosswender Strasse. When we reached the corner, she asked me not to continue. Before I could say another word she gave me a peck on the cheek and hurried away.

Before I arrived home that night I was already anxious to see Isle again. The following Saturday, with a twinge of trepidation, I knocked on her uncle's front door. Like most of the factory workers in Hanover, Herr Klaus was a long-standing party member and an ardent supporter of the Reich. This devotion, however, had been sorely tested during the turbulent years of the National Socialists' rise to power followed by the harsh economic hardships of the depression. But in the late thirties, with the dispossession of the Jews—those filthy usurers had been ordered to pay over one billion marks in reparations for *the property damage associated with* Kristallnacht—*the loyalty of men like Herr Klaus finally bore fruit.*

So it was as a comrade in arms that Isle's uncle greeted me at his doorstep, then offered me the seat of honor at his table. After pouring us brimming steins of dark Bavarian beer, he invited me to toast to Der Führer and the greater glory of the Fatherland. A lively discussion about politics, economics, and Social Darwinism ensued. And it wasn't until the candle on the mantle had burned down to a tiny stump that he finally patted me on the back and wished us well. But the hour was late and we barely had enough time to stroll around the block before our first date came to an end.

But there were other nights, many of them. As my world expanded and I reveled in the glow of my adopted family, the months flew by. My relationship with Isle grew in depth and scope. During countless hours I shared the great lessons I'd learned in the Jugend, *imparting wisdom about the Nazi party, its ideals, goals, and programs. Then, in January of 1939, when she joined the* Bund Deutscher Maedel *or League of German Maiden, she seized an opportunity to make her own contribution to the Reich.*

My eighteenth birthday, in September of that year, signaled the point where I would take my place alongside millions of loyal young Germans dedicated to the greater glory of the Fatherland. My options seemed restricted to officers' training school or the youth labor corps. A letter from Father, however, opened up a whole new possibility.

At the behest of Otto Ohlendorf, a former colleague from Hanover, he had transferred to the nation's capital in the spring of 1937. There, he joined a branch of the SS, the Sicherheistdienst *or SD, an elite corps of young intellectuals which, from a small building at Eight* Wilhelmstrasse *in downtown Berlin, engaged in the crucial task of tracking the lifestyle, attitudes, and activities of what were loosely called "enemies of the State." Under the direction of Reinhardt Heydrich the organization eventually became known as the Reich's Great Secret Service.*

In his letter Father related how this clandestine organization meticulously gathered intelligence, coordinated field-agent activities, and made decisions as to the actions to be taken. One of his less covert responsibilities was to act as liaison between the SD and the press, specifically the national SS newspaper, Das Schwarze Korps. *Learning that the paper needed fresh, young reporters, and with my reputation as creator and chief writer for the local newsletter, The*

Gerald Myers

Student Voice, he knew it would be a perfect job for me. Thus, in December of 1939, I packed two suitcases full of clothes and manuals and set off for Twenty-three Zimmerstrasse.

On August 6th, 1940, with me firmly established as a research assistant for a reporter named Rolf D'Alquen, Isle finally visited me in Berlin. By then Der Führer's invincible Wehrmacht had demonstrated its military might by smashing the inferior forces of Denmark, Norway, Holland, Belgium, and France. Our nation was rapidly approaching the height of its glory.

As the train slowed to a stop, I found Isle in the last passenger car, struggling to squeeze her large suitcase down the narrow staircase. "Isle, my love, let me help you with that," I called, running up to ease her burden. "Der Führer be praised, you're here at last."

"Oh, Hans," she murmured draping her arms around my neck. She pressed her soft body hard against me. I felt he fullness of her abdomen through my brown shirt.

"Been eating too much strudel, *liebschun?" I teased, lightly patting her belly.*

"No Hans," she replied a tad more serious than I expected. Then blushing, she added, "But I see you have inadvertently discovered my surprise."

Confused at first, the significance of her comment hit me like a thunderbolt. "Isle, my darling," I stammered. "You mean you're..."

"Yes, Hans," she replied, finishing my sentence, a tender look in her eye. "You're going to be a papa."

Overwhelmed by amazement and joy, I gathered her up in my arms and hugged her.

"This means we're to be married," I declared authoritatively.

"If you want to, dear Hans. Of course, I would never force such a thing on you. But you will notice that I've packed more than a weekend valise."

"So you plan to stay?"

"It does appear that way."

"Then it's settled," I agreed, hoisting the suitcase in one hand and taking hers in the other.

Isle moved in with Father and me, occupying the small back room in the corner of the building. We two men shared the larger bedroom next to the parlor.

52

Having my fiancée around added an entirely new dimension to my life. Soon I anticipated a home cooked meal after a hard day at the paper followed by quiet evenings sitting in the parlor or strolling Kreuzberg *or through* Tiergarten *Park. Each day, as her belly grew tauter, she would allow me to set an ear on her belly so I could appreciate the strong steady heartbeat of my unborn child.*

Approximately two years after my arrival in Berlin, on a chilly Saturday afternoon in November of 1941, within the quaint confines of Berlin's St. Matthäus Church, we were married. Although my superiors at the SD frowned on such religious ceremonies, I complied with the wishes of Isle's parents who had remained devout Catholics.

Six weeks later, our child was born. A healthy boy with a cheerful smile and arresting gray-blue eyes, we named him Dieter Ernest after both of our grand-fathers. During that, his first winter, I particularly enjoyed watching him grow and mature. He showed me something special every day. After a few months, he was sitting up on my lap, reaching for my keys, and pulling them toward his mouth. Initially his grip was weak and tenuous. But after a few months, he suc-ceeded in holding on until I pulled my hand away and he toppled to his side.

After those first few months, we settled into a regular routine. With spring the weather turned warm and balmy. During the waning hours of the day, Isle and I would walk our son in a used perambulator around the crystal blue lake in Tiergarten Park, *down what would eventually be called* der Strass des 17 Juni, *past the* Reichstag *Building, and out through the* Brandenburg Gate. *In Deiter I sensed what Der Führer meant when he spoke of the Thousand Year Reich. Boys like my son, Aryan, healthy, and strong, would grow up in the new, greater Germany, and be destined to lead the nation to even greater glory. My job was just to make sure he arrived where he was going safely.*

The next phase of my life began innocently enough. In the summer of '42, I was asked to write a feature extolling the effectiveness of the SS's interrogation methods. I could cull little from the files at Haumptamt SD, *which dealt with the day-to-day activities of native Germans, not with how the agents gathered their information. Eventually I became aware of a building that housed a collection of unique interrogation chambers which had been operated by the SS since the early thirties. With some persistence, I managed to secure an appointment with the center's director.*

The dilapidated, three-story, brick edifice was located in a deserted part of the warehouse district. Arriving early for my interview with Dr. Baron Von Ribbencoff, first SS-Rotenfuhrer *Hohn gave me a brief tour. First he led me down a long, narrow, dimly lit hallway, the air heavy and rancid, smelling of excrement. We then turned right near the back of the building. In the distance I heard a muffled scream. Muted as it was, it still made the hairs on my back stand on edge.*

Each room he showed me was different, one had electrical equipment, a second water hoses and blowtorches, another whips and chains. Each was apparently put to good use against the infidels of the State. At no point did I actually get to see an interrogation in progress, but my imagination supplied the details. And then, I met the mastermind behind the operation.

After I knocked on his half-open door, Ribbencoff, a portly old Austrian with a reddish-gray goatee acknowledged me with a curt nod. Hunched over a massive oak desk in that cluttered, dimly lit office, the brilliant senior psychiatrist resembled a Scrooge-like character poring over ledgers and lists, sniffing through his bulbous nose and grunting roughly under his breath. He glanced up and frowned deeply as his monocle slipped to his chest.

"What is it that you want?" he inquired, his deep voice gruff.

"I have an appointment," I replied.

"I no longer see patients."

"I'm a reporter for Das Schwarz Korps. *Gunter d'Alquen arranged the interview."*

"Ah, d'Alquen, that self-righteous trumpeter from a gossip-infested rag. Why would I let him arrange an interview?"

"Because you'd benefit from the publicity?" I inquired with an audacity I didn't know I possessed.

"Perhaps," he replied, the hint of an amused smile on his thick lips. "Perhaps." Then straightening to stretch, he added more amiably, "Vell, my young journalist. What's your name and what can I do for you?"

"Reichman, sir, Hans Reichman. I've come to gather information about the valuable work you do here for Herr Reinhardt and the Sicherheistdienst. *Herr Ohlendorf feels that some favorable publicity may help the secret service's image as it fights a recruiting war with the* Wehrmacht."

"Oh," the portly physician replied, smoothing his tie and giving his brown wool vest a tug. "And you think an article about torturing prisoners of war will provide that aide?"

"Probably not. But there is a certain sinister mystique about this place, one that may attract some of our more hardened patriots."

"And these are the recruits Herr Ohlendorf covets?"

"Precisely."

Rising to his feet Ribbencoff strolled over to a rack in the corner, extracted a pipe and a pouch from his overcoat pocket, and prepared himself a bowl. Returning to his chair, he leaned back, took in a couple of draughts and began his story.

The building that harbored these unique interrogation chambers was constructed in 1906 as a small textile plant. Then, in the late-twenties, as Hitler consolidated his power in the National-Socialist German Workers Party, the need for a loyal, personal militia and the subordination of Jew-loving political rivals, arose. Then, in 1930, the SS was formed, separate from the old guard, called the SA. One of Reichfeührer Heinrich Himmler's first directives was to find a place where subversives could be effectively interviewed.

Ribbencoff emphasized that from its outset the facility entertained some of the most brutal, degrading, and heinous activities known to man. Nothing, it seems, was too harsh or violent for those early taskmasters. Involuntarily, I cringed as the veteran psychiatrist catalogued them for me. However, Ribbencoff assured me that ever since he arrived to head the agency after leaving the University of Austria in 1935, its methods had become task-specific and more productive.

"We've learned," he continued, after taking a moment to refill his pipe, "that a maimed, dead enemy is a worthless specimen. In order to extract the information we seek, we must utilize skills similar to those of a master surgeon."

"And that's what goes on in those rooms?"

"In a broad sense, yes. Using psychotropic medicinals like sodium amytal and mescaline, combined with potent, strategically directed electrical shocks, we can encourage even the most resistant detainees to come to their senses."

"And these techniques have originated here?"

"Some, but not all."

"Where, then?" I persisted.

Gerald Myers

"Have you heard of the Minsk detention center in Eastern Poland?" I shook my head. "A colleague of mine, Dr. Roland Friesburg, has created a unique experimental laboratory there designed to accumulate psychological data about the limits of the human psyche. With access to such a large number of subjects, he is positioned to test multiple theories simultaneously. Each month, I receive progress reports. On three separate occasions I've visited his laboratory. Let me assure you, comrade Reichman, his data is impressive."

Soon after that he wished me well, making it clear that our interview had come to an end.

Chapter 7

Back in Berlin, while working at the paper, highly classified documents dealing with the missions of our brilliant military, the Waffen-SS-Wehrmacht *came to my attention. With each success my soul ached to join the fray. Driven by my military training in the* Jugend, *in November of 1942, when Der Führer authorized the formation of four brand new* Waffen-SS *divisions, I enroll in The* Hitlerjugend.

Soon after that I entered the Academie, *the nation's premier SS Cadet School, located just north of Brunswick and began a four-month crash course on military tactics, weapons operation, and leadership skills. Housed in a modernized medieval castle, the school stood on the knoll of a gentle hillside two kilometers north of town.*

During my first afternoon, a military strategist named Gunther Lev oriented me to the basic structures, the rigorous demands of the academic schedule, and the remote location where field exercises and war games would take place. That evening, in the cavernous mess hall, I met some of my class of four hundred, which consisted of a large number of young idealists, a small vocal group of boisterous, streetwise junior SS officers, and at least a hundred former Jugend *members. In addition to native Germans, several dozen enthusiastic young foreigners had enrolled, conscripted into the service from the occupied territories of Belgium, Holland and Norway.*

The days were long and the training schedule grueling. We rose at 5:30, participated in field didactics, compulsory night drills, a two-hour study hall, and eventually bedded down at eleven p.m. sharp. In class, the focus was two-pronged, military theory and German culture. Much of the Social Darwinism I had been introduced to in high school and at SS lectures I'd attended with my father. The majority of the instruction dealt with Aryan superiority over the sub-human Slavic populations to our East.

In the outdoor exercises, under simulated battlefield conditions, I learned what it took to be a military man. Huddled in small huts called on-sight command centers, we were instructed on making accurate weapons assessments, coordinating massive troop maneuvers through tactical operations and anticipating the actions and intentions of the enemy.

Isle wrote frequently that winter. I answered as best I could. Dieter's first birthday came and went. I regretted not being able to attend the celebration. Later that month, however, in February 1943, my family paid me a visit on its way back to Hanover from Berlin.

It was truly wonderful being together again. With Dieter bundled up in my arms and Isle clinging to my side we strolled from the train station to the old town center and back again, stopping briefly on the way at a small pub near the Steinwegstrausse Theatre. Sitting around the small wooden table, dining on knockwurst and sauerkraut, I shared my experiences at school with her. And Isle, in return, reported on Father's health and how things were progressing in Berlin.

Our few precious hours together evaporated in the course of that chilly afternoon. Before I knew it, we were back on the train platform saying good-bye. Our parting was tender and painful, leaving me with a sharp ache in my chest and a tear in my eye.

Final exams concluded on a balmy day in mid-April. Four days later we graduated. Regrettably, my wife and son could not attend. My boy was sick with an ear infection and although the doctor assured Isle he would readily recover, it was not in his best interests to make the four-hour train ride from Hanover to Brunswick. Father however, promised to attend the ceremonies.

The day dawned clear and mild. I spent much of the time after breakfast and before the processional shining my shoes, smoothing the bed, and cleaning my living quarters in anticipation of final inspection. I passed with flying colors. Afterwards I stepped out into the sunlight and joined the rest of the graduates on the far side of the commons. Commencement would begin with a formal march across the courtyard. From the stage and bleachers faculty, senior officers, and family members would review our parade.

Peering toward the podium, I discerned my father's profile. He was standing next to Commandant Shlossdorf, the school's head. As they conversed, Father handed him a piece of paper. The older man seemed to frown, nodded, then commented briefly before turning to greet some of the other guests. Father walked away, stepping down onto the concrete and hurried across the broad courtyard and took a seat in the second row of the bleachers.

Twenty minutes later, my company commander lined us up in formation at the edge of the walk. My cadet uniform was spotless and wrinkle-free. In white-gloved hands I cradled a rifle. With crisp movements I set it snuggly on my shoulder. Brimming with self-satisfaction I acknowledged that this was the day I would become an officer in the elite corps of Waffen-SS.

Once the formalities had concluded, Father, appearing proud but anxious, met me halfway across the courtyard. He shook my hand firmly and gave me an awkward hug.

Referring to our guest speaker, he said brightly, "Brigadeführer *Berger certainly knows how to inspire his troops."*

"He's been to the front, Father. He's seen combat first hand. As for me, I can't wait to be where's he's been."

"Perhaps he's withholding part of the story, my brave son," Father commented curiously. "There are many ways to interpret field reports you know?"

"I doubt that, Father. Remember, I've seen many of those reports myself. I've let others fight my battle for long enough. Now it's time for me to show my own bravery and determination."

"Certainly, Hans, certainly. But just be careful, that's all. Remember, you still have a family to think of."

"My family will do fine while I'm serving my country."

The next morning arrived gray and overcast. As I finished packing my few belongings into a green canvas duffle bag a fine mist covered the opaque barrack windows. Leaving my bunk in the corner of the long rectangular room for the last time, I strolled slowly around the room, bidding farewell to my comrades. An air of nervous excitement mixed with foreboding hung heavy over the room as we wondered where the next weeks and months would find us. And despite our optimism, we knew that once we arrived at our respective destinations, some of us would not return for our first reunion.

I walked into Commandant Shlossdorf's office, my heart pounding. Images of armored tanks, artillery guns, and marching soldiers filled my head. Soon, I would be commanding such an assembly. Fittingly it was Gunther Lev who handed me the sealed envelope with my orders. When he wished me well, I detected limpness in his congratulatory handshake. Feeling a little bewildered I stepped through the massive oak double-doors of the administration building, then paused to lean up against one of the circular pillars. It was with trepidation that I broke the seal on the long white envelope and extracted the single sheet of paper.

"By order of SS-Reichführer Heinrich Himmler, you, Hans Wolfgang Reichman, are hereby ordered to report to Detention Center 112, Lubartów, Poland, on or before May 1, 1943.

"What!" I shouted into the crowded courtyard. "Detention Center 112!"

What kind of nonsense was this? It had to be a mistake. I hadn't spent four grueling months training to be a battlefield NCO just to end up at in some Polish refugee camp. Confused, furious, and preoccupied with my plight, I barely noticed my father's approach. Slipping off his wire-rimmed glasses to wipe the mist with a cloth he asked casually, "Your orders? They have come?"

"What?" I retorted, still disoriented.

"Your orders? You are going where you wanted?"

"Hardly," I replied tersely. "No, it's not what I wanted. It has nothing whatsoever to do with what I wanted."

I glanced up and noticed Father's nervous expression. Suddenly, his brief conversation with Shlossdorf he'd had just prior to the processional came to mind.

"This is your doing, isn't it?" I demanded.

"My doing?"

"My orders. My orders, dammit, Father! You urged the Commandant to change my orders!"

"Why would I do a thing like that Hans?"

"Because you're more concerned with me being the family man than with my serving the Reich as a soldier."

Shaking his head he replied, "No, son. There's more to it than that."

"Like what?"

"Like this," he said reaching into the inner pocket of his overcoat. He unfolded a sheaf of papers. The official seal of the SD director's office was in the bottom right-hand corner of the top sheet. Handing the papers to me, he continued. "These are official documents from the Waffen-SS officers on the *front. They've been reviewed by both Himmler and Ohlendorf. They relate to the real story about the Eastern campaign. The truth my dear, brave Hans, is that the accursed Bolsheviks are decimating our troops. Hitler has permitted our supply lines to become overextended. Soon they will be shredded. And after that all of our superior equipment and machinery will rust in the snow-covered fields next to the poor, brave soldiers who are starving and freezing to death. I'm afraid there is precious little glory left to be had out there on the front, Hans—only martyrdom."*

I stared at him in disbelief. Glancing through the pages, I realized that they were authentic. The reports catalogued dwindling supplies, useless equipment, and overwhelming human losses, both for the Wehrmacht *and the* Waffen-SS. *Sending reinforcements was a futile attempt to salvage a doomed campaign.*

"But even if defeat is imminent," Father continued, "that doesn't mean Hitler will allow us to retreat. His newest policy is called, last man, last round. That means the army will be forced to fight on until every soldier is killed. And if you go to the front, my son, you will be one of the casualties. So, you see, it's not that I don't want you to fight for our dear Fatherland, it's that I don't want you sentenced to a certain death."

The shock of this revelation began to sink in. As it did I regarded the hundreds of my classmates who were mulling around the commons. With a sweeping gesture toward them, I asked my father sharply, "But what about them? Have they drawn insulated positions like mine?"

"I'm afraid not," my thin, frail papa replied. "By me appealing directly to Herr Ohlendorf himself, yours were the only orders I was able to influence. He, fortunately or unfortunately, while leading the Eisengruppen *into Russia, has witnessed much of the carnage himself. Although he supports Der Führer whole-heartedly, he is not without a conscience. When I petitioned him with my request, he granted it immediately."*

"And so your connections have saved my skin, while my classmates march to their collective death. Is that something you want me to live with, Father? Do you think I am that insensitive?"

"Son, I can only be responsible for your welfare. It is becoming clear that the course we are on is doomed. As I see it, at this juncture, our only chance is to pursue an honorable peace."

"My God, Father, are you speaking treason? If overheard you could be sent off to one of those detention camps in which you've arranged for me to serve."

61

Gerald Myers

"I'm aware of the gravity of my statements, son. But the truth is the truth. I must regard it authentically. I only hope you will do the same."

"Once I learn what that truth really is, Father," I replied.

"You will, son, as long as you grant yourself the luxury of growing old enough to experience it."

Chapter 8

At precisely 6:45 AM on May 2, 1943, a bullhorn sounded and the hordes of living skeletons awoke from their morning meal. Then, after their meager repast, amid cries of, "Macht Shnell!" punctuated by whips cracking and nightsticks thudding, the inmates evacuated the cavernous mess hall. I accompanied the throng out into the sprawling courtyard of Lumbartów detention center. Suddenly, I felt a sharp tap on my shoulder.

"Not you, Reichmann," was the comment. Pivoting, I encountered the piercing gaze of Herr Obersturmführer Maltz, the camp's Commandant. "Others will march the rabble to Lublin. Today, you've been assigned elsewhere." My heart leapt into my throat. Why had I been singled out from the group of newly recruited guards? "Follow me," he continued, clicking the heels of his black boots together sharply.

He led me across the grassy commons to a building labeled, Scientific Research and Development. We passed the front gait where several thousand Yudin were being herded up the country road toward the small eastern Polish town of Lublin. Lumbartów, situated near the bank of the Wyrst River, had evolved differently from its infamous neighbor, Treblinka. Rather than send funeral pyres high into the night sky, this camp functioned, instead, as a labor and research facility.

In 1941, Lublin's foundry, iron-works, and shipbuilding center had all been retooled as a German munitions complex and military-vehicle plant. Almost overnight an extensive search for capable young laborers was initiated. But with the vast majority of loyal Germans committed to the war effort, the government was forced to conscript a portion of the millions of relocated Polish, Czech and Hungarian Jews, to meet this need.

As we entered the Research Center, a rustic, brown brick building on the edge of the barracks, a young Rottenführer noticed us and bolted to attention.

Maltz regarded his salute perfunctorily then asked if Dr. Friesburg was available. The nervous corporal indicated that he was busy working in his office. Without another word, the camp Commandant strode past the guard, down the narrow hallway that bisected the building, and walked directly into the physician's office. I followed.

As I had learned from Dr. Ribbencoff, Friesburg was the psychiatrist conducting the mind-control experiments at Lumbartów. Perched behind his cluttered metal desk, he resembled a thinner, more compact version of the man with whom I'd interacted in Berlin. After looking up, he regarded Maltz intently.

"Ah, Herr Commandant, to what do I owe this pleasure?"

"Herr Doctor," Maltz replied in a cool, formal tone, "Here is the assistant you requested. His name is Hans Reichman. He's three weeks out of training at the Academia. *From today on, he will report directly to you each morning after the A.M. meal." Then Maltz nodded curtly to the psychiatrist, turned on his heel, and disappeared out the door.*

"So, you're Reichman?" Friesburg said, appraising me with raised eyebrow. "I've been expecting you for a week now. My last assistant was reassigned to the Eastern Front in early April." Then, appreciating my nervousness he added, "Relax. It's Hans, isn't it?" I nodded. Taking a full breath I assumed a looser posture. "That's better, lad. My friend and colleague, Dr. Ribbencoff, wrote me to report he found you both intelligent and forthright. Checking further, I've learned that you joined the SS officer training program several months ago, eager to continue your service to the Fatherland. It was decided that there is no better way of serving the Reich than assisting with research that will help shape its future. Simply stated, lad, here at Lumbartów we are engaged in top secret scientific mind-control experiments which, if successful, will make governing in post-war Germany effortless." He stood up and walked by me. I remained at attention. "Come, I'll show you where you'll be working."

We proceeded down a series of dark, musty hallways, and past a row of numbered doors. He finally turned into a dimly lit observation room cluttered with panel after panel of dials, switches, and gauges.

"It's almost time for the first experiment of the day," he stated, proudly sitting down on one of the wooden chairs. "This demonstration will afford you a fitting orientation."

At his command, a pair of prisoners was escorted into the chamber. It took me a moment to realize one was female. They were immediately strapped into chairs facing each other. On the table before the male prisoner was a small box with a row of buttons. His hands had been left unbound. The woman remained completely restrained. Friesburg gestured toward a bundle of wires that coursed from the control room to the male prisoner's chair and then from the male prisoner's box to the woman's chair.

"Der Führer has determined," he related, "that following our great victory, Germany must have effective methods to bring the sub-humans in the conquered territories under our total control. It is our job, yours and mine, to perfect these methods. Our present phase of experimentation," he commented, walking over to the row of machines, "is devised to scientifically determine the human breaking point." After sitting down before the most sophisticated control panel, he offered me the seat beside him.

"Before you are two relatively healthy Yudin transported here from the Warsaw ghetto. They are of opposite genders. Also note, they are husband and wife. The male will be permitted access to a simple control panel from which he can inflict electrical shocks of ever increasing intensity to his spouse. In a moment, he will be instructed to do so. If he refuses, he, in turn, will experience the shock himself."

Friesburg then leaned forward and spoke through an aperture in the observation room window. "It is time to begin Herr Stanislov," he said, his tone mockingly formal. "Before you is a simple row of labeled buttons, each corresponding to ever increasing electrical voltages. At my signal, you are to press the first button and deliver a small shock to your wife. Naturally, since you might be somewhat reluctant to comply, we have created a small incentive. If you refuse, you instead, will receive the jolt."

The frightened prisoner listened intently. Then, he turned toward the observation room and flashed us a defiant glare. Friesburg hardly reacted. Instead, he continued "It is time to inflict the first shock, Herr Stanislov. You may begin with the button labeled twenty-five volts."

Stanislov, his arms folded across his chest, sat still as a statue. Unfazed, Dr. Friesburg pressed his own button and instantaneously the emaciated Jew started thrashing in his chair. His wife looked on horrified.

"Get the point, Herr Stanislov?" the scientist inquired. "You may save yourself further discomfort by complying with my instructions. Shall we try it once more?"

Defiantly, the subject refused. Again he was electrocuted, this time to an inch of his life. His wife, looking grotesquely hysterical, bound a mere six feet from him, yanked desperately at her restraints. After a third series of jolts, Stanislov lost his bowels and bladder. The stench wafted toward the glass and through the opening. After the next jolt, he passed out.

"Wake him up," Friesburg calmly ordered the two Ukrainian guards who'd been stationed in the corners of the room. They doused the prisoner with a bucket of water. The conditioning resumed. Turning to me, he commented, "Obviously we've yet to reach the level which constitutes this Jew's breaking point. This time, I'll try utilizing smaller increments but prolong the discomfort."

The shocks commenced again. The Jew thrashed and screamed. Finally, after the current was turned off, he begged my mentor to terminate the experiment.

The doctor smirked triumphantly. "Now, do as I say Herr Stanislov," he commanded. "Administer the shock marked twenty-five volts to your spouse." Reluctantly, the coward complied.

After this initial demonstration, I was rapidly immersed in the fascinating world of mind control. My daily routine proved simple. Each morning I'd rise with the cock at 5:45, assist with roll call, and monitor the first meal of the day. Then, as the hapless Yudin trudged off to their labor, I hurried off to the research building for the day's experiments.

Once I became familiar with the various switches, dials, and gauges, I was stationed at the control panel while Dr. Friesburg provided instruction and recorded results. From this data reams of graphs and charts were compiled. These, in turn, were secured in sturdy mail pouches and forwarded to the SS-Central in Berlin.

Eventually, the scope of the studies broadened. First, we worked on eliciting the breaking point of parents who were ordered to shock their children. Then, Friesburg put out a call over the occupied lands for what he felt was the quintessential subject-pair, identical twins. Observing these unique subjects, so physically matched and crucially linked mentally, as they struggled with the dilemma of accepting the pain or inflicting it on the other, was much like watching someone administer torture on himself. In three of the four cases, the executive, or the person ordered to deliver the shocks, accepted a fatal jolt rather than accede to our commands.

In the following months, I participated in several unique kinds of experimentation, electrical motivation being only one of them. By utilizing a variety of psychotropic drugs, such as sodium amytal, mescaline, cocaine, opium, and peyote, in conjunction with deep mesmeric suggestion, any form of the behavior could be elicited.

One afternoon, I had the opportunity to witness a rather dramatic demonstration of the power of one of these techniques. I carefully observed Dr. Friesburg compel one of his subjects to kill his own brother. The technique was simple. All he had to do was create, while the subject was in a trance, a realistic scenario having him believe he was acting in his own self-defense or defending someone to whom he had sworn allegiance.

Eventually, after mastering the techniques I'd witnessed in the brain-modifying lab, it was I who became the practitioner. Once acquainted with the effects and side effects of the drugs, the doses and combinations needed to elicit our desired effects, I would skillfully puncture the vein of the protesting, tightly restrained subject and inject the clear, drug-laced liquid directly into its circulation. Then, once the psychotropic effects became evident, I would recite, in a controlled monotone, a carefully worded induction sequence rendering these mindless creatures completely helpless.

But as quickly as the fascinating daylight hours flew by, that's how slowly the night-time passed. When the lights were extinguished at 10 PM, the darkness of the barrack created an appropriate backdrop for the parade of images that flashed across my mind's eye. Sometimes I pictured the two-story Tudor home in which I was raised, playing with my sister Margaretta and brother Wolfgang in the small fenced-off back yard inside our clubhouse high up in the old maple tree near the edge of the garden.

More often, Isle and Dieter would occupy my musings. Memories from those brief months in Berlin were branded into my memory. In my mind's eye, I saw my beautiful son, my flesh and blood, my present and future, inquisitively crawling along the living room carpet or gurgling contentedly as we played in the park. Later during those imaginary evenings, after the child was asleep, Isle and I would lounge around before the fire, reading, talking, or listening to the works of Wagner or Schubert on the gramophone. But the memories that tormented me the most were of the hours before dawn, when my wife and I would lie together in our bed, with Dieter in his crib nearby, in the small room in the *rear of my father's apartment. As I recalled how the downy softness of my beloved's hair brushed against my cheek and the gentle curve of her thinly-clad body nestled against my chest, my very soul longed for her. Had I sought cheap release with the farm girls in the area, perhaps my psyche would have been spared the agonizing despair. But instead I proved faithful. And for my loyalty I remained an emotionally charged volcano set to explode.*

Chapter 9

April 25, 1944. It was almost a year to the day from my arrival at Lumbartów when the messenger arrived. I was hurrying across the rain-soaked field to the research facility when I noticed the sleek, mud-caked BMW motorcycle with its canvas-covered sidecar parked outside of the administration building. Standing casually beside it and smoking a cigarette was a tall, fair-skinned soldier in a black SS overcoat.

Later that morning, Maltz called an emergency meeting of the on-site guards and officers. While we sat on folding chairs in the meeting room next to his office, a weary Obersturmführer reported that a Soviet-backed Polish Committee of National Liberation was being formed in nearby Lublin. Its purpose was to pave the way for the arrival of the Russian Army, now bivouacked in large numbers along the Cruzan Line just sixty kilometers away. As a consequence, the Lumbartów Labor and Research Center was in danger of being overrun. In neat, block letters on the blackboard, Maltz outlined his Extermination, Demolition, and Evacuation Plan. If executed properly it should take seven to ten days to complete. Things were set to commence at eight PM that evening.

Just north of the camp, bordered on the east by the Wieprz River and to the west by the Warsaw-Lublin road, stretched a broad, flat meadow. Later that day, in accordance with Maltz' specifications, a large portion of the field was cordoned off. By twilight, the perimeter of the massive field could be identified by kerosene lamps. Encouraged by our snapping bullwhips, a thousand prisoners from Barrack IV marched to that pasture with shovels in hand. There the digging began.

I did not feel sorry for these individuals. They had been the fortunate ones, having avoided extermination by working the twelve-hour shifts in Lublin. Now, their toil appeared more arduous. Some feigned exhaustion, but my comrades *and I were quick to react, encouraging them with whips and steel-tipped boots. And then there were the Ukrainian guards, animals especially adept at meting out motivation, who could be called on to dispose of anyone refusing our not-so-gentle coaxing.*

Thousand-man work details labored eight-hour shifts around the clock for more than two full days. Finally, on the morning of April 28th, Maltz inspected the crater and declared it adequate. The pit's dirt floor was then covered with a wide variety of combustibles, dry timber, tons of paper, clothing, and linens, anything flammable and disposable. Next this layer was saturated with thousands of gallons of kerosene.

A mass execution ensued. The Yudin were lined up in two long perpendicular rows, roughly five hundred at a time, facing the pit. Using rapid-fire submachine guns, the demonic Ukrainians, taking great pleasure in their exercise, strafed the gaunt bodies until they crumbled in place. Frequently, the first sound of gunfire would send the horrified sub-humans scurrying in all directions, but never far enough away to avoid the shower of bullets. Many plunged conveniently into their freshly dug grave. The rest were tossed on top.

Despite executing over 1500 prisoners an hour, it still took us nearly three days to eliminate all sixty thousand. The process took from dawn until near midnight. During the remainder of those nights, the day's corpses were cremated. The stench from the burning bodies reminded me of the odor I'd smelled through the railroad car window as we passed Treblinka on the day I arrived at Lumbartów. Finally, by the morning of May 2, there was no sign any Jew had ever existed in the camp.

When the extermination was complete, despite the frenzied activity that continued in its wake, the camp felt strange and desolate. Literally, overnight, Lumbartów had become a ghost town, empty and eerie. I shuddered to envision those thousands upon thousands of hopeless souls passing through the ashes of their common funeral pyre in route to their final reward.

My reverie was cut short by the shrill whistle blast indicating an immediate assemblage of the guards. Phase II of Maltz' plan was about to commence. Quickly, we were divided into two equal groups, the first assigned to building demolition, the other sent back to the Lazerett to participate in camouflage operations. Later that morning, a convoy of trucks arrived, each with some type of heavy-duty equipment in tow, bulldozers and shovels, cranes with giant wrecking balls, land tractors with hoes, and several dump trucks. An SS-

Untersturmführer, *who lived next to Dr. Friesburg, was placed in charge level-ing the barracks and administration buildings. Maltz supervised the work at the pit.*

Even with the assistance of the earthmovers, filling the giant hole proved to be backbreaking. The rancid odor that wafted up from the bowels of the pit made us dizzy and weak. The dirt, still heavy from an early morning shower, strained our muscles to exhaustion. Occasionally the crack of an overheated coal could be heard from the depths of the mass grave, perhaps an exploding shinbone or skull. But for the most part, other than the scraping of metal shov-els against the soft, moisture-laden earth, and the grunts of a two hundred men laboring, all was hauntingly still.

After twelve hours of continuous shoveling, hundreds of tons of displaced earth had been dumped into that sizzling abyss. Maltz then ordered the bull-dozers to spread a layer of soil smoothly along the surface. Next the tractors hoed the field into narrow furrows and mounds, giving the impression that all that existed there was a plowed field. What, only hours before had been the gravesite of sixty thousand Jews, was now, to the untrained eye, an innocent farm.

Work on the remainder of the camp went according to schedule. By night-fall, the dozens of wood and glass buildings were leveled. A column of dump trucks then hauled the refuse toward the countryside. After the ruins were removed, only several acres of barren field devoid of evidence of human habi-tation remained.

Early on the next-to-last morning, we packed a spare uniform, our weapons, and any personal belongings, leaving them piled up in a cordoned off area by the barbed wire fences near the perimeter of the camp. That night, we slept on the cold ground with knapsacks for pillows and thin, woolen, olive-green army blankets for cover. The next morning, upon awakening stiff and damp, Phase III of Herr Maltz' evacuation plan went into effect.

With no further need for the close to three hundred Ukrainians, they were discharged to return to their homes. Maltz then formed all but his rear guard, about forty-five of us, into a tight marching formation. Assuming his position in his personal jeep, the only vehicle left, he briskly signaled the troops to head out, initiating our forced march to the Waffen-SS *encampment west of Warsaw.*

Our course hugged the waterways, first the Wieprz River, *then the muddy* Wiska *still swollen with the early spring rains. The nearly two hundred-kilome-*

ter journey took a little over five days. In two innocent looking villages we were unexpectedly ambushed by small bands of the Polish Home Army or Armia Krajowa, forcing us to battle our way through. It was during those vicious encounters that I finally got a taste of the combat I had been deprived of since I'd left the Academia. The violent and gory death of many of my comrades, proved sobering. By the time we reached the large detachment of Waffen-SS near Plock, our original number had been depleted by half. With their passing my enthusiasm for battle had waned.

From this point on things moved rapidly. Maltz seemed anxious to return to Berlin. Dr Friesburg, with his brown leather attaché case crammed to bulging with scientific papers and books, volunteered to accompany him. I was chosen to drive them to the train station. There, after handing Friesburg a letter for my father, I bid these two officers farewell.

My role in the military camp was to drive SS Standartenführer, Erich Krannhal. With the summer of 1944 upon us, daily reports of the Polish resistance, along with eyewitness accounts of Russian troop movements, reached my new commandant's desk. Although I was not privy to the specifics, my regular contact with Krannhal and his junior officers allowed me to piece together what had occurred.

On July 21, the newly formed Polish National Committee signaled the Soviets advance. This, in turn, drew the massive Russian army into our sector. Within a week, their soldiers reached the outskirts of Warsaw. We rallied to confront this onslaught. Although the Russians had vastly superior numbers and weaponry and could have easily decimated us, they halted their drive at the border of the city and refused to proceed farther, forcing their supposed allies, the Polish army and resistance, to defend their capital and surrounding countryside.

Confronted with only one poorly equipped enemy, we unleashed our crack forces upon them, administering the beating they deserved. While cowardly crying out for their Soviet comrades for help, these inferior Poles readily succumbed to our superbly trained forces. It was a field day, almost like target practice. In no time we destroyed a significant percentage of their inferior armed forces and deported the majority of the civilian population.

From the statistics to which I was privy after the war, of the nearly one million civilians who resided in Warsaw prior to the insurrection, we managed to *eliminate almost two hundred thousand. Immediately after the capitulation, another seven hundred thousand were evacuated to Auschwitz and Belsen. By late November, as the early snows of winter began to fall, all that remained of the insolent city of Warsaw was empty, unpopulated streets and smoldering, hollowed out ruins.*

The last half of 1944 was an extremely stressful time for me. There was the danger inherent in the Polish conflict compounded by concerns about an imminent confrontation with the Russian Army. There was also my family, who, back in the Fatherland, remained in extreme peril.

By mid-July, graphic details of the Allied invasion at some obscure French beach called Normandy finally reached our SS-Waffen *encampment. After that, with each passing supply transport, we garnered updated information about the Western attack, as the well-supplied, numerically superior American and British forces pushed our* Wehrmacht *back across the Rhine.*

Then, in early December, a letter from Berlin reached me. It was from Father.

November 14, 1944

My dearest Hans,

After failing numerous times in the past several months to contact you, I'm forwarding this letter with more confidence this time, now that I have your address with the Waffen-SS encampment in Plock, Poland. That bit of information was delivered to me by the venerable Dr. Friesburg, who stopped by our apartment last month. Arriving late one rainy afternoon, he conveyed your belated regards, apologized for the delay in following up on your request, stayed through supper, and spent some time describing, in general terms, the fascinating research in which you two had engaged at Lubartów. He referred to you in superlatives and seemed impressed by the quality of your work. In response to your inquiry, yes, except for a nagging cough and some recent unexplained weight loss, I am well. In comparison to our poor Fatherland, you might say I'm excellent.

Unfortunately, the Allied bombing raids have taken their toll. Here, in Berlin, our water, electric, and communication systems are in shambles. The accursed Americans, with their monstrous Flying Fortresses, pollute our skies every night, dropping thousands of tons of explosives. Several sections of the city have been totally demolished. Many of the local industrial centers are badly damaged. Despite all this, hope still remains. Just yesterday, Der Führer announced that the V1 and V2, our new super bombs, are ready for deployment. Once the British and Americans taste these weapons, the allied armies should be thoroughly demoralized. This, no doubt, will permit us to reverse the course of the conflict.

Several of the cities in Lower Saxony are receiving their share of abuse. Our beautiful Hanover has been attacked several times, putting your mother, brother Wolfgang, and sister Clara in a precarious position. Just last week, the *Harrenhausen Palace*, that beautiful mansion just two miles from our house, was almost completely destroyed. Isle's father has generously offered the three of them refuge at his small farm near Wunstorf.

As for news about your other sister, Magarette called me last month—a minor miracle given the abysmal condition of the telephone system—and reported that after she left the BMD, she secured a job in Leipzig working as a secretary to the local *Gauleiter*. She sounds well and misses you very much.

News about the Polish uprising in Warsaw and its successful containment by the *Wehrmacht* and your *Waffen-SS* divisions reached us. I'm certain of your valor and pray for your safe return. Speculation about the Russians restrained support of the Poles at the banks of the Vistula is circulating around the intelligence community. Word has it that Herr Stalin, intent on showing the belligerent and beleaguered Polish Nationals how dependent they truly are on their Russian neighbors, decided to use us to teach them a lesson. Now that that mission is complete, the Big Red Bear will certainly resume his counter-attack.

That fact brings me to my next concern. The political situation in Berlin deteriorates in direct proportion to the increasing demands of our two-front war. Believe it or not, the possibility of the Fatherland's capitulation is actually being discussed in the inner circles. Of course, Hitler, still convinced that some miracle will occur to shift the momentum in our favor, will not entertain talk of defeat. Herr Himmler, on the other hand, seems more realistic. Suffice it to say that, under his direction, secret efforts toward an honorable peace have been initiated.

Hans, I'm acutely aware that as a soldier of the Reich, your responsibility in this time of need is to fight for our great country. However, in addition to the battlefield, please remember that noncombatant arenas exist where this role can be played. Your presence back here in the capital, near the seat of government, would prove invaluable for the present as well as the uncertain future. Please take that into consideration

A glance at my watch tell me the hour is late. Tomorrow I meet with Herr Ohlendorf to discuss efforts of the *Gestapo* and the *Wehrmacht* intelligence agencies to cooperate. Despite our ideological difference we have been commanded to work together. Unfortunately, since the assassination attempt on Hitler, our positions have been polarized further. Cooperation may not be possible. However, my role is to work toward this end. My preparation for the meeting is far from complete. Thus, I will conclude this correspondence now.

Dearest son, be healthy, be brave, be valiant, and seriously entertain my request to return home.

Your loving father.

While reviewing the letter a second time, I tried to read between the lines. Certainly, if the military effort was going that poorly, and defeat was imminent, a concerted effort to secure the best possible peace would be appropriate. The Allies, I'd heard, were insisting on an unconditional surrender. That was something no loyal German would consider. However, if Heinrich Himmler was truly spearheading efforts to secure an honorable peace—and he succeeded—the stock of the SS would certainly increase during the post-war period.

My thoughts then turned to my father's health. Although he tended to minimize it, his casual references to a chronic cough and weight loss were bothersome. Suddenly, my yearning to stand against the Bolshevik offensive was tempered by a genuine regard for my family's safety and well-being. On the day after my father's letter arrived, I applied for transfer to the Western front. My request was denied.

On the morning of January 12, 1945, amidst a thick, almost impenetrable fog, the long anticipated Russian offensive began. Two droning air squadrons were followed by seventy infantry and armored divisions. It took them three days, but they finally broke through our Warsaw defense line.

Theirs was an awesome display of power. Wave after wave of Russian tanks and soldiers streamed across the countryside. Our Waffen-SS, *in support of the* Wehrmacht, *managed to inflict a huge number of causalities on the burly peas-*

ant army. But in the end, our numerical inferiority, almost one to four, proved critical. On the second day of the conflict, as we stood at the edge of the battlefield, I overheard Kraanhals complaining to a pair of his junior officers about the situation. He related how, on the eve of the Russian attack, Der Führer, in a desperate attempt to relieve a besieged garrison in Budapest, diverted two of our best Panzer divisions southward and away from eastern Poland occupation force. This action substantially weakened our already precarious position. Then, when it was apparent we were to be over-run, our commanders requested permission from Hitler to roll with the punch and retreat to a more secure position. His response: "Stand and fight."

To this day, I still have nightmares about those battalions of T34 tanks stretching back to the horizon. Although our smaller, quicker PzKwIV's made a brilliant account of themselves, the sheer volume of the onslaught quickly overwhelmed them.

Next we tried to impede their progress by planting dense minefields in their path. But the Russians had a unique way of sweeping these booby-trapped fields. So numerous and expendable were their troops, that the Bolshevik commanders sent column after column of infantrymen across the expanse, systematically triggering the mines until they were all detonated.

On the third day of the Russian offensive, the Red army flooded Warsaw's western suburbs. That's when my minor role in the conflict came to an abrupt end. It occurred while I was transporting Standartenführer Kraanhals to near our defensive position on the line from Plock to Lód. With artillery exploding in the distance and the soldiers deep in their trenches, we inspected the Waffen-SS division called Hitlerjugend. While making a quick sweep along the rear of the line a shell from a seventy-five millimeter turret cannon exploded five feet behind my jeep. The vehicle leapt up into a toppling spin. As it flipped over I was thrown clear. Kraanhals, on the other hand, was not so lucky. He ended up pinned under the hood.

For a few moments, I felt dazed. Finally recovering my senses, I glanced around and appreciated what had happened. When I went to shift to my commanding officer's side excruciating pain radiated from shin to groin. Glancing down I saw my bloodstained battle fatigues. Fighting off the waves of nausea I rolled up the pants-leg and found my shin fractured just below the knee. The longbone, white and bloody, protruded from itself at an impossible angle. The splintered ends of the compound fracture made me vomit before I passed out.

When I regained consciousness, I was off the battlefield lying supine in the rear of a canvas-covered transport truck. By my side knelt a pleasant looking medic. A rolled blanket under my leg partially cushioned the rough ride. But the motion of the truck bouncing over the rough roads still sent successive waves of unbearable pain up my leg. Involuntarily, I screamed.

"I know it is difficult mein freund," the medic shouted over the roar of the truck's engine. "But the quieter you remain the less the pain." I nodded and bit on the sleeve of my army jacket. Sweat poured down my forehead. "Unfortunately, I have no analgesics to offer you. Our supplies were exhausted during the Polish campaign and the replacements have been diverted to the western campaign in the Ardennes." I nodded, not really caring about this explanation. All I wanted was a shot of morphine—or some of those wonderful psychotropic drugs I had access to at Lubartów. "Perhaps some Russian Vodka will help," he suggested, handing me a bottle of Stolchinian, three-quarters full. "This could be the only thing we have to show for our precious Eastern campaign."

The clear liquid burnt the back of my throat. It went down leaving a slight bitterness behind. Soon welcome warmth washed over my body. Temporarily, I forgot about my leg. "Where are we headed?" I asked, in a voice that sounded hoarse and halting. "Westward, I hope."

"Westward it is, away from the accursed Russians. Just across the river in Frankfurt an Der Oder is the closest military hospital."

One of the most eastern cities in Germany, it lay about sixty kilometers from Berlin. I actually knew of the small town. My transport train had made a stop there on its way to Lubartów. How long ago was that? It seemed like an eternity. Peering out the rear of the truck, I noticed how the road was lined with refugees, some burdened by bundles of clothes, others pushing carts full of household items or carrying babes in their arms. "Where is everyone going?" I inquired through my alcoholic haze.

"Isn't it obvious? They are fleeing the Russians. With the tales of Bolshevik atrocities streaking like wildfire across the countryside, even loyal Poles, those uncivilized simpletons who are being liberated, choose to flee."

Soon after that I began my convalescence.

Chapter 10

With its giant wheels screeching, the massive, steam-driven locomotive eased out of the small Frankfurt An Der Oder station, then merged with the main line just west of the small border town. After a brief ten-kilometer swing southward, it turned eastward toward Berlin. After more than three long years away, I was going home.

Although the calendar read March 25th, this was not a typical spring day in Germany. The temperature was mild, the flowers were in bloom, and scores of birds populated the azure sky. Gazing out the grimy window, my casted right leg awkwardly propped up on the vinyl seat beside me, I catalogued the devastation wrought by the Russian bombs on my beloved Germany.

The pastoral countryside with its once formidable farmhouses, plush forests, and the cheerful meadows appeared worn and weathered. Deep craters pocked the roads. Wildfires smoldered in the fields. The demolished buildings, long since deserted and forgotten, seemed ghostly. And worst of all, my proud, stalwart landsmen, so cruelly uprooted from their homes and villages, had morphed into a frightened mass of nomads fleeing the onrushing Slavs.

Just past the village of Furstenwalde, where the track paralleled the Spree-Odor Kanal, I finally lost sight of the depressing scene. Drained by despair, I reached into my faded army jacket and extracted my father's last letter, a correspondence which had arrived at the tiny military hospital in Frankfort while I was recovering from emergency surgery on my splintered shinbone. The tone of the letter matched my mood.

Father began by conveying his worst fears. With the two opposing armies relentlessly pressing down upon Berlin, the war was lost. He went on to express a deep concern he had about the safety of my mother and siblings who stood directly in the path of the Allied forces bearing down on Berlin.

Next he reported on Berlin. The capital was in chaos. The populace, shell-shocked and shaken, scurried around searching for food, water, and shelter. Compliments of the relentless Allied bombings, our once proud city had been reduced to a battered shell.

Despite the inevitability of defeat, our disillusioned Führer, along with a small cadre of loyal Generals, seemed determined to fight to the end. Unfortunately, now that all the able young men had been called to the front, only children, their mothers, aunts, and a feeble band of elderly remained behind, conscripted to man the streetside barricades and crumbling buildings. And as my steam-belching train clanked past those eastern city limits, I couldn't help but notice some of those pitiful defensive lines, preparing for the final battle.

The Bahnhof Friedrichstrasse *seemed deserted as the train came to a stuttering halt. Rising unsteadily, I slung a small canvas bag over my shoulder, set my crutches on the linoleum and negotiated the narrow steps down to the platform. No boisterous hero's welcome awaited my return from the front. Instead, a few elderly Germans stood in a huddled mass and nodded toward me as I passed the stationhouse.*

Out on the sidewalk, I glanced around. I was immediately struck by the magnitude of the devastation. As far as the eye could see, mounds of bricks and rubble lined both sides of Friedrichstrasse. *Northward, I searched for a familiar row of apartment buildings. To my dismay it, too, had been leveled. Through the clearing I noticed the remains of Berlin University's administration and library buildings. Hunched over, weary-looking civilians poked through the giant piles of debris, scavenging for anything that could improve their chance of survival. In the distance I heard the mournful cry of an air-raid siren. No one seemed to notice.*

Little traffic filled the street as I hobbled unsteadily toward Father's apartment. A man driving a rusty blue pick-up must have seen me struggling and pulled over to offer me a lift. He introduced himself as a dairy farmer from Eberswalde, north of the city. He had just left his wife and son, a boy of fourteen, off at the eastern perimeter of the city to stay at a relative's house. While we talked, he reached behind his seat and pulled out an old hunting rifle. Proudly, he indicated that he was headed for the barricades, determined to help Hitler stave off the hated Russians. Then, after admiring my uniform, although he knew nothing of me, he praised my valor and heroism.

Due to the scores of wrecked vehicles and hundreds of aimlessly wandering individuals, it took us nearly fifteen minutes to reach Father's place. He pulled up in front of the familiar building. After struggling to my feet, I thanked him warmly. As he drove off I couldn't help admire this example of a loyal German, who despite overwhelming adversity, could still hold his head up high.

I pushed open the unlocked door. The small apartment smelled rank and musty. There was evidence of habitation, but no signs of life. An egg-smeared plate sat on the kitchen table beside a piece of moldy bread. A mug with dried coffee stood on the counter next to a sink full of dirty dishes.

I headed toward the living room, stopping to open a window, letting in the late afternoon breeze. The air washed away some of the stench. I called out for my father, whose room was just down the hall. When I reached the door I knocked twice. No one answered. Perhaps he was at his usual place, SD headquarters. Then I sensed there was nothing usual about the way things were. Finally, I turned the handle and entered the room.

Resembling little more than a flesh-covered skeleton, I found him lying very still in the narrow bed. A soiled sheet covered his chest. His face looked pale and gaunt, his eyes staring vacantly. For a brief, horrible moment I thought he was dead. But the gentle rise and fall of his thin chest indicated otherwise. Then he began coughing, a harsh, guttural sound that rose from the depths of his soul. The force of this spasm forced him upright. Leaning over, he deposited a glob of bloody mucous onto the floor. Exhausted, he sank back onto his gray, stained pillow. I approached. He seemed to react to my shadow.

"Is that you Hans?" he inquired in a hoarse whisper. "I feared you were dead."

"It is me, Father," I replied softly.

As if this brief conversation was already taking its toll, he took a deep breath and said, "That's good."

"You're pretty sick, aren't you?"

"Just a lingering cold, son. Nothing to worry about."

He turned his thin face in my direction, fixed his filmy eyes on mine, but seemed to find difficulty focusing. Once again mucous rattled noisily in his chest. After breathing deeply another violent coughing spasm gripped him. Wrapping a supportive arm around his frail, bony shoulders I offered to help.

"There is nothing to get son. Just pull up the chair and sit a while."

I steadied him on the side of the bed. Sitting there I gradually I eased into the muted rhythm of that quiet afternoon, lulled by the familiarity of the apartment and Father's labored breathing. Outside the sun dipped behind the crumbled buildings. Shadows inched across the darkening room. Now, distant from the demands of the Reich and the frenzied commotion of the battlefield, we remained father and son, bound in silent communication. Gazing at him, I refused to see a diseased shell of a man. Instead I imagined the healthy, energetic lawyer and politician who had shared his life with me, believed in me, and made me the man I'd become.

"Hans," he said looking up slowly, his raspy voice wrenching me from my reverie. "It's appropriate that you've returned just now. Now you can make a final contribution to the Reich." He coughed again. "We have both given our deepest hearts and souls to the cause," he continued. "This should be a source of great pride. But with the enemy breathing its rancid breath down on us from all sides, we must make our final stand. We can't be vanquished without a fight."

I was about to dismiss his ramblings as those of a sick, old man. Then he said, "Hans, over the years, my department has amassed a wealth of valuable information, much of it highly classified. We possess secrets that, if exposed, could compromise the future of the Fatherland for decades. Great men in important positions function in mysterious ways. In the process, they sometimes engage in deeds that if publicized would destroy them. All evidence of those deeds must be destroyed." He paused for a moment, took a moist breath and added, "And you're the only one who can do the job."

"Me?" I was about to protest but caught myself. Here I was, regarding what may very well have been the last request of a dying man. How could I refuse? Instead I asked, "What must I do?"

The glimmer of a satisfied smile crossed his lips. "While you worked at the newspaper," he told me, "you had security clearance to review files in the top secret record room. You were familiar with the information and knew its location. Those records must be destroyed. The room that houses them is more secure than a vault. But I have one of three special keys along with the combination to the lock on the door. Both are taped to the underside of the top drawer in my bureau. With them you can gain access to the room."

He was panting now and eased back down against his soiled pillows. Finally, he continued, "Hans, my son, retrieve the key and the combination. Tonight, after dark, go to Fifty-three Wilhelmstrasse. A guard will be there, but you should be able to subdue him. Admit yourself into that record room and destroy every scrap of paper you can find. Whatever you neglect may spell doom for some loyal patriot."

With that my father inhaled deeply, gasped harshly, and then curled up into a ball on the edge of the mattress. A few moments later, with his eyes still open, he died.

With the curfew and air raid alert still in effect I approached SD headquarters. Struggling with my crutches I ascended a flight of concrete steps. A sliver of yellow light snuck out from behind the drawn windows. I knocked on the door.

"Who's there?" barked a gruff voice.

"Herr Reichman, son of SS-Obersturmbannführer *Richard Reichman."*

"State your business?"

"Open the door and I shall."

The latch from the deadbolt lock clicked. The door split a crack. A stocky guard, no older than twenty, dressed in a brown SS uniform, sized me up. The light from a desk lamp framed him in the doorway. When he saw my uniform and noticed the cast on my leg he seemed to relax. Stepping back, he gestured me in. Then he saw the lieutenant's bars on my shoulders and snapped to attention.

"My apologies Herr Obersturmführer. *What can I do for you?"*

"At ease Rottenführer," *I replied dismissively. "As you know, my father is the deputy director to Herr Ohlendorf. He sent me down her to retrieve papers he requires for a meeting he's chairing in the morning. I will only be a minute. And by the way, in his haste to send me out, he neglected to inform me of the number to his office. If you could be so kind?"*

"Why certainly Herr Obersturmführer. *The list is on my desk."*

He turned his back and started walking away. Carefully balancing myself on my left leg, I raised my right crutch and with all my might struck him on the back of the head. He stumbled then fell to the floor, his forehead glancing off the edge of the metal desk. Hobbling over, I confirmed that he was unconscious. Then, with some difficulty, I secured his limbs to the desk supports. Lastly I gagged his mouth.

Guided by my flashlight's beam I shuffled down the long hallway. At the stairwell, I descended two flights to floor B. Inching toward the front of the building, I finally located the record room. A thick metal door protected it. I felt for the combination lock. In the fading light, I worked the combination. After running through the sequence a half-dozen times I finally got it right. The inner door yielded to my father's key. I entered the chamber.

Once the door was shut behind me, I swept the flashlight beam across the interior. The shelves and carousels were exactly as I remembered. Far in the corner I located the bank of metal cabinets, so high they nearly grazed the ceiling. After shuffling over, I opened one of the drawers. Rifling through the green, red and yellow-tabbed manila folders, I pulled out a few. After reading off the familiar names, Hesse, Goebels, Canaris, printed so neatly in black block letters, I knew that the vital and incriminating records were still intact. Next I glanced through a few of the other drawers. They contained charts on all the major SS officers and executives. What I had before me was an invaluable collection of data. I couldn't begin to speculate what it would be worth to the enemy. Father had given me the task of protecting the reputation of the Third Reich.

Any fire would create a copious amount of smoke and fume. I scanned the room for an exhaust vent. I located its grated cover at floor level along the outside wall. Setting my cheek against the metal I felt the gentle updraft. Next, I found a large waste can, dragged it over near the vent, and began emptying the contents of the first file cabinet into it. When it was half full, I withdrew a pint-bottle of kerosene from the inside pocket of my coat. Half went into the trash-can. A moment later an angry yellow flame leapt out. Quickly I smothered the flame with another pile of papers. It burned through seconds later.

Instantly, the room was filled with smoke. Involuntarily I coughed. Using a bottled-water dispenser in the corner of the room, I wet my handkerchief and draped it over my nose and eyes. Once I could breathe again, I began feeding the fire.

So engrossed was I in the job at hand that I failed to hear the hinge squeak. Suddenly, with a loud bang, the door swung open. Turning quickly, I watched two bulky figures holding powerful flashlights enter the room. In the rim of light I noticed drawn revolvers. Speaking broken German, the shorter one shouted, "Stop immediately! Arms above your head!" I reached for another file. The gun spit fire. Papers flew from my hand.

"Away from there, I said! Next time, the bullet will blow your fuckin' Nazi head off!" I raised my arms and eased away.

Then the short man spoke in English to his partner who nodded and started searching the room. Coming upon the water dispenser in the corner, he yanked it from its metal support, hoisted it onto his shoulder, and carried it to the can. A cloud of steam hissed from the red-hot receptacle as he doused my blaze.

The tall, thinner intruder made another curt comment in English. The shorter one patted me down for weapons then reached into his pocket and pulled out a picture, compared the face in the photograph to mine, then addressed me in his broken German.

"You're Hans Reichman, aren't you? We suspected you'd return from the front to see your father. And he sent you here. We've been looking for this SS stash for months." He paused for moment then continued. "You've performed quite a service for us, Reichman. For this alone we should be grateful. But the fact that you're a filthy murdering Nazi negates all that. In fact, if I had carte blanche in this matter you'd be dead. However, my department has rules against murdering people in cold blood. And with your background in the SD, you may have some value."

He paused. When he spoke again his tone was slow and deliberate.

"Now that we've captured you alive, Herr Reichman, I've been authorized by the American government to offer you a choice. Either you consent to function as an Allied intelligence service operative during the post-war period or you will be arrested and tried as a war criminal caught in the act of destroying critical government documents."

Everything was happening so fast. My head spun. Would their threat stick? With reports of Allied and Russian atrocities toward innocent Germans, I couldn't be sure. For all I knew, the tall one would order his partner to murder me on the spot. I needed to buy time.

"What specifically would you have me do?" I asked cautiously.

"That has yet to be decided. All that is required now is a simple yes or no."

"Yes," I replied.

The taller one nodded. Shorty was then ordered to bind my hands. With them secured behind me I was shoved toward the door. My cast weighed a ton. I stumbled and almost fell. They told me to point toward the back door. A few moments later, we were outside. A canvas covered transport truck raced up the back ally. A trio of men jumped out. Whatever files I hadn't destroyed were loaded onto the truck. The vehicle was sent off. I was then led me back to the stairwell. Near the front door we passed the young rottenführrer, *still bound and* gagged by the front desk. But now, besides the bruise, a bullet hole and a pool of dark blood soiled his forehead.

The late model Mercedes streaked through the shrouded Berlin streets. For me, the tight blindfold that covered my eyes intensified the darkness. With each turn I leaned hard, first to the right, then to the left. The mad driver continued this serpentine motion for almost a half hour. Finally, the car came to a stop.

The passenger-side door opened and a blast of cool, night air rushed at my face. With the help of a vise-like grip on my upper arm, I was assisted out of the automobile and led up two flights of steps. There were nineteen to be exact. The door to a corridor was opened. At the far end, I was forced into a wooden chair, bound, and abandoned.

An unspecified time later, probably forty-five minutes, maybe an hour, I heard shuffling feet and the murmur of voices. Equipment was shifted into place. The blindfold was removed. Suddenly I was staring into harsh yellow light, its brightness intensified by the hours my eyes had been covered. From near the light, a man who spoke fluent German, his accent suggesting that he was from my part of the country, Lower Saxony, addressed me.

Beginning with a few simple questions, he confirmed my name, age, birthplace, and background. I answered his inquiries honestly and without hesitation. Next, he explored my training with the SS and my work following graduation. It was then that I became cautious. I avoided specifics, offering only generalities.

He wanted names. I recalled none. He wanted a description of the activities in the camp. I offered him ambiguity. Despite being a prisoner who'd agreed to work for the enemy to save his life, I wasn't about to reveal information that was hazardous to what remained of the SS and the Reich.

Finally, after delivering the same sequence of questions a dozen times, my polished, German interrogator paused. He conferred with someone in English. During this brief interlude, I tried to discern who was around me. At least three individuals stood near the light. Another, I sensed, was a little behind me off to the right. I could smell cigarette fumes on his overcoat.

"You know your answers are unsatisfactory, Herr Reichman," continued the man with the impeccable German accent. "Suffice it to say, eventually you will talk. Make no mistake about it. We have methods of interrogation that are at least as effective as Dr. Friesburg's. But that must wait for another time."

At the mention of my former mentor's name, a pang of anxiety gripped my chest. My secrets, it seemed, weren't so secret after all. Suddenly, the blinding light was extinguished. My restraints were removed and my visitors departed leaving me alone on that uncomfortable wooden chair. While massaging my wrists, I assessed my surroundings.

My prison was quite bare, roughly cuboid in shape, and devoid of furniture, carpeting, window-covering, or pictures. A frayed, white shade covered the only window and partially blocked the moonlight. Iron bars were welded to the outside of the frame, their shadows on the cloth. After stretching my limbs and being without my crutches, I was forced to hop around the room. After running my hands along the walls and floorboards, I inspected the bars. They were solid and immobile.

Peering outside, all I could appreciate was the rear of a broad, redbrick, five-story building which stood about twenty feet away. From its generic appearance, it could have been any one of ten thousand apartment buildings or warehouses in the capital. Below, a narrow alley separated the buildings. There were broad thoroughfares on both ends. A group of dumpsters, overflowing with trash and garbage, stood ten yards away.

A knock on the door startled me. Three men re-entered the room. One switched on the interrogation lamp. This time its harsh beam was directed toward the dirty plastered wall to my right. "Herr Reichman," began the one who spoke flawless German. He was thin and short with wire-rimmed glasses and close-cropped steel-gray hair. "My colleague tells me that you've agreed to switch allegiances and join our cause. I congratulate you on your wise, insightful decision. Now that the psychotic megalomaniac who has mesmerized this country for the last fourteen years is about to plunge to his final defeat, it is time for you to save your precious Aryan skin. Never for a moment doubt that the Allies will deal harshly with the perpetrators of the atrocities committed under that sick, little Austrian's rule.

"Suffice it to say that your membership in the SS implies your participation in these atrocities and effectively seals your fate. In the event that you should prove your innocence of any military-related crimes—such as claiming you were just following orders—there is still that little act of destroying top-secret government documents. That alone will be enough to hang you from the highest tree in Germany."

As he spoke, his eyes seemed to gleam with malicious delight. He was like a weasel, stationed by the rat hole, waiting for his evening meal to emerge. After strolling over to the only chair in the room, he sat down.

"Thus, Herr Reichman, your future is by no means secure," he continued. "But, at least, if you switch stripes, you won't be summarily eliminated. And who knows, with the quirky peculiarities of post-war politics, along with conscientious service to our cause, you might prove your worth and eventually find yourself in a much more favorable position."

Next, he gave me some background on the ongoing military situation. An anti-Hitler, German intelligence network headed by a man named Reinhardt Gehlen was in existence and fully operational. I would be assigned to this organization. There, I would function as a foreign-based agent, gathering data concerning Communist activities in countries the Soviets were certain to control during the post-war period. Logically, he told me, the Americans had a strong investment in creating a balance of power with the Bolsheviks. The Gehlen organization would be vital pending the creation of an American-based operation in those countries.

Next, the German interrogator introduced me to the American who had engineered my capture. He went by the code name, Sigma. Sigma functioned as a liaison between the Americans and Gehlen. Whenever I garnered information about the Communists, he would function as my liaison. In addition, he was in the process of setting up a meeting between Herr Gehlen and myself.

Twenty-four hours earlier, I had been a loyal member of the SS, an injured German soldier returning home from the eastern front. Now I was being conscripted as a spy for the Americans against the Russians. The world I knew was disintegrating. The country I loved dearly had been systematically destroyed. My sense of self was decomposing with it. But there was more than Germany which shaped my identity. Isle and Dieter came to mind.

"Gentleman," I said in my most conciliatory tone. "Since it is obvious that I have little alternative but to accept your offer, I do and thank you for sparing my life. Needless to say, I find myself trapped in a dramatic turn of events. With my background in intelligence, I suspect I can be of service to you. But before I can fully dedicate myself to this new cause, I am preoccupied with concerns that go beyond my personal safety."

"And what may those be, Herr Reichman?" inquired the German.

"All of Germany is in flux. Two huge armies are bearing down on Berlin. Amid this harsh reality my paramount concern is for the safety of my family, my wife and child."

"Ah," chimed in this American with the code name Sigma, "your family. And where are they now?"

"The last I heard, they were living a few miles west of Hanover in Wunstorf with my wife's parents. I haven't seen them for over two years now, not since my training in Brunswick at the Academie. That last letter from my dear wife Isle arrived over a year ago."

"Hmm," Sigma continued, "perhaps I could get word of them from the forward regiments of General Simpson's Ninth? His forces will be passing through that sector any day now. Last I heard they were at the eastern border of Teutoburger Wald."

"That would be extremely helpful," I continued somewhat hesitantly. "However, until I see them with my own eyes, I could never be truly reassured. I realize that in my current position I have no right to make such a request, but I am appealing to your sense of compassion in this matter."

After a brief pause the American replied, "I'll see what I can do."

Two days later and less than seventy-two hours since the last time I'd traveled by rail, I was back on the Trans-Allemagne, heading west out of Berlin toward my boyhood hometown of Hanover. It was just after dawn on April 1, 1945.

The two days after my capture had been bearable. Demonstrating some sense of civility, my new employers dredged up a small wooden table, a kerosene heater and an old, lumpy mattress for me to sleep upon. After exterminating the concomitant bedbugs I succeeded in making the cell habitable. To pass the time I read German translations of the books and propaganda literature Herr Sigma gave me.

While lying awake in my drafty detention cell, I allowed my prisoner-agent role fade quietly into the background. Naturally thoughts drifted back to memories of Isle and Dieter. I imagined how my son had grown since I'd seen him last and wondered if he'd know me when I arrived. I was confident that Isle was doing everything in her power to keep him safe from the raging conflict that surrounded them. But I also knew that sometimes circumstances have a way of overwhelming good intentions. I prayed they were safe. The uncertainty made my longing more desperate.

And what of Isle? With no recent photo or a letter in the mail, all I could draw from was my memory. I knew she missed me as much as I missed her. We had a special bond, the kind that great romances were written about. I had no doubt she'd been faithful and would welcome me home—however briefly—with loving arms. I wanted desperately to let her know I was coming, yet the thrill of an unexpected visit seemed just as exciting.

Our time together in Wunstorf would be brief. Unrealistically, I wondered if somehow it could be arranged that my family could join me in Switzerland. Perhaps an apartment in my new destination would be acceptable. They could be part of my cover. Perhaps a cottage in the woods...?

"Wake up, Reichman," Sigma said in broken German. "We're in Wunstorf."

Shaking off the shroud of sleep, I straightened. He handed me my crutches and helped me off the train. Having never visited Isle at her parents' home during our brief courtship in Hanover, the tiny station was foreign to me. Hobbling over to the stationmaster, I inquired about a cab or car that could take us to the farm. With the town bracing for the approaching Allied army there were no vehicles in sight. However, Herr Strickland, the blacksmith, had a livery stable on Herschstrasse and might have a buckboard and a pair of horses to loan us for the ten-mile excursion.

I thanked him and we started off in the direction he'd pointed. Almost immediately we were flanked by rows of stores and shops, most locked and boarded. Peering around, I noted with some relief that the small town had been spared the full fury of the Allied bombings. Being a farm town, without the burden of heavy industry, it wasn't on the military target list. This realization increased my confidence level regarding my family's safety. Incredible as it seemed, after two long years, I would finally be seeing my wife and son again.

Herr Strickland was out when we reached the front door of his locked establishment. A sign on the window noted he would return after dinner. It was five-thirty in the early evening. I noticed a small tavern two doors down and suggested we pass the time there.

The interior of the bar was dimly lit. It took a few minutes for my eyes to adjust. A paddle fan, suspended from the center of the ceiling, circulated stale, smoky air. A low-pitched hum of conversing voices engulfed us. I spotted a table in the far corner of the room. We claimed it.

A waitress wearing a soiled white blouse and black apron took our order. As we waited for our food I surveyed the room. Most of the patrons were elderly farmers or farmhands, slouched upon barstools or clustered around the wooden tables. A few comely, middle-aged women provided a welcomed con-

*trast to the crusty faces of the old German men. Then, just as I turned back to
Sigma, one of the farmhands stood up and approached our table.*

*"Excuse me sir," he began, his Lower Saxony accent pronounced. He shift-
ed an old, worn hat back and forth between his dry, calloused hands. "You
wouldn't happen to be Herr Reichman, would you? I've only seen a picture, but
the one I was shown bears a striking resemblance."*

Somewhat taken aback, I answered, "As a matter-a-fact, I am."

*My reply seemed to make him even more anxious. He began to speak but
the words got caught in his throat. "If you are, in fact, Herr Reichman," he continued his voice barely more than a whisper, "then I have terrible news."*

*Anxiety burned in my chest. "What are you talking about, man?" I
demanded. "Out with it!"*

*"Something t-t-terrible," he repeated. "It happened just yesterday. Out on
the farm where I'm a helper. I was the only one to see it. I was planning to find
you, but didn't know where to look. I thought of Hanover so I bought a ticket on
tomorrow morning's train."*

"What happened man? Stop jabbering and get to the point!"

*"They're dead, sir. They're all dead. It was the Americans. The American
soldiers. They shot them. One of them dropped this."*

*With a trembling hand he showed me a set of what the Americans call dog
tags. I snatched them from him. I began to study the numbers etched in the metal
plate. But my tears soon obscured the symbols. I tried to focus on what to do
next but...*

Thoroughly engrossed in the manuscript, the sharp knock on the front door startled Carmen. Annoyed with the interruption, he set the papers down. Who the
hell can that be? he wondered. "Hold your shirt on," he grumbled. "I'm coming." Glancing at his wristwatch he was amazed to see the time was after four
A.M. Snatching his revolver out of its holster he called loudly, "Who is it?"

No one answered. "All right," he said, moving to the door. Holding the gun
out before him he flipped the lever to the deadbolt lock. "This better be worth
it," he mumbled under his breath. As he grabbed the knob he was surprised to
find it suddenly turn swiftly against his palm. In the next instance, he was
bounced forcefully off the adjoining wall. "What the hell!" he exclaimed.

A burly man with steel gray hair wearing a red flannel shirt and a goalie's
mask rushed him. Carmen stared into his attacker's cold gray eyes. In one

smooth motion the intruder grabbed the detective's wrist, whipped his arm around clockwise, and forced Carmen's torso to pirouette. The gun fell harmlessly to the carpet. Trapped in a tight hammer lock, Carmen was pinned against the wall. Swiftly another revolver was raised. Its butt then came down sharply on the detective's right temple. Carmen saw stars.

It was well past dawn when Carmen finally regained consciousness. In a dazed stupor he surveyed his living room. His vision was blurred. Pain pulsated through his head. Reaching up, he fingered the throbbing, golf-ball size lump above his ear.

"Whew," he moaned. "What hit me?"

Slowly the image of his unexpected visitor penetrated his consciousness, answering his query and also clearing up any confusion as to why he found himself sprawled out on the carpet by the front door. Assuming that the purpose of the attack was robbery, Carmen took inventory. Rising unsteadily to his feet he noticed his television and stereo were intact. Inside his bedroom nothing seemed amiss. Without much cash or jewelry lying around, he apparently didn't have much to steal. Returning to the living room, he slumped back down on his reading chair and wondered what the masked visitor could have wanted. Suddenly he knew.

After a quick check of the table and the rug around the chair he exclaimed, "Oh shit, it's gone!"

Now painfully aware that the old Nazi's manuscript had more significance than he'd originally suspected, Carmen considered his options. It was obvious that he needed to find that old German woman but had no clue to her whereabouts. Could she have anything to do with the Rosenberg case? Then, it was Abe Cohen's face that popped into his head. Something the old Jew had said about Malcolm Rosenberg's past struck him. What the heck, thought Carmen. It's worth a try. I got nothing else to go on.

No one answered his knock as Carmen stood on the stoop outside Cohen's small redbrick house in the Squirrel Hill section of Pittsburgh. Once he was finally convinced that no one was home, the detective assumed the role of an insurance adjustor delivering a check from the estate of one of Cohen's recently deceased cousins and began checking with the neighbors.

91

From a pleasant, middle-aged Jewish housewife next door he discovered that the former president of Rodef Shalom congregation frequently spent long weekends at his cottage in the mountains just south of Ligonier. With fluttering eyelashes and a firm grip on Carmen's hand, the helpful woman shared that Cohen had indeed packed up his Buick last evening, just before charging his friendly neighbor with the task of taking in his mail. One mandatory cup of coffee and several deflected passes later, Carmen finally escaped from the pleasant, though persistent, woman's clutches, holding a Westmoreland County address and a crude map in his newly perfumed hand.

Chapter II

The hour-long ride to the western Pennsylvania town of Ligonier was bitterly nostalgic for Carmen. Cruising along on the four-lane bypass road that skirted the quaint town of Greensburg, with its colonial style red brick houses, multi-colored shops, and domed county building, he fondly recalled the Arlo Guthrie concert he'd taken Rachael to at the Palace Theatre in 1970. Although his driver's license was a mere nine months old at the time, her father had permitted the event.

While listening to Woody Guthrie's famous son croon songs like *City of New Orleans, Mr. Customs Man*, and excerpts from *Alice's Restaurant*, they'd snuggled in the last row of the aging concert hall. Later that evening, they stopped in Schenley Park for an hour to make out. That night with Rachael, Carmen knew, was one of the sweetest of his life.

No sooner had the memory of that precious high school concert fade did he pass the Mountain View Lodge, just west of Latrobe. That's when his reverie turned sour. In May of 1976 Carmen's younger brother, Vincent, had tied the knot in the ballroom of that charming, rustic inn. The detective, then a senior at the Police Academy, would have loved to have had Rachael as his date. Unfortunately, she was out of his life by then, back in Philadelphia, a newlywed herself. So instead of sharing the special evening with the woman he loved, Carmen had been forced to watch the festivities from a table in the corner, alone, half-drunk, and feeling sorry for himself.

The sun broke through the clouds giving the asphalt a dappled look as it filtered through the dense trees that bordered both sides of the road. Leaving the fast food restaurants, motels, and service stations behind, Carmen felt invigorated by the woodsy smell of the brisk, autumn air. After passing Laurel Mountain State Park, he slowed to a stop at the intersection that marked

Jennerstown. A right onto state route 985 led to a gentle climb into the hills. Checking Cohen's neighbor's directions, he searched for Willowcrest Lane.

The two-lane country road was almost deserted, except for an occasional pick-up truck rattling past in the opposite direction. Dense woodland lined both sides of the road, which is probably why Carmen didn't appreciate the smoke until he was almost on top of it.

He located Willowcrest, a deeply furrowed dirt road full of rainwater pot-holes. After turning onto it, he slowed to a crawl, negotiating the windy path carefully, trying not to reactivate the throbbing from the blow to the head he'd received early that morning. Then, unexpectedly, his eyes began to burn. Suddenly he was engulfed by a dense cloud of smoke. Two hundred yards ahead a small white cottage was in flames.

He pulled over and watched in fascination as tongues of angry yellow fire leapt from the front windows. Approaching on foot, he'd just reached the clearing near a perimeter of trees when the slate roof shuddered and collapsed. Orange sparks escaped through the opening.

If Cohen had been in the house he was certainly burned to death by now. But Carmen needed to be sure. Off to the side of the conflagration he spied an outdoor pump. Shaking out his handkerchief, he saturated it with water. Placing the cloth over his nose and mouth he took three long strides toward the front window. The flames confronted him. He had to retreat. Next, he tried the front door. Using the moistened cloth he turned the knob and kicked.

A waft of hot hair rushed out, singing the hairs in his nose and nearly blinding him. With broad sweeping arcs he waved away the smoke, trying to discern the inside of the room. At first all he could make out were rough shapes, a chair, a table, and perhaps a couch in the corner. Ignoring the searing heat, he advanced slowly. Eventually, he found what he was looking for.

On the floor by the fireplace was a prostrate body, its head facing the door. On the carpet, next to a small bullet-hole in its forehead, was a puddle of blood. Despite the smoke and haze, Carmen recognized the tufts of gray hair belonging to Abe Cohen.

Since he was still conducting an unauthorized investigation that had suddenly become complicated by the appearance of another corpse, Carmen decided discretion was the better part of valor. Protocol insisted he should report the murder. He would do this, but with an anonymous call, once he was far from the scene. After making a mad dash for his car, he whipped through a tight U-turn, then sped down the dirt lane and onto route 985.

So intent was he on putting distance between him and the burning cottage, Carmen barely noticed the Westmoreland County Sheriff exiting a convenience store near the intersection of Route 30 and 985. The deputy had apparently received word about the fire was preparing to investigate. Abruptly caught between the urgency of checking out the blaze and flagging down the speeding motorist he decided that the former took precedence and only trailed the detective's green Fiat for a half-mile. Then, when Carmen was forced to pause at a stop sign, the officer recorded the plate number for future reference.

Carmen's mind was racing as he made his way back to his apartment. Another fire. Another body. The damn trail was becoming littered by corpses. And he was no closer to figuring out why.

Easing into the short driveway of his nine-story high-rise, Carmen pressed the garage door opener. Nothing happened. He tried again, but to no avail. Cursing his luck, he tossed the dead transmitter onto the passenger seat, backed out onto the street and searched for a parking spot.

Highland Avenue seemed tightly packed with parked cars, forcing the detective to drive around the block. Spotting an opening on Walnut, he claimed it. A few minutes later, he was back in his little one-bedroom apartment. And as the early afternoon sunlight peeked in through his blinds, Carmen reassessed his situation.

As Carmen frequently did when he was stymied, he settled himself in his easy chair and mentally retraced the course the investigation had taken. Checking his dog-eared note pad, he studied the comments of Kathy Bentley, the young nurse at Pittsburgh Memorial and then those of Howard Peterson, her no-nonsense hospital administrator. The former dwelled mostly on the young Dr. Rosenberg, Malcolm's son. The latter seemed more appropriate for a press release then an in-depth interview. Then there was Cohen. The old man had been very helpful when discussing Rosenberg senior's achievements and his stature in the Jewish community. However, when Carmen began digging into the eminent surgeon's past, Cohen had become vague and distant. Was there something he didn't want Carmen to know, something that might get him back on track?

And what about the journal? As far as Carmen was concerned, it was mostly a load of self-centered, egotistical drivel that glorified its author in the context of the most racist, homicidal dictatorship in the history of mankind. What relevance this had to the present, Carmen had no idea. But how could he forget how adamant the old German woman was about its significance. Unless she was just plain nuts, which was always a possibility, he couldn't just dismiss her out of hand. But without the manuscript—or a clue to where its deliverer was hiding—he was stuck. Disgusted with his dilemma, he got up and went to the fridge for a beer.

As he tossed the twist-off cap into the trash basket, he happened to glance down and notice the wrinkled brown paper in which the manuscript had been wrapped. Although he had originally thought the paper was blank, regarding it more intently he noticed the advertisement. Retrieving it from the basket, he smoothed it out on the kitchen table. It was a cut up grocery bag.

"Miller's Stop and Shop," he read aloud. In the lower right corner was, "Zelienople, Pennsylvania." Stopping a moment to reflect, he recalled that Zelienople was a small community northwest of Pittsburgh just off I 79. He fished out a map of Western Pennsylvania and confirmed that the small town rested just south of Moraine State Park. Feeling that old familiar tingle of excitement in his loins, he knew he'd picked up the scent.

"It's not much," he reminded himself. "But it's a start."

While pacing across his living room, he mapped out a plan. At one point in his ruminations, he paused by his rectangular picture window, split the blinds, and glanced down Highland. Mid-afternoon traffic seemed backed up all the way to Alder by a delivery truck driver taking his good old time backing into the Allen's Carpet Warehouse. A pair of teenagers strolled the pavement opposite a wrinkled old woman towing a shopping cart. A black-haired, Asian pushed her baby carriage past a group of plaid-skirted young girls from Sacred Heart Parochial School. Carmen was about to turn away when he caught a glimpse of a dark-haired man in a black suit coming out of the luncheonette next to the carpet store. For some reason his stiff gait and business-like attire seemed incongruous with the neighborhood. Carmen wasn't used to seeing many businessmen, bankers, or even lawyers spending their extended lunch hours on Highland Avenue. Perhaps he was a traveling salesman taking a quick break?

Then casually, the mystery man glanced directly up at Carmen's apartment building. With a start, the detective recognized him. It was Jeffries, one of the two Feds he'd sparred with in Powell's office.

What the hell's he doing here? Carmen wondered, feeling a little annoyed. And then he knew. Moving to an adjacent window in the dining room, Carmen scanned the row of parked cars across the street. He spotted the olive green Chevy Impala, a standard make and model. In the driver's seat sat McCormick, Jeffries' partner. As he observed the FBI vehicle, Jeffries joined McCormick in the car

I guess I'm not as invisible as I thought, Carmen thought grimly. It's a good thing they don't have much imagination when it comes to surveillance vehicles. A new plan of action instantly took form in his head.

The basement level garage where Carmen lived was designed to accommodate almost twenty-five cars. A rear door opened into a narrow alley. With the brown paper grocery bag from Miller's Stop and Shop in his pocket, Carmen slipped outside and headed toward Walnut.

Concerned that since the FBI was suddenly interested in him, Carmen assumed they must also know his car. He needed to switch vehicles. Careful to avoid Highland, he made a U-turn on Walnut and headed out of Shadyside. Recalling that the Exxon station on Forbes Avenue near CMU operated a small Budget Rent-a-car concession, he turned onto Fifth Avenue and headed there. Forty-five minutes later, with his green Fiat tucked safely away down one of the myriad of tiny east Oakland side streets, the resourceful detective turned a rented two-toned, gray Pontiac Grand Am west on Fifth Avenue and headed for the Parkway and Interstate 79 north.

Chapter 12

Matt stared out the window of Jane's room in Braddock General Hospital's Psyche Unit and surveyed the dilapidated slums of the aging industrial community. In the distance he caught a glimpse of the Monongahela. A weather-beaten tug coaxed a trio of barges piled high with coal and iron ore up the murky black surface from the strip mines of West Virginia toward one of the few remaining steel mills that dotted the borders of one of Pittsburgh's three rivers.

He reflected upon how, just over a week earlier, this hearty young woman had plummeted into those icy waters and survived. For ten days now he'd faithfully tracked her course, checking on her condition with the ICU nurses during the evenings and in the mornings when he'd worked the ER. A couple of times, he called the house doctor, an old buddy from his internship, and garnered more technical updates.

As far as the hospital's medical records department was concerned, she was still known as Jane Doe. A witty ICU RN, claiming that the young woman's hair reminded her of the famous historical figure, had modified this moniker to Jane Godiva. The nickname had stuck.

To Matt, such a sustained lack of identity seemed unusual. In all his years in medicine, he'd never dealt with a *real* Jane Doe. Whenever a patient showed up without identification, someone eventually showed up to claim him or her. In fact, from that very first afternoon when this drowning victim was dragged half-dead from the river, everyone on staff expected a worried family member or a concerned friend to step forward. And even if no one was initially aware of her absence, certainly, after Sharon Winslow's story aired on Action News that late September evening, someone should have recognized her. No one did. And if some elucidation from the patient herself was expected, this also became a source of disappointment.

For two days after her suicide attempt, Jane lay intubated on a respirator. Although she was encouraged to communicate with facial expressions or even by writing on a notepad, she refused to respond. Then, after the plastic tube was finally removed from her airway, she reported in a hoarse, croaking, hesitant voice that she knew nothing of the events that brought her to the hospital—and little else of her life before that. The neurologists confirmed that she was amnesic. The psychiatrist concluded she was depressed, withdrawn, easily agitated, and borderline psychotic.

Matt paid her a visit during that first week in the ICU. After escorting a heart attack victim from the ER to the unit Sunday night, he paused to inquire how she was doing. Squeezing between the squadron of support apparatus lined up along the side of the bed, he reached out and tapped her lightly on her arm. Her eyes opened with a start, then she glanced around wildly. After focusing on him, her alarm seemed to melt into something that resembled contempt. Eventually, the blaze faded into that vacant stare he recalled from the day she arrived. There was no recognition, no curiosity, and apparently no regard for her condition. All he perceived was withdrawal and despondency. Feeling somewhat self-conscious he tried to project a professional demeanor and explained who he was, reassuring her that if she hung in there everything would turn out all right. Finally, with a gnawing sense of uneasiness, he turned and left the cubicle.

After that initial unsettling interaction, he chose to track her course from a distance. From his house doctor friend, he learned about her transfer from the ICU to a general medical floor. There, she continued to require intravenous antibiotics to treat the aspiration pneumonia. On two occasions during that part of her stay she became so agitated and combative that she had to be sedated. One evening it became so bad that a security guard and two burly orderlies were summoned to hold her down while the IV team reinserted the line she had pulled out earlier in the day.

Finally, after four more days on med-surg, her condition stabilized to the point where she was transferred to Jeff Hurley's service on Psych Unit. Hurley, a middle-aged staff psychiatrist who advertised his casual disposition by wearing solid wool ties over plaid or pin-striped shirts, also sported a bushy brown beard, an oblong face, and compassionate, puppy-dog brown eyes. Matt knew him from Western Psych, where the venerable clinical psychiatrist had delivered several insightful lectures on the practice of psychiatry in a community hospital setting. Matt liked his affable, easy manner and found him readily approachable for a question or comment during the post-lecture period.

As Matt stood by the window, waiting for the patients to return from dinner, he tried to clarify what he was doing there. What was so fascinating about this strange young woman who'd taken a near-fatal plunge off the Rankin Bridge? Was it her frenetic temperament, her wan attractiveness, or the possibility of a mysterious past that kept her foremost in his thoughts? Or was it that unique scar he'd noticed on her inner thigh that intrigued him? Whatever the attraction, he knew he wouldn't rest until he explored the matter further.

A wheelchair squeaked by. He turned just in time to see one of the psychiatric nurses push a patient past the open door. Two ambulatory patients followed, both exhibiting the sauntering gait that medicated psychotics frequently show.

It *has* been a while since I was on the wards, he reminded himself. He thought about the sterile, untainted research world of the Weimar Clinic. Sequestered there, he'd almost forgotten what it was like to be around really mentally disturbed inpatients. But now, with this visit, the details flooded back. And as he waited in Jane's room, like eerie ghosts on Halloween eve, the blank, yet somehow curious, stares, the musty, slightly pungent odors, the screaming, senseless carrying-on, and above all, the purposeless wanderings devoid of intention or plan, revisited his pensive mind.

And then she appeared. A wraith, but with form and substance, she stood framed by the doorway, pausing momentarily to appreciate that she had a visitor. Rather than acknowledge him, she glided past the foot the bed and walked over to a hard-backed wooden chair in the corner. There she sat down.

"Hi," he said. She showed no inclination to return the greeting. "I'm Dr. Carson. I treated you in the emergency room after the divers pulled you out of the river. I stopped by to see how you were doing." She continued to stare ahead of her, with no hint of recognition. "It's good to see you up and around. You were in pretty bad shape when you were wheeled in."

Her lack of response was annoying, but he could understand it. Either she was so clinically depressed and despondent she wasn't capable of interacting with another human being, or she just wasn't interested in talking to him. If it was the former, perhaps a little persistence would break the ice. If it was the latter, he was wasting his time. He reached into his clinic coat and pulled out a small, rectangular box.

"Here," he said, holding it out to her, "I brought you a little present." While his arm remained extended, she continued to ignore him. "Come on. Take it. It won't bite."

She seemed to regard this as a taunt or a challenge. There was defiance in her expression. Then, she turned toward him, gave him a cold glance, and took the box. Grasping the edges she opened it. Inside, set against the black cloth lining, was an old-fashioned comb with tortoise-shell teeth and a mother-of-pearl handle. He watched with hopeful anticipation as Jane regarded it. Then, she gently lifted it out of its case.

"It's from an antique shop on Ellsworth Avenue. That's in the Shadyside section of Pittsburgh. Do you know where that is?"

Since no one knew where Jane was from, he figured this was as good a way as any of trying to find out. While studying the comb she ignored his question. Finally, after turning it over in her hands, running her fingertips over the handle, and gently scratching her palm with the teeth, she lifted it up to her head and ran it through her hair. The effect on him was scintillating. He thought about Eric Clapton's song, *Wonderful Tonight*:

"It's late in the evening.
She's wondering what clothes to wear.
She puts on her make-up and brushes her long blond hair.
Then when she asks me, 'Do I look all right?'
And I say, 'Yes, you look wonderful tonight.'"

But instead of being appreciative, she remained distantly cool, seemingly pre-occupied with the act of combing her hair. Her actions, a bit hesitant at first, became methodical and repetitive. She walked over to the bathroom mirror and watched herself grooming.

On one level, he was thrilled that she'd reacted to him. On another he craved more. Impatience gnawed at his sensibilities. But he knew better than to push. This odd relationship had to progress in tiny increments—in baby steps. He must exercise restraint.

This will be good training for me, he told himself. I've never had a patient quite like this before—even if she isn't really my patient.

He took a breath, then sighed. On his way out the door he passed the bath-room. Pausing, he placed a gentle hand on her shoulder and squeezed it lightly. Softly he whispered good-by.

Just past noon Matt sat across from Dr. Jeff Hurley in the Braddock Hospital's doctor's dining room. This was when the first floor lounge looked out onto Holland Avenue, long before UPMC purchased the hospital in the mid-nineties, sinking millions into a major renovation, and changing the appearance of the institution forever.

Scheduled to be sequestered in the research lab that night—another full moon was expected—Matt had volunteered for the ER's daylight shift. During this mid-day lull, he'd decided to grab a bite to eat. At one end of the rectangular table, the Chief of Psychiatry was reading the paper. Matt checked the row of food trays lined up on a counter by the wall, slipped a Reuben and some chips onto a plate, and sat down across from him.

"It's starting to get chilly out there," Matt commented as he bit off a corner of his sandwich.

Hurley glanced up. "What?" he mumbled.

"The weather," Matt clarified. "It's getting colder. We never seem to have much of a fall in Pittsburgh. Last week was Indian summer. Today, the high's only forty."

"Right," Hurley agreed and returned to the Post-Gazette's Op-Ed page.

Intent on not letting this opportunity pass, Matt persisted. "I stopped by the unit last week-end to visit one of your patients. She's that young woman the nurses call, Jane Godiva."

Hurley glanced up again, this time with a tad more interest. "You visited Jane? Why? She's not yours."

"True enough," Matt confirmed. "Honestly, I find her condition remarkable. I've never ever seen such a profound case of post-traumatic amnesia. Have you?"

Hurley seemed to consider this for a moment. "No," he admitted, "but then again, I'm not sure her amnesia resulted from her dip in the Mon. I've started to speculate whether she was having trouble with her memory before she took the plunge."

"Interesting," Matt conceded. "That possibility hadn't occurred to me."

"Nor to me, at least not initially. But now that we've worked together for a few weeks, I'm not sure when she blanked out. At best, she has a hazy recollection of the events leading up to being on the Rankin Bridge—and nothing of her life before that—which makes me think that something may have transpired right before the suicide attempt to set this all in motion."

"Fascinating," Matt commented. "I wonder what."

"At this point we both can only guess."

The two men peered at each other a moment longer. Then, Hurley seemed to lose interest in the conversation and returned to his newspaper. Matt, left alone with his thoughts, finished his sandwich while considering how to broach the idea he'd been toying with for several days now.

"About Jane," Matt interrupted again, "do you have any idea how soon it'll be before she's ready to leave the hospital?"

Pausing ever so briefly, Hurley, without looking up replied, "Now that's another interesting question." Then, as if resigned to hearing the younger man out, he set down his paper and regarded his colleague. "Medically speaking, Matt, my pulmonary friends tell me that the aspiration pneumonia has pretty much cleared. And strictly from a psychiatric standpoint, she's approaching a point where she's no longer a danger to herself or others. So, since the State's paying the freight here, and we can barely justify keeping her, it won't be much longer before they'll start pushing us to discharge her."

"But to where?" Matt inquired, his concern genuine.

"Well," Hurley replied, drawing out the word, "this is how I see it. I don't think it's appropriate for her to be on her own. Despite her inpatient progress, I doubt she possesses the necessary tools to survive in an unsupported, unsupervised environment. The other extreme would be an institution—like Mayview, for instance. But she's not psychotic, and even if she qualifies, a place like that would probably do her more harm than good. To continue to improve she needs to be around healthy people, not the mentally ill."

"How about a halfway house?" Matt suggested.

"That's a possibility," Hurley conceded. "It would certainly give her the proper mix of supervision and independence. In fact, just the other day, I asked the social service people to check into some such options."

"All predicated on the assumption that no one from her family shows up to claim her," Matt reminded him.

"Which seems unlikely at this point," Hurley countered, "unless they've been out of the country or living in a cave for the last few weeks."

"I hear ya," Matt agreed.

There was another pause in the conversation. But this time, Hurley didn't return to his paper. Instead, with a pensive look on his face, he gazed past Matt out the window. Matt patiently waited a few moments before interrupting.

"Dr. Hurley," he said slowly, "how would you react if I mentioned that I'm considering having Jane move in with me?"

The psychiatrist's head turned slightly. Staring at Matt, his puppy-dog brown eyes uncharacteristically cool, he countered, "Dr. Carson, I hope you're joking."

"No. Actually, I'm quite serious."

"Well, if you are, I think you'd be making a huge mistake, one fraught with all sorts of impropriety. But before we explore the social ramifications of your suggestion, let's explore your motivation. Why would you assume such an undertaking?"

"Because, as strange at it might seem, I think she might be in danger."

"Of injuring herself? Of repeating the suicide attempt?"

"Possibly," Matt agreed. "But I'm actually referring to something more insidious—and potentially something much more serious."

Hurley's expression reflected surprise and intrigue, but mostly skepticism. "My dear fellow, what on earth are you getting at?"

"Dr. Hurley," Matt replied, "did you happen to notice a scar on the inner aspect of Jane's right thigh, about midway between her knee and groin?"

"As I'm sure you're aware, Dr. Carson, when patients are admitted to our unit we in the psychiatry department rely on our internists to provide us with comprehensive examinations. I would have had little chance to appreciate a lesion in an area that for all intents and purposes is private."

"That's fair," Matt conceded. "And if it weren't for my working in the ER the afternoon she was brought in, I'm sure I wouldn't have seen it either. But I did and it concerns me."

"Why would it?" Hurley inquired.

"Because it reminds me of something I learned about while I was in college. If I'm not mistaken, the location of Jane's lesion resembles a reservoir technique the CIA used to employ during the early years of the cold war when they wanted to deliver mind altering agents over extended periods of time."

Hurley's cold stare became incredulous. "What? You are pulling my leg, Carson. And even if such a thing exists—and I seriously doubt it—how in the world would you be even remotely familiar with it?"

"Because, Dr. Hurley, my father is Mathew Carson Jr., the CIA's Deputy Director for Intelligence." Matt fully savored the pregnant pause that followed. Hurley was apparently having a tough time processing this disclosure and its concomitant implications.

"You're serious, aren't you?" he finally uttered, his voice little more than a croak. Matt nodded. "Then what do you think this all means?"

"I'm not sure. I hope nothing. But if the wound is what I think it is—and not the result of coring out some benign tumor like a fibroma or a lipoma—then we'd be foolish to let Jane out of our sight."

"Why?"

"Because, even though the CIA abandoned this kind of mind control activity almost twenty years ago, that doesn't mean other groups haven't."

"Like who?"

"That's where I'm stuck. I really have no idea. But you can bet that whatever outfit it is, their members are not nice."

"Which is why you think she's in so much danger?"

"Precisely." Matt had to laugh to himself. He was certain that Dr. Hurley, not in his wildest dreams, could have conceived of the kind of luncheon conversation he was having that afternoon. "Plus," he continued, "if I had Jane all to myself, I might be able to get her to trust me enough to reveal who those people are. That's assuming, of course, that she recovers enough of her memory to do so." Hurley nodded, obviously engaged in the possibility. "Which brings me back to my original suggestion," Matt said. "Don't you think it be in her best interests for your patient to move in with me?"

Over the next few weeks, Matt found his quest to have Jane Godiva Doe establish residence with him both arduous and complex. Since the young woman had no family or guardian she was, in fact, a ward of the State. And it was from this station that Matt had to extricate her.

After conferring with the hospital attorney, Matt decided that the most practical course to pursue was one of guardianship. Although technically Jane wasn't a minor, her amnesia had generated enough deficiencies in her mental and social competence that she was lumped in with what the current literature called, mentally challenged. Using this as a premise, Matt petitioned the court and argued that, just like any other mentally compromised person, she needed a responsible adult to help care for her.

When the time came to present his case, the judge, the Honorable Beverly Kaplan, voiced the same considerations Dr. Hurley seemed to imply by his initial reaction to Matt's plan. "Don't you think it's a little suspect, Dr. Carson," the slim, dark-haired judge queried, "that you, a single, young male, are offering to house this attractive young woman, without any history, relationship, or commitment? Just like in a potentially volatile experiment, one might contend that the elements exist here for a bit of interpersonal fireworks."

"Your Honor," Matt replied, standing nervously on the hardwood floor before the massive bench. Beneath his blue blazer perspiration soaked through his blue oxford shirt. "At first glance it might appear that way. But, I assure you, my intentions are completely honorable. My motivation is based solely on establishing a safe, supportive environment for this severely compromised individual. Furthermore, in my capacity as a psychiatric professional, I contend that I, above almost anyone else, should be qualified to contribute to the patient's recovery."

"You might not believe this, Dr. Carson," Judge Kaplan replied in earnest, "but I do appreciate that aspect of your argument. And I even tend to regard it favorably. But at the same time, without appropriate supervision, almost in a chaperon-like capacity, I would hesitate to grant your petition."

"Which is understandable Your Honor," Matt countered without hesitation. "And that's why my counsel and I have come up with a potential solution to the problem. As suggested in the brief Mr. Lebovitz submitted with the petition for guardianship on my behalf, perhaps daily visits by a court-appointed social worker along with a part-time housekeeper or even a private-duty nurse could perform the overseeing function the court seems to deem necessary in this instance. These individuals could then submit regular reports confirming that propriety was being observed."

"Your suggestions are well-taken Dr. Carson. I will take them under advisement and plan to have a ruling for you by Monday morning. Until then, we're adjourned."

Three days later, Matt was granted sole guardianship of Ms Jane Godiva Doe.

Chapter 13

t wasn't until nearly four weeks later that Matt finally got to take Jane Godiva Doe home from the hospital. Their destination, however, was not the residence he'd occupied since returning from Canada in 1981, but instead, one better suited for his new role as guardian.

Immediately following Judge Kaplan's ruling, Matt realized that a one-bedroom Shadyside apartment was much too small for the two of them. So, with the assistance of a real estate agent he'd met one Sunday morning at Starbucks, he located what he considered the perfect flat.

The three-bedroom, second-floor, Squirrel Hill unit was listed as an apartment. But with its front and side street accesses, it seemed more like half a duplex. It was owned by an elderly Jewish couple who had retained it for its revenue producing potential even after relocating to Florida in the late seventies.

As he stood in the hallway waiting for the charge nurse to finish Jane's paperwork Matt thought about his new place. It was situated on the portion of Beechwood Boulevard that stretched from the top of Browns Hill Road to the entrance to the Parkway East, a busy section through a residential area that was never without its share of traffic—especially during the morning and mid-afternoon rush hours. At the top of the long staircase that led up from the front door, one made a left, passed under an archway, and entered a spacious living room. To the left, a row of waist-high to ceiling windows looked out upon the busy boulevard. To the right, a fair sized dining room telescoped into a narrow corridor off of which were three bedrooms, two to the left and one to the right. The kitchen and the sole bathroom completed the side with the single bedroom.

Although Matt knew the size of this residence was an important consideration, it wasn't nearly as critical an issue as its safety. If Jane had, in any obscure way, been associated with some radical organization, she would need protection. And in order to accomplish this, he had been compelled to address the security of the unit. This aspect of the plan had required the cooperation of the building's property management company.

Ten days before the scheduled move, Matt had approached the lease property coordinator and requested that the building's security be upgraded. He supported his argument by referring to a rash of break-ins that had plagued the predominantly Jewish neighborhood over the previous six months. This, coupled with the influx of a number of skinheads, intimidating, bareheaded, young white men who'd recently become quite visible prowling Squirrel Hill's commercial district, reinforced his argument. As a final point of reference, he reminded the young woman of the explosion that had destroyed the Rosenberg home in nearby Murdock Farms and how the papers had hinted this tragedy could have been a covert act of terrorism.

His line of reasoning proved convincing. The manager agreed to the upgrade. But rather than waiting for the company to contract out the work, Matt negotiated a reduction in his rent in return for financing the project himself. In this manner, he was able to accelerate the installation process and, at the same time, exercise control over the quality of the workmanship.

In keeping with the court's ruling, the last order of business was to hire a housekeeper. Given the rigors of his training schedule, he realized that there would be long stretches of time when Jane would be left alone in the apartment. Although she was ostensibly an adult, he couldn't expect her to act like one—at least not yet. And so, he required a responsible individual to supervise her daily activities. His salary, he knew, was insufficient to include compensation for such a seasoned professional. So, instead, he took a stroll over to the Jewish Community Center and scanned the bulletin board mounted in the lobby near the front desk. Sure enough, several postings by elderly women seeking part time work were displayed. After jotting down names and numbers, he interviewed a few. Three days later he hired Sadie Hurowitz, a widow who happened to live on Caton Street, just two blocks away. Now it was the Monday afternoon following Thanksgiving. The stage was set. All that was required was the players.

At the nurse's station counter, Matt signed the discharge form. He then headed down the hallway to Jane's room where one of the aides was helping her get ready. Pausing by her doorway he watched as she set her belongings into the small valise he'd dropped off the day before.

There wasn't much; a couple of nightgowns, a pair of jeans, sweatshirts, t-shirts, a long sleeved blouse, and a few sets of underwear. A navy blue peacoat was draped over the wooden chair near the far corner of the room. Since she'd arrived with just the clothes on her back, some of the employees had donated the other items. A few, Matt learned, had come from the Goodwill Store in Wilkinsburg. Although there was nothing stylish, for now they'd have to do. Once he got her settled, he could clothe her more appropriately.

As she leaned over the suitcase sorting through her meager belongings Jane looked thin and wan. Sensing his presence in the doorway, she glanced up. From her expression he could tell she recognized him, but didn't seem particularly excited. Resignation clouded her eyes, as if she regarded herself a prisoner being transferred from one facility to another. Sensing this, he vowed to modify this perception as soon as possible.

Despite his resolve, however, he knew he was facing an uphill battle. Judging from his most recent visits, he gauged that they were making progress. At times she actually seemed pleased to see him. That's when she answered his inquiries, albeit monosyllabically, but still a distinct improvement over the cool indifference she'd displayed during their initial encounter. He might be inferring too much from her less-guarded demeanor, but he had to believe that on some level she still longed to discover who she really was and how she'd become an inpatient of Braddock General Hospital's psychiatric ward.

As they left the building by the ER entrance he noted, it's almost as if she's groping, racking her memory for some sign of recognition, some hint of a past. Her amnesia seemed pervasive, but it couldn't be absolute. Her ability to incorporate social norms, communicate needs, and master basic tasks reassured him that she was struggling with a mental block that he would chip away at until the key that would unlock it surfaced.

His Nissan 300ZX's engine roared to life. Matt glanced over and noted Jane's reaction. She appeared apprehensive, even frightened. He asked if she'd ever been in a sports car before. He wondered if she recalled being in any type of automobile before. She said she didn't remember.

"Don't worry, it's quite safe. And I'm a very good driver." She nodded, but he could tell by the way she clasped her hands in her lap and peered out through the windshield that she wasn't convinced. He turned out of the ER parking lot, then made a right onto Braddock Avenue. A few blocks ahead loomed the Rankin Bridge. After looping around the on-ramp, he checked for thru-traffic then headed across the expanse. Without glancing her way he sensed she knew where they were. Like a deer caught in the headlights, she stared through the windshield. When they reached a point about midway across, her head whipped around.

That's gotta be the spot where she jumped, he decided. They continued on by. Her attention remained on that point in space, turning to watch it fade into the distance.

"That's where it happened, didn't it?" he asked. Almost imperceptibly, she nodded. "But you're all right now. You survived. And soon we'll discover why you felt compelled to do it in first place."

He expected hostility or even contempt at this comment—as if he were prying into matters that didn't concern him. But instead, when she turned toward him, it was with hopeful expression on her face. With a hesitant smile on her thin, pale lips she said, "Yes."

The music came on at 6:45, but it wasn't until seven AM that Matt finally dragged himself out of bed. Then he recalled how this morning was different from any other he'd ever experienced. He thought about Jane sleeping in the room next door.

The night before had been awkward but passed without any major complications. After giving Jane a tour of the apartment, he let her settle into her bedroom, the one next to his toward the rear of the building. She unpacked while he cooked. It was a little past six when they sat down to dinner at the dining room table under the harsh yellow light of the antique iron chandelier. Conversation remained sparse.

Positioned across from him, Jane remained withdrawn and a bit anxious, a napkin spread upon her lap, her elbows propped up on the wooden table. He set a plate of stir-fried vegetable and noodles before her. Tentatively, she lifted her fork, sampled the offering, and then began eating in earnest. He sighed.

Chatting with her still proved difficult. Most of the time, he felt like he was delivering a monologue. He mentioned Mrs. Hurowitz and how she would be staying with her while he worked. He described their neighborhood and suggested possible places they could go during the day, like visiting the stores along Murray Avenue or taking a stroll through nearby Frick Park. He promised to upgrade her wardrobe and encouraged her to make a list of things she needed for the bath.

For a while, he talked a little about himself, about the Northern Virginia neighborhood where he was raised, about and how he came to be doing what he was. He reiterated how safe she would be living with him, pointing out the reinforced windows and doors he'd had installed, the closed-circuit surveillance equipment that monitored the entranceways.

As he referred to these, he glanced over at the twin monitor screens resting side by side on a small table in the corner of the living room. Squinting, he noted the two staircases that led to his unit, the straight one just inside the front door, the other divided into sections, ascending from inside the side portal. Both were unoccupied. Finally, when he couldn't think of anything else to say, he commented on how dreary it was outside and predicted the kind of weather she could expect living in Pittsburgh through the winter.

When they were finished, he cleared the table and offered her coffee. She declined. It pleased him when she helped him wash and dry the dishes, regarding it as a good sign. When the last plate was put away, she asked if it was okay for her to go to her room. There was no reason to object. He sensed that they were just working their way through what he hoped would become more natural, or at least, routine. After wishing her a good night, he read for a while, watched most of the Monday Night Football game, then went to bed himself.

Now, less than seven hours later, he stood by her partially open door watching her sleep. In peaceful repose, her fine blond hair in gentle disarray, her thin chest rising and falling with each breath, she appeared innocent and untroubled. But this must be a thin veneer. What seething waters bubbled under this deceptively calm façade?

They heard the doorbell ring while they were still having breakfast. Matt had made eggs, toast, and bacon, delicacies he usually reserved for more leisurely weekend mornings. But he considered today a special occasion and made an exception.

He walked over to the intercom, pressed the black button, and asked who was there. A raspy, disembodied version of Mrs. Hurowitz's heavily accented voice came over the speaker. He released the security lock and checked the monitor. The door opened. The short, stocky Jewish woman he'd interviewed a week earlier awkwardly made her way through the doorway.

Waddling into the living room she greeted them, "Good morning, good morning." He thought she sounded like Dr. Ruth Westheimer, but looked more like Shirley Booth when she had played Hazel on TV. After plopping her satchel

111

down by the archway, she unburdened herself of several layers of clothing. "The weather is so nasty," she informed them. "Be sure to bundle up when you go out, Dr. Carson. And you might want to take an umbrella with you, too. It smells like rain."

"We were just finishing breakfast," he told her. "Care to join us? There are still some eggs in the frying pan."

"Ugh," she said wrinkling her nose. "Not cooked with bacon, Dr. Carson. We Jews from the old country still manage to keep kosher. Not like the young people today who are—what do you call it—assimilated? But thanks. I had something at home before I left."

"Well, at least come over here and meet Jane."

Stripped down to a sweater, housedress with a garish floral pattern, support stockings, and black leather shoes with thick rubber soles, the new housekeeper appeared as wide as she was high. Approaching them she spread her arms wide and said, "Ah, Jane. Dr. Carson has told me much about you. What a lovely young woman you are." Jane, who'd been regarding the elderly Jewish woman with mild curiosity, now shrank back. "Don't be afraid, dear. I won't bite."

But despite this lighthearted assurance, Jane seemed apprehensive. Mrs. Hurowitz, however, continued her unabated approach. She reached the young woman, took her thin frail hands in her larger, rougher ones, leaned forward and gave her a kiss on the cheek.

"You seem very sweet. I'm sure we'll get along fine."

"I'm sure you will, too," Matt offered, pushing his chair back from the table, then announcing he had to get to work.

"You go right ahead, Dr. Carson. I'll tidy up around here. Then maybe Jane and I can get better acquainted."

"That sounds like a great idea," Matt agreed.

Secure with the knowledge that the somewhat awkward introductions had been made and that Jane would be well supervised, he packed his briefcase, grabbed his jacket from the coat tree in the foyer, said goodbye to the two women, and left for the hospital.

When Matt returned home that evening, it was to the aroma of a home-cooked meal and the cleanest apartment he could imagine. Mrs. Hurowitz was perched on the sofa in the living room, her feet not quite reaching the floor, crocheting an afghan. Jane, meanwhile, sat on the leather recliner watching a Star Trek rerun on TV. With darkness having descended outside, the room was bathed in the soft yellow light from a pair of end table lamps he'd picked up at Kaufmann's the week before.

"Whatever's cooking smells great," he said in a manner of greeting. "Hi, everyone."

"Dr. Carson," Mrs. Hurowitz replied glancing up from her work, "I thought I'd make you something before I left for the evening."

"You're not joining us?"

"My apologies, but no. As I mentioned this morning, your kitchen is traif. Lunch was no problem since I brought my food in one of those little Tupperware containers my friend Sadie got me at that party she went to a couple of years ago. But, oy, bringing dinner would be too much of an ordeal. So I'll just leave you two young people here and go back to my little house on Caton. I'm sure you won't miss me too much. And if you do, I'll be back here in the morning, bright and early."

"If you say so, Mrs. Hurowitz," Matt told her. "But you know you're welcome to stay."

"Some other time, maybe."

He glanced over at Jane, who seemed intent upon the action on the television. "So how was your day?"

"We had a wonderful time," Mrs. Hurowitz offered, her thick Eastern European accent made the w's sound like v's. "We stayed around the apartment all morning cleaning and watching television. While I was in the room, we watched the quiz shows. She especially likes *The Price is Right*. Then, once she found that *MTV*, I couldn't get her to turn the channel. Which isn't so good, Dr. Carson since some of what they show there is pretty disgusting."

"I know. I've seen it."

"Anyway, after lunch I made her a nice bowl of soup and a chicken salad sandwich, then we took a walk on the avenue."

"Buy anything?"

"Bathroom stuff—deodorant and toothpaste at Rite Aide. Then we stopped at the Pussycat on Forbes Avenue and Jane picked out a bra and some panties. Very feminine looking I might add."

113

"You went all the way to Forbes?" The old woman grinned, then nodded proudly. As she gathered up her belongings she allowed Matt to help her on with her coat. "I'm impressed."

"That gave me a chance to stop at the JCC and kibbutz with my girlfriends. They play bridge on Mondays. Then we came home."

They were standing at the top of the front staircase, Mrs. Hurowitz bundled up for the cold with her cloth satchel hanging by her side, its bottom almost grazing the runner. With Jane out of earshot he asked, "How was she? Anything unusual happen while you were out?"

"Not really. She seemed okay out on the street, curious but not frightened. After a while she started asking a lot of questions."

"Like what?"

"Simple things like, what's the difference between jitneys and buses and what kinds of things were sold in the different shops. She remembered me saying I kept kosher and when we passed Prime Kosher was curious about grocery stores that only sold food like that."

"What about the neighborhood? Did she seem to recognize anything?"

Mrs. Hurowitz considered the question for a moment. "Not really," she replied. "She seemed curious about some of the people we passed on the streets, especially the Hassids. When I told her they were very religious Jews it seemed to annoy her. She was almost angry with them. I asked her why and she said they were evil. I didn't know what to make of that, so I let it go."

"Interesting," Matt commented. "How about any other groups? Did you run into those skinheads while you were out?"

"Ugh," Mrs. Hurowitz retorted disgustedly. "Plenty. And you know what, it didn't seem to faze her. While we were waiting to cross to the JCC, a bunch of those Nazi bastards were standing on the corner of Forbes and Murray. I took Jane's hand and told her not to be afraid."

"How did she react?"

"She said something like, 'Oh they're not so bad, Mrs. Hurowitz, once you get to know them'."

"She said that?"

"Pretty close."

"Hmm."

The brief pause that followed seemed to cue the housekeeper's departure. "I suppose I'll be on my way, then. Same time tomorrow, Dr. Carson?"

"Same time tomorrow, Mrs. Hurowitz." She started down the steep staircase. "Oh, one more thing," he called after her. She stopped and looked up. "If you can think of anything else unusual that happened on your walk, let me know. It may help me when we work on getting her memory back."

"No problem, dear. I'll tell you if I think of anything." A moment later she was gone.

Chapter 14

ortunately, Brian McMurty owed Carmen a favor. Stopping by the precinct building earlier that afternoon, using the pretense of needing an item from his office, the detective noticed that the Brillo-like gray-haired sergeant was sitting at the intake desk.

Pausing by the counter he chatted amiably with the veteran cop before casually alluding to the night the old German woman had confronted him in the foyer. McMurty hadn't been on duty at the time, but he'd gotten wind of the incident. Carmen confirmed the story, then embellished the tale a bit by informing the veteran cop that he was in the process of tracking down the woman.

Aware that the stationhouse used closed circuit TV with video storage to monitor the waiting area, he wondered whether the tape from that night might still be available. McMurty didn't know. Leaving Carmen at the desk while he checked in the back, he returned a couple minutes later with a small black rectangular box.

But when Carmen indicated he wanted to borrow the VHS tape, the sergeant balked. Instead, he allowed Carmen to take it to Audio Visual room and view it there. Recently Captain Powel had sprung for a state-of-the-art set-up where the detectives could capture still pictures from raw footage. Vaguely familiar with the process, Carmen scanned the fuzzy tape and identified a few images that best captured the old woman's likeness as she sat nervously on one of the chairs against the waiting room wall. After snapping the stills, he printed the pictures using the station's color laser HP.

But Carmen wasn't done yet. Slipping the freshly minted material into a long, flat, brown envelope, he thanked McMurty and left the station. Next he stopped at Rico's Photo Processing Lab in Edgewood. There, using some sophisticated computer graphics equipment, the technician, a thin young man with a scruffy goatee and black pony tail, loaded the images onto his Macintosh, retouched the flesh tones and shading, added some background, then printed out the finished product on glossy Kodak photographic paper.

Carmen eased his rental off Interstate 79's Zelienople exit and easily found his way into the heart of the small western Pennsylvanian town. He stopped at the first service station and asked a teenage boy in grease-stained coveralls about the location of Miller's Grocery Store. A couple of minutes later, with directions in hand, he was parked at the corner of Green Lane and West New Castle Street.

With its two long rows of stores and shops, West New Castle seemed like the small community's main commercial district. The grocery store occupied a corner lot catty-cornered from where he'd parked. Casually easing out of the gray Pontiac Grand Am, he strolled around to the sidewalk. Heading along the pavement, past the parking meters and well-spaced maple trees, Carmen mentally recorded some of the store titles; Rikker's Hardware, Olga's Dress Emporium, Caldwell's Flower Stop and, or course, Starbucks coffee. Across Green Lane, he noticed an old-fashioned luncheonette with a neon Coca Cola sign blinking on and off in the window.

Classic small town America, he observed. Checking his breast pocket for the picture, he waited for the light and crossed.

Although the photograph had been an afterthought, now that he was actually standing in the small town looking for the old woman, he was glad he had it.

Despite its harsh fluorescence, the lighting in the grocery store seemed muted. Carmen took a moment to orient himself. Long rows of shelving filled up most of the floor space. Refrigerated and freezer cases were pushed up against the walls. Near the front of the store was a checkout counter with two large machines and a collection of displays. Carmen noted the late-model cash register and lottery ticket dispenser. If any shoppers were in the store, they were remote, either browsing the aisles or hidden from view toward the back. To Carmen's right, in front of the produce racks, a tow-headed boy swept the floor. By the front counter an old woman was purchasing lottery tickets. Her two-wheeled wire cart, about three-fourths filled with brown paper bags, teetered against the base of the counter. An angular man with a severely receding hairline tended her detailed requests.

"That be all, Thelma?" the counterman asked. Carmen thought his smile looked patronizing.

"I think so, Gus," she replied tucking the tickets in the inside pocket of her black patent-leather purse. She hooked the straps onto the side of the cart and reached for the handle. "See you at the Vets' Saturday night." With that she tugged at the cart and wheeled it unsteadily past the automatic glass door.

Carmen approached. "Somethin' I can do for you, sir?" the man she'd called Gus, offered.

"I hope so," Carmen replied in greeting. "You Mr. Miller?"

"The one and only." The disingenuous smile returned.

"Perhaps you can help me with a problem I'm having." Gus Miller's bushy eyebrows arched. "I'm looking for an elderly German woman. I think she lives in this town. The trouble is I don't know her name. All I have is a picture and a little story."

"First show me the picture," suggested Mr. Miller, "then you can get to your tale."

Carmen withdrew the retouched photo from the inside pocket of his trench coat. While Mr. Miller scrutinized it, he began, "You see, I had this Aunt Isabella. She went on one of those island cruises about four years ago. On the boat, I think it was a Royal Caribbean, she met another elderly woman. From what she told me, they hit it off real good and ended up spending a lotta time together. That picture there was taken by my aunt of this woman in one of the ship's lounges." Mr. Miller looked up from the picture and began studying Carmen's face. "Well, it turns out Aunt Bella wasn't real good with names," the detective continued, "which wasn't a problem until about a month ago."

"Older folks lose their memory a lot," Mr. Miller commented without much compassion. "Why is that a problem in your aunt's case?"

"The problem is," Carmen continued, "Bella died in October. When her will was read, it referred to this old German woman from Zelienople that she'd met on the cruise. She instructed the lawyer to pass along some specific mementos to her. The stuff's out in the trunk of my car. But all I got is this picture we found in one of Bella's photo albums."

"And you're sure she's from Zelienople?"

"As I said, she mentioned it in the will."

"Fascinating," Gus replied stroking his narrow chin. "Unfortunately, I can't say she looks familiar. And I've been living here for thirty years. I thought I knew everyone in this town."

"I would've thought so, too. You sure you don't recognize her?"

"Nope," Gus repeated shaking his head. "Not even close. Sorry. I wish I coulda been more help."

"That's okay," Carmen told him. "Thanks for your time."

"No problem."

With his best lead disappearing down a blind alley, Carmen stopped outside the grocery store. If Miller didn't know who the old German hag was, he doubted if any of the other merchants on the street would either. But he couldn't take that for granted. So he was about to embark on the next phase of this fact finding mission when his stomach reminded him that he hadn't eaten since breakfast. Recalling the luncheonette across the street, he crossed Green Lane, stepped inside and ordered a sandwich. While leafing through a day old copy of the *Zelienople Dispatch* at a corner table, waiting for his pastrami on rye, he felt a tap on the shoulder.

"Um," a hesitant voice said. "Excuse me for interruptin' mister, but I couldn't help overhearin' your conversation with Mr. Miller." Carmen turned to see the tow-headed kid who'd been sweeping by the produce counter.

"And," he prompted.

"I think I know that lady you're lookin' for."

"You do?"

"Can I see that picture before I say for sure?"

"Certainly," Carmen agreed and held out the photo. The boy reached for it, his fingers long, the skin soiled, the nails grimy. He scrutinized the image, his expression intense.

"Yep," he said sounding more certain, "that's her."

"And who's her?"

"Mrs. Shindle. I believe the first name is Margaret. She lived on Marion Drive, 'bout a half-mile outta town."

"Is that so?" Carmen said, struggling to conceal his excitement. "How come you know about Mrs. Shindle and your boss doesn't?"

The young boy seemed flustered. Carmen guessed he wasn't more than sixteen. "I s'pose that's because Mr. Shindle did all the shoppin' for the two of 'em. I met the missus when I made a delivery there a couple times last winter when the snow was so high he couldn't get his car outta the garage."

"So Mr. Miller never met Mrs. Shindle?" Carmen persisted.

119

"I s'pose not. People say she's a shut-in. You know, just sits around the living room and watches TV. At least that's what she was doin' when I brought the groceries."

"These Shindles," Carmen continued, "any idea how long they been married?"

"Can't be more'n a couple o' years," the boy offered without hesitation. "The old man lived by hisself since I was a kid. My family lives on West Road near the Conrail line, just a few blocks from Marion. I used to ride my bike past his place a lot back then. Then, about two years ago, my brother and I noticed this woman sittin' on the porch. We just figured she was some relative."

"But now you think she's his wife?'

"That's what I think 'cause she wears a weddin' ring."

"Astute observation," Carmen remarked. The teenager seemed to regard Carmen's comment as a compliment. "Any chance you could give me directions to Mr. Shindle's house so I can drop off this stuff I have for her?" Using Carmen's napkin, the teenager sketched him a map. The detective thanked him for his help and handed him a five-dollar bill for his trouble.

After lunch, Carmen returned to the Pontiac. After checking the map, he headed west on New Castle, past Grandview Boulevard and out to Marion Lane. As he drove he found himself doubting whether Gus Miller had, in fact, no knowledge of Mr. Shindle's bride. This was a small town. It was hard to believe that a merchant who'd been such an integral part of the community for over thirty years wasn't aware of every single person who lived there—even if the individual had only arrived recently and was, for the most part, a shut-in.

Carmen identified the small, white-paneled cottage near the end of the narrow dead-end street and parked his rental. The front door was locked. After pounding once, then a second time and getting no response, he set his ear against the thick wood portal and tried to detect the sound of anything inside, a radio, a television, a washing machine. But the place was quiet. Cursing his bad luck, he retraced his way back along the gravel walkway.

Instead of returning to his car, Carmen walked down the Belgium block street and paused at the house next door. It was starting to get dark. A row of metal lanterns marked the edge of the windy path. He decided to try his luck at this boxy two-story structure.

A chunky middle-aged woman with unkempt grey hair answered his knock. Carmen used the same cover as with Mr. Miller, telling her he was interested in locating Mrs. Shindle. Looking skeptical, she asked why. But once he shared a shortened version of the Aunt Bella story with her, she seemed friend-lier.

"That's so sweet of your aunt, Mr.—uh."

"Bucci," Carmen chimed in, "Arthur Bucci."

"Unfortunately, Mr. Bucci," she acknowledged, reaching up and twirling a long hair growing out of a mole on her cheek, "three days ago poor Mrs. Shindle was taken by ambulance to the hospital. From what I understand, she had a stroke. Gladys Spitts—that's our neighbor on the other side—says she bled into her head. She died before she got to the emergency room. Her obit was in the *Dispatch* yesterday."

Carmen felt genuinely upset with this news. His expression probably con-veyed his disappointment. The woman quickly added, "We was all distressed to hear the news, too, though none of us knew her that well. It was still sad that it happened—and so sudden-like."

At this point, from deep inside the house, someone beckoned the woman. Carmen took this opportunity to make a graceful, though hasty, exit. He offered his condolences, thanked the woman for her time, and retreated down the lantern-lined path.

Trudging through a layer of decaying leaves, Carmen worked his way back to the Shindle cottage. If he couldn't speak to the woman in person, maybe he could get some sense of her from what she left behind.

The house was still dark when he returned. Never adept at picking locks, initially he tried the first level windows and found them latched. Feeling thwart-ed and frustrated, he returned to the rear of the house, picked up a softball-sized rock, and smashed the backdoor window. Wrapping his fist in a handkerchief, he reached through the jagged aperture, slipped the deadbolt lock, and turned the knob. The door creaked open.

He entered the kitchen. In the waning light he discerned white appliances and wooden cabinets. A small dinette table surrounded by three folding chairs was pushed up against the back wall. A doorway led to the remainder of the first level.

Carmen regretted that since having stopped smoking several years ago, he no longer carried a lighter. Then he recalled the penlight he'd slipped into his shirt pocket before leaving his apartment earlier that afternoon. Was that just a few hours ago, he asked himself? It seems like a week.

Except for a table, chairs and a waist-high buffet, the dining room was small and relatively bare. "Nothing unusual here," Carmen muttered, "or particularly interesting, for that matter." A bowl of plastic fruit served as the centerpiece. On the buffet a trio of decorator plates mounted in iron wire stands were set on a long thin doily. Carmen squatted down and slid aside the wooden doors. Inside he found stacks of dishes, a case of silverware, various pieces of silver, placemats, and two pairs of candleholders.

"More standard issue," he said to himself. Then, after rising back up straight, he wondered, if I was manuscript, where would I hide?

Passing under a low archway Carmen entered what he imagined was the living room. Despite a chill in the air the place still smelled dank and musty. He called it old people's smell, a mixture of liniment, dead skin, and dried urine, an odor he'd noticed the last time he visited his Uncle Tony's place in Bloomfield. The cloth sofa and plush chairs—furniture probably culled from a low-end antique store or the community flea market—seemed to exude it.

Using his miniature flashlight, Carmen scanned the space. The front windows were shaded and curtained. An antique rolltop desk and a set of bookshelves filled up much of the wall space to the right. Off to his left, beside the staircase, stood an upright piano. Atop the piano, mounted in ornate silver and gold-plated frames, was a collection of photographs.

Carmen cursed himself for forgetting gloves. Taking out the handkerchief again, he reached up and took down the largest photo, a traditional wedding portrait of an elderly couple standing beside one another, their pose stiffly formal. A white layer cake occupied the foreground. The woman, tall, broad-shouldered, and buxom, wore a beige dress hemmed just below her knee, a broad-brimmed spring hat, and modest square-toed heels. Although her face was partially concealed by the bonnet, Carmen easily recognized her. Yep, it was the same old crone who'd forced the manuscript on him at the Penn Circle station. Her mate, a thin, older man, stood an inch or two shorter than she and was clad in an ill-fitting black suit and red paisley tie, his smile more strained than jocular, as if being forced to participate in some distasteful endeavor.

The lovely couple, Carmen thought wryly. From the looks of it, the picture was probably no more than a few years old. The boy was right. These two hadn't been married long.

He set the photograph down on the piano and reached for a second. This one, probably five-by-seven, had an outdoors setting in front of a large Tudor style house. Carmen recognized Mrs. Shindle. This time she was in a spring dress and stood between a tall, handsome, dark-haired man and a very pretty, young woman. The young woman's fine, blond hair swirled in mild disarray around her sun-drenched face. The man held his open hand up to his forehead salute-like in order to shield his eyes from the glare.

Carmen wondered about these three people and how they were related. Was it her first husband and a daughter—or a brother and a niece—or some mixture of the two? And more critical, was that Hans Reichman, the malevolent author of the Nazi manuscript? If only he was so lucky.

Carmen was able to examine one more picture before the interruption. This particular photo also portrayed Mrs. Shindle and the young woman, this time seated next to each other on an antique sofa under a floral watercolor painting. In this photo, the pretty blond seemed a little older, possibly in her twenties. And something else in the picture seemed vaguely familiar. After focusing in on the antique sofa, he then scanned the parlor with his penlight and confirmed that this same piece of furniture was lurking in the shadows off to his right. The photograph had been snapped in this very room.

Taking some care to position it properly, Carmen returned this last picture to its piano top perch. As he turned toward the rolltop desk, he heard the sound of someone walking up the front path.

From the racket this person made, it seemed obvious he had no concern about making his presence known. The slurred crooning suggested he was drunk. Unwilling to be discovered—just yet—Carmen looked for a hiding place.

He ruled out the coat closet by the front door since, if the new arrival lived here, it would probably be the first place he'd go. Beyond that single enclosure, the first level appeared open and easily accessible. The second floor was a possibility, but the occupant would probably make his way up there eventually. Carmen wondered about a basement. He skirted around the far side of the staircase, located the door, and disappeared onto the landing. Just as the darkness engulfed him, he heard a key in the lock. A moment later the newcomer was inside.

Crooning a singsong melody, that to Carmen's ear sounded like a German drinking song, he wandered from one room of the cottage to another. Carmen imagined him among a group of Aryan cronies perched on barstools in a musty beer hall with their steins held high.

123

Then the man called out, "Marga, I'm home. What's for dinner?"

Carmen, with his ear pressed against the inside of the door, thought, well, either the old fart is senile, or he likes to talk to ghosts. Into the silence that ensued the old inebriate slurred, "You *dummkopf*, Gerhard. Don't you remember? The old girl's gone. Kaput." He sounded close now, probably by the coat closet. "You just buried her."

Then old man's voice trailed off, his footfalls suggesting that he was on his way back through the living room. A few seconds later the commentary started again, this time on the opposite side of the landing's rear partition, from the vicinity of the kitchen.

"Ah, Marga, my *sheina*," penetrated the muffled voice through the thin wallboard. "What a pity you're gone. These last few years, we certainly had some good times." Carmen could almost imagine the wistful sigh. "The honeymoon cruise to Alaska. The trip back to our Fatherland. And after that Lila joined us. That part was the most satisfying. Training her for her mission. The planning. The coaching. Then seeing her pull it off. What a triumph."

Carmen wondered whether these ramblings were pertinent to his investigation. He cursed himself for forgetting his tape recorder. Gradually, the old man moved out of earshot, his voice becoming muffled and unintelligible.

Carmen appreciated that this might be his only chance to interrogate this old fart. Mustering some resolve, he reached back, unholstered his service revolver, and opened the landing's door. Proceeding with a stealth that seemed inconsistent with his stocky stature, he worked his way around the staircase and across the empty living room. Then, tucking himself in the recess on the parlor side of the archway, he extended his neck and peered into the dining room. Except for the assortment of furniture gathering dust, the room was also unoccupied. But unwashed and reeking from alcohol, Carmen could still smell him.

The old fart's gotta be in the kitchen, he decided.

Proceeding with caution, his gun clutched chin-high in both hands, the detective advanced. In less than four strides, he reached the kitchen. Peering inside, he confirmed that the old man was sitting hunched over the dinette, eating. His large head was covered with steely gray hair. He was wearing a red plaid flannel shirt and jeans—like a farmer or a factory worker. Carmen suspected that the soiled clothes accounted for much of the old man's rancid odor. As he spooned what looked like soggy Shredded Wheat into his mouth, a rivulet of sallow-colored milk dribbled down his stubbly chin.

Entering into the small kitchen, the gun held out before him, Carmen commented, "Not much of a meal."

The old man started. Shoving his chair back from the table, he began to rise.

"Not so fast, Shindle," Carmen instructed. "Stay right where you were. In fact, set your hands face down on the table, if you will."

"Who the hell are you?" the old man demanded. Without the wall to filter the sound, his accent sounded thick and guttural. "And how do you know my name?"

"Let's just say I'm a friend of the family. I stopped by to pay my respects."

"Bullshit!" Shindle retorted. "You're that wop detective that Marga gave that manuscript to."

"Gracious me," Carmen joked, "my reputation precedes me. I didn't know I was so famous."

"You're not," the old German hissed. "The truth is, Vitale, we've met before." This contention surprised the detective. "At your apartment, Detective, when I took that damn diary back from you." Absently Carmen reached up and felt the back of his head. It was still sore from the whack the Kraut had delivered. "Don't get me wrong, Detective," the old man was saying, "I loved my wife. But she could be a real *dummkopf* sometimes." He paused for a moment before asking, "So how much did you read?"

"Enough, Shindle."

"What's enough?"

"Enough to suspect that there's a link between your wife and the author Hans Reichman, that mass-murdering SS officer."

Shindle's eyebrows rose just enough for Carmen to know that he'd struck a chord. But the old man recovered quickly and commented, almost defiantly, "Don't get so condescending, Vitale. Hans was SD. He only killed Jews. And after the war, he flipped his stripes for you Yankee bastards. He became one of the good guys."

Carmen recalled something he'd read in the manuscript. "That made him OSS?"

"You did digest a lot of the garbage Hans wrote, didn't you?"

"Like I said, enough." Carmen sighed. This verbal jousting was starting to bore him. He needed more concrete information from this old Kraut. And he

125

needed it fast. Grabbing one of the kitchen chairs, he spun it around and sat down facing Shindle, resting his arms on the edge.

"Who's Lila, Shindle?" Carmen demanded.

There was another rise out of the old man. Shindle seemed surprised to hear Carmen utter this name. "I don't know, Vitale," he parried. "Who's Lila?"

"Somebody you were rambling on about before I interrupted," Carmen reminded him. "Let's try again. Who's Lila?"

"None of your God-damned business," Shindle growled.

Carmen was getting annoyed with the old man's attitude. What's more, he still owed the asshole some retribution for that attack in his apartment. What a perfect time to even the score. The detective rose to his feet, toppling the chair in the process, its back slapping against the linoleum floor. Shindle seemed unfazed.

Grabbing the old man's shoulder, Carmen yanked him roughly to his feet. "Let's take a little stroll, asshole," he instructed. Burrowing the nozzle of his revolver in the small of the old man's back he prodded him through the dining room and into the parlor. They paused by the piano. Carmen picked up the wedding portrait. "That you Shindle," he inquired, shoving the picture in front of the man's bulbous nose, "you and your blushing bride?"

"That's us, Vitale," Shindle confirmed. "But you knew that already."

"Of course I did." Grabbing a second picture he demanded, "How about this young woman here? Five'll get ten that's Lila." Shindle remained mute. Carmen persisted, "And I bet the guy with them is Reichman. What do ya say Shindle? Is that the author of the famous Nazi manuscript?" Carmen pushed the butt end of his revolver through the old man's flannel shirt, right between a pair of thoracic vertebrae. "Well?"

"Why don't you ask your CIA buddies, Vitale?" Shindle retorted. "They know all about him. He worked for the bastards for forty years."

Carmen struggled to conceal his amazement. Forty years was a long time.

"So that means Reichman was one of us," Carmen goaded.

"He was never one of you, Vitale," the old man spat back. "He did what he had to do to survive."

"That's right, Shindle. And what are you going to do to survive?"

With a look of controlled fury in his eyes, the old man turned. Carmen was about to squeeze the trigger when he felt a jolt of agonizing pain in his groin. The bastard had kneed him in the nuts. In agony, Carmen doubled over. A moment later, a solid uppercut caught him squarely in the chin. Careening into the piano, he crumpled to the floor just as another kick targeted his abdomen. But this time Carmen reacted quickly enough to grab Shindle's boot and give it a twist. The smelly Kraut dropped like a roped calf.

Despite the excruciating pain, Vitale managed to pounce. Shindle wriggled into a supine position, his back on the rug. Carmen, still clutching the revolver in his right hand, pointed it at the older man's head. Shindle worked his left arm free and grabbed Carmen's wrist. Violently, they struggled.

The stalemate ensued for several moments, an inverted arm wrestling match where neither contestant could gain any ground. Then gradually, Carmen's strength waned. He watched his wrist being forcefully rotated so that the gun was now pointing, instead of at Shindle, at him. All the older man needed to do was find some way to work the trigger.

Gathering a measure of strength he wouldn't have anticipated, Carmen overcame Shindle's counter-resistance and swung the gun in a broad rotational motion. Then, just as the barrel of the gun entered the crevice between the two men's torsos, Carmen squeezed the trigger. The ensuing blast sent a sleek, nine-millimeter, full metal-jacketed bullet into Shindle's barrel chest.

The acrid smell of gunpowder mixed with the rusty odor of blood. Shindle gasped. Carmen relinquished his position astride the old man's torso. Suddenly the flannel shirt was drenched with the blood.

"You son of a bitch," he managed to croak out, his voice little more than a rattle.

"Takes one to know one," Carmen retorted callously. "Any last words, Shindle?" He hoped the old man had enough left in the tank to deliver a dying remark. He knew the bastard wouldn't last long.

"Only this," Shindle gasped, his breathing short, his words clipped. "I didn't torch the Rosenberg mansion."

"Then who did?"

Shindle gazed up at him, his eyes starting to cloud over. Then, for a brief moment they became eerily bright. "That one, Detective I'll take to my grave."

A moment later, he was dead.

Chapter 15

It took Carmen some time to get his bearings. Here he was, standing beside another dead body and saddled with more questions than answers. But inquiries had to wait. More pressing was massaging the setting so he could avoid dealing with the consequences of his action.

He considered the fate of Shindle's bloody corpse. He could attempt to stage it as a robbery attempt gone awry. He wiped off anything he could remember touching. The gun would also have to go. If the cops discovered the body, they would search for the firearm. Since it was registered in his name it would create a direct link. He also had to worry about any visibility he had inadvertently gained in this rural community. Once the questioning started he would probably become a suspect.

So, disposing of the body became paramount. After that, even if the stained carpet and signs of a struggle were discovered, the nature of old man's death would still remain a mystery. And Carmen callously hoped that Shindle had no one left behind who gave a damn.

The detective surveyed the carnage. With fresh blood on the carpet and piano legs there was no way to eliminate some of the evidence. But if he could remove the bullet from the scene, the police would have one less item with which to work. Fired at such close range, the slug should have gone straight through his victim. Carmen knelt down and rolled the body onto its side. Sure enough, a thimble-sized hole brimming with drying blood marred the threadbare carpet. The poor stiff's blood was oozing from both sides. The bullet probably pierced an artery. And judging from how quickly the old man expired, it must've been a major one. Once he disposed of the corpse, no one would ever know for sure.

Carmen rose slowly, his arthritic knees creaking. Returning to the kitchen he rummaged under the sink. Voilá! he mouthed, ferreting out a box of plastic garbage bags, the thirty-three gallon kind, usually used to bag leaves. Borrowing a couple, he returned to the living room and shimmied Shindle's corpse into them, one over the upper half, a second up to his waist. In a utility drawer he found some twine which he used to secure the remains.

At least, whatever was still oozing would end up in the bag not the rug, he reassured himself. Next he headed out to his car, still parked on the narrow rural street, and realizing that, the shorter he had to drag the thing the better, he backed it up the driveway, and popped the trunk. Back in the house he began the arduous task of moving Mr. Shindle from his humble home to his last resting place.

This effort took a considerable amount of time and energy. In death, the old man had become as unwieldy as a concrete slab. Carmen estimated that his dry weight was over two hundred pounds. Simultaneously grunting, sweating, yanking, and pulling, Carmen managed to drag the bagged body out the door, down the two steps, and onto the dry, frozen lawn. After sliding it across the patchwork of crabgrass and dirt, he finally reached the car. With another gargantuan effort, he deposited his victim into the rental's spacious trunk. By the time Carmen finished his task he was drenched with sweat.

It took him another hour to tend to the house. The carpeting was wall-to-wall, so he couldn't just roll it up and take it away with him. In the basement he found some carpet cleaning concentrate and a shampooer. Thank God Marga was a tidy little bitch, he commented as he dragged the appliance up the steps.

After scrubbing the bloodstains as best he could, he examined the carpet again. This time the bullet hole, which looked about a half-inch in diameter, appeared nice and clean. Using the tip of his penknife he probed the matting and extracted the slug from the hardwood floor. Holding it up admiringly he declared, "This little baby's mine."

Before leaving the scene, he wiped down the furniture, returned the loose items to their proper places—as well as he could recall—and pocketed the dirty rags. Lastly he checked the landing and kitchen for telltale signs of his uninvited presence. He considered resuming his search for the manuscript but decided that a moment longer in this accursed house might be a moment too long. Instead, feeling satisfied that the cottage would pass all but the most exhaustive inspection, he flipped off the lights and pulled the door shut. When he heard the latch click, he felt reasonably certain the place was secure. A couple of minutes later, he was gone.

Needless to say, for most of the evening Carmen had been running on pure intrinsic adrenalin. Now, as he glanced at the digital readout on the rental's dashboard and noticed that it was almost 2:30 AM, the weight of the long day hit him like a sledgehammer. But he still had one more task left before he could rest. Resolutely he willed himself to remain alert.

Hastily he considered where to dispose of the body. One option was to drive directly to the Allegheny River and toss Shindle into the deep swell where a tributary, the Kiskiminetas, emptied into its bigger brother just above Natrona Heights. But since he was planning to head up route 28 anyway, why not venture all the way to West Winfield and deposit his load in the Thompson mine shaft near County Line Road?

He'd become familiar with the site a few years ago while weighing in on a serial murder case that involved three of the four counties north of Allegheny. Even now, he vividly recalled the afternoon when his friend Jason Caldwell, a Butler County Police detective, directed him to the bituminous coal operation situated a couple of miles west of PA 28. At that time, the company was still operational. With the advent of nuclear power it had since gone under. Even in the inky black of this moonless night, Carmen was pretty sure he could still find the site.

His confidence, however, was severely tested, as he drove for nearly forty-five minutes along the twisting Armstrong county roads. Finally, he spotted the fenced off entrance. Using the crowbar he kept nestled between the seat and the driver's side door, Carmen pried off the rusty padlock and opened the creaky gate. Then, with the aid of the rental's headlights, he explored the scene. Eventually he located the abandoned mine shaft, which was also secured, this time like a shattered window with boards and nails. After twenty minutes of grunting and prying, he splintered enough lumber to create an aperture that would accommodate his cargo. Hoisting the bulky corpse up onto the narrow ledge, he gave it a gentle push. Gravity did the rest. Then he replaced the loose boards and beat a hasty retreat.

During what was left of the night, Carmen slugged through lurid, eerie dreams. At one point, he saw himself standing on the edge of a mine shaft peering down into blue-black darkness, a putrid smell wafting up toward him, repugnant but compelling. A disembodied voice, deep, almost metallic, called his name, echoing cavernously off the well walls, beckoning him to jump. His curiosity compelled him to find out who was calling. There was a mystery to resolve. There were clues at the abyss' bottom. And then he was falling.

He awoke drenched in sweat, the blanket kicked off, the sheets twisted like a pretzel. Rolling flat onto his back, he felt his heart race. A few deep breaths seemed calming. Having no idea how long he'd slept, he was surprised to see it was only nine AM. His head had hit the pillow after five. It took a few moments more to clear the cobwebs. A cup of black coffee completed the task.

So much had happened in the last twenty-four hours he hardly knew where to start. In venturing to Zelienople, he'd quickly picked up the thread of his investigation. But now it was starting to encompass a much larger scope. If what Shindle had contended were true, and Hans Reichman were really an operative, then he was, in fact, entering into forbidden, and potentially dangerous, territory. This was The Agency he was dealing with. And if he was hardheaded enough to expand his inquiry, it might cost him dearly. At the very least, he would need help. But currently, he was way up on his own superiors' shitlist, let alone in the good graces of the Feds.

He racked his brain for some useful connection. It'd been ages since he'd made contact with anyone in the CIA. Local Pittsburgh detective work almost never crossed paths with the intelligence community. Oh, occasionally, in the late seventies, he'd been queried about some of the local leftist organizations and whether they had ties to the Commies. But that was just routine canvassing and he usually forgot the name of the agent calling before they hung up. No, this had to be more personal, someone with whom he had rapport, someone who owed him. Then he thought of Jarvis.

Although it proved relatively simple to get in touch with his old war buddy, it did take time. It wasn't that Carmen was confronted with layers of red tape or had to clear security or even had to offer appropriate passwords and phrases. It was that four months earlier, after serving twenty-one years as Assistant to the Deputy for National Intelligence Officers, Jarvis Lundy had finally retired from The Agency. He was now residing in the temperate Outer Banks of North Carolina.

According to Cleo, his wife, an exotic, black-haired Eurasian Carmen had the pleasure of meeting back in seventy-nine during an almost surrealistic reunion of Carmen's Vietnam Assault Helicopter Company, Jarvis was deep sea fishing for Spanish mackerel off Hatteras Island and wouldn't be back until late that evening.

Resigned to the delay, Carmen reviewed his notes, reflected on what had recently transpired in Zelienople, and napped in his easy chair. During one of the twilight-like stretches between sleep and wakefulness he recalled the day he'd first met Jarvis and the debt the CIA agent owed him.

It happened In Country, during the winter of 1968. Carmen, fresh out of boot camp at Fort Benning, Georgia, had only been in Vietnam for a couple of months. And although he was a gunner who'd opted out of flight training, he'd still been assigned to the 76th AH Company stationed north of Saigon.

He'd arrived in Southeast Asia with the reputation as a tough, stoic Italian with a wry sense of humor and a deadly shot. By early January, he came to the attention of Seth McQuire, the company commander, a tall, sandy-haired Texan who was leading a squadron of Hueys on daily reconnaissance missions as far north as Kon Tum.

At that point, Carmen had precious little time to get acclimated to his new role. On February 1st, word of the Tet—a.k.a. the Vietnamese New Year—offensive reached the southern capital. Initial reports estimated that two days earlier at daybreak nearly one hundred thousand Vietcong soldiers poured out of their bases in the north and systematically raided dozens of cities and towns below the DMZ. Before the South Vietnamese Army, supported by the US military, could react, several major cities and a few provinces capitulated. As wave after wave of Vietcong overwhelmed the poorly trained southerners, it became obvious that Charley would soon threaten Saigon, the southern capital. US military strategists became desperate for a way to turn the tide.

Late on the evening of February 4th, the 76th received its orders. At four A.M. the next morning, the entire company was dispatched to provide air support for a counterattack at an obscure little place in the Mekong Delta called Khe Sanh. It was a location the company commanders thought critical to the control of the Northern provinces and more importantly, the site of a small, but pivotal, US army base.

Carmen was tapped as one of the dozen or so men who would ride in the lead chopper. As the powerful engine hummed and the pre-dawn wind blew in his face, he peered out from the gunner door and watched the fiery orange sun rise slowly over the lush woodland. Beyond the thick stands of trees, he could make out a misty haze on the South China Sea. Now he knew why some of his buddies compared this region to his family's native Tuscany.

As the company approached the target area, a furious battle was already in progress. The rat-ta-ta-tat of machine fire was mixed with a cacophony of mortar explosions surrounding them with puffs of white smoke resembling miniature clouds. The pilot dipped down to about two hundred yards. As he did, Carmen could make out the row of rectangular barracks, some with black gaping holes in their walls, others spitting angry orange flames through holes in their roofs. Off to the east, sitting by itself, was a smaller building with a U.S. flag flying from a nearby pole. A shower of explosives rained down. Soldiers seemed to be scurrying everywhere, but mostly toward the densely wooded jungle south of the base.

They were now close enough to appreciate how the North Vietnamese insurgents had attacked from several points north of the camp. McGuire ordered them to fire. Lying prone on the floor of the copter Carmen began picking off enemy soldiers. After felling a half dozen, he noticed a band of gooks bearing down on what he assumed was that command hut he'd noticed earlier. The lead VC reached it, unhooked a pear-shaped explosive from his belt, pulled the pin, and tossed it through the open window. As he spun into a crouch with his back against the front wall, an angry explosion erupted. A choppy wave of bright yellow flared, then rapidly engulfed the roof and back wall. The grenader, now reinforced by a few of his comrades, held back, waiting for the flames to die down before investigating the torched building.

In formation with three other Hueys, Carmen's copter veered southward, made a sharp turn, and came in for another run. As they approached, Carmen noticed a man in a green pith helmet, but otherwise dressed civilian garb, crouched by the rear corner of the burning hut. Suddenly, as if chased by the burning structure heat, he stood and sprinted for the trees. He was a big man, well built, but from the way he ran, Carmen decided he wasn't a soldier. As he followed this fugitive's dash for safety, out of the corner of his eye Carmen saw that the gooks had spotted him, too. Instantly, a trio took up the chase. Another pair knelt by the burning building and opened fire.

Instinctively Carmen took aim. In rapid succession, he picked off the three gooks. As the last one fell, his two VC comrades rose from their crouch and began shooting at the helicopter. But by now, the chopper had finished its pass by. Still, Carmen heard their Russian made bullets ping off the rear portion of the reinforced metal fuselage. The pilot completed another hairpin turn. Carmen once again had the attackers in sight. Without wasting a single bullet, he leveled them both.

Beyond Carmen's personal triumph, the battle of Khe Sanh continued for several days. Huge casualties mounted on both sides. Finally, despite the breath and scope of the North Vietnamese onslaught, the southern forces prevailed. And it wasn't until over a month later, weeks after the invading VC army had been driven back north, and the American Embassy in Saigon was wrested back from the small group of commandos who had seized it during Tet, that Carmen discovered the identity of the big, clumsy civilian in the green pith helmet.

After hiding out for the better part of two weeks, Jarvis Lundy finally reached a safe haven at another US army base near Buon Me in mid-February, 1969. He rested there for a couple of days, then hitched a ride to Saigon. During the transport, his driver, a staff sergeant named Collins, shared with him the scope of the battle. After entering the capital, he made further inquiries. It took another week before he identified the members of the 76th AHC.

On the first of March, he rapped on the doorjamb of Carmen's barrack. Strolling with a swagger that Carmen soon came to recognize as unique to Jarvis, he passed between two rows of parallel beds, paused midway down the long, narrow corridor, turned, and awkwardly saluted an enlisted man sitting on his bunk reading. Respectfully, he then introduced himself to the man he'd already nicknamed as The Sniper.

It was just past ten o'clock when the telephone rang. Carmen, who had been engrossed in a made-for-television movie, started. Cursing under his breath, he lifted the handle and said, "Hello."

"Well if that don't beat all," the familiar voice on the other end declared. "Carmen Fuckin' Vitale. After all these years." Although Jarvis had been Eastern Establishment all his professional life, Carmen knew how easy it was for him to slip into his native southern drawl.

"It's about time you returned my call," the detective countered. "Catch anything?"

"Nothing contagious. Oh, and a couple hundred pounds of tuna, if that's what you're referrin' to." Carmen sensed the pride in his voice. "Nothing like nailin' KGB spies, Sniper—but a lot less dangerous."

"Unless one yanks you over the rail," Carmen offered.

"I might be pushin' fifty, Snipe, but I still got enough strength in these forearms to prevent that sorta thing."

"I don't doubt it, Jarvis," Carmen agreed picturing his old friend's six foot seven frame, the sculpted torso, the broad shoulders. Part Afro-American, part Carmen didn't-know-what, in his prime, Jarvis Lundy had been one tough customer. "Just don't try making a run for it." Carmen hoped this quip would help remind his old friend of his outstanding debt.

"You're right about that one, old pal," Jarvis replied implying he was man enough to acknowledge the obligation.

Briefly, they exchanged pleasantries. Carmen learned the details of Jarvis' recent retirement from The Agency, the status of his two children, and the health of Chloe, who he assumed was still a knockout. The detective, when it came to his turn, shared about his solitary, yet not totally isolated, existence, his years on the force, his promotion to detective, and some wins he'd recorded along the way. This last disclosure segued nicely into the purpose of his call. "Which leads me to why I tracked you down to the Outer Banks, Jarv," he commented.

"I was wondering when you'd get around to that," Jarvis countered candidly.

"It's actually pretty simple. I'm in the middle of a murder case. But I've run up against a brick wall. Much of what I've learned so far seems to revolve around a German expatriate, some guy named Hans Reichman. I think he's former SS—or maybe SD—who, right before VE day, defected to our side. From what I can tell, he's been working for your bosses ever since."

Carmen waited out the pause on the other end. He could almost feel Jarvis mentally weighing what he would say next. Finally, the retired CIA agent suggested, "Maybe you should fill me in on the details of this case of yours, so I can be sure about tellin' you what I know."

Aware that if he had any hope of getting some relevant information from his old friend, Carmen had little choice but to comply. So, as succinctly as possible, he shared the details of his investigation into the Murdock Farms bombing, the appearance of the manuscript, and the trip out to Abe Cohen's burning rural cottage. The only thing he withheld was the culmination of his most recent adventure in Zelienople. Apparently, whatever he confided was sufficient to gain Jarvis Lundy's confidence.

"I'm going to assume that this is most of what you need to know," Jarvis offered. "You're right on about the guy you call, Reichman—although he changed his name to Harvey Richman when he came to the States. He was one of a host of yellow-bellied Krauts who flipped their stripes just before Berlin fell in the spring of forty-five. We used to call them Zebras. And from what I understand, Reichman was one of the best.

"After the war he was set up as a mole in Hungary monitoring the Soviets while they solidified their puppet government there. He took the cover of a student at the University of Budapest, got his undergraduate degree and even went on to medical school. But before he could finish, the Hungarian revolution erupted and we had to airlift him outta there."

"Nice for him," Carmen commented, trying to square this part of the story with what he already knew of Reichman from his journal.

"Once he got stateside," Jarvis continued, "our ex-SD officer gave up field work, settled in Northwest Baltimore, finished up his medical degree, then went on to take a residency in Psychiatry. From what I'm told he had a knack for that kind of stuff."

"Fascinating," Carmen said, recalling the section of the diary that dealt with brainwashing. "But how come you know so much about him? You didn't join the agency until the mid-sixties."

"You got a better memory than I gave you credit for, Snipe. My first contact with Dr. Richman was in sixty-six, during my briefing for the Phoenix Program. Officially, he was in private practice in Baltimore. But he never severed ties with the Agency. In fact, back in the late fifties, before he got married, he was heavily involved in our brainwashing research."

"Brainwashing?" Carmen asked, trying to sound incredulous, not letting on what he already knew.

"Sounds corny, doesn't it?" Jarvis replied, apparently buying Carmen's response. "Seems that after our GIs returned from Korea in the early fifties, some of them started acting weird. Rumors ran rampant that the North Koreans had broken them down mentally and turned them into puppets for the regime. Remember the movie, *The Manchurian Candidate*? The boys in Washington bought the notion and thought it posed a major threat to our national security. That's when they authorized a heavily financed research program of their own, testing all kinds of stuff—drugs, sleep deprivation, hypnosis—you name it—in order to prove that you could break someone down and make him your slave."

"You gotta be shittin' me," Carmen declared. "They really believed in that crap?"

"Not only did they believe in it, they thought they could reproduce it."

"Could they?"

"Not really," Jarvis admitted. "But that didn't stop them from trying."

"Amazing."

"In a sense it was," Jarvis agreed. "Anyway, getting back to Richman. He was somewhat of an expert in mental manipulation—that's what the guys at Langley like to call it. So he was the one they asked to brief us on some appropriate techniques before we went to Nam in support of Phoenix."

"And once you got In Country, that's when we met?"

"You could say that. Turns out that in the process of carrying out my mission, I had the great misfortune of straying right into the teeth of the Tet offensive."

Carmen said, almost parenthetically, "I think I can predict the answer to this one, but what exactly was your mission?"

"Sorry Snipe, but until they declassify that data, I'll have to take that one to my grave."

"That's what I figured, Jarv, although my bet is you'll outlive the confidentiality of the matter."

"I hope so. It's hard sittin' on that kinda stuff."

Thoroughly fascinated by this information, Carmen was anxious to incorporate it into what he already knew. Candidly he asked, "So where can I find this Richman, a.k.a. Reichman, now?"

Jarvis paused again before commenting. "Last I heard he was still in private practice in the Baltimore area. But that was five years ago. The old boy's gotta be in his seventies by now. In fact, he's probably retired and living in some resort area somewhere. Just like me."

Carmen pictured the proud grin on Jarvis' boyish face. A warm rush filled his chest. He wished that instead of being separated by hundreds of miles and chatting on the phone, they were sitting next to each other in a bar somewhere, sipping beer and swapping war stories—just like the old days.

"Suppose I happen to wander down to Maryland and try to track down our friend, Richman," Carmen commented. Here was an opportunity for the retired agent to begin to repay his debt. "Any words of wisdom?"

Jarvis didn't respond right away. If Carmen were asked to label the interlude, he would call it a pregnant pause. Finally, in a hushed serious tone, his old friend warned, "This is all I can share with you, Carm. Once you get done snoopin' around for a while, the last thing you may want to do is locate a tavern in Northeast Baltimore called, *Der Bavarian Bierserver*. It's usually full of crusty old Germans slobbering into their Bock Lager and waxing nostalgic about the good old days."

Sounds like us, Carmen thought.

"Once you make your inquiries," Jarvis continued, "if anyone gets suspicious and asks you what you're up to, try saying, 'Adolph's looking for me.' That might buy you some time—and some more valuable information, if you're lucky." Before Carmen could thank him for the advice, Jarvis added, "And don't bother to let me know how things turn out. I don't wanna know."

With that, the retired CIA agent hung up.

Chapter 16

armen's trip to Baltimore began in Pittsburgh, at the Penn Circle precinct building, early the next evening. Thursday was Powell's poker night, always leaving the office before five to stop at home before meeting up with the boys. Still a *persona non grata* around the office, Carmen had no desire to run into the Chief.

After climbing the back staircase to the fourth floor he weaved his way amongst a hodgepodge of empty cubicles before reaching the far side of the building. At his office door, he noticed with some satisfaction that his nameplate was in place. Easing into his padded leather chair, the one sporting a three-inch rip down the edge, he took a moment to settle in. Swiveling around he noted with odd affection the scratched oak desk, the metal shelves, the dented four-drawer filing cabinet, and the wedding picture of his parents mounted on the wall. The photo, given to him by his mother just months before she died from breast cancer in 1981, functioned as the only piece of sentimentality he would allow himself in this den of detection. It might be Spartan, Carmen acknowledged, but to him the austere alcove felt warm, musty, and familiar.

From within the filing cabinet's second drawer he removed a weather-beaten manila folder. Inside were several pages of phone numbers. He sifted through the pile and found the one he was seeking. It listed the backlines for the motor vehicle bureaus in each of the fifty states. Maryland's was midway down the page.

Carmen dialed the number. The receiver picked up on the third ring.

"Maryland Bureau of Motor Vehicles," came an official sounding greeting. "Gordon Pershing speaking,"

"Oh, hi," Carmen responded a bit hesitantly, still stale from the lay-off and concerned that he sounded unsure of himself. He cleared his throat and added more authoritatively, "This is Carmen Vitale. I'm a detective on the Pittsburgh Police force. Is…," Carmen glanced down at the sheet, "Al Capers there?"

"Sorry, detective," Pershing replied amicably, "Al's gone home for the night. Anything I can help you with?"

"I hope so—what did you say your name was?"

"Gordon."

"That's right, Gordon," Carmen acknowledged. "Anyway, Gordon, let me start by admitting that this inquiry is somewhat unofficial. Let's just say that a friend of a friend has asked me to do some *pro bono* work for her. The woman in question was adopted at birth. Recently, after having a kid of her own, she's become obsessed with tracking down her birth parents. Genetic concerns and all that malarkey. But all she could give me was a name, an approximate age, and a possible location. So, before I go off on some wild goose chase, I thought I'd lay the groundwork. That's where you come in."

"I'm starting to get the picture, detective," the Maryland official replied. "And by the way, we've already traced this call back to your station on Penn Circle in Pittsburgh. So I'm assuming you're legit."

"Nice to see you're thorough," Carmen conceded, feeling a little anxious at being so transparent. "Anyway, here's what I have." Carmen passed along the information about Harvey Richman, estimating him to be about sixty-nine, and residing in the Northwest section of Baltimore. Without a make, model, or a plate number, the search took some time. Finally Gordon came back on the line. He had teased out three individuals by that name, all in their late twenties or mid-thirties, none living in the Baltimore area. Carmen felt disappointed but not discouraged. While he waited for Gordon he thought about his interaction with Shindle. Something about the way the old German alluded to Reichman hinted that the former Nazi might not be alive anymore. He asked the BMV official to expand his search to include vehicles registered during the last five years.

Gordon got back on the phone a second time and reported, "This looks more promising, detective. A Harvey Richman, who lives in the Pimlico section of northwest Baltimore, owned a 1979 silver Mercedes 240D, tag number XGE-775, until 1985. The car was sold at auction in the spring of '86 to a man in Columbia, Maryland. After that there's no record of another vehicle being registered in the state of Maryland in Richman's name."

As the official reported this information Carmen could feel his heart pounding. "Is there an address for Richman?" he inquired.

"You bet," replied Gordon, now sounding as friendly as ever. "He lives at 2310 South Road. The zip is 21209."

Carmen scribbled down the information. "That's great, Gordon. You've been a big help."

"No problem, detective. Let me know if you get the family back to together."

Carmen hesitated for an instant then replied, "I sure will."

On a chilly Friday afternoon in early December, Carmen packed up his Fiat and set out for the east coast. His buddies in the surveillance vehicle outside his apartment building had departed days ago, apparently convinced that the detective wasn't planning to breach his 'parole'. Little did they know he'd just begun.

Carmen accessed the Pennsylvania turnpike in Monroeville and remained on it as far as Exit 12. Although the broad stands of leafless trees swayed in the thirty mile-per-hour gusts and the dark gray early evening skies seemed threatening, the only precipitation he encountered was a brief snow squall on the west side of the Blue Mountain tunnel. After stopping at the Dutch Pantry in Breezewood for what his mother would've called a hearty meal, Carmen eased onto Interstate 70. Less than two hours later he reached his destination, a Holiday Inn near the Social Security Administration Building in Woodlawn, just west of Baltimore proper.

After registering, Carmen hung around his motel room restlessly surfing the television channels for a while. Although the pitch blackness outside would make the visibility poor, he still decided that reconnoitering the area would be better than this inactivity. Returning to his Fiat, he headed in a northeasterly direction, soon finding himself driving along a series of windy roads through residential sections that seemed vacant and foreboding. As he cruised by, he watched a few brave residents, bundled up in parka-like winter coats, walk hastily along the deserted pavements. Stray canines poked through toppled trash cans left out after what Carmen assumed was the day's pick-up.

At the intersection of Gwynn Oak and Liberty, he entered what appeared to be the neighborhood's commercial district. Service stations segued into a row of street level stores, a few eating establishments, and some meetinghouses like the VFW center and a banquet hall. Working his way further north, he skirted the community of Glen, accessed the West Northern Parkway, and soon entered the quiet community of Pimlico. He wondered if the racetrack of the same name was nearby.

Consulting his local map, he estimated that the Richman home was a few blocks away. From the road signs, so was Sinai Hospital. He wondered if the old psychiatrist was on staff. Wouldn't that be a kicker, the Nazi an attending at a Jewish medical center? More likely, at sixty-nine, he was retired. That was another detail to check out while in town.

After turning left onto Greenspring Avenue, two blocks later he came upon South Road. As it frequently happened when he was closing in on a suspect, Carmen's heart started to pound. By the light of the single street lamp he searched for addresses. Soon he discovered that he was, in fact, on the 2300 block. Inching along on the curb, he began counting houses from the far corner. Finally he stopped across the relatively wide street, cut the engine, turned off his headlights, and studied what he guessed was the house he was searching for.

From what he could determine in the pale amber light that spilled from the living room window, the Richmans occupied a two-story Tudor with white stucco walls and a gray slate roof. Half of the first level was dark, probably housing a dining room near the front and perhaps a kitchen toward the rear. He assumed there were four bedrooms on the second floor and possibly, from the way the roof sloped to a sharp peak, an attic above that. Through a tangle of trees and bushes, he made out the outline of a free-standing garage at the end of a narrow concrete driveway that ran parallel to the path leading to the front door.

Along Carmen's side of the street a man in an overcoat walked his dog. While the black Lab sniffed around the bushes, its owner eyed the detective suspiciously. Finally, he moved off. Wouldn't it be a coincidence if that was Richman, Carmen imagined. If it was, he'd probably have a Shepherd or a Doberman. Glancing into the side mirror on the Fiat's passenger side, Carmen saw the man stop again, about a hundred yards down the street, turn slightly, and peer back toward the parked car. Carmen decided that he'd already overstayed his welcome.

The next morning dawned brighter with a hazy sunlight typical of early winter in a temperate climate like Baltimore's. After showering and dressing, Carmen stopped in the coffee shop for a bite. It was still too early on Saturday morning to go visiting, but he also feared waiting too long, risking that his target would be off doing week-end activities and errands, possibly Christmas shopping now that Thanksgiving had passed. Finally, after killing an hour sitting in the lobby reading the *Baltimore Sun*, he returned to his room, grabbed his overcoat, and set out for Pimlico.

This time, as he drove along Gwynn Oak Avenue, he got a better sense of the area. It appeared mostly residential with a mix of single homes, duplexes, and even a few blocks of row houses. A typical urban melting pot, the locals a mix of Blacks, Whites, and Hispanics. Small signs marked the various communities—names like Howard Park, Gwynn Oak, and West Arlington, places he recalled from reading his map. This time, after turning left onto Liberty, he went northwest for a few blocks, made a right onto Rogers Avenue and found the racetrack. It too, like the neighborhoods he'd canvassed the night before, seemed deserted, almost abandoned. Horse racing season, he reasoned, had long since ended for the season.

Less than a block up, Rogers merged with the Northern Parkway. A few minutes later, Carmen parked on South Road across from that same two-story Tudor. Taking a deep breath, he grabbed the door handle of his green Fiat, gave it a twist, and pushed it open.

Walking up the path, he passed between two rows of vacant flowers beds bordering halves of a well kept lawn. On the small porch, he was surprised to see an array of toys and other playthings strewn about. Unless Richman entertains his grandchildren a lot, Carmen considered, this might not be the place after all.

He pulled open the iron-rimmed storm door and searched for a bell. Through the thick oak door he could hear the disembodied sounds of Saturday morning television intermingled with the clamor of playing children. A lion-shaped knocker mounted just above a peephole announced Carmen's presence with a staccato rap. About thirty seconds later, the deadbolt released.

Expecting an elderly man or woman, Carmen was surprised when he was greeted by an attractive young woman holding a small infant in her arms. Her soft auburn hair and bright brown eyes complimented her pleasant smile. Apparently some residents in this neighborhood didn't seem wary of strangers. This might make his job easier.

"Yes?" the young woman asked. Carmen judged her to be in her late twenties or early thirties. The baby, with a pacifier in its mouth and a cherubic face caked with the remains of what looked like oatmeal, couldn't have been more than fourteen months. "Can I help you?"

Carmen cleared his throat. "Hi," he began. "I'm looking for a man named Harvey Richman. I was told he lives here."

"Harvey Richman?" the woman asked, her expression confused, even dubious. "There's no one by that name living here. You must be mistaken."

"This is 2310 isn't it?" Carmen persisted. The young woman nodded. "That's the address I was given by the people at the Bureau of Motor Vehicles. At least, he lived here until three years ago."

"That might explain it," the young woman said, looking relieved. "My husband and I bought this house in January of 1987. The former owner wasn't at the closing so I really couldn't tell you if his name was Harvey Richman or not."

"Oh," Carmen said, suddenly at a loss for where to go next.

From inside the house a minor altercation erupted characterized by a fair amount of yelling and screaming. A small child with plump freckle-filled cheeks and carrot-red hair tied back in pigtails came running toward the door. She was crying. "Mom, Zach hit me," she reported, her voice tinged by a manipulative whine.

"And what did you do to provoke him?" her mother asked patiently.

"Nothing."

"Now we both know that's not true, Sarah. What did you do to make him mad?"

Pouting, the little girl replied, "I took the remote," then she hastened to add, "but I just wanted to see if the Barbie Show was on. He always watches those stupid GI Joe cartoons all Saturday morning."

"Why don't you watch in your room?" her mother suggested.

"'Cause the big TV's down here. Why can't *he* watch in *his* room?"

"Because he doesn't have his own television, Sarah. You know that."

"It's still not fair that he gets to hog the TV down here."

"Why don't you give me a minute to finish up with this nice man here and then we can work out a compromise between you, your brother, and the downstairs television?"

Mollified, but looking less than satisfied, the little girl mumbled, "All right," and walked back into the house.

"Sorry about that," the young woman told Carmen. He smiled sympathetically. "Where were we?" she asked. "Oh, yes, Harvey Richman. As I was saying, we never had the opportunity to meet the people who lived here before us. The house was multi-listed. When we asked our realtor about their story, he couldn't find out much. There was some old German gentleman at the closing, though. If I'm not mistaken, *his* name was Kruger. But he wasn't the owner, just their—what do they call it—power of attorney."

"Was he a lawyer?"

"I don't think so," the young woman said frankly. "But he was authorized to sign all the papers."

"Who'd you write your check to?"

"Now that you mention it, I think my husband made it out to the Richman Estate. So it must've been that Richman guy you're looking for who lived here." Then she paused, looking a little pensive. "But if we made the check out to his estate, wouldn't that imply that this Harvey Richman is dead?"

"I was thinking the same thing," Carmen agreed.

The young woman took a moment to shift the baby from one hip to the other. With a sweet, inquisitive expression on her face she asked, "Would I be prying too much if I asked why you're looking for him?"

Already planning to stay with the same story he'd used with Maryland BMV, Carmen replied, "Not at all. I'm an off duty detective with the Pittsburgh Police Department. A recent acquaintance of mine asked me if I'd help her find her birth parents. Apparently, she was adopted at the age of three weeks. Somehow, she was able to come up with a name, an age, and an approximate location."

"Well from the sounds of it, you might have reached a dead end," the young woman suggested, "that's if he died or something."

"True," Carmen agreed. "But I think I'll keep on looking." It was the young woman's turn to smile understandingly. Carmen appreciated the sentiment. "Do you happen to recall the realtor you used to buy this place?" he asked.

The young woman reflected for a moment. Then she mentioned a name and the agency. Their office was in nearby Mount Washington. Carmen wrote down the information.

"And finally," he said, "there must be some people on this block who've lived here longer than you and your family. Your next door neighbors for instance? Would they have known the Richmans?"

"Oh, I'm sure they did. They're the Markhams. They've been here forever. But they keep pretty much to themselves, so I don't know much about them."

Backing out into the early December cold, Carmen suggested, "Maybe I'll see if they can help me. Thanks for your time."

"Sorry I couldn't be of more help."

As the storm door closed softly Carmen turned to leave. Glancing back he saw the pretty young woman standing on the other side of the glass, the young child on her hip, raising her hand and giving him a brief wave.

The elderly couple next door, a pair of septuagenarians, proved to be more helpful. Standing across from him at the front door they confirmed knowing the Richmans since 1962 when they moved from Durham Park, right after Harvey Richman had married Dora.

"Dora?" Carman asked.

"Oh yes, Dora Levenson," related Harry Markham, a man about five-four, with a bald, freckled scalp and a wrinkled, grayish-yellow complexion. At least, he thought Dora's maiden name was Levenson. Her mother was Sylvia Levenson. That much of which he was sure. Sylvia had only been married once, to Abe.

Carmen's head started to spin. After moving to the States, Reichman married a *Jew*? *Why*? But before he could sort out this startling piece of information, Molly Markham, a pert little woman with a stern, serious expression and dyed, brown hair interjected, "They—I mean the Richmans—kept pretty much to themselves, especially after Lila was born in the fall of 1963." The mention of Lila Richman excited Carmen's interest. But before he could ask another question, Molly cleared her throat and suggested, "Perhaps, Mr. Vitale, you'd like to conduct this interview away from the front door where the cold wind is blowing into the house? Come join us in the parlor. I'm brewing a fresh pot of tea."

"That would be great," Carmen agreed, starting to get tired of standing in doorways. A couple of minutes later, the three of them were seated around a rectangular coffee table in the Markhams' living room, Carmen on a dark wood chair, Harry and Molly on a maroon, deep-cushioned sofa a few feet away. Molly had placed a silver serving set on the table. In addition to the tea, she offered him coffee cake that looked like saucers of flaky, sugary batter filled with a fruity paste. Rachael, he recalled, used to call them Danish.

While he waited for her to pour, Carmen took note of the Markhams' neat, prim home. Had someone asked him to characterize the style, he would have called the furniture antique colonial. He thought that the pieces seemed appropriate to the white two-story structure, with its Victorian flair, solid but cozy, filled with deep pile carpeting, thick velveteen curtains, and shelves and tables cluttered with photos, paintings, figurines, and other knickknacks.

"So you're tracking down a birth parent?" Molly reiterated, leaning forward on the edge of the sofa, her black pumps on the carpet, her elbows resting on her knees. "It always gives me a thrill to see families become reunited. Adoption always seems so hard on the child."

"Well this woman is hardly a child," Carmen clarified. "The one time I met her, she looked to be in her mid-forties."

"Still," the elderly woman persisted, "wouldn't it have been a blessing if she could have met her father before he died?"

"So Harvey Richman is dead?"

"I thought you knew," Harry chimed in.

"From my conversation with your next door neighbor I suspected as much. I just wasn't sure."

"Well you can be sure," Molly confirmed. "I think it was cancer. And he must have died at home. I remember seeing the people of Shueler's Funeral Home take away the body right before the High Holidays in 1986."

"Was there anyone else living with Mr. Richman at the time?" Carmen probed.

"Not that we could tell," Harry offered, "not since his daughter moved in with her aunt in Pennsylvania."

Involuntarily, Carmen's heart began pounding again. "When was that?" he asked.

But Harry didn't seem to know for certain. He glanced over at Molly for guidance. After placing a crooked, arthritic finger to her thin, pursed lips she announced, "I think it was late in the summer of 1985. She'd already graduated from the University of Maryland. Mrs. Bates down the block mentioned she was thinking about enrolling in The School of International Studies at the University of Pittsburgh."

"Was her father already sick?"

"I don't think so. Although, who knew? Once Dora died, the whole family kept pretty much to themselves."

"Dora Richman died?" Carmen queried. "When?"

Molly, who was turning out to be a wellspring of information, reported, "In the winter of 1969."

"That's right!" Harry interjected, his face beaming. "She had a heart attack on Super Bowl Sunday. I remember the ambulance at their house. I almost missed the end of the game, which might have been just as well since that bastard Namath led those upstart New York Jets over our Colts. To me it'll always be Black Sunday, just like the movie that came out in the late seventies."

No, Carmen thought, it wasn't anything like that. But he didn't want to dispute a loyal Colts' fan's musing, not when he was being so generous with his time. "So Richman raised his daughter alone for, let me see, sixteen years," he commented instead. "That must've been tough on him."

"Oh, I'm not so sure," Molly refuted. "He had plenty of help."

"Help?" Carmen repeated.

Molly nodded. "From what I could tell. And this, Mr. Vitale, is only hearsay, since anything neighborly we tried to do after Dora died, was politely rebuffed by the good doctor." Despite her bright informative manner, Carmen detected the disdain in her tone. "Soon after they buried Dora, Dr. Richman would schlep over Lila to one of his colleague's houses, then pick her up after work. Gladys Schwartz—she lives two doors down on the other side—told me that his name was Cutler. The two men worked at Sinai."

"You mean Dr. Cutler, the urologist?" Harry asked.

"That's the one," Molly confirmed.

"I never knew that."

"Well, if you'd listen to me when I talk to you, Harry Markham, maybe you'd learn a thing or two. I'm sure I mentioned it several times back then." Molly then turned her grey speckled eyes on Carmen and smiled primly. "Anyway, Mr. Vitale, I think the Cutlers had a daughter Lila's age. Gladys said the two girls went to the Lutheran Day School in Mount Washington."

"But I thought Richman was Jewish?" Carmen asked, although he knew full well how fallacious that was.

"That's what we thought, too," Molly confided, "especially when Dora was alive. They used to light candles on Chanukah and go to shul on the High Holidays. And with a name like Richman, we just assumed he was Jewish, too."

"Not so," Harry offered. "I think he was really German. And from the way he acted toward us after his wife died, I wouldn't be surprised if he was secretly anti-Semitic."

More than you'll ever know, Harry, Carmen said to himself. More than you'll ever know. Aloud, he reiterated, "But it still sounds like Richman raised the girl alone."

"Not really," Molly disagreed. "That shuttling back and forth to the Cutlers only lasted about a year. Then this middle-aged German woman moved in with them. It took me a while, but eventually I found out that she was Dr. Richman's sister, Margo.

"Her sister," Carmen repeated, a ploy to contain his excitement. "Interesting. And what was she like?"

"Just like her brother," Molly said caustically, "quiet, unfriendly, almost stand-offish. She kept even more to herself than he did—if that was possible."

So we've come full circle, Carmen noted with grim satisfaction. "And how long did she live with him?" he inquired, feeling pretty certain of the response.

"Until around the summer of—let me see...." He watched as Molly counted on her fingers. "Lila was born in '63. She started college in the fall of 1980. I think Margo stayed to help through her freshman year. That means she left in 1981."

"Why was that?"

"I'd like to say, because she wasn't needed anymore," the elderly woman said vindictively. "But I think it's because she got married."

"She did? At what age?" Carmen asked.

"That was information I wasn't privy to," Molly said, her tone confidential, almost conspiratorial. "But she had to be in her late fifties."

"And looked ten years older," Harry said smugly.

"Oh, you hush, Harry Markham!" Molly admonished, slapping the back of his splotched, wrinkled hand.

Carmen couldn't help but smile. Apparently the Richmans hadn't done much to endear themselves to their next-door neighbors. "Any idea who she married?" he probed politely.

"Now this is just local gossip again," Molly admitted, "but it was some friend of a friend who was visiting from Western Pennsylvania. I think his name was Shindle. In fact, that's probably who Lila went to live with the year before her father died."

"Which makes sense to me," Carmen agreed, watching the puzzle pieces fall into place. At this juncture, Carmen suspected that he'd probably exhausted the Markhams' ability to assist him. Conceding this fact, he tactfully brought the interview to a close. Glancing at his watch, he was surprised to note that he'd been conversing with the kindly old couple for almost two hours. Letting out an exaggerated sigh, he rose to his feet.

"Well, I can't thank you enough for all the help you've been," he said appreciatively. "But I still have another appointment scheduled for one o'clock, so I'd better be running along."

The dismayed look on his hosts' faces told him how disappointed they were to see him go. How often did they have a chance to spend a morning with a stranger from out of town chitchatting about a neighbor toward whom they had such animosity, he wondered? "One more thing," he said as they joined him at the front door. In the background he heard a cranky hot water radiator hiss. "Dora's mother?" He consulted his notebook. "I believe you said her name was Sylvia Levenson. How much do you know about her?"

"Well, she's still alive," Molly offered, "if that's what you're getting at. I know that for a fact since I still see her at synagogue on Friday nights. We both belong to Beth El in Glen. The last time I talked to her she mentioned that she lives in the Fox Glen Apartments, just a few a blocks away from Park Heights Ave, so she can walk to shul. Me, on the other hand, have to get my son, Stanley, to drive me. But he's pretty good about that. Which is what a son does for his mother."

Carmen couldn't help but smile. "What's the name of her street?"

"Glen," she replied, "which seems appropriate, if you ask me."

"Me, too," Carmen conceded. With that he said goodbye, turned, and was once again back out in the blustery, Saturday afternoon chill.

Chapter 17

The Markhams' tea and Danish had long ago worn off when Carmen sat down at a nearby diner off Northern Parkway to grab a bite to eat and collect his thoughts. From his conversations with the young mother and the elderly couple he was beginning to get a picture of Harvey Richman, a.k.a. Hans Reichman and his domestic family.

As frequently was the case in his investigations, Carmen found it helpful to devise a psychological profile of the perpetrators before he could hope to track or apprehend them. Where Richman was concerned, the dead Nazi's memoirs had been a start. But the story had terminated abruptly with a blow to Carmen's cranium after which Shindle relieved him of his prize. Now he'd picked up the trail of the former SS officer who might possibly be involved with a heinous crime that occurred almost forty-five years later. If Richman had, in fact, succumbed to cancer three years earlier, he couldn't have been the bomber. Still, his death didn't dissociate him completely from the crime.

The more Carmen reflected upon the situation, the more he kept returning to Lila, Richman's daughter. How did this mysterious young woman fit into the murky picture? He'd amassed isolated facts about her: age, snippets from early childhood, a hint about the direction her education took, and finally, her move to Pittsburgh two years before her father's death. His intuition told him that by filling in more of her story he would come closer to solving the mystery.

He thought about the conversation with Jarvis and his friend's reference to the neighborhood German tavern. Flipping through his notebook he located the name, *Der Bavarian Bierserver*. This establishment, of course, warranted a visit. But any of the 'boys' he'd be interested in interviewing would be more likely to wander in after dark. It was still Saturday afternoon. Another option would be to call on Mrs. Sylvia Levenson. Molly Markham had related that Dora Richman's mother lived in the Fox Glen apartments. Removing a now tattered map of Greater Baltimore from his overcoat, he discovered that the community of Glen was nearby— at most a mile or two southwest of where he was parked. Eager to get in motion again, he finished his tuna fish sandwich, paid the check, and before leaving, confirmed the exact address in a frayed copy of the White Pages by the pay phone near the door. A few minutes later, he was on his way.

As he drove along its narrow tree-lined streets, Carmen decided that Glen was a charming community lined with small single homes and split-level duplexes. A few public schools, several churches, a municipal building, and one large synagogue rounded out the scene. On Glenn Avenue, partway between Park Heights Boulevard and Rusk Street, he located the apartment complex. After parking the Fiat by the Leonard Luchman Memorial Park, he crossed the street and surveyed the collection of beige-brick, three-story buildings linked together like dominos, the end of one perpendicular to the side of the next. He counted twelve units per building all accessed from a common main door, each with its own small balcony. Finally, after checking out a cluster toward the rear of the complex, he located 3B. Inside the outer door, he scanned the names on the mailboxes and confirmed that Sylvia Levenson did, indeed, live in apartment 3205. He pressed the intercom.

"Yes," came the response, "who's there?" The elderly voice had an Eastern European accent.

Deciding to drop some of his pretense from the outset, Carmen announced in a loud clear voice, "My name is Detective Carmen Vitale, Ma'am. I've driven down here from Pittsburgh. I'm investigating the disappearance of your granddaughter, Lila Richman."

Even through the static laden intercom, Carmen could hear the old woman catch her breath. "Did you say Lila?"

"Yes, Mrs. Levenson," Carmen confirmed. The pause that followed seemed interminable. Finally, Sylvia Levenson instructed, "Come up, detective."

The door latch buzzed. Carmen pushed. After mounting the steps two at a time, on the second floor near the back of the building, he found apartment 3205. The door was already ajar.

Her age notwithstanding—Carmen guessed she was in her mid-to-late seventies—Dora Levenson's mother was a handsome woman. Small, but not stooped, she stood by the door and invited Carmen in. Despite being home alone on a Saturday afternoon, she was smartly dressed in a navy blue dress with a starched white collar, stockings, and black pumps. Her hair, a soft, silvery gray, was combed to one side and secured with a pair of red clips. Peering up at him through bright eyes, she seemed alert and teeming with aliveness, her complexion remarkably smooth and wrinkle-free. The expression on her face conveyed interest and concern. If anything betrayed her age, he decided, it was the flabby skin on her neck, which she stroked with arthritic fingers.

"It's not every day I have a visitor such as you, detective," she greeted him. "Truth be told, it's not every day I have a visitor at all. So, please come in and tell me more about your little mission." Carmen considered this an odd little term, but, on second thought it did define, as accurately as anything, what he was up to.

Sylvia Levenson's apartment seemed bright and cheerful. He noticed the hues were all whites and light grays with a few pastels woven into the fabric on the sofa and chairs. She directed him to a small breakfast nook off the kitchen. He draped his overcoat on one of the wrought iron chairs by an oval-shaped dinette table. She offered him coffee. He opted for water.

"So you're searching for Lila," Mrs. Levenson began after joining him at the table. "What's happened to her?"

"I'm not sure yet. I learned of her existence and subsequent disappearance while investigating an explosion at a residence in one of the more affluent sections of Pittsburgh."

"An explosion? How horrible. Was anyone hurt?"

"An entire family, Mrs. Levenson. Six people were killed."

"Oh, my heavens!" the older woman exclaimed. "And you say that Lila may have had something to do with this tragedy?"

"To tell you the truth, Mrs. Levenson, I really don't know who or what's involved here. I'm just following up leads."

"And your leads led you to Baltimore, Detective Vitale?"

He nodded. Continuing to forgo any pretense, he proceeded to enlighten her about the surfacing of Nazi Reichman's diary and how it led him to the Shindles' house in the small community of Zelienople. He then reported on his encounter with Mr. Shindle, finding the picture on the piano but conveniently omitted the part about the old Kraut's demise. "From there, it was relatively easy to track Richman, alias Riechman, back to Baltimore. Right now your

153

granddaughter is just another character in the story. I don't know who did what, if anything, yet."

"Fascinating," agreed Mrs. Levenson, her eyes alive with interest. "The old German woman was probably Harvey's sister, Margo. She moved in with him after my daughter died in 1963 and lived there until Lila was in college. Then she met that Shindle you were referring to. I think his first name was Dexter or Dieter or something like that. Anyway, things apparently become serious enough for her to pack up and move with him to that town in Western Pennsylvania that you mentioned."

"Zelienople," he clarified. "Which squares with what the Markhams told me this morning."

"You met Molly and Harry?" Sylvia asked, looking genuinely pleased. "I run into them sometimes on Friday nights at Beth El."

"I know," Carmen confided.

She gave him a look that suggested she was wondering what else he already knew. But instead, she continued her story. "That was in 1981, I think. Reagan was already president."

"Okay," Vitale prompted supportively.

"Lila went to live with them in 1985."

"Any idea why?"

"It's hard to say. When she stopped over to say good-by she told me that she was interested in a graduate degree in Political Science. Pitt's School of International Studies is apparently one of the best in the east. Eventually, she wanted to work for the federal government, maybe even the State Department. It was that or go into teaching."

"Zelienople's a pretty long commute for someone going to Pitt."

"I wouldn't know about that. In fact, I'm not sure she was actually going to live with Margo and her husband. But she just was happy to have some family in the area."

Carmen nodded. This info seemed consistent with what he'd learned from Barry Rosenberg's co-workers at Northbanks. If Lila was the woman Barry had been dating prior to his death—and it was starting to seem so—she apparently lived on or near Pitt's campus, not with the Shindles. Carmen then decided to shift gears. "What about Lila's childhood?" he inquired of this prim, mentally sharp, elderly woman. "Can you tell me anything about that, Mrs. Levenson?"

"Not as much as I'd like to," the older woman confided. Carmen detected disdain in her voice.

"Why's that?"

"Because after my Dora died, I had very little to do with it."

"Why not?"

"Because my dear son-in-law, the venerable psychiatrist, thought he could do the job all by himself. Not that I didn't offer, mind you, Detective. At first Harvey just rebuffed me—politely mind you—but regularly enough that I finally got the message."

"The Markhams mentioned a couple called the Cutlers?"

"Harvey's friends? Oh, they were just bit players in my granddaughter's story, Mr. Vitale. Dr. Cutler was a colleague of Harvey's at Sinai. He had a daughter Lila's age. I didn't mind her spending so much time there. But what did gall me was that they supported Harvey's decision to put my granddaughter in a Protestant elementary school. And she being Jewish."

"But her father was Lutheran," Vitale reminded her.

"But her mother was Jewish!" Sylvia Levenson, clearly needing no reminding, shot back. "And according to our religious laws, Mr. Vitale, if your mother's Jewish, you are, too."

"I think I knew that," Carmen conceded.

"I bet you did. And Harvey knew it, too. After all, he was born in Germany. He grew up during the Third Reich. The details of Jewish lineage were drummed into his head from childhood. Hitler made damn sure of that. My son-in-law couldn't help but know what Lila was!"

"Despite that," Vitale said, knowing he was stating the obvious, "he seemed determined to raise her as a Christian."

"He sure did," Mrs. Levenson concurred. Carmen suspected that if she wasn't so polite, her response would have been more acerbic.

"So while Lila was growing up, you were, so to speak, out of the loop."

"That's one way of putting it. Except for an occasional shopping spree and those obligatory visits for birthdays and holidays, after Dora died, I had very little contact with my granddaughter."

"Despite that, any insights into what went on in that house?"

"It's hard to say," Mrs. Levenson admitted. "I can only get a sense of it from what Lila shared on those brief times we were together over the years. For the most part, her Aunt Margo was a good woman. She treated my granddaughter well. Apparently, before coming to the states in the mid sixties, she'd had a hard life. Her husband and a small child had been killed in the bombing of Germany in May of 1945 just before VE Day. After the war she was forced to remain in East Germany for nearly twenty years where she did mostly domestic and factory work under the Communist regime. Until Shindle came along, she never remarried."

"How did she finally defect?"

"I'm sure you could never prove it, but I think Harvey pulled some strings." She lowered her voice and moved in closer. "You know he worked for the CIA."

"He did?" Carmen replied, feigning surprise.

Sylvia nodded, looking like a little girl telling a tale out of school. "Consulting work in psychiatry, I'm told. Not too much after he married Dora, though. But more, I believe, back in the fifties, at the height of the cold war."

"Fascinating. How do you know so much about that?"

"Dora," Sylvia admitted, her head nodding, her lips forming a tight, straight line.

Carmen nodded along while mentally retracing the steps that had gotten them there in the first place. "So you don't think Margo was a bad influence on Lila?" he offered.

"No," Sylvia agreed, "not as much as that Kruger."

"Kruger?" Carmen asked. This was the second time this name had come up in two days.

"I suppose he was another one of Harvey's friends. Someone he knew from back in Germany. After coming here I think he worked as a longshoreman on the piers."

"And you believe this guy Kruger had a negative influence on your granddaughter. Why?"

"Because after he started hanging out at their house on South Ave, Lila seemed to change. All of a sudden she wasn't my sweet, innocent granddaughter any more. She developed this sharp, almost caustic edge to her personality."

"How old was she at the time?"

"Around twelve."

"Maybe she was just being a pre-teen?" Carmen suggested naively.

"This was more than pre-adolescent rebelliousness, Detective," Sylvia informed him. "We're not talking about cursing in public or going around being rude to your elders."

"Then what are we talking about?" Carmen inquired.

"We're talking about becoming a racist bigot, Mr. Vitale. It's about regurgitating that white supremacist propaganda the Nazis were so famous for during Third Reich. And believe me Mr. Vitale, I know all about where it came from. I've read books on the Holocaust. Not to mention my first hand experience. You see, my husband, Abe—God rest his soul—fought in Europe from late '43 through early '45. He landed with the second wave at Normandy and died, a hero, near a place called Hanover, just before the war ended.

"During the war I was forced to work in our little grocery store near Druid Hill Park fifteen, sixteen hours a day, just to pay the mortgage and put food on the table. *Vey is meir!* My children were so young and innocent at the time. Dora was only thirteen when her father enlisted. And my Michael, my sweet, gentle, Michael, who is now a most respected Park Ranger in Colorado, was only eight." All Carmen could do was offer was a sincere, sympathetic, encouraging nod. "Abe used to write to me from the front about those Satanic Germans," Mrs. Levenson continued, barely pausing to take a breath, "what they said about the Jews and Blacks, what they taught their children in their schools. Don't get me started, detective." But Carmen knew she was well on her way.

"Not to mention Hitler's Final Solution," the petite Jewish woman vented. "Back then we only heard rumors about those death camps. Now we know the truth about what those subhuman animals did to our people. And after Kruger showed up on the scene, there was my beautiful little Lila, spouting the same racist rhetoric."

"That must've been hard to take."

"It was brutal, Detective—hearing venal, bigoted epithets pour out of that pretty, little mouth. And her father did nothing to stop it. He may have even encouraged it. Which makes it easy to believe that he was a Nazi, too—back in Germany, before they lost the war, just like you mentioned when you told me about the diary."

Carmen tried to be tactful. "So it sounds like your son-in-law and this crony of his, Kruger, tried to influence the way Lila regarded minorities."

"It was more than influence, Mr. Vitale. They brainwashed her."

"Is that what you really think?"

"It's not something I think," she replied emphatically. "It's something I know. And there's more. They started teaching her about guns."

"Guns," Carmen repeated, once again taken off guard.

"Yes detective, guns. You know, firearms, revolvers. It started right after her thirteenth birthday. By the way, Lila was born on November 22, 1963, the day President Kennedy was assassinated. Maybe that was a bad omen. Anyway, in the fall of 1976, Harvey and Kruger began taking her up to his hunting cabin near Gunpowder State Park. Great name for a retreat, huh? There they taught her how to use hunting rifles and revolvers. She bragged about it on the first night of Chanukah that year when she stopped over to get her presents. After she left I called Harvey and confronted him about it. The schmuck wouldn't even admit I was right. Instead, he claimed that girls were just as entitled to learn how to use firearms as boys. He even mocked me by saying he was raising Lila to be the son he never had. Of all the unmitigated gall!'"

Dropping his objectivity Carmen commented, "What a bastard,"

"And there's more," she continued. "Starting the next summer Harvey sent Lila to this camp in Western Maryland. When she first described it to me, it sounded pretty normal. But then, she related how part of her daily activities involved self-defense, marksmanship, and war games. That didn't sound like any camp I'd ever heard of—more like a military school, if you ask me. But all I could get out of Harvey was how it provided a healthy, outdoor environment for his daughter and kept her off the Baltimore streets during summer vacations."

"This is all beginning to suggest a pattern," Carmen said pensively, more to himself than to his hostess. Then directing his attention at Mrs. Levenson he asked, "Did she ever talk about explosives?"

"Not that I can remember."

"Unfortunately, that doesn't prove anything."

An uncomfortable silence ensued. The weight of the implications of what Sylvia Levenson had revealed about her granddaughter was taking its toll. If Lila wasn't a viable suspect prior to this interview with her grandmother, she certainly was now. While flipping the pages of his notebook forward, Carmen said, "One more question before I get going. With all the animosity and bigotry she articulated toward that same people how did Lila reconcile the fact that she was half-Jewish?"

"She probably denied or rejected that part of her heritage," Sylvia Levenson reported frankly. "That's the only thing I can figure." A somber, almost despondent note had crept into her voice. "I guess," she added slowly.

"That's what I would have guessed, too," Carmen agreed.

Feeling weary from this emotional encounter, Carmen pushed himself back from the table and rose to his feet. Sylvia Levenson stood too, resembling a mere shadow in the late afternoon light. Reaching over, she flipped the wall switch. The frosted glass chandelier suspended above the dinette table came to life. But whatever light it shed on the situation, Carmen realized, was too little and much too late.

Chapter 18

Feeling unusually weary from his day on the fact-finding circuit, Carmen left Sylvia Levenson's Fox Glen apartment and returned to the Holiday Inn. As he pulled into the parking lot, a comment Mrs. Levenson had made about Lila triggered an avenue of inquiry he'd hadn't considered before.

Less than an hour later, refreshed by a shower and shave, he headed for the large suburban mall situated only a mile from his motel. After parking the Fiat near the ground level food court, he opted for a couple of slices of Sbarro's pizza and a Baskin Robbins' ice cream cone before heading for the Daltons bookstore, two corridors over. Once inside the brightly lit establishment, he worked his way back to the modern history section and quickly located the item for which he was searching.

As it happened, two years earlier, in the fall of 1987, a band of white supremacists called, skinheads, had chosen to loiter on a popular street corner in the commercial section of Squirrel Hill. There, beneath a cracked Gulf sign, and tauntingly close to the local Jewish Community Center, these unwelcome agitators perpetrated a range of rowdy antics that caused anxious shoppers and enraged locals to give them a wide berth. This unnerving situation created consternation among the leaders of the predominantly Jewish neighborhood. In due course patrolmen stationed at the local precinct became involved in keeping things from coming to a head.

Six months later, in the spring of 1988, the teenage daughter of a prominent Jewish physician was found murdered in the back yard of her parents' Squirrel Hill home. As the case unraveled, the main suspect, in addition to being a classmate and boyfriend of the victim, was also a card-carrying member of this unsavory hate group. Three weeks later, on a sunny morning in May, during the final phase of the homicide investigation, Carmen arrived at his own precinct building on Penn Circle in East Liberty and noticed that the intake sergeant had a book called, *Armed and Dangerous*, opened on his desk. Written by an investigative reporter named, James Coates, the book dealt with the survivalist movement, a loose collection of hate groups that included the Ku Klux Klan, neo-Nazis, and various other ultra-conservative, quasi-militant organizations.

At the time, Carmen, usually with little tolerance for any group of self-righteous dissidents, was preoccupied with other matters and afforded the notion only passing interest. Now, little more than a year later, the possibility that this detestable movement was germane to his current investigation crossed his mind. So, with Coates' handy reference tucked safely under his arm, Carmen left the mall.

Now what should I do, he wondered? Perhaps a visit to the boys at that Jarvis' German pub was in order? But he sensed it was still too early in the evening. May not on Saturday night at all. The clientele would be wrong. Too many couples.

Continuing to meander down the midway, littered with commercial kiosks and small concession stands, he noticed a six-theatre Cineplex toward the far end. After checking the offerings, he opted for the Kevin Costner's baseball movie, *Field of Dreams*. "Build it and they will come," had become the pop-culture motto.

The plot unfolded. Carmen related nostalgically to the appeal of our national pastime. Eventually he was transported back to his sophomore year of high school, while playing American Legion ball at a local park on Fifth and Penn in Squirrel Hill, the starting shortstop for the Mellon Marauders. A short, compact teenager, quick and strong, clad in a black, white and gold uniform, he stood a few feet from second base, smacking his freshly oiled glove, pawing the dirt with his spiked shoe, waiting for Dicky Connelly to toss him some warm-up grounders. Between throws, he glanced toward the stands. Rachael waved back from the top row. When he noticed her, a smile blossomed on his olive skinned face. He'd mentioned the game to her in passing, the invitation to attend implied but not stated. Desperately, he'd hoped she'd come to see him play. And now she was there, in the stands, set to cheer him on.

While cloaked in the anonymity of a local Baltimore movie theatre, a tear formed in the corner of his eye. Silently it welled, then trickled down the side of his nose. Sweet Rachael, he lamented, his first true love, the highlight of his adolescence, the keeper of his heart. Now she was gone, a victim of some ruthless terrorist act, perpetrated by who knows who? But he'd find out. That, more than anything, was why he'd driven all the way to Baltimore, hot on the trail of a cadre of suspects, determined to narrow down the field and get his man—or woman, if that be the case. Justice would be served. This time, it was personal.

It was just after nine o'clock on Monday evening when Carmen finally negoti- ated the route he'd mapped out to *The Bavarian Beermeister*. As he drove the shrouded streets of North Central Baltimore, he thought about what he'd already accomplished.

Much of the day had been spent at the local branch office of the Anti- Defamation League. There, a friendly, no-nonsense woman named Beatrice Lehrer, a middle-aged Jewish housewife who volunteered for what she consid- ered one of the more worthy causes, educated Carmen on the state of the White Supremacist movement in the USA.

After supplying him with a pile of pamphlets, folders, and spiral-bound intelligence reports, she summarized the widespread, and sometimes violent, activities of the Skinheads, The American Nazi Party, The Aryan Brotherhood, The National Socialist Liberation Front, The Ku Klux Klanners, and the Brüder Schweigen—also known as the Silent Brotherhood. In 1987 members of this last group of dissidents had been indicted for the murder of Denver's outspoken, Jewish talk show host, David Berg.

In due course, Mrs. Lehrer provided him with the details that the Coates book had lacked, including how the ADL tracked the activities of these groups in Western Pennsylvania and Maryland. Lastly, she briefed him on what the local authorities were doing to keep these groups in check. While cruising the Northern Parkway over Interstate 83, then south on Falls Road, he shuddered to think how pervasive these hate mongers were.

Tucked away on Thirty-Seventh Street near Roland, *Der Bavarian Bierserver* seemed like a seedy pub at the fringe of a once-classy German neighborhood. After parking the rental at an expired meter on the opposite side of the street, he waited for the traffic to clear, then approached the entrance. A pair of filthy windows faced the street, both featuring neon signs advertising beers with which Carmen was unfamiliar. Glancing up, he noticed the slatted metal panel which slid into a sleeve above the jamb. As familiar as he was with this type of drinking hole, the nature of its location and the character of its clientele, it was with some trepidation that Carmen reached out and pulled open the heavy wooden portal.

Inside, an oddly comforting odor greeted him, a blend of heavy German beer, dark varnished wood, insecticide, and the stench from that particular segment of society that frequented this type of gathering place. The majority of the patrons seemed elderly and male, dressed in an assortment of flannel shirts, woolen sweaters, soiled khakis, and jeans. A long bar occupied most of one wall. Still in his overcoat, Carmen claimed an empty stool toward one end and sat down.

A hefty, ruddy-faced, round-shouldered man in a soiled apron stood by the far end of the bar drying glasses and slipping them into a wooden rack that hung from the ceiling. His chiseled features and close-cropped, steel-gray hair reminded Carmen of Austin Cooley, a drill sergeant he'd sweated under at Fort Benning back in 1968. Approaching, the bartender asked, "What'll it be?" His voice was gruff but not unfriendly.

"What's on tap?" Carmen asked easily.

The man listed them. Carmen chose a dark lager. From a spigot with a lever-like handle, he filled Carmen's schooner. The detective savored his beverage, impressed by its thick head, rich, full-body flavor, bitter after-taste. Gradually, the lager grew on him. By the time he'd emptied his first pint, he felt warm and pleasantly mellow.

Beside the half-dozen men flanking him along the brass-railed bar, clusters of patrons, mostly in pairs and trios, congregated at small tables or in booths along the opposite wall. Rickety, wooden paddlefans hung from the stucco ceiling, their warped blades lazily circulating dank, stale air. A smattering of recessed bulbs shed a misty amber light through the cloud of cigarette smoke. The bartender walked over and offered Carmen a refill. As he poured, Carmen casually inquired, "Anyone here acquainted with a guy named Harvey Richman?"

Carmen sensed the hesitation. "Who wants to know?" he finally asked.

Carmen had expected this. "Name's Jack Carter. I used to be a beat reporter for the *Washington Post*. Now I freelance. Let's just say I'm doing some research."

"There's nothing to research here," the barman commented wryly.

"What if I told you, 'Adolf's looking for me?'?"

163

This time, the pause stretched out for a few seconds. "Is that so, Mr. Carter?" he finally replied. "What do you want with Dr. Richman?"

"I'm writing a book. He's one of the characters."

"No foolin'?" Carmen couldn't tell if his tone reflected sarcasm or piqued interest. "What's this book of yours about?"

"It deals with former members of the Third Reich who, at the end of World War II, switched sides and worked as American operatives."

"That's gotta be a small group."

"Larger than you think."

"Sorta like the good guys' version of the *Boys from Brazil*."

"Sorta," Carmen agreed, familiar with the late seventies movie about displaced Hitlerites. But this was a start. The least he could do was follow the path.

"And you think Dr. Richman is one of these—what did you call them—operatives?"

"I know he is."

"Oh, really?" the older man said with a smirk. "What makes you so smart?"

"I met Dr. Richman back in the mid-seventies," Carmen replied, dryly. "The *Post* was doing a series of articles on the effectiveness of the CIA's Phoenix Program during the Vietnam war. The public relations man mentioned that Dr. Richman was one of the department's experts on psychological warfare and had been since way before the war. By then, much of the data dealing with that campaign had been declassified, so they let me interview the players. The doctor was one of them. And truth be told, he was very generous with his time."

"No shit?" the bartender inquired, a hint of skepticism lingering in his tone. "And what exactly did he tell you?"

"You'll have to read the book to find that out," Carmen rejoined lightly.

Rebuffed, the bartender slipped away, ostensibly diverted by requests from other patrons. But his curiosity must have kept him engaged. A few minutes later, despite the fact that Carmen was only halfway through his second beer, the burly man stood across the bar from him. "Sorry to inform you, pal," the barman commented without preamble, "but Dr. Richman's been dead for nearly three years."

Carmen, expecting this revelation, feigned upset. "That's too bad," he said. "I was really looking forward to seeing him again. The last time we met he promised to share his story. Now it looks like I'll have to get it second hand."

"If that," the bartender commented wryly.

"You mean none of your regulars knew Richman well enough to give me some background?"

"Some did. But why should they talk to you?"

"Because he was a friend of theirs. And he has a story to tell. And I'm the man to tell it." The barman grunted smugly. "Anyway," Carmen continued, "got any suggestions who I should approach?" Knitting his bushy eyebrows and pursing a pair of thin, pale lips, the bartender considered the question. Then, with a cock of his head, he gestured toward an old man sitting alone at a booth near the far corner of the room.

"Thanks," Carmen said and took out his wallet. He paid his tab, adding a generous gratuity for the barman, whose assistance, albeit grudging was appreciated.

Carrying his partially-filled glass of beer in an outstretched arm, Carmen weaved his way around the randomly positioned tables until he reached the dimly lit booth. Standing by the edge of the table, he waited for the lone occupant to acknowledge him. The man, who seemed engrossed in a tattered looking oversized paperback, finally glanced up, looked puzzled, then annoyed. Before he could comment, Carmen slipped into the booth.

"That friendly bartender over there," he explained, "told me you and Harvey Richman were friends. I'm in the process of researching a book about German World War II expatriates who immigrated into the U.S. He mentioned that you might be able to help me find out more about him."

The man, who up close appeared to be in his late fifties, had a thin torso, an oblong face, and arresting blue-grey eyes. It was through these that he regarded Carmen suspiciously. With measured deliberateness, he shut his book and eased it toward the condiment caddy near the inside edge of the table. Through the corner of his eye, Carmen read the title. *One Day in the Life of Ivan Denisovich*, by Aleksandr Solzhenitsyn. Carmen had heard of the author, a banished Russian dissident, but was unfamiliar with this particular work. He sighed, looked over, and braced himself for another arduous effort of extracting information. He was a dentist pulling teeth without anesthesia. That's why he felt a bit relieved when his table-mate fixed him with those striking eyes and smiled.

"So you want to know about Harvey?" was his opening comment. Carmen was so startled he just nodded. "That wasn't his real name, you know. It was

Hans Reichman. But in 1957, when he was forced to emigrate here from Hungary, he felt compelled to Americanize it to Harvey Richman."

"Hungary?"

"Yeah. He was a CIA operative. As part of his cover the government put him through medical school, there. But once he got to the States he couldn't find a job. In Baltimore in the late fifties the local medical establishment was run by a bunch of Eastern European Jews still smarting over what happened to their brethren in World War II. They knew Hans was German and ignored his medical degree from the University of Budapest, not to mention his psychiatry training in Austria. Freud, himself, was Austrian, for Chrissakes. So he changed his name and enrolled at Hopkins. Eventually he had enough letters after his name to even impress the bigoted credentials committee at Sinai."

Wow, Carmen marveled. This is much better than I ever dreamed. "Name is Jack Carter," Carmen said as a belated introduction. "And you are?"

"Gerhard Strauss," the older man replied, reaching out his right arm. "Call me Gerry." The two men shook hands. "Hans and I met at Hopkins while I was a medical student moonlighting as a tech in the radiology department. Turns out we were both German expatriates trying to find our way in a new land. I was the guy who shot the X-rays, mostly skull and vertebral films, spinal taps, and angiograms, way before CT scanners and these new-fangled MRI's. While he was hanging around the department waiting for his studies, we got friendly."

Carmen nodded politely. "You get to know each other pretty well?"

"Well enough. That was before he met Dora and bought the house near Mount Washington. Until then, we were together all the time."

"Did he continue to work for the CIA here in the States?"

"He didn't like to talk about it, but yes. Hopkins took up most of his time. Then, one weekend a month, he'd train down to D.C. and sit in on the Agency's brainstorming sessions. I heard about it in generalities. The operatives would gather information on spies and insurgents then forward the data to Langley. There a group of psychologists would analyze it. That's what he called himself, an analyst. Apparently, after eight years in Hungary gathering information about the Reds and his subsequent training in psychiatry, they considered him a bit of an expert on the Russian psyche. As for me I don't know how he found the time. I know how busy I was. And I was just a radiology resident." Carmen gave him an empathetic nod. "Oh, yeah," the radiologist continued, as if he'd been prompted, "twice during the years before Hans married Dora, he spent entire

166

summers in Canada at a place called the Allan Memorial Institute, working under a guy named—I think it was Cameron—doing CIA funded research on brainwashing. From what Hans told me, they tried experimenting with mind altering drugs, shock therapy, and even sleep deprivation, all designed to control the way people think. Can you believe it? Back then the government really thought that kinda stuff was possible."

"Wasn't it?" Carmen prompted.

"Not like in the *Manchurian Candidate*. You can bet about that. Sure, using well-tailored suggestions some people can be influenced. Madison Avenue types do it all the time. But you can't turn people into robots or mindless operatives using drugs or even hypnosis like the science fiction writers would have you believe."

"That's reassuring."

"I thought you'd think so," the pleasant man said with a grin.

"So Gerry, when did you say Richman was in Hungary?" Carmen reiterated.

"I didn't. But it was forty-seven to fifty-five."

"Any idea what his role was there?"

"Mostly spy stuff," Strauss replied matter-a-factly. "For the first couple of years, by day he worked in a print shop in downtown Budapest. At night, he kept the U.S. government abreast of the Communists' activities. Then, in late 1948, after Stalin sent in troops to consolidate his control over the country, he took a more active role, mostly utilizing CIA funds to bankroll the Hungarian resistance movement."

Carmen nodded. "Mind if I take notes?"

"Suit yourself." Carmen pulled a pad. "Of course, despite some rumblings, nothing of consequence happened until fifty-six," the radiologist continued. "That's when a large group of student dissidents staged a march on the Soviet's puppet government. What started out as a peaceful demonstration turned into an armed conflict. As if by magic, guns and rifles appeared. Then, the local militia joined the protesters. Overnight, the Soviets had a full-fledged revolution on their hands."

Carmen leaned forward. As if spurred on by the detective's attention, Strauss continued. "A former Hungarian leader, a pretty popular guy named, Imre Nagy, took control of the government. The first thing he did, after assuming power, was negotiate the evacuation of all Soviet troops from Hungary. And believe it or not, Moscow seemed ready to comply. For the first time in over a decade, it looked like the Hungarians were going to have their country back. But when Nagy threatened to withdraw Hungary from the Warsaw Pact, he had taken one step too far. Stalin reacted with an abrupt about face and used his military to squash the uprising."

Strauss leaned back, folded his hands on the table and briefly closed his eyes. "I remember sitting with Hans back in 1959, in a bar just like this, while he described how the Soviets reacted to the revolt, showing off their might. There he was, standing on the sidewalk of one of the main streets of Budapest, watching row after row of Russian tanks rumble by. He remarked how intimidated he felt by this show of strength and how he sympathized with the helplessness the Hungarians must have felt. During some of the street fighting, Hans' cover was blown. That's when he decided to forsake the continent and flee to America."

Gerhard's gaze lingered on Carmen's face for a moment, then glanced at the empty glass. Picking up on the cue, the detective asked, "What are you having?"

"Scotch," the radiologist replied. "Cory always stocks a fresh bottle of Glenlivet for me."

"Glenlivet it is," Carmen offered. He searched the darkened room for a waitress. Seeing one socializing with a group of men two tables over, he gestured toward her. A few minutes later, Dr. Gerhard was, once again, casually sipping the high-priced Scotch whisky. Carmen tackled his third lager.

"How about your political persuasion?" Carmen commented casually. "Were you a Nazi, too?"

"Hardly, Mr. Carter," Strauss retorted. "I was born in 1935 in Bremen, a city in Northern Germany. That made me ten when the Reich fell. My father was killed in the battle of Stalingrad. But he was Wehrmacht, not Nazi, just another loyal German soldier sacrificing his life for some megalomaniac's fantasy of world domination. My mother was also killed in the war, in early '45, during Allied bombing raids. I had family in Dresden, so I went there to live with my aunt. In 1955, after I earned a science degree at the University, I packed my bags and moved to the States. Medical school started a year later."

"It sounds like you made the best of an awful situation," Carmen said supportively. "Did Reichman ever talk about his family back in Germany?"

"Not much," Strauss recalled. "I know his parents were dead when he got over here. I think he had a brother who died in the war and two sisters who he lost touch with. Why?"

"Just background for the book," Carmen replied. Strauss nodded. "How about a wife back there?" Carmen persisted. "Or kids?"

"A wife and one child, a son. They were both killed during the Allies last push toward Berlin," Strauss related.

"In the bombings?"

"No," Strauss related solemnly. "Actually, they were murdered by a band of GI's sweeping the farmlands for hidden German soldiers."

"Did Reichman have any idea who did it?" Carmen probed. "I mean, specifically?"

"I'm not sure. He had this set of dog tags. He thought that they belonged to one of the soldiers who killed his family."

"Did he ever find out for sure?"

"I couldn't say."

"Hmm," Carmen murmured. "That's quite a burden to bear."

"I'd say so."

For a while after that, the two men drank in silence, each absorbed in his own musing. Finally Carmen, almost thinking out loud, suggested, "From what you've told me, Reichman must've harbored a fair amount of resentment toward the very people who saved his life. I wonder if, since coming to the States, that's shown up in other ways."

Strauss, whose attention had been wandering, fixed his gaze on Carmen's face. "What are you getting at?" he asked pointedly

"I've been reading up on something called the Survivalist Movement," Carmen commented without preamble. "It's a loose amalgam of some very diverse white supremacist groups. Did Hans have any connection to them?"

"You mean the neo-Nazis? Or the Skinheads?" Strauss retorted, blood rushing to his angular face.

"To name a few," Carmen replied coolly.

"That's pretty deprecating, Mr. Carter. My friend was a respected physician, a dedicated father, and a loyal American. Those attributes are inconsistent with neo-Nazism."

"Some would disagree," Carmen retorted, aware that he might alienate this helpful witness, but finding it impossible to check his anger. "From what I've learned, Gerry, most of these so-called survivalists wrap themselves in the flag like it's a cloak of honor, while they make up all kinds of lies to justify their hatred of Blacks, Jews mostly, and anyone who's not Caucasian and a multi-generational American."

"But why lump Hans Reichman in with all those illiterate hate-mongers?" the radiologist said defensively.

"Because I can't help but believe that once a Nazi, always a Nazi."

Strauss appeared ready to rise to the challenge. Then he paused, took a deep breath and replied, "That's terribly naïve of you, Mr. Carter. People change. They see the error of their ways and modify their views—especially political. People embrace new ideological positions all the time."

"And you think Reichman was one of these people?" Carmen asked, cutting him some slack.

"I do."

"Well, Gerry, I'll take your word for it. You knew him better than I did." Strauss nodded with a solemn, almost appreciative expression on his thin face. "After all," Carmen added lightly, "he did marry a Jew. That has to say something about his willingness to change."

"Precisely," Strauss agreed.

Carmen still had a few more questions for this helpful expatriate. But as he glanced down at his notebook, Dr. Strauss reached out his hand and set it upon Carmen's. "No more questions, Mr. Carter. It's a school night. My wife is expecting me home. The dog needs walking."

Carmen, concealing his disappointment, didn't persist. He'd garnered more from this amiable Dr. Strauss than he'd ever expected. As the older man started to ease out of the booth, he suggested, "Can we continue our conversation at another time?"

"I don't think so, Mr. Carter," Dr. Strauss replied. "I believe this conversation has gone on long enough."

Chapter 19

Carmen remained in the narrow booth with its red vinyl covered seats sipping beer and considering his situation. A picture of Hans Reichman was gradually coming into focus. What Dr. Strauss reported squared with what the German expatriate had chronicled in his self-serving diary. Then there was a smattering of random facts reported by other interviewees that seemed consistent. But still, gaping holes in the story remained. For instance, he didn't buy Strauss's assertion that Reichman wasn't sympathetic to the white supremacist movement. What about sending Lila to that camp? Once a Nazi, Carmen concluded, always a Nazi.

With a weary sigh Carmen slid out of the booth and rose to his feet. As he started toward the door, he glanced over toward the bar. The row of regulars seemed the same, fixed in place like group of mannequins in a storefront display. The bartender—Strauss had called him Cory—was chatting with one of the 'usual suspects', a bald-headed man in a dark gray overcoat. Judging from the way their faces were just inches apart, their conversation appeared intent. Carmen was about to dismiss them when the newcomer turned his head and regarded Carmen.

Even at this distance, perhaps ten to twelve yards, the detective appreciated the icy stare, perceiving unconcealed emotion on the older man's face, an expression of unmitigated hatred. It was enough to send a shudder through his frame. For some reason, this man had some issue with him. Did it have something to do with Cory sharing how Carmen had been inquiring into the life and times of Hans Reichman? The newcomer may have taken exception with the intrusion. In the brief time it took him to reach the door, Carmen gave this notion some credence.

For an instant, he considered confronting the man. Then, simultaneously a sense of weariness overcame him. He doubted he had the strength for another interaction this particular evening. Adopting a "discretion is the better part of valor" stance, Carmen shoved the metal bar and a few seconds later, he was outside.

The bitter cold air felt numbingly refreshing. He fumbled in his pocket for his key as he approached the row of vehicles lining the tavern side of the street. He was just about to cross when he noticed one particular automobile parked under the streetlamp. Something about it seemed familiar—or it should—he thought. He stepped back onto the pavement.

It was a late-model Mercedes Benz with a layer of rust rimming the wheel wells and an ellipse-shaped dent on the passenger's side door. Parked under the harsh fluorescent light, it looked silver. Casually strolling around to the rear Carmen noted that it was a 240D. But why should this particular vehicle be so intriguing? It certainly wasn't his style. Then, just on the off chance that he could glean some significance from it, he jotted down the license number. Trained to recall plate numbers, this discipline served him. He sensed that this particular series of letters and numbers had special meaning. He'd check his notes back at the room and try to make some sense of it.

Turning his collar to the howling wind, Carmen crossed the deserted Belgium block street. He then slid into his rental and shivered while the engine revved. A few minutes later, he shifted the transmission into gear and gladly left the eerie neighborhood of Rowland Park behind.

Carmen indulged himself the next morning by sleeping in until ten. Then, after packing his few personal items into a rolling duffle bag, he checked out of the Holiday Inn on Security Boulevard west of Baltimore. Back on the Interstate, he passed through the Maryland countryside, a washed out December sun hovering unobtrusively in the pearl white sky. His traveling companions seemed to be mostly truckers and traveling salesmen. With a host of time on his hands, he reflected upon his extended weekend on the trail of the late Harvey Richman, alias Hans Reichman.

Being brutally honest with himself, Carmen had to concede that he was no closer to apprehending the Rosenberg bomber than he'd been before arriving in Baltimore. What appeared possible, however, was a connection between the Nazi and that wanton act of violent destruction. And although a dead man couldn't have perpetrated the act, Carmen's instincts told him that he had something to do with it.

But who was the bomber? How about Margo, Reichman's sister, a German expatriate who resided with her brother in northern Baltimore before moving to Zelienople to become old man Shindle's wife? But if Margo was the culprit, why did she deliver Reichman's diary-manuscript to Carmen in the first place and focus attention on her brother and indirectly on herself? Perhaps, in her mind, the police would eventually associate the bombing with Reichman. By making the manuscript public, this would somehow justify the crime, maybe even exonerate her brother through his story, which somehow revealed a creditable motive for the despicable act. But what could this motive be? Carmen still hadn't a clue.

The miles passed. As he crossed into Pennsylvania, Carmen considered other possible suspects. Old man Shindle had to be one. He had opportunity, and through his association with the Reichman family, motive. But his last utterance to Carmen before he expired firmly denied any involvement in the actual act. For some intuitive reason, to Carmen, this quasi-deathbed revelation seemed believable.

Then, there were Reichman's 'associates' in Baltimore, people like Strauss, the Cutlers, and this mysterious Kruger fellow, individuals who'd known the Nazi both before and during his marriage, had remained friendly with him after his wife, Dora, had died, and then when he had been forced to raise his daughter as a single parent, helped him out. Where did these folks fit into the drama? Were they accomplices or just innocent bystanders, ignorant of the menace with which they were associating or co-conspirators? Carmen had no way of knowing.

The Pennsylvania turnpike stretched out in front him like a never-ending concrete expanse. His head feeling weary, he tried to pick up some music on the radio, but all he could pull in were talk radio stations out of Bedford and Johnstown. His thoughts migrated back to the case at hand.

Of all the players, Kruger intrigued Carmen the most. Apparently, Reichman's mother-in-law, Mrs. Levenson, wasn't too fond of him. Hadn't she mentioned that after Kruger entered the picture, the tenor of the household changed and along with it, the nature of the granddaughter, Lila. Instead of dealing with a pre-teen immersed in a world of innocence and exploration, a streak of evil and violence had been introduced into the young girl's daily life, coldly symbolized by firearms and the military-like atmosphere that had invaded the Reichman household. But where did all that come from? And why? And more importantly, where was Kruger now? Carmen sensed that with the answer to that question, he'd be much closer to unraveling what had actually transpired on that balmy Yom Kippur evening in early October.

But truth be told, the most interesting character in this malevolent play seemed to Reichman's daughter, Lila. She was the common thread that wove through this multi-city search. She was the elusive suspect, chaste and innocent during a troubled childhood, then evolving into—what? The son Reichman never had? Her father's little soldier? Had her father sent her to Western Pennsylvania commissioned with the task of befriending Barry Rosenberg, the son of Malcolm Rosenberg? Had she been instructed to infiltrate Rosenberg's family and then facilitate its annihilation? Was there some remote connection between the Nazi and this successful thoracic surgeon and outspoken, almost militant, leader of the local Jewish community? Could this heinous act of violence be a manifestation of Reichman's enduring Nazi hatred toward the Jewish race, covertly harbored and faithfully nurtured through the years?

But bombing the Rosenberg house seemed like too random an act to Carmen, especially if it just silenced an outspoken Zionist. That would constitute a heretofore unpublicized act of terrorism, hardly a warning or an example. Carmen rejected this explanation. Just like his own motivation for solving this crime was personal, he suspected the compulsion to commit it was, too.

With the setting sun just under his visor, he exited the turnpike at Monroeville. The amiability of the toll taker seemed oddly refreshing. Checking the dashboard clock, he noted it was just after four. An early dinner at Minetello's seemed like a nice option. Then he would head back to his apartment.

Wearily, but with a certain sense of contentment, Carmen fumbled with the lock to his eighth floor unit. Pushing open the door with his hip, he reached for his rolling duffle. To his surprise, near the sofa, a light was lit. His sense of caution roused, he eased into the living room. What he then noticed was the person with the shaved head sitting in his easy chair.

"It's about time you got your sorry ass home," came the greeting. It was a voice that, although he'd only heard it once in the last ten years, he easily recognized. "I been waitin' on you for hours." The deep baritone reminded Carmen of the guy in the Cola Man commercials.

"If I knew you were here, Jarvis, I wudda skipped dinner and come right home," Carmen replied lightly, genuinely pleased that his old friend had decided to pay him a visit. "To what do I owe this pleasure?"

"Oh, this ain't no pleasure call, Carm," Jarvis said pivoting on the recliner. As the big man squared around, Carmen found himself starring into the barrel of a standard issue revolver. "Unfortunately, my good buddy, I got some business to attend to."

Confronting this lethal menace from such an unlikely source caught Carmen way off guard. "You gotta be shittin' me, Jarvis," he replied, the pitch of his voice a tad too high. "Someone put you up to this? One of the boys from the squadron? Or maybe from The Agency?"

"None of the above, little buddy," the huge, part black man replied. "I been sent," he clarified, "but not as a prank."

Now Carmen's heart, which had started to race, felt like it had jumped into his throat. This wasn't a joke. He needed to think fast. Suddenly survival was his top priority. "Now, what on God's green earth could I have possibly done to warrant this kind of treatment?" he asked, shamelessly buying time. "You act like there's a contract out on me."

"In a way there is," Jarvis agreed, then rose to his full height, an intimidating six-foot-seven. Although he'd softened over the years, especially around the middle, he still appeared gargantuan to Carmen, broad-shouldered, thick-muscled and a whopping two hundred and seventy pounds, if an ounce. "You see Carm, you refused to follow orders. You were told to cease and desist. Instead, you persisted."

"You mean with the Rosenberg bombing?" Carmen asked, knowing full well what Jarvis was referring to. "But what's that got to do with you? Or with The Agency, for that matter? I presume that's who you're representing here—someone, or a group of people, at Langley."

"Sorry Carm, but of that I'm not at liberty to say. I'm just here to do a job. And unfortunately for you, I'm gonna hafta do it."

"This must be a pretty important contract, Jarvis. Vital in fact to negate what I've meant to you, how you owe me. Remember pal, I'm the one who saved *your* life. Now you're threatenin' to take mine. There's a certain injustice there, don't you think?"

"You might be right on, Carm," Jarvis agreed, his arm steady, the weapon trained directly on the police detective's chest. "Unfortunately, it don't matter what I think. It only matters that I follow orders."

"But I thought you were finished with all that," Carmen persisted. "When we talked last week you told me you were retired, living on a pension."

"I was," Jarvis confirmed. "But seems the pension has strings."

"And killing me is one of the strings?"

"That's one way to look at it."

"I suppose you can understand why it's not a way I'm particularly fond of."

"I understand that, Carm."

For the moment Carmen felt stymied. He was one bullet away from being history and had no idea why. Perhaps he'd gotten dangerously close to revealing something with his investigation, something that had to do with the Agency. But what could it be?"

"Since I'm going to eat it anyway," he stalled, "you can at least tell me who sent you. Given our history together, it's gotta be someone important. As unorthodox as it might be, you owe me that Jarvis—for saving you from the Cong."

The former agent seemed to consider this request. Carmen had always known him to be a good person, a man who played by the rules, even if the rules had been honed by the spy business. He wondered how his pension could be more important than sparing Carmen's life. Jarvis couldn't be the only one in play here. It must be Cleo, his beautiful wife, who was also pulling the strings. She must be the one with needs, the wants, and desires. She must be the one insisting he retire from The Agency with his pension intact. These were demands Jarvis had to obey. And if Carmen was the price of marital harmony, the big man seemed willing to pay it.

"Sorry Carm, but I can't name names," Jarvis replied. "But I will admit that this directive comes from way up high in the department."

"How high?" Carmen persisted, curious whose prestigious tail he'd stepped on.

"Associate director," Jarvis revealed.

"For covert activities?" Carmen added.

Jarvis nodded.

Carmen whistled. He tried hard to recall who this person could be, but wasn't that familiar with who occupied what office in the upper echelons of the CIA these days.

"So, now you know," Jarvis commented releasing the revolver's safety, "for what good it'll do you."

Carmen's mind raced. His desire to discover who authorized this contract burned as brightly as his will to live. But he had no time to pursue this course. Jarvis stood less than fifteen feet away, his long legs in faded black jeans spread in a classic attack stance.

"Any last words, Sniper?" Jarvis asked raising the revolver to eye level.

How touching. Jarvis had used his wartime nickname, just as he was about to blow him away. "Not really," Carmen replied unbuttoning his overcoat and letting the lapels drift away from each other. "Except," he added, arching his back and spreading his raised arms. "Don't you think you should relieve me of this first?" Jarvis could now see Carmen's pistol tucked snugly in a leather holster under his left armpit.

"My goodness, Carm, I must be slippin'. I been so intent on my mission that I didn't even think to check if you were totin'. But you're right. I don't want you doin' anything stupid with that thing. How about removin' it from its holder and slidin' it over to me, real easy-like."

Which was exactly what Carmen wanted his potential assassin to say. Keeping his right hand in view he reached across his chest, flipped open the holster cover, and slipped the gun out of its sheath. Then he squatted down on the throw rug, placed the weapon on the tight pile surface, and gave it a push. It slid awkwardly, in the general direction of Jarvis' feet, spinning to a stop about a yard in front of the big man. But instead of reaching over to pick it up, Jarvis glanced down with a satisfied smile on his face. But at this point, Carmen really didn't care about the big man's reaction. Instead, while leaving the hand he'd used to propel the gun on the rug, he grabbed a handful of fabric, and gave it a yank. The entire carpet moved toward him, including the portion on which Jarvis was standing. Suddenly, the big man teetered. This split second of unsteadiness gave Carmen a chance to dive to his right and roll toward the end of the sofa.

A shot rang out. Then another. The first hit the door behind where Carmen had been standing. The second whizzed past his nose. "Don't pull this shit on me, Sniper," Jarvis growled, angry, but also sounding a little flustered. "This is one small, fuckin' pad you got here. You ain't gonna get away from me."

Now flat on his belly under the wooden end table, Carmen listened for the big man's approach. Reaching into his pants pocket, he extracted a compact spring-operated device. Seconds later, a giant foot passed his nose. Before Jarvis could fire his third shot, Carmen flexed at the elbow and sent the point of his switchblade through his old friend's calf.

The big man crumpled to the floor. Carmen seized the opportunity and scrambled out from under the end table. He then dove past the writhing giant who was on his side in a quasi-fetal position clutching for his pant leg. Scooping up his gun, Carmen rolled leftward. In one slick series of motions, he half rotated, flexed at the abdomen, forced his upper body into a sitting position, raised his right arm, and fired. The first shot caught Jarvis on the shoulder. The second nailed him between the eyes.

Chapter 20

Over the course of the next few weeks, Matt, Jane, and Mrs. Hurowitz fell into an easy routine. On weekdays, the two women cleaned the apartment, watched game shows and soap operas on television, strolled the neighborhood shopping the local stores, and occasionally visited nearby Frick Park. One cool, sunny afternoon they walked all the way to Phipps Conservatory for the annual Holiday Flower Show. On another, they hopped a Port Authority bus to the North Side and joined scores of boisterous preteens waiting to see the miniature train display at the Buhl Science Center. Later that night, Jane, betraying a hint of excitement in her voice, related to Matt how, after viewing the trains, they'd reclined in cushy chairs in the cavernous Planetarium and saw a simulation of the Christmas sky in the year four A.D.

Despite his demanding job as a psychiatry resident at the University, Matt retained a remarkably manageable schedule. His weekdays stretched from eight to five occasionally supplemented by his evening research projects. And although nighttime and week-end hospital coverage was obligatory, he took calls at home and almost never had to go in. And since Jane had moved in, he'd cut back on his moonlighting, making him available most week-ends, an important reality since Mrs. Hurowitz refused to work on the Sabbath.

Matt sensed that, as Jane became more familiar with her own routine, she seemed less apprehensive and withdrawn. Familiarity fostered less temerity. And after a week of living in the Beechwood Boulevard apartment, she even started offering suggestions about things she could do with Mrs. Hurowitz or with him.

In the evenings, after her caretaker left, Matt and Jane frequently went out. On one occasion, a brisk Tuesday night early in December, they visited the surrounding neighborhoods and surveyed the Christmas displays. The elaborate lighting, multicolored Santas, motorized reindeer, life-size nutcrackers, and full-sized sleighs propelled Matt back to his own childhood in Silver Spring, Maryland where his parents had exposed him to similar sights. On another star-lit evening, they took the Parkway East out to the Monroeville Mall and there, while browsing the shops, Matt offered to supplement Jane's meager wardrobe with new clothes and accessories.

Matt quickly discovered that movies were one of Jane's favorite pastimes. Conveniently, the Squirrel Hill Theatre, a bank of four, small screens, was situated only a few blocks from his new apartment. Either with Mrs. Hurowitz on a slow afternoon, or with Matt on a Friday or Saturday evening, Jane quickly exhausted the current offerings. To Matt's amazement, her penchant skirted the typical chick flick—schmaltzy romances or historical dramas—and gravitated instead toward suspense thrillers and action films. Strolling out of Gibson and Glover's, *Lethal Weapon 2*, highlighted by a series of spectacularly incendiary scenes, Matt couldn't help wondering where her affinity for cinematic mayhem came from.

Although much of what they did was purely for entertainment, on a more professional level he hoped that something to which she was exposed during one of these little excursions would inadvertently trigger a recollection that might jump-start her dormant memory.

On holiday season week-ends, they had an opportunity to spend longer stretches of time together. On the very first Sunday after she moved in, Matt took her to the Highland Park Zoo. There they spent a blustery afternoon mean-dering along the wooded, hilly paths that cut through the animal preserve. On the second Saturday in December, Matt planned a full day. First they checked out the holiday season sale at the Pittsburgh Center for the Arts on Fifth and Shady and purchased a collection of colorful, artsy ornaments along with some novel knickknacks. Then, they headed across the Fortieth Street Bridge to the small town of Millvale where a local garden center offered the best blue pine Christmas trees in the county. Later that evening, after unloading the tree and setting it in its red metal stand, they had dinner and spent the rest of the evening decorating.

The next night, back in Monroeville, it was an early dinner at *TGI Fridays* then a stop at the Showcase Cinema to see *A Christmas Story*. Afterward, while walking to the car, as the brisk suburban air blasted them, Jane timidly set her gloved hand in his and snuggled close. This spontaneous expression of famil-iarity, this subtle hint of affection, delighted him. From a practical standpoint, it was an explicit sign of transference, more than he could have hoped for at this stage of their relationship. He was also aware that this tender scenario toyed with the question of impropriety, suggesting potential repercussions if their relationship were to veer into murky, more unprofessional waters. But despite these considerations, Matt couldn't help but covet this tender moment and fantasize about the possibility of genuine intimacy in the not-too-distant future.

Matt, clad in black Burberry pants, a white dress shirt, and a red paisley tie, sat on the living room sofa watching a CNN special on the fall of Communism. Just three days earlier the Soviets had been forced to open the Brandenburg Gate allowing free passage through the Berlin Wall. In the news footage a steady stream of East Germans filed through this physical and symbolic barrier that had, since the end of World War II, divided Germany in two. Among the pedestrians and automobiles moving were a few individuals on motorcycles. Noticing the distinctive two-wheeled conveyances, brought to mind the powerful BMW R90S upon which he'd crossed the country back in the summer of '86. Talk about feeling alive and free. Come to think of it, he really missed that bike. But having the 'Z' did help ease the pain.

A few minutes later, Jane emerged from the long hallway and crossed the dining room. He turned to watch her approach dressed in the blue wool dress he'd helped pick out at *Adele's* last week, her freshly shampooed, fine blond hair resting lightly on its white starched collar. He thought she looked fetching. Appreciating how she'd made the effort to apply some make-up, a hint of eyeliner, a brush of blush, and a thin coating of shiny lip gloss, further enhancing her already arresting features. He wondered how this ability, along with a modicum of other skills and memories, had survived whatever catastrophe that triggered her partial amnesia.

Checking his watch, he noted that it was just after eleven on Sunday night, Christmas Eve. They still had plenty of time to make Sacred Heart's Midnight Mass. All week long, as his own sacred holiday approached, Matt kept wondering about Jane's religious training. Her fair hair, blue eyes, and angular face with those prominent cheekbones and clear, pale skin, made her appear Scandinavian or possibly German. This suggested a Protestant, Presbyterian, or possibly Lutheran background. Speculation of this nature was unusual for him. He took his own Catholic background for granted. His grandfather had emigrated from Ireland in late-nineteenth century fleeing the potato famine. His grandmother was a second generation American Italian from Genoa and had been born in Pittsburgh. Matt, as a young single physician in the later part of the twentieth century, dwelled in the secular world. However, in his capacity as this mysterious, young woman's guardian, the nature of her ethnic origin became germane.

The late night air felt windy and cold. Fighting off the bone-numbing chill, he opened the passenger door and waited for Jane to slide onto the leather-covered bucket seat. Once she was settled, he scurried around to the driver's side, slipped in beside her, and warmed the engine. Suddenly feeling anxious, he wondered how well his sports car would negotiate the slippery streets of Squirrel Hill. He glanced over at her. Despite her powder blue parka zipped, she was trembling. Then, when she noticed his glance, she smiled, as if sensing his anxiety and trying to reassure him. She did.

Their drive proved uneventful. Cruising along Matt marveled at the serenity of the setting as multi-colored holiday lights illuminated deserted streets and darkened stores recovered from the frenzy of last minute shoppers. The snow fell, offering an extra layer of insulation over a landscape already blanketed by restful stillness.

After crossing Fifth Avenue, Matt located a parking spot near the corner of Walnut and Shady. Sacred Heart Catholic Church, an impressive black stone and stained glass edifice, stood catty-cornered to them. After helping Jane onto the curb, he took her mittened hand and led her toward the steady stream of parishioners arriving for the service.

The church was nearly packed when they entered. Matt paused at the entrance, dipped his finger in the porcelain bowl, and crossed himself. Jane looked confused.

"You don't need to do that," he reassured her. "Just follow me."

He escorted her down the carpeted corridor finding a pair of seats about a third of the way from the pulpit. Before entering the row, he genuflected. This time, Jane, imitated him. Unsteadily, they then slid between leather padded kneelers and the wooden bench-seat.

Nestled in an alcove off to the right, a musician dressed in a black suit sat before a huge, antique organ, its sonorous pipes occupying much of the church's rear wall. Members of the choir, a formidable group of black-robed carolers, stood in parallel rows near the pulpit facing each another across the corridor. As the congregation settled, they delivered traditional versions of *Do You Hear*

What I Hear?, *Little Drummer Boy*, and *Little Town of Bethlehem* with inspirational gusto. These tunes, Matt recalled, were the same selections he'd performed along with the rest of his Silver Spring High School glee club at the White House tree lighting ceremony during his senior year.

The choir switched to a moving rendition of *Silent Night*. On cue, the processional began, its pageantry reminiscent of a wedding ceremony. But instead of a bride, groom, their attendants, and family, the entourage consisted of a set of altar boys followed by an assortment of deacons, junior priests, and finally the head priest.

The assemblage passed their pew. As it did Matt detected the sweetly acrid odor of incense wafting from a pair of ornate metal urns swung by two of the altar boys. After the deacons, the high priest strolled slowly down the aisle, pivoting from side to side, solemn yet amiable, greeting the parishioners with a brief smile or a nod. He was regally clad in white flowing robes, an ornate, prayer shawl, and what looked like a miter's cap.

Once the processional was complete and its members took their designated positions on the dais, the choir sat down in unison. Next the priest welcomed and blessed everyone. Matt couldn't help but glancing over and gauging Jane's reaction to all the pomp and circumstance. What he sensed was rapt attention, similar to her reaction to an especially spectacular scene at the movies. But her expression was also devoid of recognition or understanding. She responded like a young child experiencing the world anew, lacking prior contact, judgment, or interpretation. Her perceptions, unbiased by the filter of her past, made her a kind of tourist visiting a foreign land, sampling culture and traditions, but not connecting with any of it. The notion seemed freeing and frightful. She was like a hot air balloon, floating around in the clouds, a witness to all but not tethered to anything.

The formal service commenced. Ingrained in him by familiarity and repetition Matt recalled the incantations and the congregational responses. Buoyed by the fervor of this religious dialogue, he sang along with the hymns, familiar Christmas carols like, *Hark, The Herald Angels Sing, Oh, Come All Ye Faithful*, and *Joy to The World*. Adding his voice to the assembled multitude felt oddly inspiring. The readings were also rote. The first was culled from Isaiah in the Old Testament, a second from a letter written by Titus, the last, from the gospel according to Luke. In one form or another, they all retold the story of the birth of Jesus.

Matt regarded Jane intermittently throughout the service. At one point, her expression suggested a hint of recognition. Had some repressed memory been accessed? Could this hook help him pull up the threads of her repressed past? Then he frowned. Hadn't she heard this same ancient tale just two weeks earlier at the Buhl Science Center Planetarium? Oh well, he thought with a sigh, at least she's making associations.

With the first part of the service concluded, the priest walked over to a spiral staircase and ascended to a speaking platform. "The Lord be with you," he blessed.

"And also with you," the congregation replied.

"My warmest holiday greetings to one and all. Firstly, allow me to acknowledge each and every one of you for braving our Pittsburgh winter weather to participate in this, one of the holiest masses of the year. The turnout is truly inspiring. It reinforces my faith in the religious fervor of our Shadyside parishioners.

"With all due respect to the scripture readings, I'd like to stray from expanding upon their meaning and focus my remarks on more topical areas. Don't get me wrong. The prophetic words of Isaiah, the insightful correspondence of Titus, the gospel according Luke, while referring to events that occurred in ancient times, have timeless appeal. If you doubt that, observe how we are assembled here today, on the eve of the last decade of the second millennium, still recounting the significance of what transpired back then. But as monumental as the year of our Savior's birth was, so are the times in which we now dwell."

That's what I like about Sacred Heart, Matt thought approvingly. The priests aren't so absorbed by their holiness that they won't venture beyond the narrow confines of traditional religious rhetoric and incorporate the community and current events in their sermons.

"Witness for example the monumental events which have taken place in this, the year 1989, the forging of friendships, the crumbling of walls, the uprisings and their suppression, the glorification of democracy, and the demonization of tyranny. It was a year when Romanians revolted and Hungarians established their independence. It was a time when, with the opening of the Brandenburg Gate, the Cold War was delivered a blow from which we hope it will never recover.

"It was also a year when, in its effort to perpetuate a merciless dictatorship, the Chinese government utilized soldiers and tanks to mutilate young university students taking a stand for personal freedom and liberty. This occurred in a place called Tiananmen Square."

Matt noticed himself nodding in agreement, appreciating the contrast while marveling in how monumental the year 1989 truly was.

"It was also a year of natural disasters," the pastor continued. "Earthquakes rocked northern California, tornados and floods ravaged the Midwest, hurricanes pummeled parts of the southeast."

Matt's attended assiduously to the priest's comments. Only when the pastor paused to check his notes did he steal a glance at Jane. Satisfied that she was still paying attention, he waited for the priest to continue.

"Those were some of the current events and natural cataclysms that played out on the global stage," the priest began again. "They were most notable—but certainly not the only ones deserving notice. Focus your attention, for example, on a particularly troublesome incident that occurred much closer to home. It was a tragedy that took place in nearby Murdock Farms. It occurred on Yom Kippur, the evening of the Jewish Day of Atonement, when our Jewish friends celebrate their holiest day of the year. The event I'm speaking of, of course, was an explosion that destroyed the Rosenberg home, killing the prominent physician and five members of his family."

Matt recalled discussing the tragedy with that Post Gazette reporter out at the ER triage desk. What was the guy's name? Frank something. No, Franks. Russ Franks.

"Perhaps you'll take issue with my depiction," the priest continued, his tone ironic, almost satiric. "The members of the media have implied that the explosion was an accident, some unfortunate mishap, albeit catastrophic, caused by a faulty furnace or a leaky gas line. Perhaps that is so. But I stand here, as your symbol of spirituality and morality, prepared to offer a more heinous scenario." The high priest paused for effect. "Suppose," he continued in a whisper that gradually attained arresting force and volume, "that this was a premeditated act of terrorism, a murderous hammer presumably striking out from a place that oozes cruel prejudice and blind hate. Such an accusation sounds unrealistic, maybe preposterous. How, you ask, can I even suggest it? Where is my evidence? Where is my proof? Certainly not merely in material clues and frag-

185

ments. But more abstractly—encrypted in the nature of the world in which we live.

"And if dealing with this type of ethnic conflict is too remote for you, or too theoretical, or too historical, let's look more provincially. For instance, many of us have had the experience of strolling down the streets of Squirrel Hill and passing clusters of shaven-headed, swastika-tattooed young men. These, too, are hate-mongers, card-carrying members of some of the most heinous groups in the world, many dedicated to the destruction of all non-Caucasian minorities.

"Yes, my fellow parishioners, we are confronted with a legacy of hate that utilizes the politics of destruction. Their existence is a testimony to an evil that still dwells in the world, an evil that we, the followers of our beloved Lord Jesus Christ, are bound to exorcise." Matt involuntarily shuddered. "Imagine the horror," the priest continued, "if tonight, during midnight mass, or on Good Friday, or on Easter Sunday, the integrity of our religion, the sanctity of our faith was disrupted by the infusion of this sort of violence and hate. Imagine a bomb exploding in a house on Howe Street or Highland Avenue or in the Village of Shadyside, while some of our beloved parishioners were enjoying their Christmas Eve repast. At one moment, they would be gathered around a linen-covered table, candles flickering in the breeze, silver serving plates full of aromatic food. The very next, they would be blown to smithereens. Imagine vital, thriving, robust human beings, transformed by some senseless act into a molten tangle of limbs, torsos, and skulls, their very being destroyed beyond recognition. Imagine these not as faceless strangers, but as our friends and relatives.

"My message to you, my fellow followers of our Lord, Jesus Christ, is simple but poignant. If we consider ourselves even the least bit Christian, we have a mandate to follow the word. Solemnly charged with the task of taking a stand for goodness, we must rededicate ourselves to the eradication of evil. And to achieve that reality we need more than thoughts or words but deeds. We are surrounded by the forces of destruction. We must root them out, expose them for what they are, and punish them accordingly. Our neighbors are like the helpless flocks of old, hiding under our spiritual wings, dependent on us for security and protection. If we stand as a force, united for the good of humanity, no amount of evil could overwhelm us. If we don't, tragedies like the brutal death of Dr. Rosenberg and his innocent family will continue to flourish." And with that, he stepped back.

Whew, Matt thought. Glancing over at Jane, he expected to see some evidence that she was moved by the sermon. Instead, he sensed the opposite. Her expression suggested that she was frightened, perhaps even terrified. Reaching over he gave shook her shoulder.

"Jane," he asked, "what's wrong?"

Spellbound, immersed in her dreamlike state, she simply ignored him. He shook her arm again, this time more forcefully. Finally, she wrenched her eyes away from the lectern and regarded him.

"What?" she said, her fear fading into to confusion. "Did you say something?"

"What's on earth is wrong?" he asked again.

"Oh," she mumbled, "nothing."

"From the look on your face, I know it's not nothing."

"I'm fine Matt," she said. "Really. Can we talk about it later?"

As much as he would have liked to pursue the matter then and there, the priest had resumed his position on the pulpit, indicating to Matt and the rest of the congregation that that the final portion of the service was about to begin.

Chapter 21

Matt sat in bed under a blue velour blanket with January, 1990's issue of *Men's Health* open on his lap. Amber light rested softly on the pages. But it was Jane's strange behavior near the end of the priest's sermon that preoccupied him. During the drive home, he'd expected some elaboration, but she'd remained mute. Now, a little over an hour later, he was still waiting.

He glanced at the nightstand clock. Two-thirty a.m. Wearily, he reached over and flipped off the lamp. The room plunged into inky darkness, absolute, except for a sliver of silver peaking past the drawn shades.

He wasn't sure if he had been dozing or was fully asleep when the door hinge squeaked. He turned toward the sound. A moment later, she was standing there, appearing wraithlike in her loose fitting flannel nightgown, her fine blond hair tied back. She stepped closer, her bare feet gently whooshing on the carpet. "Matt?" she whispered. "Are you awake?"

"Huh?" he replied, the weight of his voice betraying his state. Now the clock's fluorescent read-out said four. "What's up?"

"I couldn't sleep."

He nodded. Courteously, hopefully, he shimmied over, freeing up a narrow strip of mattress. "What's keeping you up?" he asked. While she delayed her response his eyes gradually adjusted to the darkness. There was consternation clouding her pale countenance. Patiently, he waited for her to speak.

"Do you remember what that priest said at Mass tonight," she began, "about the explosion in Squirrel Hill?"

"Of course," he replied.

"Was Barry Rosenberg one of the people killed?"

The reference to this specific person caught Matt off guard. His heart quickened. She was forming an association about an event which had occurred before she lost her memory. This was major. Anxious to respond, he strained to recall the details. His bantering conversation with Russ Franks came to mind again. Then, later that night, there was the report on Action Four news. The video of the explosion scene rolled through his mind, fire and policemen scurrying about, apprehensive onlookers huddled behind hastily erected barriers. The camera cutting to a row of body bags, black, glistening cigar-shaped bodybags, probably made of reinforced plastic. A female reporter droned in the background.

Photos appeared on the screen, the first of the respected heart surgeon; full-faced, double-chinned, receding hairline. Next to him, in split screen, his wife, petite with perfectly, coifed gray hair, bright, gray eyes, a narrow, face, a pleasant smile. United in marriage, he thought, united in death, and finally united posthumously for the viewing public. Next, a photo of their daughter; pretty, facial features that resembled her mother, probably around thirty, with brown hair stylishly cut shoulder-length. Her soft brown eyes looked oddly troubled. Perhaps, she'd had some premonition about what was to happen.

The children's pictures came next, probably the young woman's, the older couple's grandkids, dressed in their best clothes as if posed for a holiday portrait shoot, the girl standing behind the boy who was seated on a wooden stool, all displaying compulsory, almost unnatural smiles. The last picture could have been of the children's father, a man about the young woman's age, perhaps a little younger, with a round, boyish face and a crop of curly brown hair. In his mind's eye Matt studied him more closely. He decided that he resembled the sister and parents. He must have been the son, Barry.

Gradually the images dissolved. Her question was paramount. He felt poised on the threshold of a breakthrough. Reaching over, he took Jane's hand and gently eased her onto the bed beside him. Sliding up and leaning against a pair of pillows, he inquired softly, "Why do you want to know?"

"Please, Matt. Just tell me."

"I think so," he offered. "It was a while ago. I can't be sure. But I think so."

She sighed. Her chest fell as her shoulders sagged. Her hand felt chilly and frail. "Why?" he repeated.

"I think I knew him."

"Whoa," he said softly and almost whistled. "You knew him? But how?"

"I think we met at a dance—at some community center. I remember a bunch of people milling around. The music was loud. The food wasn't good. This guy Barry had a friend with him. The two of them came up and started talking. They were both very nice. The friend was cuter and more outgoing. But Barry seemed special. He was more, you know—what's the word—authentic. He told me he was a medical resident at one of the local hospitals. But he wasn't cut out for that kind of work. He really wanted to do something more humanitarian."

"You remember all that?"

"Yes. I remember all that," she repeated, not sounding offended.

"What else to do you remember?"

"About what?

"About anything?"

"Well," she said, drawing out the word. "I think, after that, we dated for a while. I know I saw him again, several times. I can't remember the details, but just the sense of him. He was very sweet. I wanted to sleep with him. But he resisted. I think he was shy. We finally made love though. When we did, he was very gentle." Her voice remained calm. But he could tell she was affected. Despite the pre-dawn darkness he could still appreciate the moisture around her eyes. "And now he's dead."

With as much tenderness as he could muster, he reached over, wrapped an arm around her narrow shoulder, and pulled her near. She didn't resist, instead easing her upper body against his chest. As he held her close, he felt the vibrations of her weeping. Tears soaked through his t-shirt and onto his chest.

They remained like this for several moments, connected in a way they'd never been before. Matt's head, meanwhile, ached from the muddle of conflicting thoughts, feelings, and emotions. He was breaching both the doctor-patient relationship and his charge as her guardian. On another, purely academic level, he coveted this unexpected bond, the very pinnacle of transference between a therapist and his client. Finally, on a more personal note, he anticipated the flood of emotions and perceptions she was engendering, her touch, her smell, the heart-wrenching sound of her weeping. Above all, he knew that at this critical moment he had to help her, a woman, who up to a few hours ago hadn't appeared capable of displaying any such deep-seated feelings, to deal with an unexpected emotional breakdown.

She reached up and stroked his face, her fingers warm and gentle against his stubble. He enveloped her hand in his, his arousal stirring. Rotating her head slightly she burrowed her face into the cleft between his chin and shoulders. She brushed her lips against his neck.

This tender gesture, so innocent, yet explicit, only served to tantalize his pent-up desire. He arched his back. She raised her chin. They kissed, softly, gently at first, then with a passion that was usually reserved for seasoned lovers. His arms held her tight.

He folded back the blanket. She slipped underneath. After helping her with her nightgown, he shed his shirt and boxers.

The touch of her skin against his seemed electric, its texture satiny soft, its temperature like bathwater. Shivers coursed the length of his body, intensified at each point where they caressed. Desire fed his arousal. They kissed and fondled. Despite her recent flight from reality she seemed experienced and skilled, in complete control. His analytical assessment was soon overwhelmed by the rush of pleasure.

Their loving-making was rapid, intense, and passionate. Once he ventured into this wonderfully unexpected territory, he exercised little restraint. Rather than resist, she seemed to welcome him eagerly. Briefly, he wondered what she was expecting from him, what she required. Was it just this—or more? But that consideration, like all the others, quickly dissipated like moist breath on a frigid morning.

When he awoke the next morning, she was still beside him, her head on the pillow, the pungent odor of sex in the air. The digital readout said, 10:15. Focusing, he recalled that it was, indeed, Christmas morning. But on this auspicious occasion, in contrast to when he was younger, he had no need to see what Santa had left him. In spite of the festively wrapped packages nestled under the tree, he'd already received the best gift of all.

He hesitated to rouse Jane, curious how she'd be. Were they in the wake of some unexpected breakthrough or had their love-making simply been a pleasurable detour along an uncharted path? His patient helped mitigate his confusion by opening her eyes, rotating slightly, and rewarding him with a warm, sleepy grin. Instantly he wanted her all over again.

"Hi, sleepy head," he said.

Stretching her arms over her head, she yawned. "Hi," she said.

"Sleep well?" he asked

"Uh-huh."

"Me, too," he agreed. "Hungry?" She nodded. "Why don't you stay in bed a while? Let me make breakfast."

"What about the presents?"

"We can do that first, if you want."

"Good."

An hour later they were at the dinette with plates full of scrambled eggs, lightly greased bacon, and buttered whole wheat toast. Matt glanced into the living room at the remains of their gift exchange; empty boxes, torn wrapping paper, and colorful ribbons. Despite the meal waiting to be consumed, Jane seemed preoccupied with the tri-colored gold necklace, the Isotoner gloves, and the fluffy moccasin-like slippers he'd given her. He, too, was proud of the crushed velour robe she'd purchased with the allowance he'd given her.

They'd had dozens of meals together. But to Matt this one was different. For the first time they were a couple. He gazed across the small table, marveling anew at her natural beauty, genuinely displayed in the harsh morning light, unadorned by make-up or jewelry, except, of course, for the brand, new necklace. His chest ached. In his heart of hearts, wasn't this what he'd hoped for from the first minute he'd visited her in the psychiatry unit at Braddock? Probably. But beyond the realization of his yearning, more seemed at stake here. A glimmer of light had penetrated the murky darkness of her clouded consciousness. A memory from her shrouded past had surfaced. She'd identified someone she'd known before the amnesia had taken hold. A vital key to unlocking the rest of her mind was at hand. It was his job to utilize it.

"Remember what you asked me last night?" he began.

She hesitated, then replied without looking up. "About Barry?"

"That's right."

Now regarding him she asked, "What about him?"

"Do you recall anything else?"

"So, Dr. Carson," she quipped, "you're planning to spoil our first Christmas morning together by playing psychiatrist."

"Not totally," he hedged. "I'm just trying to get to know you better. You had a breakthrough of sorts last night. I think we should expand on it. You do want to remember your past, don't you?"

She hesitated. That glimmer of brightness in her eyes dimmed. "I suppose so," she conceded. "It just hurts. That's all."

"I know it hurts," he offered and reached over to stroke her hand. "But the more you remember, the better you'll understand, and the easier it will be to cope with what shows up later."

Appearing to accept this she set her fork down and nodded. Then glancing up again, she peered into his eyes. "Barry was such a nice guy," she said wistfully, "almost a throw-back, kind and gentle, not like so many of those self-absorbed macho-men you meet these days. I loved the way he would hold the door for me when we walked into a building or my chair in restaurants. I know it sounds a little corny, but he treated me like a princess."

"And you became more than friends?" Matt interjected, trying to be as tactful as possible.

She smiled. "Yes, Matt, we were more than friends. I mentioned that last night. Why?"

Feeling a little flustered, he clarified, "I was just curious if you recalled the details of your times alone with him?"

She hesitated, as if straining. Then her face brightened. "Matt, I used to live around the University! I was going to Pitt, in their Graduate School of International Studies, working on my masters. I was a political science major in college."

Swept up in her excitement, he inquired, "And you lived on campus?"

"I don't think so. At least, I can't remember having a place of my own. Pitt's in Oakland, right?"

"That's right. Remember when we drove past the Cathedral of Learning near the Public Library and Carnegie Music Hall? That's where the main campus is."

"You took me to that music hall to see the Men's Glee Club perform their holiday show?"

"That's right."

He waited politely for her new reality to take hold. His patience over the last few months had paid off. She was beginning to reclaim her past. While wondering how extensive her recovery would be, he had an intriguing notion. "If you knew Barry Rosenberg," he offered, "you must have also met his parents. Were you ever in their house, the one that blew up?"

"I've been thinking about that ever since the priest referred to that horrible explosion. I seem to recall Barry wanting me to meet his mother. They were apparently very close. But where his father was concerned, it was different. He was scared of him. They weren't on very good terms."

"Interesting. What did you say Barry did for a living?" Matt asked, trying to recall.

193

"He was a physician, just like his father. They both worked at one of the downtown hospitals. I think he called it Northshore or Northview?"

"You probably mean Northbanks," Matt offered, "across the Allegheny from downtown. We call that area the North Side."

"That does sound familiar," she admitted. "But Barry didn't like being a doctor. I remember him saying once that if he had it to do all over again he would have joined the Peace Corps or gone into social work."

"His father couldn't have been too thrilled about that idea," Matt offered, recalling heated arguments regarding career choices he'd had with his own father.

"Probably not," Jane related. "And his father could be a real bastard at times, very authoritarian and controlling."

"So he must have been closer to his mother," Matt reasoned.

"I know he was."

"How can you be so sure?"

"Because I met her. And him, too."

"You met them both? When?"

"On Labor Day. There is something called Labor Day, isn't there?" He nodded, amused with her sketchy familiarity with some of the more basic notions. "Anyway, from what I remember, Barry invited me over to his parents' house for a picnic. They lived in Squirrel Hill. Now that I think of it, ever since you brought me to live with you, this area sounded familiar. Now I know why."

"Do you remember anything about that day?" Matt probed.

"Well, first of all, he picked me up."

"Where?"

"In my dorm room," she replied, excitedly. "Now I remember. I had a room in the Quadrangle. My window looked out on two big white buildings." Probably the Hillman Library and David Lawrence Hall, Matt thought. Now we're getting somewhere. "So he picked me up and we drove to the house," she reiterated. "The drive took about ten minutes. We passed another university along the way."

"Carnegie Mellon," he confirmed. "That's where I went to college."

She nodded, politely acknowledging this bit of information. Then, as if afraid she'd derail her train of thought, she plowed on. "When we arrived," she continued, "it was obvious that the Rosenbergs didn't just live in a house, they lived in a mansion. And although Barry seemed a little nervous about having me be there, afraid we'd run into his father before he could get up the courage to introduce me, I also think he was proud."

Matt nodded, impressed with her insight. "So what happened once you got into the house?"

"Well, first I got the tour," she revealed. "The place was truly amazing, with all those big rooms with high ceilings and walls full of expensive artwork. All the furniture seemed expensive, mostly traditional with a lotta antique chests, bureaus, and credenzas. I especially liked the grand piano in the family room and the Victorian bed in Rachael's old bedroom."

"Rachael?" Matt inquired.

"Barry's sister."

"His only sister?"

"I think so."

"Then, she must be the one who died in the explosion—along with her two children."

Jane's hand went to her mouth. "Oh, my God!"

"I know," he sympathized. "It was a real tragedy all around."

Jane took a moment to integrate this data into her rapidly expanding memory bank. Taking a deep breath, she continued. "Well, it was some tour. Barry even showed me the basement where he used to play as a child. Then, back in the first floor hallway, we finally ran into his mother."

"What was she like?"

"Nothing like I expected—short, almost petite, with dark gray-streaked hair, a narrow face, and very warm, friendly eyes. After Barry introduced us, instead of shaking my hand, she reached out and gave me a big hug. It made me feel accepted, welcomed. We stood around in the hallway for a while chatting. She acted very interested in what I was studying. But with all the other guests around, she seemed anxious to move on. She apologized for not staying longer, but promised to spend more time with us later in the day."

"Did she?"

"I never saw her again."

"Why not?"

"Because, before I could, I was asked to leave."

"Asked to leave?" he repeated. "By whom?"

"By Dr. Rosenberg, senior."

"How'd that happen?"

Gerald Myers

"Let's see if I can remember," she offered, setting her chin on her slender hand and peering off into the distance. Then, as if returning from some far off place she began, "We had just finished eating out on the back deck. I think it was Rachael's husband, alan, who did the grilling. I got the urge and went to look for a bathroom. After I finished, instead of returning to the deck, I walked back into the living room and paused by the piano. It was a baby grand with a gorgeous black lacquer finish. I sat down on the bench and starting picking out something simple, *Chopsticks* or *Jingle Bells*. That's when this older man walked up behind me. I turned and noticed he was wearing Kelly green golf pants and a Westmoreland Country Club polo shirt. I assumed he was one of the guests, you know, an uncle, or a neighbor, or maybe a friend of the family. So he walked up and demanded to know who I was. I told him my name. He retorted something like, 'That's who I thought you were'."

"Which was pretty rude," Matt commented.

"That's nothing compared to what came next."

"What came next?"

"Well, to the best of my recollection—and you know my memory isn't the greatest these days—he continued with something like this: 'I told Barry not to bring you anywhere near his house or his family. I'm sure my wife has been very gracious to you. Well don't expect the same kind of treatment from me. I've got no intention of having my son contaminate this family with a *shiksa*. And I don't give a damn how much he cares about you. As long as I run this household, there will be no intimate relationships with anyone outside our faith. Our people have become too assimilated in this country already. The line has to be drawn somewhere. And in my family I draw it right here!'"

"Wow. What a jerk. What did you do?" Matt asked.

"Well, I think I tried to defend myself. I told him he didn't know anything about me. I was an adult. And so was Barry. We were both old enough to make our own decisions, especially about relationships."

"You told his old man that?"

"I think so."

"How did he take it?"

"He told me this story about the survival of his people. Where that was concerned the desires of any individual was secondary. By keeping Barry from straying he would help ensure the future of the Jewish people."

"How did you respond to that?"

"I told him he was full of crap, although I'm sure I didn't use that specific phrase. I think I took a stand for diversity and expansion of the gene pool. He, of course, wouldn't hear of it. He was so narrow-minded, there was no way a rational argument could convince him otherwise."

"Is that when he made you leave?"

"Not until I confronted him with something I knew he wasn't expecting."

"What was that?"

"I mentioned I was Jewish."

"What! You're Jewish?"

"You know, Matt, that's about the same way that old man reacted."

"But how could that be? You certainly don't look it."

"I know. But I'm pretty sure mother was."

"You remember that?"

"Yes," she said slowly. Then with more resolve she repeated, "Yes, I do!"

"That's amazing!" Matt exclaimed. Where should he go next? Then he knew. "You mentioned that when old man Rosenberg confronted you at the piano, you told him your name."

"That's right."

"What did you say it was?"

"Lila Richman."

Chapter 22

S lowly rising to a standing position, Carmen surveyed the mess. Another day, another dead body, he thought grimly. And dealing with this particular corpse was going to have repercussions—all kinds of repercussions. Unlike that old Kraut, Shindle, Jarvis Lundy would be missed, sentimentally by his wife and family, professionally by whoever took the contract out on Carmen.

Pursuant to this realization, Carmen suspected that beyond disposing of the body, he would also have to dispose of his life the way he knew it. This was an agency operative he'd iced. Yep, he lamented, once poor Jarvis was missed, the proverbial shit would hit the fan.

Attempting to inject some order into the chaos that was littered at his feet, Carmen briefly left his apartment and used the building's service elevator to access the basement. There, in the laundry room, stored alongside the row of washing machines, he located a canvas linen cart, a cloth satchel reinforced by metal rods secured to a rectangular wooden frame that rolled on plastic casters and wheeled it back into the elevator and up to his unit.

By now Jarvis' head wound had stopped oozing, which made moving him a little less messy. After wrapping his old buddy's remains in a plastic drop cloth, he summoned all his strength and hoisted the body into the canvas receptacle. Tidying up the rest of the living room proved more problematic. In the wake of the fatal head shot, blood stains, bits of skull, and a smattering of gray matter had soiled one wall and several pieces of furniture. Carmen debated whether to attend to the clean up. The first order of business, he reasoned, was to transport poor Jarvis to his final resting place. Buffing the crime scene could wait.

With the corpse hidden by a pile of dirty sheets and towels, Carmen wheeled the linen cart along the hallway and into the elevator. Down in the garage he waited for a couple of his neighbors to clear the area before lifting

Jarvis' inert body into the trunk of the Fiat. Then he dumped his laundry into the back seat, returned the cart to where he'd found it in the laundry room, and a few minutes later, breathing a sigh of relief, he headed off.

After crossing the Highland Park Bridge, he accelerated up the ramp onto Route 28, north. A half-hour later he was beyond the small western Pennsylvania town of Freeport. Approaching West Winfield and County Line Road he exited the highway. This time, he had no trouble finding the Thompson mine. As a testimony to how really abandoned the place seemed to be, the padlock he'd crowbarred loose just a few weeks earlier was still lying by the side of the gravel road with the ends of the chain it had joined dangling from the gate.

The mine shaft was a hundred yards farther down the road. Once again, after lifting a section of planks that covered the aperture, he created an opening large enough to accommodate a body. The tough part was transferring his old buddy's bulky frame from the Grand Am's trunk up over the lip of the shaft. After a fair amount of pulling, hoisting, shifting, twisting, grunting, and finally pushing, the lifeless sack of organs, muscle, bones, and congealing fluids succumbed to the force of gravity and plummeted toward the bowels of the Earth.

Carmen knew he couldn't just return to his apartment and resume his life as if nothing had happened. Like the unfortunate citizens he'd helped enter the government's Witness Protection Program, Carmen needed a new identity. After stealing five hours of restless sleep, he shook himself awake, then rummaged around the apartment until he found the pair of green canvas duffel bags—circa 1971—he was looking for. Inside of them, he stuffed as much clothing and personal effects he deemed necessary for a prolonged period undercover. Next, into a fairly large cardboard box, he packed an assortment of other items; his case notes, a few books—both reference and leisure—his spare firearms with ammo, a hot plate, a miniature coffee maker, and some utensils. The remainder of the morning was spent cleaning the organic matter off his furniture and walls. Around mid-afternoon, his duffels and cardboard box in hand, he stepped out of his apartment, uncertain whether he'd ever return.

The next order of business was his vehicle. The Fiat would have to go. He retained it long enough to drive to the Mellon Bank office on Penn Circle. There he closed both his checking and savings accounts and cleaned out his safe deposit box. After that he drove to a nearby shopping center, locked the car and

Gerald Myers

called a cab. Into the vehicle's cavernous trunk he loaded his odds and ends box and the pair of army bags, then directed the driver to take him to Tower Motors on Old Freeport Road in Blawnox. There, using a freshly printed money order, he purchased a 1987 sapphire blue Volvo 740 GLE Sedan with a manual transmission and 23,000 miles on the odometer.

From there he drove to Youngstown, Ohio, located a bank that was open evenings, and deposited the remainder of his savings into a non-interest bearing checking account under the name of Salvatore Serrano. Serrano was one of the aliases he'd created twelve years earlier while working undercover for the FBI during the Bureau's investigation of something called The Pizza Connection. At the time, the Feds had benefited from Carmen's Italian roots to infiltrate the Buffalo, New York faction of a nationwide heroin trafficking network run by the Sicilian Mafia. It was from his Mellon safe deposit box, along with the rest of his valuables, that he'd withdrawn the identification papers which had served him during that caper. Finally, at nine PM, wearing khaki slacks, a long-sleeved polo shirt, and a beige raincoat, Detective Carmen Vitale registered at the Howard Johnson's Motor Inn on the Boulevard of the Allies back in Pittsburgh as a Mr. Salvatore Serrano.

Feeling the pull of his investigation into the Rosenberg house explosion, Carmen awoke early the next morning. After a light breakfast in the motel's coffee shop, he decided to jump right back into the fray. Taking advantage of the fact that his motor inn was situated less than a mile from the University of Pittsburgh campus, and bolstered by a new sense of purpose, Carmen pushed open the front door and walked out into a crisp, clear, late-autumn morning. He squinted against the bright sunlight, crossed the parking lot, turned right, and began a leisurely stroll toward the Hillman Library.

Although it was after nine, the narrow, lower Oakland streets were only sparsely populated with students and local businessmen. He checked the calendar on his watch and noted the day, Wednesday, December 12th. Fall term classes were probably over and the co-eds were most likely studying for finals. A flyer on the library's ground level door confirmed his assumption. Inside the modern four-story structure, he consulted a schematic of the library's general stacks, periodicals, study areas, and reference sections. Locating the portion of the reference room that housed current and back-dated newspapers, he made his way over to the southwest quadrant of the first level, set his stuff on the desk in an empty carrel under a row of high windows, and began his search.

The explosion had taken place on a Monday night, October 10th. He reasoned that, although the television coverage could report it 'live at eleven', the local newspapers wouldn't be able to run the story until the next day. First he checked the Post Gazette, which had a small reference to the tragedy on the last page of the first section. In the Pittsburgh Press, however, there was a two column article on page three above the fold including a picture of the demolished mansion. A guy named Russ Franks had the byline.

After that Carmen knew where he'd be heading next. In the midst of completing the remainder of his library-based research, Carmen worked on setting up an appointment with the reporter. A receptionist at the *Press* told him that Franks was out of town until Saturday morning, gathering background information for a feature he had running in the Sunday morning edition. Carmen used the lull to accumulate data on various aspects of the CIA, the White Supremacist Movement, and the Nazi storm troopers also know as the SS.

With a pile of books and magazines at his side, for much of Thursday and half of Friday he was back at the political science section of the library. On Friday afternoon, he went reference book shopping, first at Pitt's Student Book Store on Fifth Avenue and after that, further down the street at Jay's Book Stall. Purchasing a copy of a hefty reference book called, *The Agency, The Rise and Decline of the CIA* by John Ranelagh, he garnered some background info on the Office of Strategic Services, the American spy organization that was operational during World War II and which eventually evolved into the CIA. He knew it was a long shot, but although the crime he was investigating took place in the fall of 1989, based on what he'd gleaned from Reichman's memoirs before being unceremoniously clunked on the head, he still had the notion that the seeds of discontent had been sown almost forty-five years earlier.

The fourth floor of the Pittsburgh Press edifice reminded Carmen of his own precinct building on Penn Circle. Rectangular, with white washed walls, harsh fluorescent lighting, a grimy tile floor, and dirty floor to ceiling windows, the room had a cold, inhospitable air to it. The floor space, occupied by several dozen interdigitating cubicles, resembled a prefabricated, three-dimensional puzzle. The equipment, however, seemed more current, the reporters and editors mostly working at computer terminals and electronic word processors.

Gerald Myers

Franks occupied the corner cubicle along the far wall, not traditionally a place of honor, but at least it bordered a corridor which made him seem less cramped than most of the other journalists. After taking a short drag on a filterless cigarette, he set it down on the lip of an ashtray already brimming with stubs. "I'm still not used to these damn monitors," he commented to Carmen while still peering at his computer screen. "They want me do all this cutting and pasting before I turn in one of those new-fangled, floppy discs. I'm old school, detective. I'd rather churn my story out on that Smith-Corona sitting on the floor over there and x out what doesn't fit."

"Can't say I know what you mean," Carmen replied. "They still make us type our reports the conventional way. In fact, most of the typewriters we got at the station are manuals."

"No shit," Franks said, finally looking up. "Russ Franks," he added holding out a nicotine-stained hand. "You the detective that called for an appointment?"

"That's me."

"What can I do for you?"

Carmen savored this no-nonsense attitude. He had a feeling he was going to like the crusty, old, beat reporter. Before delving into his story, he took a moment to appraise the guy. Gaunt, almost malnourished looking, Franks had thinning jet-black hair combed into a pompadour, resembling an over-the-hill greaser from the fifties. His freckled face was riddled with wrinkles, deepened by his chain smoking, making him look older than the fifty-five Carmen knew him to be. The sleeves of his white, dress shirt were rolled to the elbows. His red paisley tie was loose at the collar.

"I'm working on that Murdock Farms explosion, the one that wiped out six members of the Rosenberg family."

"You mean from early October? I thought they decided that was an accident? Something about a heater blowing?"

"That's the official story," Carmen confirmed. "But I'm pretty sure it's cover-up. There's more to this deal than a faulty furnace. But if someone like me doesn't pursue it, the truth may never come out. A lotta pretty important people don't want the case solved."

"Like who?" Franks asked, his salt and pepper eyebrows arching in interest. Forever the beat reporter, Carmen thought.

"I don't have names, but the Feds and the CIA are both involved."

"But the CIA's international. Why would they care?"

"That's what I'm trying to find out."

"Any hints?"

"A few." Carmen, knowing that to get information you sometimes had to offer some, told Franks about Margo Shindle and the Reichman manuscript.

"Interesting," Franks agreed. "But where do I come in?"

"You were the reporter who wrote the story about the young girl who jumped off the Rankin Bridge the day after the explosion; the one who they revived at Braddock General." Carman paused for effect. "I have reason to believe that she's Hans Reichman's daughter."

Franks didn't look convinced. "What makes you think that?"

"It's kinda circuitous, but I tracked this young woman, Lila Richman, to her Aunt Margo's house in Zelienople. Margo's the one who slipped me the manuscript. After that the trail led me to Baltimore where Hans Reichman lived since the late fifties. Reconciling the two names was easy. Reichman changed his to Richman when he immigrated to the States by way of Hungary in the mid fifties."

"But how does that make the Richman girl the Rankin Bridge jumper?"

"Lila Richman dated Barry Rosenberg for a few months before the explosion. He was blown up along with his parents, sister, niece, and nephew," Carmen summarized. "After that this Lila disappears. I think it's more than coincidental that a mysterious woman with total amnesia shows up at a local hospital the very next day after attempting suicide."

"You're the detective, Mr. Vitale. But don't you think your theory is a little far fetched. Rankin's a long way from Murdock Farms."

"I bet it'd only take a few hours to walk."

As if pausing to consider the route he seemed to agree. "If she wandered from the house through the CMU campus she would have ended up in Schenley Park. From there she could have crossed over the Parkway into Greenfield."

"Which gets her onto Beechwood Boulevard," Carmen commented. "Isn't there a road on the other side of the Squirrel Hill Tunnel that takes you back under the Parkway?" he asked.

"It's called Commonwealth," Franks said with a nod. "It's a continuation of Forward."

"From there I imagine it would be pretty simple to get all the way to Rankin. First you pass through Swissvale then make that first right turn onto

Main. Once you're in Rankin and near the river you can't help but end up at the bridge. It's the continuation of Braddock Avenue right at the bend before you go into Braddock proper."

"When you spell it out like that, it's certainly plausible." Franks paused for a second. "So, if your jumper's the bomber, where's she now?"

"That's what I need to know from you. I'm trying to establish some continuity here. Any idea what happened to her after she got to Braddock's ER?"

"She was admitted, of course," Franks commented, "in pretty bad shape if what the medics claim was true. You know, breathing but little else. I chatted with the ER doc a little after she stabilized. He said she was suffering from things like hypothermia and aspiration pneumonia. Apparently, a fair amount of river water got into her lungs. They never allowed me to see her. But I was told she was on a respirator."

"Do you recall the ER doc's name?"

"Not off hand," Franks admitted. "But wait. These new fangled computers are good for something. Let me save what I'm working on then I'll look it up." The reporter initiated some commands on his grimy, beige keyboard. The green paragraphs on the black screen suddenly contracted into a tiny icon in the upper right hand corner. "Now let me see…." He opened up the lower desk drawer and from a cigar box withdrew a five and one quarter inch floppy disc. Inserting the flimsy storage medium into a slot on the computer, a Macintosh SE, he tapped a few more keys. A different set of green paragraphs appeared.

"Ah," Franks said after skimming his notes, "there it is. His name, detective, is Mathew Carson. He's in the psychiatry residency program at Western Psyche but was moonlighting in the ER that morning."

"That was a week day, wasn't it?" Carmen asked writing down the physician's name.

"Yeah," Franks confirmed, "a Monday. Why?"

"What was a resident doing moonlighting on a week day?"

"I wondered the same thing when he mentioned he wasn't full time. Apparently he had some research project going that would be keeping him up all night. His program director gave him the day off to rest."

"And he spent it working."

"Residents don't make much money these days," Franks clarified.

"Especially if they have wives and families, I'd imagine," Carmen commented.

"This guy was single, though."

"How do you know?"

"He told me."

Carmen considered this. "Did you do any follow-up on the story?"

"I called the hospital a few times," Franks admitted, "and chatted with the community relations director—a nice lady named, Adrianne Costa. She told me that the young woman—your Lila Richman—eventually recovered from her pneumonia and was transferred to the psych unit. They labeled her condition post-traumatic amnesia and concluded that her memory loss occurred after the fall. I pursued it for a couple of weeks. But when it looked like nothing was happening, I lost interest and stopped checking."

"That's reasonable," Carmen agreed. "Is there anywhere else I should be looking?"

"Besides with the hospital?"

"Yeah."

"The evening news—I think it was Sharon Winslow on Channel 4—did a bit on the incident that night. It ran for thirty seconds and only reported a few of the facts I listed in my article."

"Did they have video?"

"They brought a camera crew."

"Good," Carmen said and bid the veteran beat reporter a friendly *adieu.*

Chapter 23

Despite doing his best to project a sense of the urgency to her secretary, it took Carmen a full ten days to get an appointment with Braddock General Hospital's Vice President in charge of Nursing Services, Adrianne Costa. Now, on December twenty-sixth, a cold, dry, cloudless Thursday morning, he parked the Volvo between a Volkswagen Beetle and a rusty, old Chevy Cavalier in the hospital's Holland Avenue parking lot, flipped his overcoat collar to the brisk wind blowing from the Mon, and hurried inside. A portly guard at a metal desk by the main entrance directed him down the hall, past the cafeteria, and into the hospital's east wing.

A phone booth-sized, underpowered elevator carried him to the top floor of the three-story structure where, after consulting an old fashioned black felt directory, he located the administrative office suite. A few moments later, he handed a freshly minted business card to the matronly looking receptionist and was shown into a cluttered cubicle. Not long after that, the administrator walked in.

Adrianne Costa, clad smartly in a brown print dress and stylish beige scarf, appeared pert, petite, and energetic. After flashing Carmen a hospitable smile, with outstretched hand she introduced herself, then glided around to the opposite side of her desk. Leaving her Styrofoam cup of coffee within reach, she settled herself in the black leather chair, folded a pair of tiny hands on the calendar blotter, leaned forward, and asked Mr. Serrano what she could do for him.

"As I mentioned to your secretary," Carmen began after clearing his throat, "I'm a private investigator. I've been hired by the Harvey Richman family to find their daughter, a young woman named Lila. There's reason to believe that, sometime after her rather sudden disappearance from the Pitt campus in early October, she might have been hospitalized here at Braddock."

"That's an interesting contention, Mr. Serrano," Ms. Costa commented, her narrow face assuming a serious expression. Carmen couldn't help but notice how ferret-like she looked, her tiny brown eyes almost beady. But her personality seemed vivacious and engaging. "However, when Claire, my secretary, briefed me on the purpose of your call, I took the liberty of checking with our record room. As a result of that inquiry, Mr. Serrano, I'm sorry to say that no one by that name is listed in our files."

"Which doesn't surprise me," Carmen replied quickly. "When she was admitted, I suspect she may not have given her real name. In fact, we 're concerned that if Lila had suffered some trauma, she may not have known what her name was."

"Ah," Ms. Costa seemed to concede, "that's an even more intriguing prospect. What makes you suspect something like that occurred?"

"Well, first of all, from what I'm told by the family, Lila has always been a very responsible person. She would never go off somewhere without finding a way of keeping in touch." Ms. Costa, nodded, her expression a study in rapt attention. "The last her father heard from her was on Saturday, October eighth when she called from her dorm room at Pitt, just before she was leaving for a date with a Dr. Barry Rosenberg. Does that name ring a bell?"

Ms. Costa paused, appearing to give the question an honest appraisal. "No," she finally replied. "Should it?"

"Not really," Carmen admitted. "But just so you know, I'll clarify that point in a moment." Ms. Costa smiled and nodded. "What is significant, however, is that twenty-four hours after Lila's disappearance, Barry Rosenberg was dead."

"Oh, my God!" Ms. Costa cried with a gasp. "What on earth happened?"

"He was killed while having dinner at his father's house in Squirrel Hill. The place blew up."

"Blew up?"

"That's right. The official police report claimed the explosion was the result of a gas leak near the furnace."

"That's horrible. How many people were killed?"

"Six."

Adrianne Costa drew in another breath, a shocked look on her narrow face. Then her expression softened as she commented, "Come to think of it, I do remember seeing something about that explosion on the evening news. But the story was dropped so fast, I didn't pay much attention after that. How on earth does that tragedy tie in with this Lila's disappearance?"

"Well," Carmen offered, "the family is concerned that the shock of having her boyfriend blown to pieces might have sent her off the deep end."

"So the trauma she suffered was psychological, not physical," Ms. Costa commented. "Was there a history of emotional instability?"

"Not according to her father—who by the way is a retired psychiatrist. But he was concerned that since she lost her mother to the complications of diabetes when she was a child, another loss of this magnitude could have triggered a full blown breakdown."

"It's hard to argue with a professional's opinion like that," Ms. Costa conceded. "Tell me again, why do you think she spent time as an inpatient at Braddock?"

"Because," Carmen began, fixing her with his most intense gaze, "according to the Press, after jumping off the Rankin Bridge, a woman without a clear-cut identity was brought to your emergency room by a pair of medics on the afternoon of October ninth."

To Carmen, the pause that followed seemed pregnant. He sensed that Adrianne Costa was weighing her options. If she was a stickler for the rules, she could certainly hide behind the hospital's privacy policy and refuse to provide him with any information. Then he would need to get a court order—which he wasn't sure he could justify—and force the issue. Instead, what he fervently hoped for was that he had presented his case with enough compassion that the administrator would take pity on him and circumvent the system. When she picked up the phone and asked her secretary to connect her to the record room, he quietly breathed a sigh of relief.

While they waited for the records to arrive, Carmen and Ms. Costa chatted about the possibility of emotional trauma causing mental breakdowns, agreeing that the notion wasn't that far-fetched. A few minutes later, a volunteer in a royal blue smock appeared holding the file.

To the detective's eye the chart appeared thick and well traveled, its manila cover smudged and frayed. The fold suffered from a two-inch tear. Carmen imagined that a fair amount had happened to this patient over a short period of time or that her hospitalization had been protracted—or both.

"Well, you're right about her lack of identity," Adrianne commented without preamble. "We labeled her Jane Doe when she arrived and the name was never modified. In the six weeks that she spent with us, no one appeared to i.d. her."

"That's not surprising," Carmen commented. "Her father had no idea where to look. And he didn't make the connection with Barry Rosenberg since Lila hadn't spoken about him that much. I only stumbled on the possibility after I interviewed some her friends at the Graduate School of International Studies, then checked the local papers for anything that might pertain to the disappearance during the days following it."

"Sounds like you did some pretty intense detective work there, Mr. Serrano," Ms. Costa complimented him.

"That's what they pay me for," Carmen acknowledged.

Returning to the chart, the administrator leafed through a series of sections, stopping intermittently to review some entries in detail. Finally, she looked up and commented, "Well it appears that Jane was pretty sick upon arrival, initially admitted with a bilateral aspiration pneumonia that deteriorated into full blown respiratory failure. The organism then infected her blood and caused a condition we call sepsis. In our geriatric population this is frequently fatal. But Jane—and possibly your Lila—proved to be young and in relatively good health. Once the antibiotics took hold, she fought off the infection. The medical course took almost two weeks to complete."

"And after that she was discharged?" Carmen asked hopefully.

"Apparently not. The truth was, she had nowhere to go. Not to mention that she was suffering from an almost total amnesia. Once she was stable her medical attending had the Chief of Psychiatry evaluate her. He concluded that she'd do better with a stint in the inpatient psychiatric department."

"How long did she stay there?"

"About a month."

"And then she was discharged?"

"Yes."

"To where?" Carmen asked. "And should I add, with whom?"

"Now that's the unique part," Ms. Costa revealed, "and why this particular case is starting to sound very familiar to me. Although the legal department handled most of the negotiations, I was involved with some of the specifics."

"What was so complicated about one particular patient's discharge? Doesn't your social service department regularly deal with this sorta thing?"

"Not quite," the director said, almost flippantly. "There were several aspects of this case that were both unique and somewhat challenging. And," she added parenthetically, "since you do represent the family, I suppose you'll need to know where to go from here. Apparently, one of the physicians who moon-lights in the emergency room took an interest in her."

"An interest?" Carmen repeated, more than a little intrigued.

Adrianne nodded. "He's in his second year in the psychiatry residency pro-gram at Western Psyche. The notion of her amnesia apparently fascinated him. Once Jane was transferred to the psyche unit, he began visiting her. Eventually, she started confiding in him, more than the staff or the other patients. When it came time for her to be discharged, he petitioned the court for guardianship."

"But he couldn't be much older than she is," Carmen pointed out.

"That's correct."

"How could any judge in his right mind permit such a thing? It sounds to be like thinly veiled shacking up."

"That notion seemed to play prominently in the legal considerations. But when Dr. Carson agreed to hire an older woman to act as a chaperon and over-seer, that pre-requisite seemed to satisfy the judge's concerns. She granted him the guardianship he was seeking."

Wasn't Carson the ER doc Russ Franks told me he talked to the day the jumper presented? Carmen wondered silently. Aloud he inquired, "And how has this little soap opera played out?"

"That, I can't really speak to," Ms. Costa replied frankly. "Dr. Carson hasn't worked the ER in over a month. And we're not privy to any reports he makes to the court."

"How convenient," Carmen commented sarcastically. "So Jane Doe, the young woman who I believe is Lila Richman, is shacking up with some horny psyche resident. Are you at least *privy* to his address?"

Ms. Costa ignored his flippancy and removed a notebook from her desk drawer. After consulting the discharge papers filed away toward the back of the chart, she wrote down the Dr. Carson's street and house number. "Well I've shared this much already, I guess I'd be a hypocrite if I didn't give you this infor-mation, too."

Taking the paper from her he glanced at the address. "It looks like Beechwood Boulevard is my next stop," Carmen commented.

"I wouldn't expect anything less from you, detective."

Grimly Carmen concurred. Then he rose to his feet, thanked Adrianne Costa for her time and assistance, and left the office.

Chapter 24

Matt and Lila lounged in the living room watching the movie, *Miracle on Thirty-Fourth Street* on Matt's new nineteen-inch color TV. Despite having heard so much about the classic film, he'd had never taken the time to watch it. Now, with the opportunity, try as he might to concentrate, his mind kept wandering.

Friends raved about their honeymoons. His last three days with Lila had to be as sweet. From Christmas morning on, their time together had evolved into a journey full of inquiry and discovery. Not only was he intimately involved with the wonders of her body, he was also tapping into the mysteries of her mind. Something miraculous had clicked into place at midnight mass. Matt felt like the beneficiary of its bounty.

When they were not making love, they explored her past. In addition to her childhood and adolescence in Baltimore, her undergraduate years at the University of Maryland had come into focus. Then, early yesterday afternoon, they reviewed some of her memories of Western Pennsylvania.

He compared her psyche to an onion, its translucent overlapping layers ripe for unpeeling. Or perhaps, she was a blossoming flower with petals unfurling, slowly revealing a soft, vulnerable core.

She leaned over and set her head on his shoulder. He extended his arm and drew her close. Although they'd only been lovers for a short time, he sensed a growing bond.

The movie ended. The credits rolled. He glanced down at Lila and noticed her eyes moistening. A good sign, he decided. She seemed to be sympathizing, possibly empathizing, with the joys and sorrows of the characters, even if they were merely fictitious figures on a television screen. Her emotional side was awakening. Without a word he slid across the sofa and hugged her. She leaned her head against his shoulder and wept.

"Lila, it's just a movie," he reminded her,

"I know," she replied, her voice catching in mid-sob. "But it's so touching. It reminds me of when I believed in Santa Claus."

"It does me, too."

As they sat watching the Movie Classics station preview its next feature, the pressure of Lila's body against his side aroused him. He was about to indulge his impulse when the telephone rang. With the moment undermined, he got up and answered it. Moments later, after returning from the kitchen, he commented, "Didn't you say your father died a few years ago?"

"Uh huh," she mumbled, her eyes fixed on the first scene of *From Here to Eternity.*

"That's what I thought." He sat back down on the couch.

She glanced at him. "Why?"

"A private investigator by the name of Serrano showed up at Braddock Hospital claiming to represent him. He said he was looking for you."

Her expression mirrored his grim tone. She seemed to grasp the significance of this revelation. "What do you think it means?"

"I'm not sure," he replied. "But I don't like the sounds of it."

"Who do you think really hired him?"

"I have no idea."

Lila hesitated before asking, "Who called to let you know?"

"It was Adrianne Costa. She's head of nursing at the hospital. I met her while moonlighting in the ER. She used to stop down occasionally to see how things were going."

"Did she say what he looked like?" Then, before he could answer, she added, "Did she tell him where you live?"

"Yes and yes," he replied.

Her face fell. Apprehension tainted her expression. "Matt, do you think he'll come looking for me?"

"I'm sure of it," Matt answered frankly. His heart started pounding wildly. He forced himself to think straight. "You know," he added, "if this Serrano guy's gonna show up here, you probably shouldn't be."

"Be what?"

"Be here."

"Oh."

"Listen," he said, trying to sound calm. "It's after six on Friday evening. My bet is this guy won't bother us tonight, especially if he wants to keep things civil. Tomorrow's Saturday. It's Mrs. Hurowitz' Sabbath, so she'll probably go to synagogue in the morning then be home after that. I'll call her and see if you can stay overnight, then spend the day. If she agrees, that'll free me up to deal with our unwanted visitor, whenever he shows up. I can meet you over there for dinner tomorrow night."

"If you think that's best, Matt," she said, wide-eyed. "This really scares me. I wonder what that guy wants. And who sent him."

"I really don't know," Matt admitted, trying to keep his tone even. Inside he was trembling like a leaf. "The fact that he used a bogus story about your father suggests he's not who he says he is. Maybe I can find out more when he shows up."

"But that's the point. He's going to show up. And he's probably dangerous. What are you going to do if things get out of hand?"

"First of all," he tried to reassure her, "all this fancy security equipment should help me get an idea who I'm dealing with."

"But let's say you can't tell," she persisted. "What if you let him in? Then, what?"

"Then, I'll have to deal with the situation. Remember, you're the one he's after. If you're not here, I doubt if he'll hold me hostage. And worse comes to worst, I do have a third degree black belt in Tae Kwon Do."

"Whatever that is," she replied, "I hope it's enough to protect you."

If he weren't so apprehensive, he would have been amused. "When it's all over," he declared with more bravado than he felt, "he'll be the one who needs protection."

She nodded, then eased over to him. He hugged her fiercely. Against his cheek her soft willowy hair felt like a caress. The remnants of her tears moistened his shirt. As his chest involuntarily tightened he appreciated how much this mysterious young woman had come to mean to him in such a short time. Now that he'd found her, he silently pledged that no one was going to take her away.

That night Matt slept alone. The next morning, he worked on his research project, tabulating data, refining the statistical analysis, and finally tackling the outline of the article he hoped to have published in the *American Journal of Psychiatry*. After a light lunch of leftover salad and reheated clam chowder, he sat down and watched one of the parade of college bowl games so common during the days leading up to New Year's. This one was the Tangerine Bowl with Auburn playing the Penn State Nittany Lions.

Barely into the game Matt reminisced about Saturday afternoons during his first two years at CMU when his grandfather, Mathew Carson Sr., would meet him in front of his Forbes Avenue dorm and, weather permitting, challenge him to a brisk walk down Fifth Avenue into the Oakland section and up what the locals called Cardiac Hill to Pitt Stadium. As if to validate how things came full circle, the famous football field stood a half-block southeast of Western Psych where Matt currently trained.

The door bell rang. Matt started. His heart rate quickened. He rarely had visitors. Today, only one person was expected.

He hurried down the staircase to the front door. After disengaging the deadbolt lock, he turned the knob and pulled back. Facing him was a short man in a slate gray overcoat and a felt fedora. He had a thin black mustache, brown eyes, and bushy eyebrows.

"Hello, sir. My name is Salvatore Serrano," the visitor said offering Matt a business card. "I'm a private investigator hired by the Harvey Richman family, commissioned to locate their only daughter, a woman of about twenty-six who disappeared almost two months ago while attending graduate school at the University of Pittsburgh."

"So," Matt said slowly. "How is that it you think I could help?"

"Before I continue, may I step inside, it's rather chilly out here."

"Oh," Matt said, a little embarrassed. "Sure. Sorry about that. Come in." He cracked the door wide enough to allow the private investigator to pass. He then directed him up the steps.

Once Mr. Serrano was seated on the couch, Matt offered him something to drink. The visitor asked for water. "As I was saying," he began after Matt returned and sat down on one of the straight-backed, dining room chairs, "I represent the Richmans. Their daughter has disappeared. My search, a somewhat convoluted one, eventually led me to Braddock Hospital. There I had a very pleasant conversation with the nursing supervisor, a woman named Adrianne Costa. She confirmed that a young woman meeting Lila's description presented to the hospital a couple days after the Richman girl disappeared. And since she was, during her brief period in the emergency room, under your care, Dr. Carson—you are Dr. Carson, aren't you?" Matt nodded. "That's what I assumed. Anyway, since she was initially under your care, I assume you know at least a portion of the story."

Matt wasn't sure how much of the 'story' he was supposed to know, but he managed another nod. Anxiety was affecting his concentration. Uncomfortable and unsure, he knew this Serrano guy had picked up Lila's trail, pursued it to Braddock Hospital, and was now in his apartment. What he couldn't fathom was who the man really was and why he was really here.

"That's what I thought," Matt's visitor commented. "What's more, Ms. Costa also mentioned that, upon being released from the hospital, since she was still suffering from almost total amnesia and had no viable way of caring for herself, she was discharged to your custody. In fact, I believe you even petitioned the courts to obtain legal guardianship."

"That's right," Matt confirmed.

"So, I am to assume," Mr. Serrano queried, "that Lila still lives here?"

"She does," Matt offered, realizing that denying this would only force him to fabricate some elaborate lie to explain where she'd gone.

"Is she here now?"

"As a matter of fact, she's not."

"That's too bad. Will she be back later?"

"I'm not sure."

"Why's that?"

"She's made some friends since moving in with me. She's visiting one of them," Matt said, embarking on one of those fabrications he'd sought to avoid. "They're going to be out late tonight. She might even stay over."

"Could you give me the friend's name?" Mr. Serrano asked.

"I'd rather not."

"Why?"

"Lila's not comfortable around strangers. I'd rather not have you barge in on her without me around."

"Then why don't you join me? Or call her at this friend's and ask her to come home. It's very important that I confirm that your Lila is in fact the person I'm seeking. Her family is bereft."

"I can appreciate that. But in my capacity as her guardian and mental health therapist, I think it would be best if you met with her in a safe environment among people she trusts."

"Point well taken, Dr. Carson," Mr. Serrano acknowledged. "When would that be? I assume you're talking about here."

Matt considered this. He knew putting this guy off for long would be futile. And if she and Matt really tried to avoid him, they'd have to make a run for it, which was unrealistic to say the least. But he still felt compelled to buy some time.

"Stop over tomorrow," he suggested. "Lila should be back home by then.'

"What time tomorrow?" Serrano asked.

"Give her most of the day," he advised. "How about in the evening, around seven."

"You're the doctor," Mr. Serrano joked, then rose to his feet. "You're sure you don't want to take a ride over to these friends' house?"

"Quite sure, Mr. Serrano. Tomorrow should be soon enough."

Matt followed the investigator down the steps. The heavy footfalls shook the entire staircase. At the front door Serrano turned and commented, "You call her Lila? Does that mean that you've discovered who she is?"

Despite this obvious deduction, having to confront this reality caught Matt off guard. "She's begun to reclaim her identity," Matt confirmed. "But there's still a lot she hasn't been able to recall."

"And a lot she has?" Mr. Serrano pressed.

"You could say that."

"Such as?"

"Why don't we leave that for tomorrow? Then you can ask her yourself."

Mr. Serrano frowned, glanced down at his shiny wing-tipped shoes, then back up at Matt. "Fair enough, Doc. Until tomorrow."

"Until tomorrow."

Matt looked as the dark-haired man in the gray wool overcoat made his way down to the sapphire blue Volvo sedan parked by the curb.

Chapter 25

Winding through Schenley Park enroute from Oakland to Squirrel Hill, Carmen marveled at how early in the evening twilight descended upon Pittsburgh during the last week in December. You'd think he was living in Newfoundland or something. After making the right onto the Greenfield Bridge he eased into the turning lane. While towering over the mass of Parkway East traffic creeping in and out of the Squirrel Hill Tunnel below, he wondered whether this narrow overpass did indeed, comprise a portion of the circuitous route Lila Richman had taken from Murdock Farms to Braddock following the explosion.

A rush of excitement gripped him as he eased the dark blue Volvo in front of the row of two-story houses on the 6500 block of Beechwood Boulevard. It almost felt like a first date. After two months of arduous investigation, a search that had taken him to nearby Zelienople, then to Baltimore, and had ultimately resulted in two lost lives, was finally approaching its culmination. Poor Jarvis, Carmen lamented, recalling the caper's most recent casualty. If that big, black bastard had just stayed retired, he'd still be fishing for marlin off the coast of Cape Hatteras. But he apparently valued loyalty over friendship. So, like Carmen's favorite piano man, Billy Joel eulogized, "Only the good die young."

After locking the door, Carmen paused for a moment by the side of the sedan. Glancing up at the bank of windows, a murky row of glass that comprised much of the front wall of the building's second level, he searched for some sign of habitation. With the shades drawn the only illumination came from a nearby mercury vapor street light reflected off the opaque panes.

Not much of a reception, he thought. Perhaps the cautious young couple had flown the coop or was cowering in the recesses of the unit. He recalled a sparsely furnished dining room tapering into a hallway that dissolved into shadows. They could be in the bedroom doing other things. Now that was a more tantalizing notion.

He thought about last evening after Dr. Carson had escorted him out the apartment's front door. He'd considered remaining in the neighborhood and keeping the building under surveillance. In the event that the young psychiatrist left the apartment, Carmen could have followed him, perhaps getting lucky and learning where Lila was hiding. And he was pretty certain she was hiding somewhere, no doubt warned of his imminent arrival by Ms. Costa late Thursday afternoon. But he had concerns of his own. Uppermost was the danger of his own detection, especially if he remained in one spot too long. A high ranking CIA operative had been murdered. His death would not be ignored or concealed. Carmen would be held accountable. And despite his new identity, it wouldn't protect him for long. He'd been Salvatore Serrano for over a week, now. So instead of watching the apartment, he'd returned to his motel for the night, resigned to return at the appointed time.

He pressed the buzzer once, twice, then a third time. Considering that the button might not be connected, he pounded on the door, hard. Still no answer. This wasn't surprising. Despite having anticipated this kind of cool reception, he was starting to get pissed. But before doing something rash, he decided to circle the building, checking to see if any access points existed.

He considered the entrance to the first floor unit. That particular door stood next the psychiatrist's. But what value would there be breaking into the downstairs apartment? Instead, he retraced his way back down the short flight of concrete steps and began a clockwise rotation around the building. About halfway along the south side of the building, down a narrow corridor that separated Carson's structure from its neighbor, he happened upon a side entrance. Mounting the two steps he tried the knob. Not unexpectedly it was locked. But although this door seemed secure, there were no deadbolt locks to contend with. Before attempting to break in there, he continued around to the back where he found a cinder block wall ascending all the way up to the second floor bedroom windows. The far side wall was brick and glass. Without a ladder, these alternative access points were worthless.

Back by the south side entrance, he withdrew a small file and a thin metal rod from his overcoat pocket. Inserting his tools into the conventional keyhole, he jiggled them until the tumblers clicked. He turned the knob and with a brief rush of satisfaction pushed. The partially rotted wooden door complied. A moment later, he shut it tightly behind him.

Carmen paused, engulfed in a claustrophobic darkness, estimating that he was standing on a landing somewhere between the first and basement levels. Pulling out his personal, untraceable revolver and a small penlight, he surveyed the enclosure, noting that there were three flights of steps above him and one below. Heading upward he was surprised to find that there was no door leading into the first floor apartment. That implied that the second story unit had exclusive access to the basement. Treading softly he continued his ascent. A few anxious moments later, he reached the top.

The door to Dr. Carson's unit was unsecured. In fact, examining it in the narrow penlight beam, he couldn't even find a lock. Gently turning the handle, he felt the catch release. The door opened toward him. Easing slightly backward, he paused for a moment, hoping no one was poised and waiting on the other side. Then, with his revolver cocked at eye level, its barrel at a forty-five degree angle, he peered inside.

He'd reached what appeared to be a small, square-shaped kitchen. The wall to his left was filled with cabinets and a sink. Directly across from him was a stove and refrigerator. To his right a metal cart supported a small microwave oven. There was a row of cookbooks on the lower shelf. Above him a wall clock's luminous hands showed the time. It was seven-thirty. Carmen paused again, listening for a sign that the occupants were present. Except for some generic background street-noise, there was only silence. Still, convinced he wasn't alone, he advanced warily.

Passing under an archway, he entered the dining room. Easing forward, he glanced left, then right. His blunder was not vigilance, but the direction in which he chose to inspect first. As his neck turned toward the telescoping corridor leading to the bedrooms, something attacked him. Almost supernaturally, an entity, laden with mass and form, materialized in the space under the suspended ceiling near the wall. Utilizing its full weight it descended upon him. Succumbing to this irresistible force, Carmen could do nothing but crumple to the carpet. The revolver barked. A flash of light. A loud explosion. A nine millimeter projectile whizzed across the room. With a deafening crash one of the dining room windows shattered.

Carmen struggled to right himself. Matted down in a tangle of arms and legs he felt like a dolphin caught in a fishing net. Complicating this dilemma was his bulky wool overcoat which burdened him further. Straining, Carmen thrashed and wriggled against his attacker, a person who seemed small but strong. Finally, while lying on his back, he extricated his left arm, the one holding the penlight. At that instance, he felt a stabbing pain, not unlike a wasp sting, at the angle where his neck met his shoulder. Turning to get a better look at his attacker, in the amber light, he recognized, Dr. Mathew Carson. And to his further dismay, he also noticed that the psychiatrist was holding a twenty cc syringe. It didn't take a detective to deduce that its needle had just been withdrawn from deep within the cervical muscle at the base of his neck. The implication of this discovery dawned on the Carmen just as he lost consciousness.

Carmen awoke slowly, his eyelids weighted, his body feeling like lead. He had no idea how long he'd been out. Gradually he appreciated the fact that he was lying flat on his back on a fairly large bed with his arms and legs bound. Squirming in place, he created undulations that revealed the mattress to be filled with water. On the nightstand to his right stood a Tiffany lamp and a clock-radio. The clock's read-out said ten PM. The third item, a white plastic device with an antenna and a speaker grill, was more intriguing, probably an intercom, the kind anxious parents used to track an infant's sleep patterns.

"So you're finally up," a voice from the doorway announced. "It's about time." Dr. Carson walked into the room. "I didn't expect you to be out that long. But then again, it's hard to tell how much bulk you're hiding under that overcoat. I guess I dosed you a little high."

Carmen attempted to reply but couldn't, his tongue feeling three times its normal size. Whatever Carson had injected resembled the Novocain his dentist had used to numb him that time he needed root canal work.

"Don't try to talk yet," Dr. Carson advised. "Your speech center should kick in a little while. Then we'll have plenty of time to converse."

Carmen started to resist. But the young psychiatrist seemed right. Eventually, he relaxed and waited for the drug to wear off. It was clear who had the upper hand here. All he could do was fantasize about his captor's motives and methods. Closing his eyelids, he drifted off. When he regained consciousness again, Carson was sitting on a high-backed chair by his side, a book opened in his lap.

"Can you talk now?"

Carmen opened his mouth. The cotton balls were still there, but his imaginary oversized tongue had shrunken considerably. He licked his parched lips and croaked, "I think so."

"Good," the young psychiatrist said. "Here, drink this."

Carson held out a plastic cup of water with a straw. Carmen pinched the tube with his lips and sucked. The water tasted cool and refreshing. Testing his swallowing mechanism, he gulped, savoring the liquid as it flowed all the way to his empty stomach.

"Now, Mr. Serrano," Dr. Carson continued. "Who the hell are you? Really?"

Carmen started to reiterate his cover. As he did, he discovered that although his mouth intended to form the words, his mind wouldn't permit him to do so. If he told this nice young man he was a private investigator, he would be lying. And it was wrong to lie. There was something about this young physician that inspired trust. It would be a disservice to deceive him.

"Carmen Vitale," Carmen heard himself saying. "My name is Carmen Vitale. I'm a detective for the Pittsburgh Police Department. Currently, I'm on a disciplinary leave from the force."

Oh shit! Carmen thought. I know it's noble to be honest. But isn't that a little more than I really wanted my friend here to know?

"Now why doesn't that surprise me?" Dr. Carson commented sarcastically. "So you're not a PI representing the Richman family?" Despite it being framed like an inquiry, this comment didn't seem to require a response. "And what are you really doing here?"

"I'm investigating the explosion at the Rosenberg home in Murdock Farms, the one that killed six people back in early October." Again, Carmen was amazed at how much he was sharing. Somehow, he had relinquished control over his statements.

"What's that have to do with my ward, Lila?"

"I have reason to believe she's the bomber."

As he said this Carmen noticed how his captor's expression, which had been one of placidity, now turned into angry disbelief. "That's ridiculous, Vitale! Absurd! How could you cook up a conclusion like that?"

"From what *I've* discovered," Carmen replied calmly, "she had the necessary training and the opportunity to practice it."

"And from what I've discovered, I think that's patently impossible."

Carmen appreciated where this young psychiatrist was coming from. After all, besides being a trained professional, he was also apparently a man who felt deeply for the woman being accusing. At this point Carmen really didn't want to say anything more. But once again, he couldn't stop himself.

"My theory is that Lila's father and Malcolm Rosenberg are linked. Their connection probably goes all the way back to World War II. Something happened back then that enraged Richman—really Hans Reichman—and has been burning all the way until now."

"Are you implying that Lila was the instrument of his revenge?" Carson probed, his expression betraying his disbelief.

"It sounds far-fetched," Carmen conceded, "but I think it's possible."

"I think it's bullshit!" Carson exclaimed. "That's what I think."

"I can't say your reaction surprises me," Carmen conceded. "You obviously care about Lila a great deal."

He waited for the psychiatrist to respond. The young professional seemed to be weighing how much to reveal. Finally, he commented, "You're right on there, detective. I do care about her. But there's more to it than that. We've lived together for almost six weeks, now. During that time I've gotten to know her pretty well. Based on that exposure, it's hard for me to imagine her being capable of performing such a heinous act of violence and destruction."

"What you can imagine and what may actually be true may be worlds apart," Carmen pointed out bluntly. He sensed he was starting to own his thought processes again. "By the way, Dr. Carson, what, besides a sedative, did you slip into that injection you gave me? Until the last few moments, I've had a tough time thinking clearly."

Matt glanced over at him and grinned. "You noticed. Just a derivative of Pentothal sodium I've had some experience with over at Western Psych. It helps our more recalcitrant patients deal with their inhibitions."

"I gotta admit, it's pretty effective," Carmen conceded. "I could use some over at the station. But that's beside the point. I think it's time you have Lila return from wherever she's hiding. Maybe, then, she'll help us clear up the mystery."

"There's a minor problem in that regard, Detective."

Uneasiness gripped Carmen's stomach. "What kinda problem?" he asked.

"Lila's gone."

"What do you mean, she's gone?"

"I mean, I went over to get her from our housekeeper's place this afternoon. There, I found Mrs. Hurowitz gagged and bound and Lila missing. My first notion was you had done it. Then when you showed up here tonight, I suspected you were probably as much in the dark about her whereabouts as I."

"Oh, shit!" was Carmen's only comment.

A half hour later, the two professionals were sitting in Matt's living room, nursing mugs of coffee, and chatting like old friends. A single lamp set on a chrome and glass end table illuminated a portion of the spacious enclosure. Despite the drawn blinds, Carmen could still appreciate the champagne pink light coming from the mercury vapor streetlight outside.

The effect of the drug had all but worn off. Dr. Carson's richly caffeinated coffee helped. Now that their awkward power play was resolved, Carmen convinced Matt they should compare notes, then formulate a strategy to locate and hpefully rescue Lila.

"I'm a little surprised you're not more upset she's missing," Carmen admitted to Matt after the young psychiatrist had settled onto the leather recliner. "From what Miss Costa implied, you really took an interest in her—and that's not to say you've been intimate or anything."

Matt seemed to sense the detective's discomfort and suppressed a smile. "We've become quite close," he agreed. "And yes, Detective, for about a week now we've been intimate. Don't let appearances fool you. I've been trained to hide my emotions. But make no mistake about it, when she turned up missing yesterday, I was beside myself with worry and grief. And to make things worse, I'm pretty much alone in all this." Carmen nodded grimly. "So, with no one to turn to for help, my initial reaction was to go after whoever kidnapped her. But, obviously, I had no idea where to start. So after I made sure Mrs. Hurowitz was okay, I came back to the apartment and spent most of last night working through my feelings of anger and loss. Then I considered my options."

"Which were?" Carmen prompted.

"The most obvious was to report her missing to the police. That's what Mr. Hurowitz encouraged me to do. But another notion persuaded me to wait, especially since it's now apparent to me that Lila's of value to more people than just you. In fact that's when you entered my reasoning." Amused, Carmen mouthed, "Me?" "Yes you, Detective. Although I was pretty sure you weren't who you said you were, whoever you are, you had been savvy enough to track Lila down to my place. Having accomplished that, and now that she was missing again, you probably had a better idea where to look for her than I did."

"So you hung out here waiting to see if I'd show up, then ambushed me?"

"Pretty much," Matt confirmed. "Here's my reasoning: if you had anything to do with Lila's kidnapping, then you'd be long gone by now. But if you hadn't, then you would probably show up as scheduled. This left it up to me to discover who you really were and once I established that, maybe you could help me find her."

"Remarkably simple," Carmen said approvingly, "almost elegant. And now that you know who I'm, how can I help you?"

Matt grinned, apparently appreciating Carmen's innocence act. "Who do you think kidnapped her, Detective?" Matt asked.

Carmen barely hesitated. "It could have been any one of a number," he commented, ambiguously. "If it's not her own people, then my best guess is the Feds—one of the agencies, either the FBI or the CIA."

"Really?" Matt replied. "Then we're up against some heavyweights. What could she possibly have done to have the government after her?" Then, before Carmen could elaborate, Matt blurted out, "You're not referring to that bullshit about the Squirrel Hill bombing, are you?"

"That's a big part of it, Doc."

"But what's the connection between Lila and the Rosenbergs?"

"That's where it's pretty much conjecture. My theory is that there's a link between the two fathers."

"Wasn't Malcolm Rosenberg killed in the bombing?"

"That's right, along with his wife, his children and his grandkids."

Considering the magnitude of the crime, Matt commented, "There's no way Lila could do something like that. From the time I've spent with her, I can't image a violent bone in her body."

"You may not know her as well as you think you do," Carmen commented coolly. "How far into her past did you delve?"

"By my standards, pretty far," the young psychiatrist boasted, "but only in dribs and drabs. After checking with Adrianne over at Braddock, you must know that she had a pretty profound memory loss when she showed up at the hospital. And that condition persisted through her entire hospitalization and for the first few weeks she was staying with me. Eventually, after some trial and error, I succeeded in exposing her to stimuli that triggered some images from her past. And that had a bit of a snowball effect. During the last week or so, we've uncovered many of the pieces to the puzzle."

"For instance?" Carmen probed.

"Well, she recalls being born in Baltimore and initially raised by both of her parents. Then, from the age of three or four, her mother died and her father took over. Eventually, a paternal aunt moved in to help out. Unfortunately, she's only tapped into some general experiences from her childhood. After that, there's a fairly substantial gap in her memory. Her undergraduate years at the University of Maryland are a little clearer. Then, she remembers moving to western Pennsylvania and enrolling as a graduate student in Pitt's School of International Studies."

"Which squares with what I've learned about her," Carmen revealed. "Did she say anything about an aunt and uncle in Zelienople?"

"Not that I recall. Why?"

"Because, they seem to be an integral part of this story," Carmen confided. "At least the aunt is. Her name is Margo. She's the same woman who helped her father raise her back in Baltimore. She's also the old hag who gave me something I've started calling, The Reichman Manuscript."

"What's that?"

Carmen briefed Matt on SS officer's self-indulgent memoir and how he came upon it a few days after the Squirrel Hill bombing. Despite the impulse to embellish the story, Carmen decided to skim over much of the manuscript's main content, focusing instead on the section, toward the end, when Reichman returns to Berlin and is captured by the Allies.

"Something significant occurred between the time Reichman agreed to switch allegiances in Berlin in the spring of 1945 and when he left Germany for Hungary before Christmas that same year. I'm pretty sure it has to do with a trip he made to Hanover to visit his family after the war ended. When he arrived there he learned that both his wife and son had been brutally murdered. From what I could glean from the journal, the rape and murders were being blamed on a band of American soldiers. One of the GI's dropped a set of dog tags in the barn. I have a pretty strong notion who they belonged to."

"Who?" Matt asked.

"Malcolm Rosenberg."

"No way!" Matt exclaimed. He paused, absorbing the significance of this revelation. "So if what you are saying is true, the Squirrel Hill bombing could be the culmination of a vendetta spawned all the way back in 1945, planned in exhausting detail by a psychopathic Nazi and ultimately executed by his only daughter forty years later."

"I couldn't have summarized it better myself," Carmen conceded, "or come up with a better word to describe him."

"But why," Matt continued, ignoring the sardonic acknowledgement, "if your theory about her kidnapping is accurate, is the government so anxious to hush things up?"

"You got me there, Doc. You're not the only one puttin' puzzle pieces together. There's a few of my own I haven't been able to figure out."

Matt, set his head against the rest, and whistled. After staring at the ceiling for a while he turned back to Carmen. "Once he moved to Baltimore, what did you say this Hans Reichman did for a living?" he asked.

"I didn't," Carmen corrected. "But had I mentioned it earlier, I would have told you he was a psychiatrist."

"Which makes sense," Matt commented. "And did he continue to work for the CIA after he came to the States?"

"He sure did," Carmen confirmed. "He was one of their top experts on chemical and psychological mental manipulation—what we in the lay public like to refer to as brain washing."

"I'm familiar with the term," Matt commented without a hint of condescension. "Do you happen to know if Reichman was involved in the CIA's Operation Phoenix during the Vietnam War?" he asked.

This specific reference took Carmen by surprise. With an arch of his bushy eyebrows he replied, "You might say, quite involved. In fact, from what I've learned, he was on the committee that formulated much of the psychological warfare utilized during that campaign."

"That fucking bastard!"

"What did you say?" Carmen retorted, shocked at this outburst.

But Matt didn't elaborate. At least, not right away.

Gray clouds of mist rose lazily from the thick-handled mugs. A cluster of Entenmanns' coffee cake squares had been set on a dinner plate between them. Matt was back on the leather recliner, his shoes off, his feet curled under his thighs. Carmen sat on the sofa, his tie loose and his navy blue sweater rolled up at the sleeves.

"When I first encountered Jane—," Matt began, cautiously sipping his coffee then setting the mug down, "I mean Lila—until a week ago I only knew her as Jane Doe. Anyway, after the medics brought her in, we got her stabilized. When I finally had time to examine her for signs of trauma, among the cuts and bruises, I noticed this peculiar scar on the inner aspect of her right thigh. It looked like a sebaceous cyst or perhaps a lipoma that had been surgically removed. I didn't think much of it until later that night, while I was conducting an experiment in the research lab at Western Psych; something I observed triggered an association."

"An association?" Carmen repeated and leaned a little closer.

"Yes," Matt continued. "I was observing the behavior of a patient through a one-way mirror. After acting out a bit, she finally plopped down on a chair. When she did her skirt slid up and her thighs were exposed. That's when I remembered where I'd seen the lesion before. It resembled the description of a healed surgical site I'd come across while researching unconventional methods of mind manipulation during my medical school psychiatry rotation. Much of this information comes from recently declassified government funded research that occurred in the mid to late fifties. That's when the CIA became almost obsessed with reproducing what they conceived of as brain washing techniques perfected by the Communists during the Korean War."

"A lá *The Manchurian Candidate*," Carmen offered.

"Something like that," Matt confirmed. "Apparently, the intelligence community was convinced that the North Koreans had perfected methods of breaking down American POW's and then reprogramming them to reject Democracy and embrace Communism. This paranoia spurned an extensive effort to come up with innovative and effective techniques of our own to secure the same ends—but in the interests of freedom. Sounds a little oxymoronic doesn't it?" Matt quipped. "Brain washing people so they can be free."

Carmen appreciated the irony.

"Well, despite this massive effort to discover a method of manipulating unsuspecting minds—and believe me, they tried everything, from drugs to hypnosis to sleep deprivation to repetitive stimulation—nothing ever really worked. For several years, they even bankrolled a high profile Canadian psychiatrist named Cameron, and used his Toronto clinic to conduct all kinds of long-term experiments into shock therapy and sleep-based suggestion."

"Believe it or not, I'm familiar with that campaign," Carmen admitted. "A retired radiologist named Strauss, one of the Krauts I interviewed in a seedy

Baltimore pub a month ago, claims that Hans Reichman actually visited Cameron's clinic in the late fifties. I'd have to check my notes but I think the place was called the Allan Institute—or something along those lines."

"That's fascinating," Matt agreed, "and certainly squares with what I started to share. One of the techniques the CIA experimented with was to take a fairly large volume—perhaps twenty cc's—of some psycho-active drug and implant it in a reservoir with a semi-permeable membrane under the skin of one of its subjects. The drug would then leach out slowly into the bloodstream, allowing the operator to do repetitive psychological programming without the need for daily or multi-day injections. But from what I understand, the technique was deemed ineffective and the research community abandoned it months before Kennedy took office in 1960. Now, it looks like Reichman may have experimented on his own daughter using this same kind of mind manipulation."

"What a grizzly, old bastard," Carmen declared. "Are you implying, Doc, that even though Lila could have been the bomber, her father may have programmed her to commit the crime."

"The contention's a little far-fetched," Matt admitted, "but given what I've discovered about her psyche, I can't imagine her destroying that family of her own free will."

Hearing this notion, Carmen felt compelled to offer a notion of his own. "Hey, Doc, could it have been possible for old man Reichman to indoctrinate his own daughter into the hate mentality that seems so pervasive in the White Survivalist movement these days—so much so that she *truly* believed what she was doing that night was right?"

Matt seemed to consider this possibility. "I suppose," he conceded, "but I prefer my explanation."

"Given your emotional attachment to the suspect, that doesn't surprise me," Carmen offered.

Matt didn't seem to take the criticism personally. Instead he eased back, reached up and rubbed his eyes. Carmen thought he looked weary, almost defeated. "Despite what we've been saying," he commented, "I still can't believe she did it."

Carmen, trying to tread gingerly around the young man's feelings, "Although the evidence seems to be piling up against her, I hope you're right."

Despite the exhaustion from the day's events, Carmen and his new confidant spent another half-hour considering their options. Finally, he suggested they part for the night and meet the next day to set into motion a plan to rescue the missing girl.

"Who do you think kidnapped her?" Matt said softly to Carmen as he escorted him to the front door.

"I'm leaning toward some of my old friends at the CIA," Carmen admitted.

"Really? If we've already touched on the why, do you have any idea how?"

"I got what you like to call, a notion."

"Elaborate," Matt requested.

"First, let me ask *you* a question," Carmen began. "After I left your apartment on Friday afternoon, did you happen to go out for any reason?"

Matt considered this. "For about a half hour," he finally reported. "I drove over to Mineo's to pick up a pizza."

"That's all it took," Carmen confirmed. "The guys we're up against are slick. First, let's assume that even though this Salvatore Serrano cover I've taken on is a good one, the Feds have managed to sniff up my trail. But instead of reeling *me* in, they decide to wait and see where I lead them. In this case, it happens to be to you. So, after they confirm we've made contact, what they do is stake out your place, too. Then, when you head out for that bite to eat, they slip in and install a few microscopic taps."

"My God!" Matt exclaimed. "And then, I led them to her."

"More than likely," Carmen confirmed. "I bet you called her later that evening—or she called you—just to see how she was doing, wish her a good-night." Matt acknowledged this with a nod. "There you have it. They traced the call, learned about your Mrs. Hurowitz, found out where she lived and, whad-dya know, your housekeeper's gagged and bound and Lila's gone."

"Pretty slick," Matt admitted.

"Happens all the time," Carmen replied.

"But not to the woman I love."

"To people other people love," Carmen said unfazed.

"Maybe so, detective," Matt commented. "But this is one loved one I intend to get back."

"Plan on me helping you."

As if to reinforce their mutual resolve, they shook on it.

Chapter 26

"Don't wander too far from your room," an excited Matt instructed the detective over the phone. "We just may be embarking on a little excursion later this afternoon." It was the morning following Carmen's botched break-in at the Beechwood Boulevard apartment. Matt snickered as he related these instructions, imagining the confused, possibly intrigued look on the detective's face.

"Whaddya mean, excursion?" Carmen demanded. "The way I figure it, if you're still interested in sniffing out your girlfriend's trail, there's plenty of work to do here in Pittsburgh."

"With a little luck, Detective," Matt countered, "I should be able to accelerate the process."

"You will, will you? And how's that?"

"Stay available," Matt instructed. "I'll get back to you," he added and hung up. It wasn't until after four in the afternoon that Matt finally called back. Without further explanation, he suggested Carmen pack an overnight bag and pick him up as soon as possible. They would probably be out of town for a couple of days. Carmen, still dubious, agreed. Forty-five minutes later, he was knocking on Matt's front door.

"Now what the hell's this all this about?" Carmen greeted the young psychiatrist. "Who's the detective here, anyway?"

"You're still the detective, Detective," Matt conceded, "but I might be the one with connections."

"Connections?" Carmen retorted. "What sorta connections?"

"My duffel's at the top of the steps. Do you mind driving? I'll brief you on the way."

"How far we going?"

"About a hundred miles."

"Which direction?"

"South by southeast. To Deep Creek, Maryland."

"That's not much of a trip. Sure. Go get your bag"

Five minutes later, with Matt in the passenger's seat of the Volvo, Carmen made a U-turn on Beechwood Boulevard, then rapidly worked his way onto the Parkway on-ramp. Once merged with the eastbound flow of traffic, they were on their way. "Now what's this is all about?" Carmen demanded as the sedan emerged from the Squirrel Hill tunnel. It was ten days after the winter equinox. By 5:00 PM, the sun had already disappeared behind the western hillside easing the sky into a deepening gray. Pinprick constellations attended the crescent moon which, with every bend in the road, drifted in and out of their field of vision.

"Like I said over the phone," Matt commented, "I have this connection. I think you guys call it a source."

"You have a source? Who's your source?"

"My father."

"Your father?" Carmen repeated. "How's he gonna help us find Lila?"

"In his capacity as a former Deputy Director of the CIA, he might be of some assistance."

Carmen whistled. "No shit! Your father's a big shot in the Agency. But you said, former. He retired?"

"For about four years now."

"And he lives in Deep Creek?"

"He lives with my mother just outside of D.C in Tyson's Corner, Virginia. But we've got this hunting cabin in Deep Creek. I called my mom this morning and found out he's there now."

"So why not just call him on the phone?"

"I tried. He wouldn't answer."

"You think something's wrong?"

"Not really. He got this thing about solitude. When he's at the house, he likes to keep to himself."

"What if there's an emergency?"

"My mother has a system worked out with the neighbors."

"And she wouldn't let you in on the details."

"I didn't share enough to qualify this as an emergency."

Carmen snickered. "If this isn't an emergency, I hate to imagine what is."

"Considering his former line of work, she's pretty clear about that distinction."

Carmen nodded, then pulled up to the turnpike ticket booth. A few moments later, they were cruising along the toll road, heading east toward Harrisburg. "Why do you think your father'll be able to help?" he asked.

"You mentioned the Agency might be involved," Matt reminded him. "And even if they're not, if the federal government has anything to do with this abduction, my dad would have ways of checking it out. He might know already."

"Makes sense. The Deputy Director's pretty high up in the pecking order. What department?"

"Operations." Matt assessed the detective's reaction. Carmen seemed impressed.

"And he retired in eighty-five?" Carmen reiterated.

"Early in Reagan's second term there was a major reorganization in the entire agency. Dad knew he'd never make it to the top—the job's too politically sensitive—so according to my mom, he called it a career."

"And go fishing," Carmen jested. "How old's he?"

Matt thought about this. In fact, he had to think about a lot of the material he was relating about his father. It'd been a long time since his father had been in his thoughts at all, at least the mundane, nonvindictive, biographical items. "Let's see, he was born in 1919," Matt recalled. "That makes him seventy. He'll celebrate seventy-one in May."

"Sounds like he was ripe for retirement anyway," Carmen commented. "You two get along?"

"I hate his guts!"

The reply was expressed with such venom that it prompted Carmen to glance at his passenger. "That's a pretty harsh sentiment," he commented. "What gives?"

Matt hesitated, not sure how to respond. Just thinking about his father made him see red. But how could he convey this blinding hatred to the detective? Then he remembered that seminal event.

"There was a time when I really respected my father," Matt conceded. "He was a hard working man with an important job in the Federal government. And although I was never privy to the intimate details of what he did for a living, it was obvious to me that he was a vital part of the nation's security. Knowing that was enough—enough to trust and believe in him. Which amounted to a lot. It meant accepting the ultra-conservative, no nonsense way he ran our home. It meant supporting his patriotic views while, as a teenager during the late sixties and early seventies, I had to cope with the storm of liberal protest that stirred all around us. Remember Detective, there was a very unpopular war raging a half a world away, a war where thousands of my contemporaries died in a country we had no business being. And despite all that, I still supported my father and the administration he worked for."

"Then what happened?" Carmen probed.

"I suppose it all started when I refused to enroll in West Point. Suddenly, my father's compliant, respectful son, refused to be his little warrior, too. But I just couldn't see myself as a career military man. I was a student not a soldier. I was into math and science. I was sixteen in sixty-nine, the summer we put a man on the moon. In fact, at that time, it was the space program that seemed glamorous to me, not as an astronaut, but as an aeronautical engineer. That steered me away from the military—although the Air Force Academy may have worked. That's when, without informing him, I applied to Carnegie Tech."

"Right here in Pittsburgh," Carmen commented. "So that's how you got here."

"Not most recently. But I did start out in college here. Moreover, Detective, I was born in Pittsburgh. My parents lived in an apartment in lower Oakland on McKee Street. In 1956, when I was two and half, we moved to Arlington, Virginia. My grandparents still live here. Grandpa sold his tool and die company about ten years ago. So enrolling in Carnegie Tech seemed like a perfect fit."

"But from the sound of it, you didn't finish," Carmen speculated.

"Very perceptive, Detective. That's right I didn't finish. I left before the end of my sophomore year. My lottery number was called. But I declined the opportunity to be one of those war casualties I was referring to before."

"So you were a draft dodger," Carmen commented without apparent malice.

"We used to call ourselves conscientious objectors," Matt clarified, feeling a familiar animosity fill his chest. "We were young men who remained true to our values and principles, one of which was preventing the meaningless slaughter of innocent farmers in a place our army had no business being."

"Sounds like a pretty simplistic indictment of a very complicated foreign policy," Carmen countered. "Or was that just a convenient excuse for saving your own skin?"

Matt, drawing on wisdom and maturity he'd acquired since crossing the border into Canada seventeen years ago, decided not to sidestep the challenge. "Perhaps," he conceded, "but I was also a bitter, betrayed, young man. Back then it was more personal."

"How so?" Carmen persisted.

"I felt responsible for the fact that it was my own father who authorized inhumane torture of innocent human beings."

"Torture?" Carmen repeated. "Who was tortured?"

"Viet Cong POW's."

"By whom?"

"By CIA operatives in Saigon."

"Really?" Carmen sounded somewhat incredulous. "I never heard anything about that. And I was over there."

"I'm sure very few people knew about it. It was top secret."

"Then how did you find out about it?"

"Serendipitously, you might say." Matt paused. When Carmen made no comment, he continued. "It happened during the summer after my freshman year at Tech."

"Nineteen seventy-one," Carmen clarified.

"Very good, Detective," Matt commented then added, "By the way, do you own a VCR?"

"As a matter-a-fact, I just bought one a couple of months ago. Why?"

"Probably VHS," Matt commented. Carmen nodded. "Have you ever heard of a Betamax?"

"The name sorta sounds familiar. Why?" Carmen sounded impatient. "Where's this heading, Doc?"

"Betamax was the first video cassette recorder format. It was developed by Sony Corporation and perfected in the late sixties. The technology revolution-ized the entire video recording industry. Up until then, field reporters would have to rely on newsreels to display the video portion of their features. That kind of film required standard processing, then projecting on a screen for viewing. With the Betamax videocassette recorder, these same reporters—and now, lay people like you—could record an event on a cassette tape and view it immedi-ately on a player without going through the hassle of developing the film in a lab."

"So?"

"So, the news industry wasn't the only entity that had access to the technology. The government did too, especially the CIA. You must know how much the intelligence community is fascinated with technologic gadgets. All the stuff in the James Bond movies isn't fictional."

"Granted," Carmen commented, "but what's all this have to do with hating your father's guts?"

"Everything," Matt replied.

Matt continued his story. He related how, during the summer of seventy-one he'd been home from college. On a muggy evening in mid-August after being out most of the evening, smoking pot with a buddy then driving around DC for hours, he finally returned to his parents' three-story colonial style house on Greensboro Drive in Tyson's Corner. It was well after midnight and he was still stoned. It was in this state of what he described as heightened perception, he regarded retiring to his own room way too boring. Instead, he wandered up to his father's second-floor study.

"Growing up," he told Carmen, "this part of the house had been strictly off-limits. Even my mother wasn't allowed in there, except to clean once a week. She used it call it his inner sanctum."

But Matt was a college sophomore now and, in his mind, no longer a kid. As a mature young adult he felt that no part his parents' home was off limits, including his father's den. After all, it was 2:00 AM. Who was going to stop him?

Once inside the enclosure, he marveled at the wonders he saw. Not only was there a twenty-one inch color television and state of the art stereo system, his father had recently acquired a sophisticated Betamax movie machine. He recognized the bulky, black box stacked on the rack next to the other high-tech equipment. And as Matt soon discovered, it was a cinch to use.

Instead of having to thread that temperamental thirty-five millimeter film through the guts of a complicated movie projector and show the movie on a cumbersome screen, all one had to do was pop the tape in the recorder, push a button, and watch the film in living color right on that great television. How could he ignore the prospect of such effortless visual fulfillment? Plus, from other times he'd invaded this forbidden territory, Matt knew of the stag film stash hidden behind the bookcase.

Walking over to the deep-set built-in by the far wall, he counted the books on the fourth shelf from the ceiling. Pulling out a copy of John Toland's *The*

Rising Sun, he waited for a mechanism to engage. With a whirring of machinery a section of the shelf above rotated a hundred and eighty degrees, replacing the half dozen volumes of the Encyclopedia Britannica with a collection of ten or so videotapes. Scanning the titles, Matt passed on the few he'd already seen and chose one with a somewhat more intriguing label, *The Folly of the Phoenix*.

"I couldn't imagine what the title meant," he told Carmen as they exited at New Stanton and headed south on 119. "I imagined some buxom woman dressed up in a bird costume. You know, high heels, long legs, maybe a beak-like crown and her big breasts exposed. Boy, was I wrong."

After flicking on the television and flipping off the lamp by his father's desk, Matt pressed the play button. The black leader gave way to a title page. The image was grainy, the letters in a simple font resembling something created on a standard typewriter. A young man, not much older than Matt, with dark, greasy hair that reached his shoulders came into view. He was dressed in ripped jeans and a *Peace Now* tied-dyed T-shirt. In his right hand, he held a bulky microphone. He appeared to be sitting in a basement apartment, the sofa under him worn and soiled, the carpet threadbare and faded. A staircase with a thin wooden railing ascended out of sight a little to the left. Hovering over the room off to the right was a rectangular casement window just below the ceiling level.

"Ladies and gentlemen," he began solemnly, "what you are about to witness is actual footage depicting atrocities perpetrated by the government of the United States of America on the innocent people of Vietnam. It is brought to you as a humanitarian service of the Students for a Democratic Society intended to heighten the awareness of peace loving Americans to the extent their leaders will go to harass, maim, and torture blameless civilians while pursuing an unauthorized, imperialistic agenda. Furthermore, most of these atrocities have been, and are still being, perpetrated by the Central Intelligence Agency under the auspices of the Federal government, the same government that has callously sacrificed the lives of thousands of young, healthy Americans in its demonic quest for power and prestige.

"Four years ago, in 1967, the CIA launched what was code-named The Phoenix Program, a broad-based, paramilitary campaign designed to eradicate the Viet Cong infrastructure through intelligence gathering, interrogation of civilians, and ultimately, neutralization of target members of the National Liberation Front. It has now evolved into a well-coordinated assassination operation which has murdered more than twenty thousand individuals. It also functions as a means of establishing a network of Provincial Interrogation Centers which act as primitive torture chambers the likes of which have not been seen since the Spanish Inquisition."

The narrator faded from the screen. In his place was what looked like a scene from Inside Africa. The image seemed jumpy, the focus shifting from sharp to blurred. A loud whirring sound poured out of the speakers. Matt guessed that the video was being shot from the air, probably from a helicopter panning a thick forest. Scanning the surface, the camera exhibited a broad, marshy field rimmed by thick stands of trees. Seemingly random, military activity was noted as American soldiers ran in all directions, some near the trees, others near a row of what looked like oil drums or perhaps, garbage bins. Tightening the focus, the lens zeroed in on a grappling hook attached to a thick cable hanging from the helicopter to the ground. On the surface, soldiers were seen grabbing the hook and then quickly securing it to a ring on the side of one of the bins. Next a mechanized retraction device hoisted the cargo onto the copter.

"Although this might appear to be an innocent salvage operation," the narrator intoned, "ladies and gentlemen, you are, in fact, witnessing the retrieval of living, breathing human beings, innocent men and women, who have been snatched from their small rural towns, villages, and farms, and are in the process of being transported by these American-made helicopters to the interrogation centers I alluded to earlier."

Matt shivered, trying to imagine what it would be like to be kidnapped from your home—probably at night, probably at gunpoint—sealed in a small cylindrical container, encased in pitch blackness, rolled or carried into a nearby field, attached to a hook and cable assembly, and then violently hoisted skyward, swinging wildly in the breeze, suspended God-knows-how-high above the ground, expecting at any minute to plunge to a sudden, splattering death. Instead, you were lifted onto the deck of a foreign flying machine and conveyed to a fate that, in the end, could conceivably be worse than death.

The SDS spokesman, the narrator in the tie-dyed T-shirt reappeared, peered intently into the camera, the arresting nature of his gray eyes apparent despite the poor quality of the tape, and reported, "Last summer two U.S. congressman, Augustus Hawkins and William Anderson, were permitted to visit what was billed as a South Vietnam Prison. We believe this facility also served as one of the CIA Interrogation Centers. Accompanying them was an aide, a public safety advisor, and an interpreter, who happened to be an American. For our sake, it turns out that this interpreter was also an advocate of prison reform. As a result of his covert efforts, we were able to secure this highly classified footage."

The scene shifted to a clearing in the woods. The group approached the compound in a trio of army jeeps. They were met at the gate by a South Vietnam officer. The narrator identified him as the warden, Colonel Nguyen Van Ve. The congressional aide handed the Colonel a list of prisoners the congressmen wanted to interview. The small man, his mustache bold and black, nodded. He then led the visitors toward a small building flying both American and South Vietnamese flags. But before they reached the structure, the interpreter, who had split off from the group, called them over. The congressmen, over Van Ve's heated protest, joined the interpreter near a woodpile at the edge of what looked like a vegetable garden. The disturbance prompted a guard to open a door hidden behind the woodpile.

"What you will witness now is a set of what the Vietnamese call tiger cages, stone compartments five feet wide, nine feet long, and six feet high."

Access to the cages was apparently gained by ascending a set of steps that led to a catwalk. The image that came into focus through the parallel iron grates turned Matt's stomach.

What he witnessed was up to five men shackled to the floor of each cage. From the welts on their naked bodies, the sores crusting like craters on their exposed skin, it was obvious that they'd all been beaten and mutilated. Their legs seemed withered, their faces gaunt. Matt was reminded of pictures he'd seen in his high school world history text of Nazi Concentration Camp survivors.

The prisoners noticed the American congressman staring down at them and, like human crabs, scuttled across the earthen floor. Most begged for food and water. Some pleaded for mercy. Several were crying, emitting pitiful, wailing sounds that seemed other-worldly. The interpreter translated. They were starved and tortured. A few of the more articulate prisoners pointed to buckets of lime set above each cage and complained how the contents of these containers were frequently dumped on their heads.

After a few moments of this interaction, Colonel Van Ve managed to hustle the visitors back along the catwalk and out the door. He barked an order to the guard in Vietnamese and then escorted the group toward the command hut, trying to explain away as much as he could on the way.

"In the interest of accuracy," the narrator commented, "I must report that the Colonel denied everything. He claimed that the lime was for whitewashing the walls and the prisoners were evil people who deserved their punishment because of being traitors. We, of course, are more inclined to believe the evidence of our own eyes. These were innocent farmers and villagers who had been kidnapped from their homes and spirited away to CIA endorsed torture chambers."

Matt, his stomach churning, couldn't watch any more. He pressed the power button and the screen went blank. Grotesque images of those pitiful human beings, a collection of stick figures, horribly maimed and mutilated, emaciated and diseased, lingered in his mind for a long time. These were innocent victims of a terrorist campaign conceived by the American intelligence community and carried out by an agency in which his father was a director. Which, in his mind, made Mathew Carson directly responsible for the carnage. Rather than being a patriotic hero, his father was a torturer and a murderer. Matt even wondered if the man, his father, felt justified, perhaps even ennobled, in this capacity.

"I was horrified and appalled," Matt told Carmen as they passed into northern Maryland. "Up until then, despite the liberal rhetoric I had been fed my whole freshman year at CMU, I still wanted to give my father the benefit of the doubt. I'd analyzed the war effort from his point of view, like a military strategist supporting the campaign, believing that we were obligated to stop the spread of Communism before it overran the entire Far East. But what I witnessed on that video negated whatever rationalizations I had been conjuring. This was government-authorized mayhem. And the victims were innocent farmers and villagers."

"And that's when you stopped talking to him?" Carmen asked. Matt nodded.

"Did you ever mention the tape?"

"I was planning to. But I couldn't find an opening before I returned to school. Midway through the fall term I left for Canada."

"It's been a long time."

"Almost sixteen years."

"Why now?"

Matt thought the answer was obvious. But he verbalized it just the same. "I want to get Lila back."

His tale concluded, Matt leaned back and watched the taillights of the cars in front of him. Despite his usual need to be in control, he was content to let the detective drive.

Meanwhile, the stress of the last few days was taking its toll. While closing his eyes for a moment, an image of his father came to mind. Broad shouldered with close-cropped gray-black hair, a protruding jaw, and pale blue eyes that seemed to see right into his soul, the man had been bigger than life to him his entire childhood. It was easy to imagine him commanding the respect and admiration of the hardcore professionals he supervised; the intellectuals, the strategists, the scientists, the spies. Working himself up in the organization, he'd been culled from a cadre of crack, young attorneys, fresh out of law school, enticed away from western Pennsylvania and relocated in northern Virginia like some highly recruited college athlete.

All his life, most of what he did had been cloaked in secrecy. Even his family was sheltered from the sensitive nature of his work. All Matt knew was that his father helped keep the greatest nation on earth safe. That's what made it easy to be proud of him.

But even the shiniest armor eventually tarnishes. Initially, the blemishes were modest, bluish stains prompted by comments from high school classmates parroting their liberal parents, espousing arguments against the war, sloughing off the threat of Communism, pronouncing skepticism of the Cold War drama. At first Matt felt compelled to dispute these remarks, holding fast to the party line, recounting the same right wing rhetoric he'd so often heard at home. But eventually, the logic of the left wing radicals took a foothold in his impressionable conscience. And as he gradually made more and more concessions to their peace-now position, he started to question the validity of his father's stance. Not surprisingly his father's notion of a military career for him seemed incongruous with his new state of mind. Dressing in uniform, playing war games, devising strategies of how to lead other men not much younger than himself into battle was no longer appropriate. Appreciating these incongruencies, he began searching for another career.

Matt dozed. Skimming the surface of sleep he reminisced about how, as the reborn adolescent, he began exploring alternatives to military service. His strong suits had always been math and science. He considered a career in technology, possibly aero-space engineering. He always liked visiting Pittsburgh. His grandparents still lived there. There was a great technical school there. He applied to CMU and was accepted. When he shared this development with his father, the CIA director was far from supportive.

From the iron and brass chandelier soft, yellow light poured down onto the oval table now festooned with Mother's favorite white linen. Fine china and Waterford crystal adorned the four place-settings. It was a special Friday night dinner. The head of the household was home.

The four family members passed around plates of potatoes, vegetables, and bread. Matt's twelve year-old sister, Quincy, returned from the kitchen. Leaning over she tickled his neck with her new feather earrings. Raising his shoulder to his ear he said, "Stop that," then smiled at the way she teased him.

Mathew Carson Jr. sat at the head of the table sawing through a thick, New York porterhouse. The knot of his red paisley tie was loose, his white fly-away collar spread at the neck. Silence hung over the square-shaped room like a mist. There was little conversation at the dinner table unless he initiated it.

Glancing up from his plate, his steely gaze fixed on his only son. The dark-haired man commented, "Matt, I was over at the Pentagon today and ran into General Stillhouser. He mentioned that West Point is still waiting for your application. I thought you handled that last month. Mother told me she wrote a check for the fee." Mathew Carson's eyes followed his fork as it collected a pile of peas. "Well, young man. What's with the application? Did you send it or not? It's embarrassing when I have to make up excuses for my son after assuming he's done what he said he would."

"I pitched it," came Matt's reply in little more than a hoarse whisper. He was staring at his plate, his poised fork seemingly frozen in place.

"You did what?" his father inquired, his voice rising.

"I said," Matt replied, this time a little louder, "I pitched it."

"You pitched it! Why the hell would you do a thing like that? I thought we decided you'd enroll at the Academy in September. That's why I went to all that trouble of talking to Senator Cramdon."

"We didn't decide anything," Matt clarified. "West Point was your idea. Remember?"

"Wait a minute, Mathew." Matt hated when his father addressed him by his formal first name. "Ever since you were in grammar school you've been telling me how you wanted to be a soldier. When it came time to apply, we agreed that since it was relatively close to home, West Point would be perfect. What happened to all those plans?"

"I changed my mind."

"You changed your mind," Mathew Carson repeated. "Just like that."

"That's right, Father, I don't want to be a soldier anymore. I've decided to do something else with my life."

"Is that so? Well, isn't this an unpleasant development? And when did this change of heart occur?"

"A while ago," Matt said stammering. "I just didn't mention it until now."

"If I hadn't brought up the subject, you wouldn't have mentioned it tonight, either." The Director set down his utensils and leaned toward his son. "And what makes you think I'm going to go along with your unilateral decision? There's a tradition in this family you have an obligation to uphold. Your grandfather was a soldier in World War I. I fought the Germans in World War II."

"And I suppose you want me to get killed fighting gooks in Vietnam or maybe Russians in World War III, if I make it that long? Is that what you want?"

"Oh," the CIA Deputy Chief replied. "So, that's it," Turning to his wife, who'd long since stopped eating and was sitting upright with her hands in her lap and her eyes on her hands. "Well, Lorraine, it looks like we've raised a coward here."

Matt, with moisture collecting around his eyes, looked away. This was just the type of assessment his father would reach, the exact opposite of what he needed. Anytime he tried to take a stand, make a decision on his own, display maturity and self-direction, his father would invariably cut him down. And so, while longing to be strong in his father's eyes, he always ended up appearing feeble.

"Now, Mathew," his mother was saying, "Our son's just trying to work things out for himself. Maybe he really isn't cut out for the military. He has other interests you know."

"Were you aware of this decision, Lorraine?"

"Yes," his mother admitted. "We discussed the matter."

"And you kept this all from me?"

"Not really." Her pale blue eyes managed to meet his. "I thought it was appropriate for Matt to be the one to tell you."

"Or have me drag it out him."

The six-foot tall CIA director stood up and began pacing. As his legs scissored past one another Matt heard his baggy blue pants whisper. His black wing-tipped shoes crunched the brown pile carpet. Finally, he paused. With his arms folded, he raised one hand raised to his chin and inquired, "And what may I ask is the nature of this alternative interest, oh my many-talented son?"

Despite the coolness of the late-March evening Matt felt his cheeks burning. Flushed, with tiny beads of sweat collecting on his forehead, he felt like a prisoner perspiring under interrogation lamps. He suspected that his father savored this kind of interaction, the Grand Inquisitor, no doubt having played the role a thousand times in a hundred places before. It was at times like this that he despised him. Determined not to cower he replied, "I'm not cut out for the military, Father. I like to design things and see them built. I'm going to a technical school, probably for mechanical engineering or even aeronautics."

The older man resumed his pacing. Once or twice he ran his broad palm through his close-cropped hair. "It's all well and good that you're interested in design and construction, Mathew. But how will mechanical engineering serve your country?"

"I don't know," Matt replied slowly. "Maybe it won't."

And just like that, Mathew Carson Jr. had no further questions for his son that evening. And, for several day after that as well.

"Hey, Sleeping Beauty." A voice called to Matt from a distance. "Wake up. We just crossed into Maryland. I'm gonna need my navigator."

Matt opened his eyes. The light took him by surprise. As his surroundings came into focus, he saw that the detective had stopped at a service station. "We crossed the Pennsylvania-Maryland border about ten minutes ago. I just saw a billboard advertising this restaurant in Deep Creek that's supposed to be about fifteen miles further south. Are we that close?"

Matt rubbed the sleep out of eyes. Turning to Carmen he said, "I suspect. But I'm as lost as you are. In all the years I've been coming here, it's never been from the north. You drove down 219. I've always headed west outta D.C."

"Well, you figure it out," the detective delegated. "I gotta take a leak. And while you're at it, pump us some gas. We're down to a quarter-tank."

Carmen eased out of the Volvo and a few seconds later disappeared around the side of the building. Matt opened the passenger door. If he was still suffering from any lingering somnolence, the blast of sub-freezing, lakeside air obliterated all traces of that. Hopping in place, he tended to the fueling. After the pump clicked off, he slid the nozzle into its harness, checked the total, and hurried over to the Mini-mart. Inside, he approached the cashier, a teen-ager half hidden behind an assortment of candy racks and a Maryland lottery display. He was about to ask the kid about local maps when he saw them stacked on the counter. Choosing one that seemed detailed enough for their purposes, he bought it along with the gas. While waiting for his change, he saw Carmen get back into the Volvo.

"So whaddya think?" Carmen asked as Matt, the unfolded the map spread across his lap, studied the routes.

"There," he said pointing, "when I used to come with my family, we took I 70 to US 40 then dropped down 220 from Cumberland. We're north and west, heading down 219. If I remember correctly, the cabin is at the end of White Oak Drive on Beckman's Peninsula." Matt leaned over and studied the region. "See," he said. "There it is. White Oak Drive."

"Great," Carmen agreed, "but can you get us there?"

"Shouldn't be a problem," Matt rejoined confidently.

A few moments later, they were back on the road, a black asphalt, two-lane highway, badly in need of repaving. The night, dark except for a smattering of pinpoint stars, seemed unusually black. Matt knew it was due to the paucity of houses, businesses, and more specifically, streetlamps. They passed a sign for a restaurant called, The Black Bear.

"Hungry?" Carmen asked

"Even if I was," Matt replied, "I doubt if anything's open."

"But, it's only ten-thirty."

"That's about an hour and half after most of these joints shut down for the night," Matt informed him. "And that's in the summer. It's even worse in the winter when only a handful of people still live around the lake."

"I shudda figured as much," Carmen grumbled.

They drove along in silence, Carmen concentrating on the road, Matt tracking their progress on the map. After passing a small town called McHenry they reached the northern edge of Deep Creek Lake, a narrow irregularly-shaped body of water with a half-dozen spindly appendages that sliced into the surrounding woodland. The western shore of the lake bordered the state park. The rest of the area was zoned for small businesses, homes, and lodging. After crossing a short concrete bridge they passed several old-fashioned motels, their neon signs announcing their presence, a series of single-story structures recessed by the lake on the left and partway up a gentle hillside on the right.

"Pay attention," Matt cautioned, "our turn's coming up on the left. It's where the road curves. The road's called Glendale." They crested a hill and passed two more motels. Then, just after a yellow sign warning that the road bore to the right, Matt saw the marker. "There it is."

Carmen slowed into the turning lane and made the left without stopping. If it was dark before, now, away from the main road, it was pitch black. Slowing to fifteen miles-per-hour they weaved through dense woodland, only a rare house light visible through the trees. Then the trees receded and they came upon a one lane bridge.

"This is the Glendale Bridge," Matt confirmed. Glancing past Carmen he saw the lake's inky black surface, perhaps a couple hundred yards wide. Densely packed trees bordered both banks. On his side the corridor of water seemed narrower, with lights from a few cottages visible along each shore. "The road forks up ahead. Bear to your right. We'll be turning at the first intersection." After a half-mile more on the curving, ascending thoroughfare, they came to the crossroad. It was unmarked.

"You sure this is it?"

"Not positive," Matt conceded, "but it looks right."

"Okay," Carmen said and made the right.

For the next couple miles, they stayed on the narrow road, which was more like a path, passing through more dense woodland which concealed several dozen cabins and small homes. A few of the driveways seemed more evident, with pop-up trailers and fishing boats parked on the gravel. Others were only marked by banks of dented, rusting mailboxes, assembled in irregular rows and highlighted by barely discernible labels. At one point, as they rounded a gentle curve, the trees receded, giving way to broad grassland on both sides of the road. The hillside on the left sloped gently down to the water. But as soon as they appeared, the meadows retreated again, replaced by more forest.

"If my map is accurate there should be two or three lanes cutting in from the left. Ignore them. My father's cabin is at the end of this road."

Carmen nodded, slowing the car down as the darkness engulfed them once again. As predicted, a series of narrow drives appeared on the driver's side. Carmen held steady. About a half mile further up ahead things ended abruptly.

"I think we're here," Matt declared. Carmen pulled off onto the shoulder of the road and cut the engine.

"You 'think,'" Carmen repeated.

"We're here," Matt claimed more confident this time, "although, it's been fifteen years since the last time I was here."

"Well, I hope you're right," Carmen added, sounding skeptical. "How do you get to the house?"

"There should be a path up there to the left. It leads to the front door. Now that I think of it, the driveway's about fifty yards back. We must've missed it. But the path isn't that long. We can walk it from here."

Carmen nodded. "Before we get there," he said putting on his gloves and buttoning his overcoat, "is there anything I need to know about your father."

"Only that he's a no-nonsense son of a bitch."

"That much I cudda figured out for myself."

Matt grinned. Then, almost simultaneously, they opened their respective doors and set out into the wintry air.

Chapter 27

Matt was glad he'd worn his down parka as he trudged alongside the detective. The night air was frigid. Dried leaves and small twigs crunched underfoot. He'd never been to the cabin in winter, his school holidays were spent skiing in Pennsylvania at Seven Springs or sometimes, if his father was fortunate enough to have the time off, down in Boca or on a cruise. From what he recalled, the only time his father used this place was to entertain his close buddies during hunting weekends in November. Since college, Matt was never interested in joining his father on these little outings. Besides, he was never asked.

While reflecting on this family folklore, Matt was startled by Carmen's outburst. "Oh shit! I bet that German bastard's here, too." Matt watched the detective draw his service revolver. "See that Mercedes over there? Is it your father's?"

Matt turned to where the detective was pointing. Fifteen yards away a late model silver or gray Mercedes was parked by a stand of trees. "I doubt it. At least Mom never mentioned it. Besides, my old man would only buy American. And never a car made in Germany."

"That's what I figured," Carmen commented. "Let's get back to the Volvo. There's stuff in the trunk I'm gonna need."

Although Matt was anxious to inquire further, he thought better of it. Instead, he hurried behind Carmen, who, for a man of his stature, was moving rather quickly. By the time the psychiatrist caught up, the detective was bent behind the Volvo, the trunk lid up.

Glancing up he asked, "You wearing gloves?" Matt nodded. "What kind?" "Leather."

"Good." Carmen replied. "Ever fire a gun?" Matt shook his head. "Well, there's a first time for everything. Here." Carmen then placed a sleek, silver revolver in Matt's gloved hand. The physician was about to voice his philosophical objections to handling weapons but intuitively sensed the gravity of the situation and refrained.

"Did you mention that your father's hunting cabin is sometimes used as a safe house? Is the property monitored with surveillance equipment?"

"I'm not sure. But knowing my father, probably."

"So they might already know we're here."

"Who might know?"

Carmen ignored the question. Instead he instructed, "This time, when we approach the house, we'll head down the driveway and head for the trees on the far side of that cut-out."

"Carmen," Matt asked, "what's this all about?"

"I think I know where Lila is. And she's got lots o' company."

With the mention of his charge's name, Matt's chest constricted with fear for her safety and longing to have her back in his arms. He tightened his grip on the revolver. This was more than he'd bargained for when he offered to enlist his father's help in finding her. And in some sense, what he'd hoped for. Snapping a clip of bullets in the handle of his own firearm, Carmen ordered, "Let's go!"

The two men set off back up the road, in the opposite direction from where they'd just come. About half a football field away they came upon the driveway, a rudimentary path of hard-packed earth impregnated with loose and embedded gravel. Keeping close behind the detective, Matt could feel the larger stones bite through the soles of his hiking boots. Moving furtively from one clump of trees to another they eventually reached the Mercedes. Carmen paused by the rear of the vehicle, flipped on his pocket light, and checked the plate.

"Just as I thought," he mumbled.

"Whose is it?" Matt whispered.

"It once belonged to Lila's father," Carmen commented. This disclosure heightened Matt's confusion. How did Harvey Richman's old German sedan get to his father's lake house? Before he could inquire further, Carmen added, "and now I think a guy named Kruger owns it."

"Kruger? Who the hell is Kruger?"

"You'll find out soon enough." And that was the end of the discussion.

Utilizing brisk hand signals, Carmen instructed Matt to follow. At the house, they paused by the front deck. The detective gestured to Matt to stay.

Crouching low, he hurried across the narrow opening, then along the base of the deck. A set of five steps led to the platform. Instead of using them, he hoisted himself up onto the wooden surface and in a rolling motion slipped under the wooden rail. Still moving in a modified crouch, he maneuvered his way to the front wall of the cabin and positioned himself between the left front window and the door.

As instructed, Matt stayed by the side of the house. At Carmen's signal, he followed the detective's path to the front wall. Soon they were crouched next to each other.

Carmen inched closer to the window. After placing a cautionary finger to his lips, he peered inside at what Matt knew was the downstairs family room, a combination living-dining room with the kitchen toward the back and a stair-case to the second floor almost out of sight to the right. Carmen grunted as if acknowledging something to himself. Next he motioned to Matt to take a look. Utilizing a slick spinning motion to pivot around the short stocky detective, he ended up flush with the window's edge. Easing his head slightly forward he saw enough of what had transpired inside to make his stomach turn.

From this skewed, tangential vantage point, the first thing Matt noticed were the two bodies lying at right angles to one another by the inside of the cabin's side wall. Both corpses displayed extra eye sockets from forehead-level bullet holes. Ever-so-carefully craning his neck further, Matt managed to make out the leather reading chair set at an angle facing the fireplace and the enter-tainment unit which occupied most of the back wall. In that chair, bound and gagged, sat Mathew Carson Jr.

Pressing his ear against the edge of the window pane, Matt could make out a voice. Low pitched and gruff, it had a German accent. Matt suspected this was the man Carmen had called, Kruger. Matt was desperate to survey more of the room. Carmen restrained him. Obediently, he eased back against the detective's side and awaited further instructions. Speaking so softly as to be barely audible, Carmen asked, "Is there a back door to this place?"

Matt nodded. "Off the kitchen."

"How about ground level windows?"

"There's one by that door and two on the far side of the house. Why?"

Ignoring the question, Carmen instructed, "Give me five minutes, then cre-ate some sort of commotion out here."

"Like what?" Matt said, immediately feeling stupid for asking.

Carmen looked left, then right. Finally he turned to Matt and with hand gestures, instructed him on how to crouch under the window, raise his arm high, and slap the window with his open palm. After that, they synchronized their watches. A moment later, Carmen was swallowed up by the shadows on the far side of the deck.

Matt soon appreciated how seconds could seem like minutes and minutes like a goddamn eternity. As his heart pounded forcefully, he felt every moment. Periodically, he glanced down at his *Polaris* digital watch. Its backlight could be activated by the push of a button. But he held the revolver in one hand and had a leather glove on the other. Noticing a rusty, three-penny nail near the front wall, he reached over and grasped it between his thumb and index finger. Now he could keep track of the time.

At the four and a half minute mark, he prepared himself. The window sill was low, so low that he couldn't crouch under it without exposing the top of his head. Instead, he slid down onto his back and shimmied under the ledge. Rolling over onto his side, he raised his arm in a way that his palm faced the window pane. Glancing at his watch, he noticed with horror that he'd taken about thirty seconds too long. Excitedly, he began banging on the glass.

At first, he didn't think he was making enough noise. Suddenly, the bark of a handgun was followed almost simultaneously by the sound of shattering glass. A shower of shards came pouring down. As he shielded his eyes a few pieces glanced off his cheeks and lips. Most bounced harmlessly off his parka.

More commotion erupted from within the house. Through the brand new aperture in the window, Matt heard Carmen, shout, "The game's up Kruger! Drop your weapon!"

Assuming that the detective had the situation under control, Matt raised himself high enough to glance over the window ledge. A burly man in a thick wool winter coat was standing roughly in the center of the family room brandishing an ugly looking revolver at arm's length. Carmen was positioned by the kitchen counter, his arm also outstretched, his handgun raised. Matt expected the assailant to set down his weapon and surrender. Instead, the German pivoted and fired. The bullet winged the detective in the left shoulder, its impact spinning him clockwise. Quickly righting himself, Carmen returned the fire. One of the bullets hit the mark, entering the German's chest with a soft thud. Kruger jerked backward. While doing so, he attempted to fire again. But before he could squeeze the trigger, Carmen caught him with another shot, this one square in the right shoulder. The German's report soared harmlessly into a cabin's ceiling crossbeam. Then Kruger lost his balance and crumpled to his knees. With his injured limb dangling, Carmen moved forward. He seemed to be considering a third dose of lead for the staggering German. But before he could deliver it, Kruger buckled forward and fell face first onto the cabin's hard wood floor.

The pain in Carmen's shoulder was worse than anything he'd ever experienced. It was like being branded with a hot iron. But there was no time to dwell on his own discomfort. A man was bound and gagged a few feet from him. Hopefully a young woman was somewhere else in this god-forsaken hunting cabin.

As he turned to regard the captive, a glint of metal from up on the second level landing caught his eye. A nine-millimeter Beretta crossed his mind. Just before the firearm barked he ducked. The deadly projectile whizzed past his ear. Seeking the only refuge he could find, he dove under the massive rectangular table that filled much of the dining area. In rapid succession three more bullets imbedded themselves into the thick wood. That bastard had a partner, Carmen fumed. Too much of a pussy to do the job himself.

But the logic of this reality didn't escape the detective. The German had, after all, in this attempt to recover the young Richman woman, pitted himself against a seasoned CIA director and whoever had been conscripted to help detain their victim. Glancing at the two fallen bodies by the far wall, Carmen acknowledged that the Director's recruits had not fared well. Returning to the shooter, Carmen tried to get a better line on his position. Upon entering the cabin from the kitchen area he'd glanced upward and noticed the staircase led to the second level. He thought he recalled a rail up there too.

He's got me pinned. That's for damn sure. If I move I'm dead.

Resigned for the moment to his restricted state of affairs, Carmen stayed put, He hoped the stalemate would encourage his attacker to make the next move. He didn't have long to wait. A shot rang out, then another, both hitting the table. But to Carmen's trained ear they sounded like they'd come from a slightly different location. The shooter was on the move, probably inching along the upstairs corridor, working from right to left, heading toward the top of the staircase. Or maybe worse, there might be two.

Carmen shrunk back a bit, hoping to cut down the angle. He heard the foot-falls on the steps, then the black boots appeared—paratrooper's, perhaps military surplus stuff, the kind anyone could pick up at the local Army Navy Store. The bastard's probably wearing fatigues, too, Carmen thought wryly. Coming into view, Carmen's saw his prediction realized—ebony BDU's and a black web belt. And he was big too, his torso seeming to go on forever.

Carmen was tempted to risk a shot. Another barrage of revolver fire sent him reeling. A few more feet and the shooter could shoot at him under the table. Reacting, more than acting, Carmen grabbed the two table legs which flanked him like pillars, pulled, then lifted. The huge table tilted onto its edge. The move must have surprised the shooter. Glancing over the near side, Carmen saw him hesitate. He also saw the shaved head, the SS tattoo on the side of the neck and the hate-filled expression of what only could be a member of the Skinhead cult of the White Supremacist movement.

Makes perfect sense to me, Carmen reflected as he reached up and took an awkward shot at the racist. The bullet went high and wide, hitting the top of the front door.

Carmen's blast was met by another flurry. Then, before the detective could position himself better, the Neo-Nazi rushed the table. Carmen felt himself being shoved toward the rear wall, driven like a mound of dirt by a bulldozer. Despite bracing himself for the impact, the force with which he finally hit left him dazed. This reality was compounded by the fact that his attacker seemed to have every intention of crushing him to death between two solid wooden surfaces.

Pain gave way to breathlessness. Carmen started to flail. He started slipping into a semi-conscious stupor. Then, in a panic, he anticipated the inevitability of suffocation. He heard the next shot. He assumed it was the last sound he would ever hear. But instead of blacking out, he started to revive. Gradually the pressure against his chest eased. Coincident with that, another body fell to the floor. No longer pinned like a slab of protoplasm between the two planks, Carmen's toneless frame collapsed into a heap.

The next thing Carmen knew, he was being forced to drink something out of a dented metal cup. Willing his eyes to remain open, he glanced up and saw Matt peering down at him. His head was cradled in the younger man's lap.

"What the hell happened?" Carmen managed to croak after swallowing the flavorless liquid. It was water.

"We got 'em, partner," Matt replied.

"'We?'"

"Yep. You got Kruger. And I nailed that damn skinhead before he crushed you to death."

"You actually fired that gun I gave you?"

"Isn't that what it was for?" Carmen just nodded. "You think you can sit up?" Matt added.

Carmen nodded again and made a feeble attempt at complying. On the third try he was able to lean up against the back wall without being supported. He then managed to glance around the room. The two of them were alone.

Answering the detective's implicit inquiry Matt commented, "Father's upstairs checking on Lila."

"I thought you'd want to be the one to do that," Carmen said, his voice still a little hoarse.

"I had my partner to think of first."

The warm feeling this sentiment engendered seemed to help ease the detective's pain.

Chapter 28

I t was almost twenty-four more hours before the surviving members of a group of individuals who'd found their way to a hunting cabin in the woods of Deep Creek, Maryland were able to reassemble once again. It was also New Year's Eve. As the world prepared to usher in the last decade of the second millennium, these survivors sat before a blazing fire in the lodge's living room feeling thankful to be alive. In the spirit of completion, they decided to sort out the complex set of circumstances that had brought them together in the first place.

"How's the shoulder, Vitale?" Mathew Carson, Jr. asked as he took a sip of his drink. His son, Matt III, offering to play bartender, had just distributed beverages to the assemblage. The Director had opted for Canadian Club on the rocks. Matt had anticipated this. It had been his father's favorite for as long as he could recall.

"Better, now that the percocet's kicking in," Carmen told the retired Agency man. The detective rested on the Lazyboy recliner, a blanket on his lap, his bandaged shoulder supported by an immobilizer. Seeing him like that, Matt recalled the forty-five minute drive the four of them had taken to the Garrett County Memorial Hospital late the previous night.

There, in nearby Oakland, Maryland, after an obstinate ER doc had insisted on performing the initial assessment of Carmen's gunshot wound, Bill Clements, a general surgeon living in Mountain Lake Park, and a college fraternity brother of Matt Junior, arrived. Wheeling Carmen into the Same Day Surgery Center, and with the help of the circulating RN on call, he neatly extracted a blunted, flat metal-jacketed, nine-millimeter bullet from deep within the detective's shoulder. Next he stitched together a severed deltoid muscle tendon, before aggressively cleansing the area and suturing the wound shut. Later that night, after the commotion had died down, the detective's chart, a handwritten document which had never been officially entered into the institution's permanent data bank, mysteriously disappeared.

"That brandy should help, too," the former CIA director commented. "It's from the Christian Brothers Grand Reserve, a gift I received when I retired from The Agency in eighty-six."

"It's an honor that you're sharing it with me, Director."

"It's the least I could do for someone who just saved my life."

As if deflecting the acknowledgement, Carmen said, "Don't forget your son's part in that effort."

"Oh, I haven't," the older man commented cryptically.

Actually, throughout the long day, Matt had already received his share of praise for neutralizing the ogre-like Skinhead with one well-placed shot from his vantage point outside the shattered front window. But that didn't mute the persistent image of a stocky mass of blind hatred clad in black fatigues and paratrooper boots bearing down on his friend Carmen.

After reaching over to set his tumbler on the coffee table, a heavily lacquered, smoothly beveled tree stump that supported a thick, elliptically shaped piece of tinted glass, the retired Agency man sat back, directed his piercing gaze at the young woman sitting on a sling-back chair near the fireplace and inquired, "And how's our little hostage doing?"

His son, now finished with beverage rounds, eased onto his knees beside her. Putting an affectionate arm around Lila's shoulders, he answered for her. "She seems to be getting along just fine, Father," and was about to add, "no thanks to you," but thought better of it. Grudgingly he acknowledged that, to some extent he, on some level, should feel indebted to his father for Lila's safety, having gotten to her before Kruger.

"That's good," the Director replied without sarcasm. "So we've somehow established that, besides a nonfatal wound to our Pittsburgh detective and some bumps and bruises to the rest of us, we've survived this ordeal intact. Now, perhaps we can sort out the gory details." Matt watched his father survey the occupants of the room. Their noncommittal facial expressions seemed to grant him tacit approval. Matt, for one, was anxious to hear about those details. "Why don't you start us off, Detective?" the father suggested.

"Where?" Carmen asked.

"At the beginning, of course."

255

Carmen nodded. Before embarking on his part of the story, however, he reached over and took another sip of the Christian Brothers. Matt wondered if it was a trick of the lighting or the detective's proximity to the fire, but his oval-shaped olive-skinned complexion seemed to blush a little as he swallowed. Then he settled back, took a deep breath, and began. And from the manner in which the chronology was catalogued, the events described, and the characters characterized, Matt sensed he'd related the story several times before.

It all began, Carmen reported, with the Murdock Farms explosion at the Rosenberg mansion on the eve of the Jewish Day of Atonement. Although Carmen seemed intent on sparing them the emotional upheaval he'd felt personally after discovering one of the victims was a woman he'd loved, the catch in his voice probably betrayed his true feelings. Then, after completing the description of the crime scene, Carmen's demeanor reached a more even keel. In his best professional manner, he described his subsequent investigation, the interviews at the hospital and the synagogue, and how the threads of evidence started pointing away from an accident and toward the fact that the explosion may have been caused by some incendiary device. Next, he recounted how the trail had led him to the burning cabin in the Laurel Mountains, inside of which the dead body of Malcolm Rosenberg's close friend and confidant, Abe Cohen. In passing, he hinted at the roadblocks set in his path by his own police department, culminating with his Chief, encouraged by what Carmen loosely called, The Feds, shutting down his investigation.

Matt glanced over at his father, expecting a reaction. He detected none. He, like Carmen, was hoping that his old man would eventually offer to clarify the CIA's role, if any, in the cover-up. It was at this point that the Director spoke up. "Do you happen to have your notes with you, Detective?" he inquired politely.

"Since you explicitly requested it, I brought them in from the car this morning," Carmen reported.

"Then, first of all, could you please tell us more about the dead man you found in that Laurel Mountain cabin fire?"

Carmen flipped through the weathered pages of his little notebook. As he did Matt couldn't help comparing the scene to a courtroom with the detective on the stand and his father playing the part of the prosecutor."

"As I alluded to before," Carmen reiterated, "his name was Abe Cohen, a close friend of Malcolm Rosenberg, a member of Rodef Shalom Synagogue, and a strong supporter of the Jewish Community. He and Rosenberg's relationship went back a good many years."

"Any idea how long?" the Director probed.

"Possibly to World War II. I've written something down here about the two of them landing in the second wave at Normandy, then being part of the push across France and Germany."

"Any reference to General Omar Bradley?"

"As a matter of fact, there is," Carmen replied calmly, apparently not surprised that the former CIA director seemed to already know some of the answers to his own questions. "Cohen did mention that Rosenberg was part of Bradley's division during the march through northern Germany."

"That is accurate, Detective. And so was Cohen."

Carmen's face seemed to register surprise, then comprehension. Another piece of the puzzle had fallen into place. "And how did you know that, Director?" he asked Matt's father

"You continue your story, Detective," Matt's father said evasively. "I'll fill in the details later."

"Fair enough," Carmen conceded. "What else do you want to know?"

"How about elaborating on the manuscript."

"Ah," Carmen replied, "the manuscript."

This part of the story took a while. Carmen began by describing the evening at the precinct building when the old woman shoved a package upon him then disappeared into the night. Taking what he soon discovered was Hans Reichman's personal memoir home, he related how he'd spent most of that night reading the incredible story of a young German patriot who had been recruited by the Nazis into the Hitler Youth Movement, moved through the ranks into officer training school, and was finally plucked out of his preferred professional path by an overprotective father and reassigned to a Polish work camp.

Although Carmen hadn't taken notes on Reichman's manuscript, the essence of the story was still vivid in his memory. Sparing the group some of the details, he went on to paraphrase the author's description of Lumbartów, with its overcrowded barracks, inhuman torture chambers, and mind-manipulating interrogation rooms. He then described how, as the threat of the Soviet army approached from the east, the SS had chosen to eliminate any sign that the camp ever existed, killing, then burying all of the prisoners there in the process.

257

"And where did Reichman go from the bulldozed remains of Lumbartów, Detective?" Matt's father inquired.

"If I recall correctly, after a forced march westward, he hooked up with the Wehrmacht outside of Warsaw. That was when the Russians sacrificed what was left of the Polish Army to the Nazis. After that, the Soviets rolled in to clean up the mess. Reichman, however, was wounded in the leg by a stray bullet and escaped in a Red Cross truck back to Berlin."

"Which is where we met," the former CIA director commented.

"What!" Carmen exclaimed. Matt, just as shocked, gasped. Carmen's next question was drowned out by the noise in Matt's head. Oh my God, he thought. My father knew Reichman during the war. But how? And how does that impact the rest of this?

"That's correct, Detective. I was an operative for the US intelligence community during the war, a member of an outfit called the OSS. In the late forties, it evolved into what we now know as the CIA. But back then we were just a bunch of cowboys, led by a charismatic guy called Big Bill Donovan, all of us hoping to toss as many wrenches in the Axis war machine as we could.

"In the spring of forty-five, just as Berlin was about to capitulate, we knew that the SS would be desperate to destroy whatever evidence there was of their complicity in the atrocities of Hitler's regime. Back then, although there was only an inkling of the magnitude of the Holocaust, we still appreciated that whatever we could do to stop those bastards from destroying valuable files and documents, the more leverage we'd have prosecuting them in the post-war period."

"And Reichman had plenty of experience with record-keeping," Carmen offered. "He spent a year in Berlin working with his father's people in the records department before being sent to Poland."

"Right you are, Detective."

"And those were the files he tried to destroy," Carmen continued.

"Yep. And that's when we intercepted him."

Carmen suddenly sat up straighter. "Director, that means you could be the person Reichman referred to as Sigma."

Mathew Carson, Jr. smiled. "We were really into Greek letters in those days. That's right, Detective, back in Germany during the war I was code-named Sigma. I was also the one who engineered Reichman's capture, then helped persuade him to flip his stripes. In one sense I took Reichman under my wing.

Since then, I've kept up with his life and times, privately, professionally, and politically."

"Well, now the puzzle pieces fit into a nice, neat picture," Carmen commented.

"Almost," the former CIA director clarified.

Matt, almost recovered from the shock of his father's revelation, was straining to follow the two men. Chiming in for the first time since he'd sat down two hours ago, he commented, "I get the connection between you and Reichman, Father. But why did he seem to have this vendetta against Rosenberg?"

His father smiled, then deferred the inquiry to Carmen. "Would you like to elaborate on that part of the story, Detective? Or should I?"

"Maybe it's time for you to take the wheel, Director. Remember, I got clunked in the head just as I started reading this part of the Reichman's tale."

"Fair enough," Matt's father agreed. Settling himself back in his seat, he looked vacantly toward the mounted deer head above the fireplace. "Let's see, it was a couple days after Reichman had agreed to join the Gehlan network. That's a referral to Gerhard Gehlan, a former Nazi who despised Hitler and whom Allen Dulles, one of the original members of the OSS, recruited into one of our counter-espionage networks during the Third Reich. After the war, he continued to operate in a similar capacity. With the new Soviet block an inevitability, we were still desperate for fresh operatives. We hoped Reichman would be one of them."

Matt glanced over at Carmen who was nodding appreciatively.

"But before we could transport Reichman to Gehlen's headquarters near Berne, Switzerland, he insisted on paying a visit to Hanover. That's where his wife and child were riding out the war on his in-laws' farm about ten miles north of the city. Normally, at this stage of conflict, it would have been a prohibitively dangerous excursion. But although our B52's were still sweeping through northern Germany, there wasn't much industry in Hanover, so they bypassed the region and targeted Berlin instead."

Sitting back and putting his feet up on the coffee table, the old man continued, "This is the part I remember like it was yesterday. When Reichman and I got off the train in Hanover the city was almost completely deserted. The streets and shops were empty. After wandering around for a while, we finally found a downtown tavern where a few local diehards were still holed up, content to guzzle beer and whine over the demise of their proud Fatherland.

"While we were sitting at a corner table discussing our options, this young farmhand—he couldn't have been more than seventeen—tow-headed and in over-alls, walked over. He said he recognized Reichman, and in this stumbling, stuttering voice proceeded to inform him that his wife and kid were dead, murdered by a band of American soldiers. While he was delivering the message, he took out a set of army dog tags and claimed they belonged to one of the perpetrators. He'd found them in the barn where the carnage had occurred, about twenty yards from the woman's body. It seems that before she was killed, Reichman's wife had also been raped. During the struggle she must've yanked the guy's tags off and flung 'em. He must've left in too much of a hurry to get them back."

Matt glanced over at Carmen. Silently, they acknowledged that this was the same story the detective had related while they were sitting in Matt's living room the day after Lila's disappearance.

"After that, we tried borrowing a car. It was over ten miles to the farm. But anything with a motor was busy transporting refugees eastward toward Berlin. How ironic. Although we were the good guys, the natives chose to flee right into the arms of the Reds. And they had the nerve to call themselves the superior race. Hah!"

The former CIA director paused to take another swallow. After setting the glass down again, he continued. "So we trudged along the abandoned street a couple more blocks. Finally, we came to what looked like the local smithy's shop. There we borrowed a weather-beaten buckboard and a mare that was probably too old to be much good to anybody. After that, like two homesteaders in a Wild West movie, we headed out to the farm."

"That's about where I was interrupted," Carmen interjected. "I wish I had got a better look at the asshole who clunked me. But now that I've seen Kruger up close and personal, I wouldn't be surprised if he was the guy."

"I wouldn't be, either," the former CIA director agreed. "Once he knew you had the manuscript, the last thing he would have wanted was to have Reichman's story made public."

Matt found this curious. "Why's that?" he asked.

"Because of the anti-German sentiment it would have fomented. Remember, with the Berlin Wall coming down, suddenly the Russians weren't looking like the bad guys anymore. And with Kruger so deeply involved in the white supremacist movement, the last thing he needed was an anti-German backlash from a vendetta that happened almost forty-five years ago."

"It sounds like you were aware of Kruger all along."

"We've been tracking him ever since he made contact with Reichman."

"Interesting."

"It's more than interesting, Matt. It gets personal. As recently as the late seventies and early eighties, our now-deceased former Nazi helped organize and run a training camp for young dissidents that was located just thirty miles from here. In fact, your girlfriend Lila spent a few summers being indoctrinated there. Didn't you, my dear?" Mathew Carson, Jr. flashed Lila an ingratiating smile. She returned it in kind. Matt, witnessing this pseudo-intimate interaction, realized that what his father had said was true. "Anyway, Kruger was already having trouble recruiting members for his various hate groups at the time. He didn't need any more negative publicity."

"Even if the motive was revenge for such a heinous crime?" Matt argued.

"With the way the liberal press spins topical items these days, it's hard to predict how the story would have played. I suspect Kruger didn't want to find out."

"Which is also why he was so desperate to get Lila back," Matt postulated.

"No doubt," Carmen agreed.

"Getting back to the story," Mathew Jr. interjected, "we bounced around in that old buckboard for over two hours. Once we reached the farm, we contacted Isle's parents. They were pretty much still in shock over the incident. They did confirm the farmhand's story, however, adding the part about the rape. If Reichman was angry and upset before, now he was furious. Then we tracked down a pair of elderly brothers who lived on the farm next to theirs. They were the ones who'd found the victims. They helped bury the bodies in the family graveyard on a hillside near the main house."

"So what exactly did happen?" Matt asked curiously.

"Well, from what we could discern, a small band of American soldiers, probably four or five, did raid the farmhouse looking for food and water. While two or three stayed at the house with the older couple, the other two headed to the barn. There they found Reichman's wife and kid hiding. No one could be sure if she was raped by one or both. But what is indisputable was that both the wife and the four-year-old boy were then shot and killed."

The CIA director paused, allowing this harsh reality to settle in. Then he added, "I remember like it was yesterday standing next to Reichman at the gravesite on that cool, gray afternoon in early April, paying our respects to the dead. At one point I couldn't help but stare at him. There, etched on his almost boyish Aryan face, was a mixture of sorrow and rage so profound it seemed palpable. I tried to imagine how he was feeling and what I would have done if I were in his shoes. All I could get in touch with was blind hatred, a feeling of limitless fury. I have no doubt that that's what fueled his thirst for vengeance over those next forty years."

Silence hung over the gathering like a mist. For several moments no one spoke. Finally, it was Carmen who asked, "Any idea who any of the other American soldiers were?"

"We don't know about the guys who stayed in the farmhouse," Mathew Jr. commented impassively. "We're pretty sure that Abe Cohen went to the barn. And the dog tags belonged to Malcolm Rosenberg."

"That's what I thought," Carmen replied.

Chapter 29

It was several hours later, in the corner bedroom on the second floor of the hunting lodge, that Matt leaned back against the headboard with his hands interlaced behind his head and reflected on the day. Sex that evening with Lila had been wonderful, a passionate reunion of sorts after a few fretful nights apart. The rush of intimacy seemed to embody all the fear, lust, longing, and yes, love, that haunted them while they were apart. And while he usually slipped right off to sleep after such a delicious release, tonight the experience energized him. Glancing over at his beautiful mate, he expected to see her fast asleep. To his surprise, her eyes were wide open and she was regarding him with a warm, almost whimsical, expression on her face.

"What?" he said.

"I was just watching you, that's all."

"And what do you see?"

"The man I love."

Even if he sensed this intuitively, it gave him a thrill to hear her say it. He loved her, too, but had never been bold enough to express it. Or perhaps, he feared that the spoken word, on some level, would imply a commitment that he wasn't prepared to make. After all, how well did he really know this beautiful, mysterious young woman? Despite how much of her shrouded past had been uncovered, what was left concealed? After tonight's session with his father and Carmen, he'd learned about the horrible thing she'd done. What else was she was capable of?

"What?" It was her turn to inquire.

"Just thinking."

"About what?"

"About us. About you."

"What about me?"

"I was wondering who you are."

"You know who I am."

"Do I?"

"I thought you did." She turned and propped herself up on an elbow. "What would you like to know?"

Matt paused. He knew that if he posed the question, he'd be compelled to process, if not accept, the answer. Was he prepared for that? He decided that he was.

"How could you have done what you did?"

She hesitated. "You mean the bomb?" she finally replied, her voice so flat and devoid of emotion he wasn't sure she'd asked a question.

"I guess that's what I mean."

"Well, the answer is, I'm not sure."

This, of course, didn't make sense. Was she evading his inquiry?

"Well, then, what *do* you remember? What do you know?"

"I know that what I did was terribly wrong. It was a crime so horrible I can't believe I was the one who committed it."

"But you did."

"I know I did."

"But why?"

"Because it was part of my programming."

He was ready to cut her some slack. But this was too much. "Isn't that a cop-out," he challenged, "just a convenient way to avoid taking responsibility?"

"Matt," she said, her lovely blue eyes locking onto his, "you of all people should know better. You, at least have some sense what he did to me, how he used me, how he manipulated my mind."

"But you committed the act, Lila. On some level you have to own up to that."

"I know, Matt. And I do."

"Good."

She turned away, easing back down onto the mattress and staring at the ceiling for a while. After those few, weighted moments she whispered, "It's like I was play-acting in a dream. My body did horrible things. But I can't recall being mentally present for any of them."

"Like being in a trance?"

"Sort of," she agreed, "but with direction and purpose. It was as if I was fulfilling the culmination of a lifetime of instruction, training, and conditioning. I was this human instrument of destruction, not some random person performing a wanton act of violence. I know that doesn't justify it. But it may give you some insight into why I could follow through."

"Maybe," Matt replied, his tone non-judgmental.

"All right," she countered. "I suppose I deserved that. I suppose I deserve whatever happens to me from here on out."

"I wouldn't go that far," Matt cautioned. "Share how much you recall of what happened. I'll reserve judgment until you're done."

"Fair enough," she agreed, still on her back, still not looking at him.

Matt regarded the window across from the foot of the bed and noticed a faint glimmer of light peeking between the shutters. Was it the waning winter moon or had they been up most of the night?

"It was early October. I'd befriended Barry Rosenberg. We were a couple, content to spend time together, getting to know each other better, proud of what we had, but still not accepted by his father. That was the part that really made him mad. Because of it, he seemed determined to defy the old man."

"How did he do that?"

"By sneaking me into that mansion in Murdock Farms."

"Was that all part of the plan?"

"I suppose so. But truthfully, at that point, I really didn't know why I was doing this—you know, cultivating a relationship with Barry. Uncle Gerhardt fed me the instructions. He told me this was all part of a mission I'd been groomed for. He said things like, even though the rest of world was enjoying an unsettled peace, we were at war. The Aryan race had been humiliated twice in the same century. But there wasn't to be a third time. The Germans would rise again. But in order to accomplish this influential people in this country had to be eliminated, especially powerful Jews."

"And you swallowed that garbage?"

"It wasn't a matter of swallowing, Matt. It was part of the fabric of my upbringing. Since my mother died, that white supremacist bullshit was everything I'd ever known, all my father harped on, everything he stood for. And if on some level I was conscious of the blatant racism and bigotry inherent in those notions, any resistance I might have generated was ultimately muted by that psychological brainwashing I was subject to."

"And you're aware of all that?"

"What I'm aware of Doctor, is the sessions with my father when I just lost chunks of time. One minute I'd be sitting with him on the sofa in front of a fire, or across the dining room table, the next thing I knew it was a half-hour to an hour later. And although he'd insisted that I dozed off for a while, I couldn't get the notion out of my head that somehow I'd been manipulated or influenced in some manner. And with the manipulation came ugly feelings of hatred and animosity toward Jews and Blacks. It was almost like there was a malignancy growing inside me spinning out of control. And despite the fact that the rational part of my mind knew it was wrong to think this way, I still embraced those racist ideas."

"Could he have hypnotized you or given you some mind altering medication that facilitated planting those ideas in your head?"

"If he did, I never knew it."

"That scar I noticed on your thigh the first day I examine you in the emergency room. I've read about drug reservoirs being implanted that way."

"I wouldn't be surprised, Matt. Father knew about all those techniques. In my mind, it was simpler to believe what he believed. That way I wouldn't cause a conflict and he'd be nice to me."

"Yeah, while methodically destroying your mind." He saw her nod. "So once you befriended Barry, what happened next?"

"I was primed for action. It all went into motion on a Sunday afternoon in early October. I returned home from studying at the Hillman library. A cassette tape was waiting for me on my dorm room desk. It was supposed to be from my father. He'd been dead for over two years by then, so I wondered how it had gotten there. But more importantly, I was thrilled to be holding something from the man I'd adored since childhood."

"What was on the tape?" Matt probed. He felt moved to side with her but decided to hold his ground.

"He said it had been recorded about a month before he died," she related. "After the introduction, he started sharing how much he was suffering—struggling with metastatic prostate cancer at the time. He mentioned loving and missing me. The fact that he was already dead made that one a bit hard to take. Next he shared about the long and embittered life he'd lived, of the humiliation of being a survivor of a vanquished country, a member of a race of humans who should rightfully be ruling the world. Some of it sounded a little bizarre, like the ramblings of an old man who'd lost touch with reality, who was trying to relive a past that really never existed. Then, for some reason, he stopped talking about ideals and platitudes and became very personal. He spoke about his life in Germany before and during the war. Not the military part, but the private part, about his first wife and his son. He emphasized how deeply in love he was with both of them, how devastated he'd been when they were taken away from him.

"You gotta understand Matt, these were things he'd only hinted at before, feelings and memories he'd refused to talk about, ever."

"This squares with the story my father related tonight, about how your father's first wife was raped and killed along with their son."

She nodded. "I know. It was freaky hearing about it. Everything started making so much more sense."

"It should. What came next?"

"Well, after lamenting his lost family, he alluded to how after all these years we—and he did say we—had an opportunity to set things right, to rectify this grievous injustice, to avenge a terrible wrongdoing. I remember wondering how this could ever be so. That particular crime had occurred over forty years ago. Certainly the statute of limitations had run out. Then he said something I found even more curious. He said that my whole life had been dedicated to this one goal, this one noble mission. He said my life, not his. That was the part I found strange. And then he added how, despite the fact that I would achieve my life's work in just a few hours, if all went smoothly, I'd never know what I'd accomplished. Next he said, 'so my dear *Liebshun*, go forth as the instrument of my redemption.' And that's the last thing I remember."

"What do you mean that's the last thing you remember?"

"Remember clearly."

"What do you remember vaguely, then?"

"Well, that's when this dream state descended upon me. I started performing a series of actions without any apparent purpose. It was like I was an actress playing a role. Having memorized my lines and movements sometime before, now I was carrying them out."

"And you said this happened in early October. That's consistent with when the Jewish Day of Atonement usually falls."

"So I've been told. All I remember is waiting until six o'clock one evening. It was just getting dark. I was dressed in black tights and a black turtleneck. My hair was tucked under a black ski cap. In my clothes closet was a small duffel bag. I grabbed it and headed outside."

"So you walked?"

"I suppose I did, although it was more like sleepwalking. I left the Quad and headed up Forbes. I passed the public library and the museum and continued up the hill toward CMU. Then, I headed on past the campus and into the lower part of Squirrel Hill. On some level I knew where I was going. Barry had taken me there a few times before. But on another level, I was venturing into the unknown, into a place I'd only visited in my imagination, in some sort of simulator, years before. It was familiar and foreign at the same time. But I had no trepidation, no restraint. I was on a mission."

"You certainly were."

She seemed to ignore this remark. "I think I finally turned on Plainfield, walked a couple more blocks, then made a left onto Bennington. When I saw the Rosenberg mansion, I slipped into the bushes and waited."

"For what?"

"To make sure the coast was clear."

"Was it?"

"Yes."

"Then what did you do?"

"I broke into the house."

"You did what? How?"

"Using the key that the Rosenbergs kept under the greenhouse doormat. Barry used it one time when we sneaked into the house."

"What about a security system?"

"People were in the house so I didn't have to disarm it."

"You did this while the family was home?"

"I think so."

"In some dreamlike state?"

"Let's say this; I knew what I was doing, but only as a series of unrelated actions. I had no idea how they were connected. Things were unfolding for me just as they are unfolding for you as I describe them."

"I find that hard to believe."

"That may be so, Matt, but it's the truth."

"All right," he finally relented. He imagined telling this story to a judge and an impartial jury. Despite his bias he wouldn't bet on her chances of convincing them. "So, what happened next?"

"I slipped down into the basement and planted the device."

"You remember doing this?"

"I do."

"Did you know why?"

"In all honesty, no."

"You're certain of this?"

"You have to believe, Matt, I didn't know why I was doing what I did."

"Fine," he said backing off. "Did you set a timer? Was there some kind of remote? How was the damn thing set to go off?"

"I think there was a timer. I remember setting this old-fashioned alarm clock—you know, the kind with the bells on top. This was connected to a battery which, in turn, was connected to some clay-like substance in the shape of a brick. My instructions were to press a button on the clock and get out of the basement."

"And that's what you did?"

"Yes."

It wasn't hard imagining what happened next. Less than two hours later the house was in shambles and six people were dead. The thought made him shudder, again. And here was the perpetrator of the crime—whether she knew about it at the time or not. "Do you remember anything else?" he asked, not really interested in the answer.

"Only that I walked around aimless for some time, probably hours. Finally I ended up in a park. I wandered along the trails for a while. Then I came to a statue of a man standing in front of a dry pond that was filled with leaves. Suddenly feeling exhausted, I laid down and went to sleep. That's the last thing I remembered, for weeks after that."

"And that's where I came," Matt concurred.

Near dawn, Lila had slipped off into a fitful sleep. Matt, on the other hand was wide-awake, carefully processing the incredible story.

She'd planted a bomb. Six innocent people were blown to smithereens. Whether she'd been programmed or not, she was still responsible for her actions. In the not-to-distant future she would be held accountable.

269

But despite her culpability, there was an air of innocence about her. She'd been victimized by a maniacal parent who utilized his only daughter to carry out an odious crime. Could the courts take this strange dynamic into consideration and treat her with compassion? The Rosenberg family could not be resurrected. Could their unwitting assassin be given another chance?

Whatever the cost, whatever the sentence, Matt vowed to wait. His love for her demanded nothing less.